THE TURNED GODS SERIES | BOOK 2

IMMORTALS IN THE EVERYTHING

JOYCE SERRANO

ISBN: 978-1-7340603-3-1

Cover design by Publish Pros | publishpros.com

CHAPTER ONE

It had been over a year since Grace had seen this place. The last time she had was vague as the morning after a dream. The sun wasn't up yet as she strolled over the newly paved path. She relished the walk down to the retention pond beyond the vineyard's west field. Vivienne had built a grand event hall there replacing the tiny tasting shack. She hadn't seen it yet, but that wasn't the purpose of her visit at this early hour. This was likely the last time she would see the sunrise from here. Thermos and blanket in hand, she set off, determined to enjoy some alone time. She veered off the paved portion of the path where it would turn left toward the new facility. Taking an old familiar trail cutting through a small grove of trees, she moved along, winding down to the small beach built around the water.

The grass was moist with dew but not too slippery to walk down the slope. This side of the beach was dark, but she could still see everything, including her favorite bench. It faced directly across the water toward the mountains in the west and was more of a stone chaise than a typical bench. The surface was wide and smooth, formed of gray concrete that curved with high back rests on the short sides to lounge against. She could see signs of early snow high in the peaks. Although it was late summer, you couldn't tell by the brisk air gently blowing at this early hour.

She stretched out on the bench, pulling the soft, thick blanket across her legs. Steam rose, carrying the thick, decadent scent of strong-brewed coffee, as she took the lid off the thermos to pour the hot liquid into the cup-style lid. Sipping slowly, she closed her eyes and listened to insects and frogs waking up before dawn. She remembered loving this place. Her memories were indistinct and vivid at the same time. More like watching a movie than a genuine memory. What she clearly recalled was feeling at peace on this bench. A peace that would be in short supply for the next two days. It was a happy time as well as a hectic one, and she wanted to take advantage of the silence while she could. The sky in front of her was melting from black into a deep royal blue, while overhead seeped into azure.

The direction she was facing, sunrise would be behind her. She sometimes wondered why so few people took the opportunity to watch the sun rising from behind them. Regular sunrises were beautiful, but the other side was interesting. The way the tops of the mountains took on a deep orange hue, melting pink, then slowly turning bright gold before landing on their own unique blend of daylight colors. The valley was still dark. Intricate patterns of shadow crept down the sides of the mountain, behind trees and through crevasses, while the sky above lightened to morning blue. The night dwellers turned in while other creatures became active when the sun slid across the valley floor toward her. Deep-green summer grass glistened with dew, sparkling like a carpet of emeralds. The beach shimmered like diamonds. The water, sapphires. Finally, she could feel the warmth of the sun on her back.

Ivan had asked her if leaving was the right thing to do. She wondered herself sometimes if she could have done anything more for humans. They had already been given so much at the beginning. They had all the tools to become an egalitarian society, but they never arrived at that goal; not as a whole planet, anyway. Their strong division led her to doubt their ability to ever evolve. Maybe as her light spread throughout the planet, they would be able to see how much they needed to come together for their own survival. She couldn't worry about that anymore. She had to focus on the Rasan people now. They were the key to providing balance in this universe so that every species had an opportunity to survive.

She wanted to sit a little longer before heading up to the venue to see what tasks Vivienne needed help with. Vivienne was so different now. Without memories of her friendship with Grace, she had become stuffy and formal. It was upsetting for Grace to see her this way. The one thing that hadn't changed at all was her need to be in control.

Grace could already hear some of the setup crew making their way up the narrow road to the event hall. She also caught a very familiar scent approaching.

"What are you doing down here watching the wrong way?" Violet teased.

Viewing the sunrise backward had always been their thing. The only problem was, Violet didn't remember. Even as a little girl, Grace would take her down to special places wherever they lived, holding her in her lap to watch the world wake up. That was a lifetime ago for Grace. In a timeline Violet didn't have.

In the new present, Grace had still been her blood nurse. She was still her godmother, and she was still close to both of the girls. She wasn't as close with Vivienne and had to remind herself constantly not to call her Viv. Grace wasn't a member of the family anymore, at least not in the way she had been. She wasn't Aunt Grace, and she had never lived with them. Violet and Grace worked together on community projects and incorporating clean blood, or CB, into their wines. Mostly, she only came to the vineyard when she was working with Lukkas on a contract or to move investments.

"I love watching the sunrise. I thought I had told you that," Violet said, sitting at the other end of the bench, pulling half of Grace's blanket across her lap. "There's just something so comforting about it."

"I thought you'd be overwhelmed with everything going on today. Figured I'd let you sleep in. Besides, I thought you were coming back to turn over the Napa office after the ceremonies." Grace offered her the cup, which Violet took.

"Uncle Luke is going to do the turnover. He agreed to stay another year or so, tying everything up. No reason for me to stay." She handed the cup back after drinking half the liquid.

"Jack will be happy about you staying on Rasa. He doesn't enjoy using the port to come back here. Now I am sorry I didn't wake you," Grace smiled. "At least we'll be up for the sunrise on Rasa tomorrow. Well, you will anyway. I may still be locked in." Grace was glad to be getting settled in her role on their new planet. There was still a lot of construction going on, but it was all coming together very nicely.

"I'll be happy, too. I can't wait to see our quarters. Jack says they're very well appointed." Violet preferred clean lines and monochromatic color schemes in a living environment. The real personal touches were in the art—accessories and a few well-placed decorative furniture pieces—anyway. Grace's design style was much the same.

"They are, you'll like them. Very sleek, but comfortable at the same time. Not sure your mother is going to be a fan. She'll probably bring stockpiles of old junk to fill her quarters. Although surprisingly, your wedding ceremony has an air of simple sophistication. The theme must have been your decision, then?"

"You're kidding, right? Mother has had every detail of this planned well before I was born. I didn't get to make a single decision for either ceremony. The wedding is for Jack's family and the mating is for my mother, since she never got to have one of her own. If it were up to me, we wouldn't be doing any of this in public."

"Well, you got one decision. You got to pick your dress for the first ceremony."

"True, but only because you convinced Mother that an all-white wedding with the bride in scarlet and black was something Jack's family would flip out over. I'm the only one not in white today."

Grace smirked at her. "Well, should you be? I mean ... really?" Grace taunted.

"Probably not." They both laughed. "I do love the dress I ended up with. And we're saving the scarlet one for the mating ritual, so it's not going to waste." Violet shrugged.

"I hope no one gets the ceremonies confused. An all-white wedding and an all-black mating. I'm sure Vivienne has a contingency plan for any mix-ups, though."

"My mother has contingency plans for her contingency plans. She made us wait nearly a full extra year because midnight here and midnight there line up exactly today. She will have three hours to coordinate getting everyone who isn't going to the mating out and everyone who is going changed and ported over. Both facilities have been set up for days. She has a time chart posted by the port as well as written on the inside of the guests' place cards so they don't miss their allotted slot." Violet nonchalantly waved her hand toward the event hall, where the temporary port was set up in the wine cellar.

Grace shook her head. "There's nothing wrong with having an efficient plan. Aren't you supposed to be somewhere by now?"

"Let's see. It's six thirty-five now. I have hair and makeup at two in room A. Four o'clock wedding, an hour for pictures, five thirty reception, six thirty dinner, nine o'clock start moving guests, ten o'clock Jack and I depart for our 'honeymoon.'" Violet used air quotes. "Midnight, I snap Jack's neck." Violet took a deep breath and let it out quickly. "I'm free as a bird before that. What about you? Any assignments today?"

"Surprisingly, no. I'm scheduled for hair and makeup right before you at one in room A. Asta's with me, so Viv must be with you."

"Nope. I've got Ella with me." Violet pulled out her copy of the schedule from her jacket pocket.

Ella was one of Violet's closest and oldest friends. They worked together at the Napa offices. If Asta hadn't been her maid of honor, Ella would have been. Grace didn't know Ella well. She hadn't been Violet's assistant in the other timeline.

"The rest of the bridesmaids are in room B, starting at one. I don't have Mother on my schedule at all."

"I wouldn't worry about it. I can guarantee you every second of her day is scheduled somewhere. Want to go up to the hall and see if they need any help?"

"Oh, you haven't seen it yet, have you? We can walk up if you really want, but it's best to stay out of the way. An offer of help to my mother is an insult of monumental proportions. Besides, she knows how to reach out to you if she needs to. My vote is we stay clear of that place until we are summoned." Violet's eyes grew wide in an exaggerated, ominous expression.

Grace searched her thoughts for a second. "True. And anyway, Ivan and Lukkas are with her now." She giggled as she felt Ivan roll his eyes. "They're getting instructions on the groomsmen's schedules and the seating assignments for the ushers. Wouldn't want to seat Ami next to a devout Christian, now would we?"

Violet shot her a nervous look. "Like Jack's Aunt JoAnn? Can you imagine?"

"Don't worry. Ami will be with Ben."

"That's a new twist. I thought they hated each other."

"It took a lot of convincing for Ami to realize Ben was protecting me. They get along well enough now."

"Hmm. Ty is going to be here too, so we may have to sequester them away from any humans if they get excessively loud," Violet offered.

"You may want to warn your mother about that. She may need to port them early." Grace felt that would be a decent solution.

"Yeah, right. I'm going to suggest something to her?" Violet replied with sarcasm. "I'm sure she has it on lock. She's briefing Lukkas and Ivan on the ushers' seating assignments, for heaven's sake!"

Violet sat upright, speaking forcefully while pointing toward the hall. "The ushers are service units, Grace! They're programmed with the chart. Lukkas isn't even involved with the ushers or groomsmen, and Ivan is performing the ceremony. Why would they need to have this briefing?" She craned her neck and shrugged.

"Before you answer that, they don't. It's all about the ridiculous amount of control my mother needs to have over everything. The best advice I can give you is to nod your head, agree, and stay out of the way. That's what I'm planning on doing today. Why else do you think I'm down here?"

Grace gave Violet a mock-sad look, sticking out her lower lip a bit. "Aww, and here I thought you wanted to spend time with me."

Violet gave her a shove that nearly took her off the bench. Grace grabbed Violet's arm to keep balanced as they both burst out laughing again.

"I'm starving. Let's go see what Mrs. B has laid out for breakfast." Grace hadn't realized how hungry she was.

The sunrise had been a lovely start to the day. Time alone with Violet had made it even better. They had become good friends over the last year. It wasn't the relationship they had before. It was different. They were more equal. As they walked up the hill toward the house, Grace thought to herself, *Let the chaos begin.*

They entered the house through the side door and made their way down the long hall. The smell of freshly baked pastries and bacon drew them toward the large kitchen. When they took the last turn at the end of the corridor, Grace rubbed her temples, sorting out the déjà vu sensation that had overtaken her. It was exactly as she remembered, yet completely different. It had been updated recently, but not in the modern style with the marble slab counters she had pictured in her head. The style was more old world. Warm, ornate, and colorful. The counters were black granite. White marble was only used on the center island, while Grace had remembered it being on all the counters. The commercial-grade refrigerator was paneled in dark oak to melt into the cabinets. The stove was huge, made of shiny black cast iron, and gas burning, with a flat griddle in the center. It was along the far wall next to the double ovens, not on the island. The steel farm sink was the size of a small bathtub, with a tall spray faucet set out from the wall. Vivienne had decorated the deep-green walls with a myriad of wine-centric paraphernalia. The backsplash was tiled in a hazy large blue-and-orange Mediterranean stone. It was very Vivienne. Old Italy, rich and deep. There was no glass folding wall. In its place was a set of French doors flanked by two sets of tall glass panes on either side. The word that came to Grace's mind was "provincial." Grace was snapped out of her abstraction by a welcome, familiar voice.

"Come here and let me inspect you, little missy." Mrs. B. approached Grace with her arms out wide. "Snuck in here in the midnight, did ya now?"

Grace hugged her affectionately. Mrs. B. was both motherly and stern. She treated everyone equally, putting on airs for no one.

"It's been a long time. I've missed your hugs."

"It appears you've missed my cooking, too. Look how skinny you are." She stepped back, still holding Grace's hands, and proceeded to scrutinize her up and down. Grace had lost no weight, and suspected it was Mrs. B's excuse to fill her stomach, which was the one way she knew how to show love. "Sit. Let me get you something."

Violet offered her help. "Let me get it, Mrs. B. I'm sure you have a list of assignments from Mother."

"Humph. I have my side of things under control. Don't you worry about that. You two sit and let me enjoy your company before all hell breaks loose around here. Eggs? Waffles? What can I get for you?"

"Just fruit and a little oatmeal for me, please. I have a dress to squeeze into." Violet didn't want an enormous meal before strapping into a hard-corseted gown.

"And you have eight hours before you have to put it on. You'll eat what I bring you. Don't want you passing out up there. What about you, Grace? Anything special?"

Grace already knew Mrs. B. would bring her a massive plate no matter what she asked for. "Anything with bacon."

"Good answer."

They continued to talk as Mrs. B. filled their plates full of eggs, bacon, and her special breakfast muffins. They also each got coffee and oatmeal with fruit. As they conversed, the staff swirled around, ducking quickly in and out of the room. Mrs. B. intermittently called out orders about what went where and who was supposed to do which tasks. She never lost her huge smile the entire time. She was quite pleased with the additional service staff Vivienne had hired for the wedding. They were incredibly professional. She never had to tell them anything twice. Little did she suspect they were service units on loan from Rasa. They were completely undetectable from humans. At least not by other humans. Any immortal would know the difference immediately.

While they had genetic material overlays, real heartbeats to circulate nanite-infused fluid, and breathing that allowed for internal cooling, detecting scents, and evaluating atmosphere, they emitted a mildly synthetic scent.

Mrs. B. knew a little of what was going on. Instead of knowing the family was going to relocate to another world, she believed they were going back to Italy. Galin would stay on for the five-year transition planned by the Board and the Council. He would take Ivan's place as Regent and establish a stable government for the few who chose to remain. Vivienne would travel back and forth to support him while also establishing their new home on Rasa. Lukkas would be here for another year or two to ensure properties and assets not sold off by the clans would be transferred to the remaining members. They wanted to ensure their financial security, and who better to do that than Lukkas?

Vito would be staying. He didn't feel as if he fit into the new world. He would eventually go back and take over the small vineyard the family still had in Italy. Asta had initially been planning to stay on until after the fall harvest, then travel back and forth as her mother would until Galin joined them. She hadn't yet informed her parents that Lukkas had agreed to oversee the harvest, so she didn't plan to return.

Today was the real beginning. After the ceremony, many would never come back. All of Ben's people had migrated months ago. The new immortals on Rasa would take longer as many of them still had ties outside their clans. Once they took that final step over the threshold, they were all Rasans. No more Æsir. No more vampires. They were all one people.

The remainder of the morning was very relaxing for both Violet and Grace. Violet was obviously the center of attention. Grace also held a prominent position in the festivities. She was the sacrifice for the turning ceremony. It was only a symbolic position now, but it gave her a special place. She would also receive gifts and be treated like royalty. She was to be placed into the death chamber for Jack to feed from when he woke out of his death sleep. The new ceremony wouldn't have a blood sacrifice and, hopefully, not even a need to take CB to complete the transition. Grace was still an important symbol of the old ways, and she needed to be there when he woke up. She needed to make sure if he did require blood or CB to complete the transition, he would be given only enough to become complete. She would also be responsible for calming him before presenting him to the rest of the guests. Newly turned vampires normally woke a little confused and overwhelmed by their greatly enhanced senses.

Asclepius had taken on the task of monitoring the turning. He was Apollo's son and considered by humans to be the god of medicine. Apollo hadn't stuck around long after the revelations from last year. He wasn't much of a team player and at the last minute decided not to involve himself with the CB experiment, which had made Beivve livid. Apollo preferred flitting off on his own after creating as much dramatic impact as possible.

Asclepius came over at Grace's request to help with the new way of transitioning. Beivve had objected, becoming highly offended she hadn't been asked. It wasn't that Grace didn't like her. She had just known him longer.

Jack would be the first human turned without blood or CB. At least, that was the intent. He would also be the first turned Rasan on their new world. It was crucial to make sure they gathered as much data as possible during his procedure. Asclepius had already set the chamber and the ceremonial slab with sensors. He would be placing a monitor on Jack soon. Jack's change could take anywhere from four hours to several days. No one was sure why there was so much variation in the process. Asclepius would try to find an answer to that question, as well as seeing how the change physically took place in real time.

Asclepius believed the next natural step would be to see if it was plausible to turn other immortals. The more who were able to turn, the more who would be able to spread Grace's light signature by blood or bite. That was the goal. It had taken a long time for this dimension to get so far out of balance, and it would take a long time to bring it back into balance. The only other option was to abandon it and allow it to collapse. The problem with that was they didn't know the full effect it would have on the remaining dimensions. It should have been several billion years away from collapse, and no one had any idea how it had gotten to this point. They needed to do whatever they could to save it. They needed to find out why it was collapsing so quickly.

Asclepius knew it wasn't Nyx. She only spread darkness for balance with light. She had stayed out of this dimension since she noticed it going darker. Her daughters tried to bring the light forward here, but they couldn't stay long enough and risk all the other dimensions. Maintaining balance had become a much bigger task than they could take on. It was a battle they were losing in several dimensions.

"Hellooooo." Violet snapped her fingers in front of Grace. "What color?"

"Huh?" Grace looked up, pulled out of her thoughts.

"Your nails. What color?"

They were in a small day spa Vivienne had set up in the pool house. Grace had drifted off in the massage chair while getting a pedicure. She and Ivan had ported in last night sometime after two and she had been up at five thirty for the sunrise. Grace was caught off guard by how tired she was. She normally slept about four hours, sometimes five, so the nap had been refreshing, but she was still dragging.

"What color are you getting?" Grace asked.

Violet half smirked. "I thought blood red would be appropriate."

"I'll take the same then." Grace watched as Helen, a personal service unit, popped the blood-red vial into the back of what looked to be a laser pen. She touched it to each nail, which was instantly colored and instantly dried. Grace seldom ever used colored polish, and she felt the shiny finish was a bit too glaring, although she liked the color. "Thank you, Helen. Can I get a matte finish on that?"

"Of course. Anything you wish," Helen replied.

"Ooh. I like that idea," Violet squealed. "Helen, please make sure all the bridesmaids have the same blood red with a matte finish. It will be perfect. Thanks, Grace." She reached over and touched Grace's arm, which was unusually warm. Slowly, she turned her gaze toward her.

"Grace, you don't look so good, and you're really warm. Are you feeling all right?" Violet was unsettled. Grace had never been "sick." Injured, yes, but like this, no. Her cheeks were flushed, and her eyes were a much deeper green than Violet had ever seen.

"I feel a little warm, but I thought it was just hot in here. I am tired. I need to ask Ivan if he's feeling anything. Maybe it's something we picked up on Rasa, although neither of us should be, nor have ever been, sick. Maybe I should call Leo." Leo was what Asclepius preferred to be called. Since he was already here to place Jack's monitor, it wouldn't be a bad idea to have him check her out.

Violet tried to hide a smile as the answer struck her. "Calling Leo wouldn't be an awful idea, but I think I know what your problem is."

"How could you possibly know what's wrong with me? I've never been sick before. This is something I should be concerned about," Grace retorted irritably.

"Yeah? You and Ivan merged last year, right?"

"Yes. What's your point?"

Violet was still smiling. "You got all of our little vampy things like sight, hearing, scent."

Grace rolled her eyes. "Yes. Again, what's your point?"

"Well, hot, tired, irritable, lustful. Estrus." Now Violet had a huge smile.

"No." Grace glared back at her in disbelief. "No. It can't be. I'm not ready for this. The timing could not be worse! Ivan and I haven't even discussed it."

"Better get to discussing it then. You have seven days, and who knows how long it will be until the next time? Could be a few decades, could be a century."

Grace leaned forward, placing her head in her hands. She shook her head. She really wasn't ready for this. It was too soon. She didn't think she wanted more children. She didn't know if Ivan wanted children. Even if they wanted a child, should they? They had no idea what they would produce. Nyx was a dark bringer, but two of her daughters were light bringers. What if they had a dark bringer? This dimension was too fragile for that. Her thoughts swirled. They only had seven days to decide. And what if they didn't take the chance? They may have to wait centuries to have another. But why not wait a few centuries? She didn't want children now. Maybe never. Why was it that every time she had her life in order, her feet got swept out from under her?

She sat up and leaned back in the chair. When she opened her eyes, Ivan was standing two feet in front of her. Of course, he heard her. How could he not have heard her? She could block everyone except for him.

He stared at her. He was blank. She couldn't tell if he was happy, upset, or concerned. He was stunned silent. He didn't have a single thought.

Violet looked back and forth between the two of them. "Well, this is awkward. I thought you'd be happy. I'd be happy."

Grace didn't break eye contact with Ivan. "Not a word, Violet. Not to anyone."

Ivan held his hand out to help Grace out of the chair. "We should talk."

Grace sighed as she stepped out of the chair without taking his hand. She wasn't sure she could restrain herself if she touched him. She was still barefoot when Ivan opened the port.

Violet looked at the space where they had been standing and sighed. "I'd be thrilled," she said, nodding to Helen.

CHAPTER TWO

Ivan and Grace stepped out onto the front porch of the cabin. The Three had been staying there whenever they were on Earth. It was much nicer than being cooped up in the nearly empty underground facility. Most times, it was only Alex and Mikkel. It was enough to say the cabin had been lived in for the last year and a half since Grace had left it.

Erik was overseeing the infrastructure on the new world. He had taken Jack under his wing, teaching him as much as he could absorb. The few times Erik did come back, he usually came with Jack and stayed at the vineyard closer to Jack's family. Jack's ability to retain information had already impressed Erik. Once he was turned, Erik thought Jack could even surpass him in quantum engineering.

Ivan opened the door. When Grace stepped through, she was surprised to see they had kept it much cleaner than she expected. There was still no coffee table since the last one had been destroyed. She headed to the kitchen, pulling out the coffee maker. Ivan poured a scotch. Neither of them had spoken out loud or otherwise.

Ivan stepped out on the back deck and waited for her coffee to finish brewing. He knew she couldn't hear his thoughts out there. The blockers were still in place. Now that having a child was an option, he desperately wanted to have one with her. He cared for The Three as if they were his own, but they were grown men. He wanted more, but he couldn't tell her. She was right about one big thing. There was no telling what would be produced from their union. Would a child of theirs even have a physical form? They weren't even certain what their own species was. He heard her open the door and pressed his thoughts down.

She stood close to him along the railing. Her scent was enticing. He felt intoxicated by it. She could feel him becoming aroused and stepped away from him, sitting in a chair by the fire pit. He leaned against the rail, breathing deeply to regain his composure. He didn't know if he would be able to resist her for the next seven days, even if he wanted to. They had to talk. They had to discuss everything. Their own feelings as well as the way it could affect the community they were building. Grace had been unanimously elected as their Administrator. She held the reins as the head of their egalitarian society. She was responsible for making sure everyone had the opportunity to take part in the government. Everyone had a vote, and every vote was weighted equally. If anything happened to her, the entire fragile society could fall apart. They owed it to everyone not to be selfish.

They sat and stared at each other for quite some time. Ivan leaned forward with his elbows on his knees and spoke.

"It was easier when we had a board that decided if a mated pair had a solid enough structure and temperament to parent a child," Ivan said wistfully.

"The first question for us is: do we even want a child right now? I'm not sure I want another child at all. How will one change our relationship? Are we ready? Nothing else matters unless we can answer that." She was still in shock. All she could think was: seven days. They had to make this decision in less than seven days.

"You're the one taking all the risks here. It has to be your decision." Ivan desperately wanted to tell her how much he wanted a child, but he couldn't. He couldn't pressure her into this. He kept his mind as blank as he possibly could.

"That wasn't the question, Ivan. Do *you* want a child?" She knew how painful the loss of his two children so long ago was for him. It was uncertain to her if he could emotionally manage having another without knowing what they might produce. She wanted him to answer no. She wanted him to take the pressure off her.

"Grace, I need you to answer that question first. What I want or don't want doesn't matter if you can't or don't want to do this. I would never pressure you into having a child just to please me."

She listened closely. She heard him this time. Barely a whisper in the back of his mind, but it was there. *I want more.*

She had to be honest with him. He would know if she was lying, even if it was to protect his feelings. How could she phrase her thoughts so he wouldn't give up hope in the future? She didn't want him to be hurt, but she really wanted no part in starting over with an infant. It had nothing to do with how much she loved him. Children were hard enough for working parents to raise. Raising an incredibly powerful infant that could have the ability to wipe out life with a temper tantrum was something she may never be ready for.

"Ivan, I would love to give you the child you deserve, but I'm scared, and I don't know if the right time is now or if any time will ever be right."

"Grace, I would have a hundred children with you if you wanted them. We are encouraging the community to procreate as quickly as possible, but you and I are different. I'm afraid of that too. We don't know what abilities a child of ours would have. We don't know if they could even live in our dimension. I think we need to get help from the Council with this. We have a few days. We don't need to be rash. This may not be an appropriate time, but someday it could be."

"Ivan, I'm not having a hundred children with you." Her eyes widened. The corners of her mouth turned downward. "But I would consider having one at some point. I think you're right, though. We need to get some help with this decision. It's bigger than the two of us."

He stepped over to her chair, leaned down, and kissed her. She made him incredibly happy. The dizzying rush of raw sexual energy flowed over her. She phased through her chair, breathing hard, standing up a few feet away. He backed away quickly as well. Neither looked at the other while they revived their restraint. It was even more intense than their normally elevated attraction.

Ivan downed the last gulp of scotch. "I think we should probably keep a little distance from each other for the time being."

"Agreed." She let out a final deep breath. "Let's go find Leo."

Grace and Ivan ported to the room they were staying in at the vineyard. There was so much activity, they couldn't risk porting into a public space and having a human staff member or one of Jack's brothers see them. Leo would be with Jack in the library. Ivan opened the door for Grace, more out of habit than anything else. She didn't expect him to, but he liked doing it. He placed his hand on her lower back as she exited, and they both felt a fiery spark as their skin touched. He recoiled at the intensity.

"I lived through the Crusades. Not touching you is going to be harder," Ivan groaned. Grace dug her freshly painted nails into the palms of her hands. Each touch ignited a powerful urge inside of her to mate. She had only been going through this for a few hours at most. She couldn't imagine how hard it was going to get in the next few days. They needed to find an answer quickly. Otherwise, they would have to be separated until they could figure this out. She didn't know if anything had the ability to contain or separate them.

The slate floor in the corridor outside the library was cool against Grace's bare feet. It was dark, lined with benches tufted in red velvet, and had heavily paneled walls. They were hand-crafted tongue-and-groove panels with intricate millwork, not the manufactured-sheet type of paneling. They were thick and stained with a highly polished dark-cherry finish. Jack's brothers sat slumped over the benches, waiting for him to finish with Leo. Their dad, Josh, had an affinity for "J" names. Jack was the oldest, followed by Jeremy, Jimi, and Jordan. They were all hungover and had their heads buried in their phones. They barely noticed when Grace and Ivan passed. Ivan tapped on the door to the library, then swung it open without waiting for a response.

Jack was sitting on the edge of the desk looking rough, with his shirt unbuttoned. Leo stood in front of him. He was quite tall with curly reddish-blonde hair and his father's unusually light blue eyes. He had an evenly trimmed mustache and beard, more like two- or three-days' growth than full facial hair, appearing as one would imagine a god should look like. He was a stunningly beautiful man. His clothing was casual: jeans and a blue Oxford slightly darker than his eyes. She could see part of a snake tattoo running up his arm and chest to the side of his neck with very ornate scaling. She imagined the complete tattoo was a full caduceus.

Leo had just finished stamping the monitor into the center of Jack's chest. It was barely noticeable—about the size of a quarter, no thicker than an extra layer of skin. Clear and matte. If you didn't know it was there, you would never notice it.

"Hey, Ivan, come on in. We were just finishing up." Leo put the apparatus he had used to apply the monitor back in his bag.

Ivan started to reply that they had a problem they needed to speak to him about, but he felt someone else was in the room. As he swung the door farther open, Erik was standing just outside of his original view.

"Hey, Leo. We just wanted to go over a few things with you before all the chaos gets started. Hi, Jack." He nodded. "Erik."

Jack had asked Erik to be his best man. They had become very close in the last year. More friends than a regular apprentice situation. Erik was normally so preoccupied with his research and gadgets that he had seldom made any friends. Jack had been trying to pair Erik up with Asta. They saw each other whenever he was on Earth, causing his trips to become far more frequent lately. He wanted to get to know her better before she met Mikkel with his gregarious personality. He hadn't realized it yet, but he had fallen hard for her. The best man and maid of honor were to be paired for most of the event, which Erik was anticipating eagerly.

Once Grace realized Erik was in the room, she moved through the doorway behind Ivan and hugged Erik.

"Hi, honey."

"Hi, Mom, Ivan." Erik wasn't the least bit hungover. Probably because he could drink a tanker of beer by himself. An immortal metabolism could process alcohol much more quickly than a mortal's could.

She turned back to Jack. "Jack, how are you doing? Hungover?"

"Yes ma'am. Extremely hungover." Jack spoke slowly and came across rough.

"At least you can take heart in knowing it will be your last," Ivan chided.

Leo queried Ivan, "So, you don't want me to cure him, then?"

Jack turned, the bright window behind Ivan illuminating his eyes, and he winced pathetically.

"Only because it would ruin Violet's day if you didn't. Go ahead, Leo," Ivan agreed.

The relief on Jack's face was apparent. Leo placed a pinch of something into the palm of his hand and blew it into Jack's face. The dust was absorbed through his eyes and skin. Almost instantly, Jack perked up. Bags and bloodshot eyes disappeared. He looked a hundred times better.

"Make sure you drink plenty of water. And take a shower. You reek of alcohol."

"Thank you, Leo. Are you sure it's okay to shower with this on?" Jack asked, pointing to his chest.

Leo nodded. "It won't come off until I remove it. You can do everything as normal."

Jack thanked him. He and Erik left to go get ready with an air of relief.

Leo eyed Grace and Ivan suspiciously. "What's really going on? Grace, you don't care about the technical aspects of this, and Ivan, you know more about the turning process than I do."

"It's not something we're really looking to broadcast. But yes, we have another issue. How much have you been studying our people?"

"I think I've been very comprehensive in my research up to this point."

"What do you know about the estrus process?" Grace had asked the question, which confused Leo.

"Grace, I'm not sure I understand the question. Æsir don't go through estrus. Who are you talking about?"

She continued to hold eye contact with Leo. Ivan deferred to Grace. Leo glanced back and forth between them.

"How? You? Really? From the merge?"

She splayed her hands in front of her. "I guess so."

"Let's get a monitor on you." He reached out to take her hand. "Come sit up here."

She withdrew her hands. Ivan pulled Leo's arm back. "You probably shouldn't touch her. It's getting difficult for her to manage."

Grace leaned forward, taking in a long, deep scent from Leo. "I think it's okay, Ivan. I think it's only you." She offered her hand to Leo as Ivan let go of his arm. She was tense as his hand moved closer to hers.

Leo cautiously touched her fingertips. She relaxed and took a firm grasp of his hand. "It's good. I must just be drawn to Ivan."

Leo also relaxed his posture. "It makes sense. The merge gave you all the connections of a full blood mate, plus all the other ones you gave him. I need a continuous stream of data. This planet isn't set up with sensors, so we'll need a physical attachment. Let's get a monitor on so we can see what we're dealing with."

Grace pulled up her shirt. The monitor had to be placed in the center of the chest under the sternum and between the ribs to be most effective. Leo placed the monitor on her as he had on Jack.

"All right Ivan, now you," Leo approached him.

"Why me? I thought it was a female issue."

Grace's eyes could have cut him for that sexist reply.

Leo quickly salvaged the conversation. "You two reverberate off each other. I need to monitor you both." He narrowed his eyes momentarily. "While I appreciate the data, what exactly are you two hoping to have as an outcome to this situation?" He was projecting the stream into a holographic model as he received the first pieces of information.

"We have no idea. This came as a complete surprise to both of us. We never even considered the merge would cause this to happen to her. We need to buy some time here until we can decide about it after the ceremonies." Ivan didn't know if there was anything they could do.

"Oh yeah, and the timing couldn't have been better." Grace rolled her eyes in disbelief.

Leo didn't want to reveal how extremely out of whack her readings were. "Grace, your hormone levels are quite …" He paused, searching for the right word. "Elevated." What he really meant was "off the charts." As in so high, the graph ended in an almost 90-degree upswing. "Can you tell me what you're feeling right now?"

"Mostly irritated, but that could be the surprise of the situation and me not wanting to ruin Violet's ceremonies. Other than that, I'm physically warm, tired, and hungry."

"What about being aroused?" Leo needed to understand what the trigger was.

She scoffed and rolled her eyes at him. "I always have elevated arousal around Ivan. He's far enough away that I'm in a controllable range. But earlier, when he touched me, my primal urge nearly took over. I wanted to shred him, if you know what I mean." She tingled when she thought about it.

"You don't react to me, so it's likely you will only react to Ivan. We need to have some limited exposure to others so we can test that theory."

"I was fine with Jack, although I didn't touch him. And I knew I wouldn't be attracted to Erik."

Ivan had his own theory. "I'm thinking it's because of our blood bond. We merged, but I never sired Grace, so she could be freely bonded to others as well. She has a blood bond with Lukkas and Ben. If I'm right, she is going to need to be isolated from all three of us until we can get through the next few days of ceremonies."

Leo bit his lip as he thought. "I'll mix up something to curb the hormones. Ivan, can you get Lukkas and Ben to each come in here one at a time? And you won't be able to be in here when they are."

Grace added, "Let them know what's going on, but please ask them not to tell anyone else until after the ceremonies."

"How am I supposed to explain that to Lukkas?" Ivan hadn't wanted to go into the past with Leo.

Grace thought for a second. "He knows we have a blood bond from the woods, Ivan. Just tell him."

Ivan nodded in agreement and moved toward the door.

Leo thought of something else. "Ivan, how do the other women handle estrus when they don't mate?"

"It's manageable for them as long as they aren't near their mate. Normally, either one will take a vacation or their mate will lock them in a room, with consent, of course."

"But we can't do that with Grace. Nothing can hold her, or you, for that matter," Leo added.

"You can send me to Rasa and change the port code so I can't get back. Once I'm there and in the death chamber with Jack, I won't leave him. I won't have any of their scents with them being outside, either. As far as I can tell, it's either scent or touch that is triggering me."

"I need to see what the extent of it is. Ivan, please approach Grace slowly. I need to observe the changes."

Ivan moved cautiously toward Grace, who was still seated. Her levels began to rise; her temperature, heart rate, blood pressure, even brain activity was increasing. She was breathing heavily. All his elevations were mirroring hers except for estrogen. Once he got within a step of her, both of their readings were maxed out.

"Stop." Leo made a few swiping motions. "That's enough. Go get the others, Ivan. You're going to need to stay away from her until you decide if you will mate or not."

Ivan moved to the other side of the room, panting loudly. He leaned against the bookcase closest to the door for a few minutes, waiting for their levels to drop. Grace's dropped somewhat, but far less than Ivan's had. Both stared at the floor, avoiding eye contact. Once Ivan left the room, Grace's levels went back to normal except for her hormones, which he still couldn't read, and her temperature, which was slightly elevated.

"Leo. What am I supposed to do?" Grace asked, hopping off the desk.

"We've been friends far too long for you to expect me to answer that. It probably wouldn't hurt to start with a drink, though." He poured them each a glass of red from the tray on the reading table while she moved to a chair near the windows. He handed her one and sat in the chair next to her.

"You've got to figure out a way to keep me sane enough to make it through the next couple of days. I can't ruin this for Violet." Grace's tone was desperate.

"I'll come up with something, but the reality is we may just need you to have distance from Ivan. How are you feeling right now?"

Grace took a moment to reflect before answering. "I have to say, I feel pretty normal."

"Your readings are pretty normal, too, which is encouraging."

"I guess we'll see when Lukkas gets here. You know the relationship I had with him, don't you? I mean the *actual* relationship." She knew Leo's memories hadn't been altered, but she didn't know if he understood what her history was with Lukkas.

"I know he was the one you were with here. I also know that the memory alteration couldn't have had any effect on the blood bond. What I am wondering is, was your merging with Ivan a form of sire bonding? If it was, it could have severed the bonds with Lukkas and Ben."

"My hypothetical reasoning would lead me to believe that was the case. Which likely means it's not." Grace laughed at the irony. "Anywhere there is the chance to add a complication to my life, the universe seems to find a way to take advantage of it." Grace found it ironic that all of this would be happening today. She felt she had the worst timing ever.

"Oh well. Guess I'll have to deal with it. As usual," she smirked.

They drank and chatted while Leo worked on a solution to diminish Grace's overactive mating urge. There was a light rapping on the door. Lukkas opened the door hesitantly before entering. It had been so long since Grace had seen him. The last time had been when she came last year to cash out her portfolio.

"Ivan explained what was going on. What can I do to help?" Lukkas would never know how they were really connected. Grace would have to make him believe it was only from sharing blood when she saved him. For him, their history was a family bond, not the bond of lovers.

Leo stepped forward. "Morning, Lukkas."

Grace wondered if it really was still morning since it felt like it had been such a long day already. "Morning, Lukkas. Thanks for coming down."

"Of course. Anything for you, Grace." Lukkas smiled at her.

Leo continued, "Did Ivan explain what was going on?"

"He did."

"Considering the circumstances, we need to see if your blood bond has been severed since Ivan never formally sired Grace in the traditional way. If the bond is still intact, you'll have to keep your distance from each other until the estrus is complete." Leo paused, ensuring that Lukkas understood. "Open your shirt, please. I need to place a monitoring patch on you before you approach her." Leo already had the placement device in his hand when he strode across the room toward Lukkas, who unbuttoned his shirt as Grace watched.

She admired his physique but didn't feel a draw to him. Maybe the bond was broken. She very much hoped it was. It would be hard enough staying away from Ivan, much less Lukkas and Ben, too.

It only took Leo a few seconds to place the monitor. "Well, ready then?" He glanced between Grace and Lukkas. They both said yes in unison.

"Grace, stay seated. Lukkas, move slowly toward Grace but do *not* touch her."

Lukkas proceeded forward cautiously. The readings changed little. Grace's pulse was slightly elevated.

"Grace, are you nervous? Your pulse is increasing, but nothing else."

She took a breath and slowed her pulse rate. "Better?"

"How do you feel?"

Lukkas was within a few feet of her.

"Perfectly normal."

"Okay. Lukkas, please touch her hand."

There had been no increase in Grace's readings. Lukkas's heart was racing, and his blood pressure had increased, which led Leo to believe he was scared.

A huge smile of relief passed over Grace and she grasped Lukkas's hand. "Perfectly normal," she sighed with relief.

She stood up and gave Lukkas a huge hug.

"Our bond may be broken, but you will always be in my heart, Grace." Lukkas hugged her back tightly. "You okay?"

"Much better. I don't know if I could stand being attracted to you like that." It wasn't a lie. She was overjoyed her feelings for him had diminished. "You're prettier than I am. I'd have to be jealous all the time." She winked at him.

"No truer words were ever spoken," Lukkas joked back. "I'm just glad we're okay."

"Now maybe you can find a girlfriend."

"Not on your life, sister. I'm too young to be shackled. I'm staying single for a few hundred years longer." He turned back, extending his hand to Leo. "Are we good, doc? I've got assignments from Vivienne," he grimaced.

Leo shook his hand. "All good. Let me get the monitor off."

"Oh, yeah. I forgot about that already." Lukkas opened his shirt for Leo to remove the disk. His personality was so much brighter than Grace had remembered. Had his constant worry over her made him somehow dim in the other life they had? She couldn't help but wonder. She liked him better like this. He should have been this way all along.

Once Lukkas left, Grace and Leo discussed their relief. The bond with Lukkas was broken. They were optimistic the bond with Ben had been broken too. Leo still wanted to proceed with the test to be sure.

It had taken Ben a while to get to the library. Ivan had needed to get him from Rasa. When he walked in, it appeared Ivan had dragged him from the shower. His hair was wet, and his long-sleeved shirt was stuck to his chest. On seeing the state he was in, Grace felt a twinge of lust.

She didn't know if it was because of a bond, because he had been her husband for so long, or because she still loved him. She hadn't expected that last thought to cloud her mind. But she did still love him. She couldn't deny it. It differed from the way she loved Ivan. Ivan was her destiny; Ben was her history.

The love she shared with Ivan was pure and effortless. The love she felt for Ben was muddled, volatile, and complicated. She couldn't examine those feelings without pain. She turned away from him and poured herself another drink. She drained half the glass and refilled it before sitting down where she had been. When Leo fitted Ben with the monitor, he pulled off his shirt over his head. Grace couldn't bring herself to look at him. Anguish started her heart racing. She needed to calm herself and focus.

The encounter differed from the one with Lukkas. Grace already knew this bond wasn't broken. Tragically, it would never be broken.

"Grace," Leo said for the second time.

"Yes?"

"Are you ready?"

"As ready as I'll ever be, I guess." Yeah, sarcasm to the rescue. That would really help her out of this mess.

"Ben, how about you? What do you feel?" Leo saw signs of elevation for both.

"Fine. I don't feel anything." He regretted saying that as quickly as it came out of his mouth.

"Really? That's kind of the norm for you, isn't it?" Grace didn't know why she said that. Her anger toward Ben was boiling the instant he spoke.

"Wow, way to be a bitch about it. I'm here helping you. Like I've been doing for your entire life. You have no idea how I feel. You never did." Now Ben was fuming. Her words had stung him. This fight had been a long time coming, but he hadn't been looking to do it here or today.

"Right. That's why you left me alone for months or even years at a time, treating me like property while you slept around and flaunted it in my face. You never loved me. I was a burden your mother put on you, and you resented me for it." Grace felt like someone had splayed her open, leaving her for all to see with her guts falling out.

"If that's what you really think, then you're an idiot. I loved you more than anything I have ever loved. Not because of your abilities. You couldn't use your telepathy to sway me; your charms and your light didn't work on me either. I was immune from all of that, and yet I fell in love with you anyway. The real you. And the worst part was they did not create you for me. I wasn't supposed to keep you. When you got pregnant with our sons, my mother and Freya were livid with me for getting too close to you. I did all those horrible things to make you angry with me. I couldn't stand to be close to you and not be allowed to love you, so I had to make you hate me," he yelled. His hands tightened around the edge of the desk, crumbling it to dust.

"Do you know how hard it was to kill the love inside you and see it on your face every time you looked at me? How hard it was to listen to you cry in your room when you thought I wasn't there?"

He pointed at her angrily.

"And I NEVER left you. Not once. Not for one minute. I was always there, even when you thought I was gone. At least until I went to Hel. I was relieved when you left me. Then it hurt, and then I survived on *my* pain and *my* anger. And I missed you. More than anything, I missed you." He had been yelling at her until the last sentence. His demeanor changed. He became sullen.

"But then I saw you with him. Ivan. And I knew. He was the one you were created for. You were light in each other. Your love for him is clean. Something we never had a chance to have. He's perfect for you. He's good for you. And I like him. So, forgive me if I have a hard time seeing you with him at times."

Grace found herself standing, staring at him, although she hadn't remembered rising from the chair. She said in a whisper, "I never knew."

Leo could see both of their readings were out of range. "I think we need to put an end to this. I don't know if there is an actual blood bond, but there is something significant between the two of you, and you need to be separated while Grace is going through estrus."

Ben picked up his shirt. "I'm sorry, Leo. Our bond can *never* be broken because they created her with my blood. We have always and will always be bonded. I have no choice but to protect her. That doesn't mean I can be close to her." He left the room, slamming the heavy door hard enough to shake the entire wing.

Grace didn't say anything. She couldn't say anything. She slumped back down into the chair. The extent to which she had misinterpreted their entire relationship left her in disbelief. Everything he did to her was because he loved her, and it was tearing him apart. She understood how twisted that sounded, even in her own head. She could see pain in others so clearly, but she never saw his. All she ever did was antagonize him further.

Ivan was in the hallway when Ben came out. He had heard everything, and not through Grace. He had heard their yelling through the door and was certain that every immortal on the property had also heard it.

Ben pulled his shirt back on as he stormed down the hall. Ivan looked like he was going to say something to him, but Ben cut him off, holding his hands out in a manner that showed Ivan he needed to back off.

"I can't, Ivan. Not now." Ben walked to the end of the hall and out the side door. Ivan was stunned. He sat on one of the benches. He couldn't imagine going through that for hundreds of thousands of years. It had been hard enough for Ivan to watch her with Lukkas for only seven hundred when he barely even knew her. Ivan didn't pity him, but he did empathize.

Leo gave Grace a weak smile of sympathy, which highly irritated her.

"Don't look at me like I'm some pathetic little weakling who just got her feelings hurt. Can you manage to get me through the next two days or not?" She snapped her body straight, pressing her hands into her thighs. She didn't like having her thoughts clouded by rampant, erratic emotions.

She immediately regretted snapping at Leo. "I'm sorry, Leo. I can't be around people right now." She slunk to the bar and poured herself another drink.

Leo didn't want to imagine what could happen if her temper got out of control. He didn't like the thought of an unpredictable, irrational, and angry Grace.

"I can help. I'm programming some nanites to relieve your symptoms. It won't reduce your hormone levels. What it will do is block the transmission of overwhelming signals to your brain. I'll monitor them through your patch and adjust as necessary until there is a resolution. If I reduce your hormones back to normal levels, it will take you out of estrus. I *can* do that if you prefer."

"Thanks, Leo. I'd appreciate it if you could just buy me a few days to figure this out." She was relieved she wouldn't be the ruin of Violet and Jack's ceremonies.

"You'll still have to keep a little distance from Ivan and Ben to keep things manageable."

Grace exhaled sullenly. "I don't think being too close to Ben will be a problem. How far do you think I need to be from Ivan? He's performing the handfasting while I'm performing the bonding."

Leo regarded her oddly.

She realized he hadn't been to a mating ceremony before. "Draining Violet's blood into the chalice for Jack to drink after she injects her venom."

"Oh, so you'll be on the other side of them from him? Like three or four feet?"

"About that. We will both have our hands on them at the same time. His will be on their shoulders, while mine will be on their wrists."

"As long as it's a short period and you don't touch, you should be okay with the dosage I'm giving you. I'll have you on the monitor, so I can adjust the nanites as necessary. You should be fine." Leo was confident this would work. "Let me introduce the nanites now, and we'll do a test run with Ivan here."

Leo placed the nanites onto the monitoring patch. It sucked them into Grace's body with a green glow. Her eyes lit green concurrently. As the nanites dispersed, he could see changes in the levels. Her hormones were still high, although the emotional range of brain activity was reduced tremendously.

"Hmm," Leo grunted.

"Hmm what?" Grace asked.

"I've never seen the nanites react like that. They lit green. Usually when they go in, they are more of a warm white. Your eyes lit green, too, which I've never seen before."

"I guess green's kind of my color. I emit a warm green glow when I heal others, and Ivan told me that when I went psycho goddess on the guy in the auction house, my eyes flashed green light." She didn't know what green had to do with anything, other than it was her eye color.

She squirmed from the nanites tickling her insides.

"Your readings are normal except for the hormone levels. How are you feeling?"

"I feel them moving, but then again, I feel everything moving all the time. I'll get used to it."

"Let's get Ivan in here to test this out. You stay put." Leo headed to the door to let Ivan in. Ivan opened the door and entered the room before Leo got there.

"I'm going to assume you heard everything Grace and I discussed?"

"Yes," Ivan replied. Leo made a mental note that when treating any of the turned, he'd have to take extra measures to preserve privacy.

"Okay. I am going to change the experiment slightly. Ivan, I want you to sit, and Grace, you approach him until you feel uncomfortable."

Ivan sat in a chair by the windows. Grace moved to be directly in front of Ivan's chair on the other side of the room.

"I'm ready when you are, Leo." Grace waited for him to signal her to move forward. After a few seconds, he motioned her to proceed. She approached Ivan slowly. She felt fine. When she was within arm's reach, she felt the nanites moving more quickly. She was being drawn to him mildly. She stopped, not wanting to push her luck.

Ivan looked up at her. He didn't feel her losing control. He was aroused only as much as he normally was with her. A huge sense of relief poured from her. She moved quickly to sit in the chair a few feet away and to the right of Ivan.

"I think that's good enough to get us through the next couple of days. Thank you, Leo." She was reassured and appreciative.

Leo breathed a sigh of relief. "In the event of any changes, I'll receive a notification and adjust the programming as necessary, in case the nanites are unable to self-regulate."

"Leo, you have no idea how much this means to us. Thank you." Grace was grateful he had helped avert yet another crisis. In her relief, she realized she didn't know what time it was. She checked her phone.

"Balls! I'm late." It was a quarter after one. Vivienne was going to be livid. She had missed her time slot. "I've got to go." She leaned over to kiss Ivan as she did every time they parted. He sunk back in his chair, pulling away from her.

"Nope. No touching."

She cringed slightly. "I forgot already. Sorry."

"Admit it, you never could keep your hands off me." He shook his head, joking with her.

"Which is the entire reason we are in this predicament today," she retorted. "I have to go." She stepped backward and ported out.

CHAPTER THREE

Grace had ported directly into room A. Asta sat in one of the salon chairs, while Vivienne was standing behind her with her arms folded. Vivienne was a classic Italian Sophia Loren kind of beauty. She was sophisticated and stern. She seemed much older than Grace with her proper manners and etiquette. Grace was much more fluid and adaptable. Vivienne hadn't always been this staunch and unpliable. At least, not the Viv Grace remembered.

"I apologize for being late." Grace was flustered as she sat in the chair on Asta's right.

Violet popped up from behind her. "We weren't sure you were going to make it at all. Is everything all right? Are we expecting an announcement anytime soon?"

Violet may have gotten her mother's looks, but she did not get her subtlety. Grace could tell she had already told Asta and Vivienne what was going on.

"No," she said firmly. "Leo brewed me up some nanites to hold me over until after the festivities when we can make a rational decision. Thanks for keeping my confidence, Violet! Can I assume everyone knows?"

Asta piped up, "After your little confrontation with Ben, it was kind of hard to miss."

The situation stretched Vivienne's already precarious patience. "If you ladies would set this aside for the time being, we're on a schedule."

Nonverbally, Grace said to Vivienne, *Thanks for the rescue.*

Vivienne showed a hint of a smile around her eyes. *You appeared to have needed one.* Then she said out loud, "Violet, pour Grace a glass of wine."

One of the personal service units started taking the braid out of Grace's hair. Vivienne shook her head disapprovingly at the tangled mess.

"Why am I here first? Shouldn't Violet be the one getting pampered?"

Vivienne cringed at the state of her hair. "You need a lot more help than she does."

Grace knew it was true, but she still felt a little offended. "I love you too, Viv."

Asta and Violet both laughed.

Vivienne sighed. She despised being called Viv. "Seriously, Grace. When was the last time you brushed your hair?"

Grace rubbed her throat, avoiding eye contact. "Yes—ter—day." She drew out the word. Normally, she was better kempt. She and Ivan hadn't gotten in until late. She slept three hours, then got up early and showered to watch the sunrise. Given the cold temperature, she had been averse to getting her hair wet. Not that she was concerned about getting sick as much as she was having her hair frozen. She just had so much of it that it would never dry on its own. She had decided not to take it out of the braid. Her intention was to correct it, but before she could, the day had become unmanageable.

Vivienne raised her eyebrows in disapproval. "Hence your slot being early."

"Ouch. Brutal honesty is always appreciated," Grace retorted.

"I can't let you embarrass yourself in public, Grace. It reflects poorly on all of us." Vivienne held everyone to a higher standard, including herself. She wasn't trying to be mean with her comments. In her mind, if no one told you about your flaws, you wouldn't have the opportunity to correct them.

"I've got other things to check on. Enjoy yourselves." With that, Vivienne snapped her fingers over her head, porting away. She loved the dramatic effect of it all.

Hair and makeup were as Vivienne had directed. As each of them finished, they made their way into the dressing area. There was Violet, Asta, Ella, two other bridesmaids whom Grace didn't know, and Grace. Everyone was painted up with a neutral base color, dark eyeliner, and a deep-red lip. Hair was swept up off the neck. In days past, this was for a more vulnerable kill. These days, it was only for show. All of the women had crystals sewn into their hair, and Violet wore a full tiara.

Grace had never been an extremely feminine woman. She was free spirited. Her hair wasn't always perfectly brushed, her makeup wasn't always on. She didn't much care about formal events, but this was an exception. It was important for many reasons. This would be the first turned mating without blood or CB after the turn, if it worked as expected, and Jack would be the first Rasan turned on the new world. She could put up with formal for the gravity of this event.

The dresses for the three bridesmaids were simple, long, white, and sleek. They had a draped neckline with side cuts that wove into straps at the back of the dresses. They were finished with dangling diamond earrings and white satin pumps. Very simple and classic. Asta's dress was similar, with the addition of simple crystal beading all over the dress.

Grace's dress was different. As the sacrifice, she wore something a little more special. For the wedding, she would only be an honored guest, but for the mating, she would be the only one still in white. Her gown was high waisted with silver embroidery and crystal beading from the open slit running from the waist to the top of the structured bodice. It was strapless, exposing her neck, back, and shoulders. In the old days, she would have been chained for the ceremony before being entombed with the dead. She wore thick, solid silver bracelets on each wrist, beckoning back to the shackles that had been used.

Violet's gown took a team to get her strapped in. It was a showstopper. Grace had never seen anything with so much detail. The underdress was gold with a very fine floral brocade pattern embroidered in silver throughout the skirt. The overskirt was sheer, dotted with clear, shimmering crystals. Corseted strips of silver metal that showed gold fabric between plates adorned the top, overflowing into the bodice. The sleeves were sheer gold and silver that flowed into a shimmering train. The gold tone was perfect with Violet's deep auburn hair. She was lovelier than any queen Grace had seen throughout her years. Grace realized from experience the dress alone must have weighed fifty pounds.

Before long, it was time for everyone to take their places. Grace would sit with Josh, Jack's father, and JoAnn, his aunt, in the front row of the groom's side. They had little family left, so Jack's side was supplemented with a few overflow deities who didn't fit on Violet's side. There were some of Jack's friends and people from the town. He probably only had thirty-five of his own guests on his side, not including Grace. The wedding was fairly small, with only about one hundred guests in total. The big event would be the turning later that night. Every immortal they knew would be there. It was a big event for the entire multiverse. There had never been a species that could turn a non-immortal species immortal.

With Grace seated in the front, she could feel Ben enter the building behind her. She knew he was with Ami before she turned around. They were easily the most stunning pair at the event. Ben's white tux was immaculately pointed with mother-of-pearl buttons and cufflinks. His thick dark hair was loose and combed back on the sides, much more tamed than the wild curls that usually fell from his head. Ami, wearing stiletto-heeled boots, was easily as tall as Ben. She had selected a slim-cut silk-and-crepe tux with an unbuttoned white shirt under the jacket. It played beautifully against her dark skin tone. Grace wasn't sure if it was her state of being or something underlying that had always been there. She lightly bit her lower lip, unable to help but think they were something she would enjoy getting between. Grace had to avert her eyes as they took seats a few rows behind her. She looked forward to being locked in the death chamber with Jack, away from all of this temptation.

Grace glanced around the room, waiting for everyone to be seated and for the festivities to begin. Everything was white. The flowers, the silk and crepe draping, the miniature lights, everything. They had even sprayed the flower stems and greenery white. She couldn't believe how perfectly Vivienne had gotten all the shades of white to work together without a single other color, aside from the silver metalwork in the fixtures and railings. It was something you could only imagine in a dream.

Ivan stepped out onto the altar area set in front of the rows of chairs. He had a similar tux to Ben's with mother-of-pearl buttons and cufflinks. She had never realized how much they looked alike. Ivan's hair was a lighter shade of brown and his eyes were golden brown. He was a few inches shorter than Ben. Other than that, they could have been brothers. Both were lean and muscular, both were well tanned, both had square jaws. She couldn't believe she had never seen it before, even when they were standing side by side. Ivan met her eyes. He knew what she was thinking. Since the merge, they always knew what the other was thinking.

He grinned at her. *You have to realize just how far off you are if you're contemplating a threesome with Ben and Ami.* He was trying to lighten the mood. He realized how hard of a time she was having being in between the two of them.

She blushed. *I could be imagining one with you and Ben. Although that would be closer to normal for me, wouldn't it?*

He looked at the floor so others wouldn't see him trying not to laugh. *I think it's time for Leo to up your nanite dose. You only need to hang in there for a few hours. Once you're locked in with Jack, you'll be fine.* Ivan covered his smile, looking over the audience.

Ivan cleared his throat. "Everyone, please be seated."

While guests took their seats, Jack emerged, looking quite handsome. His white tux was topped off with a gold brocade vest heavily embroidered with silver to match the skirt of Violet's dress.

The trumpeting announcement played, denoting the beginning of the bridal procession. The standard music played as the bridesmaids and groomsmen made their way to the altar. When Violet appeared in the doorway, there were whispers and gasps.

She was extraordinary. She stood tall, confident, and bold. Instead of the normal bridal march you would expect to hear, Jack had something a little more special in mind. He picked up a white guitar sitting along the side of the altar stairs and played a beautiful stripped-down acoustic version of a song Grace was familiar with but couldn't quite place. She didn't know Jack had such a beautiful voice.

It overwhelmed Galin with emotion. His eyes welled, his shoulders hunched, yet he managed not to shed a tear. Vivienne couldn't say the same. She was drowning silently under her own sobs. Even Josh was dabbing at his eyes.

The ceremony was lovely; not too long, while still conveying all the joy and love these two had for each other. At the end, Ivan turned the couple around and pronounced them married.

The wedding party headed outside for pictures while the caterers and service units transformed the space to accommodate the reception. Grace headed down to the wine cellar to get away from the crowd. On a normal day, she could feel every cell, movement, and emotion from everyone around her. She had gotten used to it. Today was difficult, to say the least, and she sought a reprieve.

She opened a bottle of Riesling since she had to stay in the white range. She found a secluded seating area in the back, kicked off her shoes, and flopped down in a giant overstuffed chair.

Upstairs, Ivan and Ben had found themselves standing back-to-back along the bar on the fringes of the celebration. Ivan preferred to observe. Not that he was antisocial in any way. He liked to see how others interacted; he was reading the room, so to speak.

Ben was the opposite. Usually, he was very sociable, often the center of attention. His charms were undeniable, but this wasn't a normal day for him.

After the confrontation with Grace, he was sullen, preferring to disappear into the outskirts of the room. Seated at the bar, he hung his head and leaned on his elbows. He hadn't even realized that he was within a few feet of Ivan. He had never wanted to say those things to her. Their relationship would be different now. They had just figured out a way to work as friends, and he had blown it up. He knew it would be awkward from now on. He didn't know how he was going to face Ivan after what he said. The two had become very close friends.

Ivan could feel Ben's deep remorse. He knew Ben was standing behind him. Ivan flagged down one of the service units behind the bar and had her hand him a decanter of his private reserve scotch with two glasses. He poured one for himself and one for Ben, sliding it down the bar so it stopped in front of him. Ben picked it up and turned to face Ivan.

"You look like you could use that."

Ben pointed to the bottle. "I feel like I could use all of that and more."

"It's not you. It's her. She normally absorbs external emotions the way she does pain. Right now, she's pushing all that out. When she was indignant with you this morning, she forced those emotions onto you, too. You were goaded into your responses." Ivan was trying to make Ben feel better about what had happened.

"I only wish you were right. She doesn't have the ability to change my emotions. Pain, yes, phasing, yes, emotions, nope. My mother made sure her emotions couldn't affect me, otherwise I wouldn't be able to protect her. Sorry, my friend, but that was one hundred percent me and my genuine anger slash love toward her. I understand if you need me to keep my distance from the two of you." He swallowed down the entire glass of scotch, staring into the empty glass.

Ivan poured him another. "Ben, if I stayed away from everyone who loved Grace, I wouldn't have any friends."

"Ivan, you *don't* have any friends," Ben replied, feeling slightly less devastated.

"I got you," Ivan said, raising his glass toward Ben.

"You're in a lot of trouble then." Ben snorted and clanked Ivan's glass with his own.

CHAPTER FOUR

Grace had finished half the bottle and was feeling calmer. It was reassuring that distance made the effects diminish. She had kicked off her shoes, hiked her dress up to her thighs, and flung her legs over one arm of the chair. It was so massive that her calves were resting on one arm, her head on the other.

She heard footsteps coming toward her. They were light. She could hear clicking, followed by the soft sole of a high heel, indicating it was a woman. It was dark, so Grace only saw the black, white, and red ranges of her night vision. She didn't recognize the woman even when she came into the low light.

Grace felt serenity coming from the woman. She could make out that she was small-framed, delicate, and shorter than Grace, with golden-blonde hair and grayish-blue eyes. Her skin was creamy white and flawless. Her dress was white, as expected for today. It was a retro-style cocktail dress, super stylish with white open-toe pumps.

It perplexed Grace as to why someone would choose to wander in this direction. Most people didn't even know this part of the wine cellar existed. She was obviously an immortal. Of what origin, Grace couldn't figure out. Although something about her felt familiar, Grace had never encountered anyone who felt like her. She was curious, although she made no effort to move or stop drinking.

"Can I help you with something? Are you lost?"

"Oh sweetie, I'm here to help you. You haven't got a clue what you're doing, have you?" The woman seemed genuinely concerned and condescending simultaneously.

Grace snorted. "I think you need to narrow that down a little. I'm confused about a lot of things."

"For starters, you don't understand how the multidimensional universe works or why it needs to stay in balance, do you?"

That piqued Grace's interest, but she still didn't turn to face the woman. No one up to that point had explained the whats or hows of the way it was all supposed to work or how she was involved with it. "And you do?" she uttered sarcastically.

"Yes, I absolutely do. And you are wasting your time turning one insignificant immortal at a time. You need to be spreading your light energy to populations of entire planets and creating stars. You don't have the time to waste figuring out the learning curve. That's why I came myself," the woman smiled smugly.

"And you are?" Grace tilted her head, giving the woman a side glance. At this point, Grace had a rough idea of who she was but was reluctant to guess incorrectly and make herself look like an idiot for a second or third time today.

The woman scrutinized Grace as if she were an insolent child. Her posture was arrogant. "I am the primordial manifestation of night. You may call me Nyx."

Next to Nyx, Grace really was a child. Nyx was one of the earliest beings to come into existence, emerging from Chaos shortly after the creation of the universes.

Grace was grateful to speak with her, or anyone who could explain what was happening. She was less assured that Nyx wouldn't be yet another one with an agenda who wanted Grace to do something for their own benefit. Her body sank deeper into the chair, subconsciously releasing tension.

"You have no idea how relieved I am to see you. I don't have a clue what I'm supposed to be doing. The Council expects me to somehow grasp my purpose innately in all of this. They created me, yet they are oblivious to how I'm supposed to do what they want me to do. Now I'm supposed to lead an entirely new species and bring light to this universe. And to top it all off, my body has decided to throw me into estrus today. I am lost and frustrated and confused. And this," Grace raised her glass, "is the only thing helping me right now."

Nyx shook her head. "You're a bigger mess than I thought. I should have come earlier." She pointed to the chair across from the one Grace was sitting in. "May I?"

"Please. Wine?"

"Yes, thank you."

Grace rolled out of the chair, went to the rack behind her, and pulled out a glass before getting another bottle from the chiller. She filled Nyx's glass, handing it to her before flopping back down the way she had been before.

"I thought you couldn't be in this universe while it was out of balance. Won't it be a problem for you to be here?" Grace wondered.

"Not while I am in this form. It diminishes me," Nyx scoffed in disgust. "It was essential that I come. If you can't understand what you need to be doing, none of this will matter anyway."

"Well then, where do we start?" Grace asked.

"We're going to start at the beginning. You need to understand how the universes are connected and how the progression works. Then we can go into specifics of your role." Nyx realized it would take hours, maybe days, to ensure Grace understood all this information.

"We have about four hours before I need to go to Rasa for the mating ceremony."

"That will not be enough time. Can't someone else do it? This is crucial." Nyx felt Grace was being flippant about her vast responsibility.

"I'm the sacrifice. Ceremonial only these days, but it's a tremendous honor. Sacrifices are picked months, sometimes years, in advance. The ceremony takes less than an hour, and then my duty is to be locked into the death chamber with the deceased until he rises as an immortal. It can be anywhere from four to forty-eight hours. You're more than welcome to sit with me and continue our conversation there. If I don't uphold traditions, they won't follow me. From what I understand, I need them to follow me." Grace wasn't being flippant at all. She was being pragmatic.

"I apologize. I misunderstood. Of course, traditions are important to lower beings, and the time is not impractical. I have allotted one day of your time for this visit, and I will also leave you instructions on how we can communicate after I leave. Just so you understand, having followers makes your task easier, but you don't *need* them to follow you. You only need Ivan. The two of you together create the light. But I'm getting ahead of myself. You need to understand the balance. After that, we can discuss how you can create light on a much grander scale. We should involve Ivan in this conversation."

Grace explained why she couldn't be close to Ivan for more than a few minutes at a time. At least not until after the turning.

"I can't see what your objection is. I think you should simply mate and be finished with it. Bringing a new life forward will only make you stronger." Nyx had dozens of children; some light, some dark, and some neutral.

"But what if our child is of the dark? Would he or she negate what we are trying to accomplish here, creating light?"

Grace's question seemed quite childish to Nyx. It irritated her that no one had ever explained even the most basic information to Grace. "Do you really have no concept of what you are? They created you from pure light as I was created from chaos. Light from every universe has contributed to your existence. You cannot die, you cannot be destroyed as other immortals can. You are neither male nor female. Only your biological shell determines your gender. You. Are. Pure. Light. You are equal to any Primordial who came before the Titans. I cannot fathom how these imbecilic primitives brought you into being, but they clearly fell upon something in their blinded and grasping state," Nyx exhaled, curling her lip in disgust.

"That's encouraging," Grace retorted.

"Grace, the energy you hold can burn through other immortals with a thought. I seriously doubt the simpletons riding their power wave on the Council had much involvement with it at all. But I do know you are my equal in strength. Even now, you don't understand how to manifest your energy into light, being as old as you are. What makes you believe any child of yours would have the ability to create darkness without any training?" She thought it laughable that Grace had zero concept of the power she held, much less how to manifest and control it.

Now Grace was getting angry. "How am I supposed to know *any* of this? I was never prepared. I was never trained. No one gave me any idea of what I was or why I was. Why wouldn't you say anything to me when you found out I existed?"

"Because I couldn't comprehend the thought that you could be so oblivious to what you were if you had truly existed. How could you not know?"

"If you were born a wolf and raised by dogs, how would you have any idea that you were not a dog? I had no reason to believe I was more than those around me. Can we both agree I am unsophisticated, uneducated, and untrained and get on with it?" Grace was quite angry now. She wasn't sure if it was because of this conversation or if it was because of her excessive hormone levels.

Her sense of the situation amused Nyx. She sighed. "Childhood education it is, then. This is going to take far longer than I had initially believed. You'll need to come to my dimension next time. For now, let's begin with the creation of the universes. Are you prepared to listen?"

"I've been ready for someone to tell me the truth since the day I was born."

"Well, this is a rudimentary way we explain the workings of the universe to children, so excuse me if I offend your intelligence, although I doubt I will. We can get more in depth later if you think you can comprehend it." The corners of her mouth turned up, but Grace thought it was more a sneer than a smile.

Nyx continued. "Think of the layers of universes as being like a water wheel. The front sections of the wheel hold content, and the back sections fold flat and hold nothing, waiting to be filled." Nyx paused.

"That sounds simple enough," Grace replied.

"This wheel moves a little differently than what you're used to. Each front section is a universe. For this purpose, we'll start with a full front side. There is only a specific amount of water that the wheel can hold and only a specific amount each section contains. As the wheel moves, the top section leaks into the section below, and so forth. Do you understand?"

"I'm with you so far." Grace could picture it in her mind.

"When the top section is nearly empty, the lowest section is completely full. As the top section is pushed over the top of the wheel, it collapses into nothing, spilling out its contents, forcing a new bottom section to scoop up the overflow in one quick burst. This shift causes one universe to collapse and simultaneously causes another to come into existence. Still with me?"

"It makes sense, but what turns the wheel?"

Nyx closed her eyes and took a deep breath. "It doesn't matter."

Grace felt she had been admonished by a teacher and kept quiet, nodding her head.

Nyx was almost certain she'd lose Grace during this next part. "As the top sections lose 'water,'" Nyx used air quotes around the word, "they become darker. The bottom sections are fuller; therefore, they contain more light. Each section from bottom to top gets progressively darker as it contains less water, or light, in this example."

Grace nodded in understanding.

Nyx continued, "The relationship between the progression of the decline of each universe is absolute. No universe can contain more light than the one below it without upsetting the balance of the entire system. Usually, I'd have a projection of some sort to show you. I didn't realize I would have to be explaining this. Hopefully, you can visualize it."

"I can. I understand the concept."

"Excellent. So, here's where the problem lies. The universe you inhabit is still young. It's in the bottom third of the wheel, which still contains vast amounts of light. But this universe has less light than the universe above it. It is upsetting the balance of the entire system. Once the imbalance becomes too extreme, or spreads to other universes, the wheel will stop."

Grace was digesting this information. "Do we know why this specific section—dimension, universe, whatever you want to call it—is so far out of balance?"

"Something is consuming the light and scattering it much more quickly than it should, and I don't mean just cloaking it with darkness. I mean, the energy is being changed back to matter in several sectors. The only resolution is to create more light from inert and gaseous matter throughout this universe until it reaches the correct percentage."

Grace's eyes widened, although her face remained blank. "Now you lost me. I don't understand the relationship between light and matter. What do you mean?"

Nyx heaved a deep sigh, unconsciously rubbing the tips of her fingers slowly over the arms of the chair, digging into the edges, while she considered the proper phrasing. "It's the cycle of all life. Energy is light. Something is consuming stars, or rather their energy, dissolving them into particles of dust and gas before their time and spreading them. You can take that same matter, in solid and gaseous states, and combine them, forcing them to collapse into themselves, creating a star and restoring the light that has been dispersed."

"Yeah," Grace said sarcastically. "What the hell gives you the idea I can create something on the scale of a star?" Grace was beginning to think this was a joke. There was no way she had that kind of power.

Nyx was visibly frustrated as her face contorted from her tightly clenched jaw and her body tensed. "Because you have the ability to accelerate particles in various ways; I have the ability to decelerate particles. You create light, or more precisely, you can control the process of fusion. You can do it alone on a small scale, but you and Ivan together can create massive stars. You just need proper training."

"And exactly who would be qualified to teach me? I accelerate particles without the addition of heat. Cold fusion technology, as we understand it, can only provide enough power for propulsion and sustainment of spacecraft. How am I supposed to figure out how to scale that up to such a massive task when none of our scientists have been able to do that?" Grace was still in disbelief.

Nyx thought Grace must be the wrong person. There had to be someone else out there who could do this. This woman sulking in front of her was an ignorant joke, but she couldn't give up. If this pathetic woman in front of her really was who she was supposed to be, Grace might be their only chance to fix whatever was happening.

Nyx laughed at her in a way that made Grace feel stupid. She got out of her chair and stood over Grace. Then her tone became aggressive.

"I knew this was going to be difficult, but this is ridiculous! You won't be generating anything with cold fusion. You need heat to create a star. Did you not hear the part where I told you that you are essentially a primordial being? Obviously, completely out of step with the creation of the rest of us, but none the less, you are equal in power. You need to suck it up. Stop feeling sorry for yourself and do what you were created to do! Do you think you can handle that?" Nyx was practically yelling at her.

"Then tell me what I need to do!" Grace yelled back. "It's not like this ability comes with a manual."

Nyx shrugged. Her tone went back to merely condescending. "Actually, it does. You're just ignoring it." She started pacing as she spoke, without taking her eyes off Grace. "Aether and Hemera have been keeping The Everything in balance since the beginning of time. Since they were children. They just started doing it on their own. But whatever has been consuming the light here has also been in other dimensions. It has become too much for them to deal with alone, which is why the High Council, as they *love* to call themselves, wanted to create you. I never thought they'd be able to do it, but here you are. Maybe they finally did something useful for once." She didn't think much of the lower deities, as she referred to them. There were a few who had her respect, but mostly they thought far too much of themselves for their miniscule capabilities.

"Think you should have led with that?" Grace asked in a condescending tone. "I mean, if there are others with eons of experience, wouldn't that be the first thing you would think about? How about, 'Let's get you to go over to them and see how they're doing it? Give you a few pointers?' You know, stuff like that."

Nyx regarded Grace with disdain. "Because they don't have time to hold your hand and wipe your nose. You need to follow your energy. You have a built-in guide," Nyx growled. "I didn't have to come here at all, you know." Nyx was not used to anyone speaking to her in the tone Grace had. She seemed quite annoyed by Grace's arrogance.

"Bullshit. I may not understand my role, and I may not know the extent of my abilities, but I know when someone is full of garbage. If you didn't need me, you wouldn't have bothered because you think this world is beneath you. You think I'm beneath you. And I'm sure I am. So, either teach me or get out of my dimension and let them all collapse. What do you care anyway? You'll still exist in the vast nothing, won't you?"

Grace leaned back in her chair, emptying the remainder of the bottle into her glass. She was done playing games with all these supposedly higher beings. They all wanted something from her, but none of them so far had been willing to help her or teach her how to do what needed to be done. Today was not the day for anyone to jerk her around.

"Someone grew a little courage, did they? When I walked in here, I thought you were some worthless little snit, wallowing in her own self-pity. Unwilling or unable to do the work that needed to be done. I wasn't even sure you were what they said you were. Speaking to me like you did, you're either incredibly brave or incredibly stupid, possibly both."

"I'm sure it's both. I have been manipulated for my entire existence, and I'm finished with it. I'm not down here wallowing in self-pity. I'm down here because I don't want to ruin what is supposed to be the best day of my friend's life. Aside from that, I like being alone. When you can feel every particle of everything around you, crowds are not always the best place to be. Especially ones filled with powerful immortals. I can tell what a person's abilities are by the way they feel to me. Yet, I can't even tell what Ivan's or my own are. How's that for irony?" Grace wasn't afraid of or intimidated by Nyx. She was envious of her knowledge. She was exasperated by spending every minute of her life in the dark.

"Why would you care about these beings at all? Your little mix of mortals and inconsequential immortal beings doesn't matter in the grand scheme of things. The only thing that matters is the balance of light and dark. Without that, there *is* none of *this*." Nyx waved her hand with an apathetic gesture and a look of disgust.

"Well, Nyx, without *this*," Grace waved her hand, appearing insolent, "the entirety of the universe or multiverse or The Everything, whatever you want to call it, doesn't matter. If you have nothing to care about, there is no point to the existence of anything." Grace couldn't figure out if Nyx was trying to make her angry or if she truly thought other life didn't matter. She was trying hard to stay calm, but she could feel the nanites keeping her emotions at bay, burning out.

"Grace, you're personalizing this as if your attachments matter. You were created to ensure the grander scale exists. Your feelings are inconsequential. Nothing will exist for anyone or anything if balance isn't restored. The only ones left will be Primordials, and we will only exist in The Nothing. So, if you want any of this," Nyx waved both her hands, "to exist, you need to get over yourself and your feelings. This would have been so much easier if they had turned you over when you were created. You wouldn't have formed any attachments, and we could have found an appropriate secondary being for you to merge with. Your entire life has been nothing but a waste of time!" Nyx was now yelling at her.

Grace felt her rage welling. She couldn't hold it back any longer. She sprung out of the chair with the deftness of a cat, stopping inches away from Nyx. Her eyes were glowing green, and her skin burned hot. Her amulet was glowing blue, locking her down. She let out an enraged scream as her entire body glowed brightly. Ivan had felt her rage and ported in beside Nyx. He reached out to Grace, but Nyx grabbed his arm, pulling him back.

"What are you doing to her?" he yelled at Nyx.

"This is what she was created for, Ivan. She has to rise."

"What do you mean, *rise?*" Ivan demanded.

"Release her essence into the universe. It's called rising."

"But Beivve said if she releases into the universe, she'll be gone."

Nyx spun to look at him. "That's nonsense. She's part of the universe and so are you. She'll never be lost out there. You'll need to rise alongside her and join her out there. It's where you belong."

Grace began to calm herself, reducing the light emanating from her. It finally dissipated as she returned to normal. Ivan and Nyx watched as the amulet darkened back to its original sapphire.

Nyx sighed, "Well, that was anticlimactic. I never thought I was going to get you angry enough to rise. With the estrus and all, I thought it would be easy. You have much more control than I had at your age. Why didn't you rise?"

Grace and Ivan were both flustered by her behavior. The experience had drained Grace's energy.

"What in all hells are you trying to pull? Why were you trying to make me rise, Nyx? I don't want to be lost to the universe."

Ivan involuntarily recoiled at the mention of her name.

Nyx leaned in, scrutinizing the two of them. "Where did you get the ridiculous idea that you could be lost to the universe? Did I not just say that it is where the two of you belong?"

The statement confused Grace and Ivan even more. "We don't understand what you're saying to us. If we rise into the universe, what happens to *us?* What happens to our bodies? Our lives?" Ivan could feel Grace being pulled to him and backed up a step as she sat down.

"Nothing. What do you mean? Your bodies stay where they are. They're designed to sustain themselves while you're outside of them. You can come back whenever you want. They're only shells, anyway. They're not what you are. I've gone through many shells. They just hold you in a tactile form and create a means for you to reproduce little biological beings. I don't understand why you didn't rise from your shell, Grace." Their complete lack of basic knowledge was much worse than she had thought. They would need more help than she had been prepared for.

"It's the amulet. It shut her down before." Ivan remembered the auction incident.

"Then take it off. I can't teach you anything if you're stuck inside of there. How did they trap you in it, anyway?" Nyx was concerned. If there was a way to trap a Primordial inside of a shell, it severely limited their abilities. More concerning, she did not want anyone to be able to do that to her.

"I can't. I should say I can't right now. It's a blood seal and I don't have the blood with me. And it also cloaks my light from being seen or tracked."

That didn't answer Nyx's primary question. "How does a blood seal trap you inside that shell, is what I'm asking you. I understand it won't let you remove the amulet. What I don't understand is how it can keep you in that." She pointed at Grace, sneering.

Grace thought for a second. She hadn't put it together until Nyx made her think of the relationship of the seal and shell. "It's Ben's blood. My shell was created with Ben's blood, and they sealed the amulet with Ben's blood. I think Frigg did it so I couldn't fully use my abilities while I didn't know who I was. Or at least not until Ben found me."

Nyx closed her eyes, rubbing her temples. Being in a biological encasement had its pitfalls. She was getting a raging headache. "I know I'm going to regret this. By the phrase 'didn't know who I was,' do you mean you didn't know who you were born as, or you didn't know that you were of the light? Second, who in any universe's version of all hells is Ben? And why would Frigg use his blood?" Nyx didn't know the background of how Grace had gotten to this planet in this universe at this time.

"We need another bottle for that discussion." Grace retrieved another bottle and opened it. "Ivan, what time is it? My port time is set for ten thirty-five. What about yours?"

Ivan checked his watch. "It's quarter to eight. I'm scheduled for ten fifteen with Erik and Asta. I'll have to get back upstairs at some point to wish the bride and groom off at ten."

"I'd forgotten about that. I'll need to be upstairs for that as well." Grace didn't want her absence to seem suspicious.

"You don't have to. Erik's been telling all the mortal guests that you had an allergic reaction to some shellfish at the beginning of the reception. They're not expecting you back."

Kudos to Erik, Grace thought. He always was the smart one. Two steps ahead of everyone else.

"Excuse me. Can we get back to the extremely boring issue of balancing The Everything?" Nyx thought it surreal they could chat about a party when the fate of The Everything was in question.

Grace stated contemptuously, "We're obviously *not* going to get unilateral balance achieved tonight. What we can do is get some basics out of the way while ensuring these ceremonies are completed properly. You know, you could have picked a less hectic day to come."

Nyx rolled her eyes. "I must agree, you're not wrong about the timing. I figured, go to a nice party, have a few drinks, chat for a moment, and then I could go home. It was a shock to me how much of a monumental task it turned out to be. Can we at least get back on point until everyone is required to move?"

"Yes." Grace sighed, then slid the bottle across the floor to Nyx, not wanting to get too close to Ivan, who had taken the seat farthest from Grace beside Nyx. She grabbed it and refilled her glass. She offered the bottle to Ivan. He took it and knocked back nearly half of what remained in one swallow, wishing it was the scotch he had left upstairs.

"I have another question for you before we start. I've been to Ami's home dimension. It's a dimension of light where we were outside of our shells. How was I able to go there as light?"

Nyx had a theory. "Was it before you got the amulet?"

Grace thought back. "Yes, but I had a bracelet that cloaked me."

"That dimension is different. You could have still had your shell, but it's a place where the light can shine through. And you were still young. You weren't at full power yet. Forget everything you ever thought you understood about the manifestation of life. Yhwh, or God as he calls himself, is a Primordial too. All the creators are Primordials born of Chaos, just as I was. His children, the angels, can look upon us as any of my children can. The ones who either come from two Primordials or the ones created autonomously from only one of us are our direct descendants. They are undiluted beings similar to what we are. The same as yours and Ivan's will be. Now, back to this Ben person and his blood."

Grace still didn't fully understand. "Are you trying to insinuate that since they created me of the light, it somehow makes me a Primordial?"

"I insinuate nothing. You are a Primordial being. It is beyond me how you could be. Nevertheless, you are. You both are." Nyx cut her eyes between Grace and Ivan.

"That's ridiculous," Grace replied.

"You would think," Nyx retorted.

"Not that I am agreeing with you," Ivan looked at Nyx. "Let's, for the moment, say your assessment is correct."

"I'm not incorrect," Nyx sneered.

"Okay, then let's accept the idea that you are correct. What does it matter?" Ivan asked.

Nyx clenched her jaw. "It matters because if she can be locked inside of a little genetic prison by a piece of jewelry, then all of us could." Nyx pointed at Grace. She dropped her hand and took a cleansing breath. "Now, Grace, continue."

Grace gulped. Whether she was or wasn't what Nyx thought she was, she realized she needed to narrate her story. Nyx may have better insight as to why things had happened to her the way they did. And it may also make Nyx less inclined to torture them to death.

It took a while to recount how her second shell had been created, her memories, Ben, and the last seventeen hundred years to present. She skipped past the boring parts, hitting only the relevant highlights, so Nyx might understand how little she really understood about the workings of technology and the universe. When it was getting close to time for Ivan to leave, Erik appeared in the doorway.

"Ivan, Vivienne needs you upstairs. Hey, Mom. Leo has been searching for you. I thought you might have been hiding down here. I only found you because your voices were carrying through the entire warehouse."

Nyx scanned the young man silently.

"Thank you, Erik. Please let him know where I am when you go back up." Grace assumed Leo wanted to replenish her nanites before the second ceremony.

Ivan rose to stand beside Erik in the doorway. "Grace, I'll see you on Rasa. Let me know if you need anything before then. Nyx, it was ..." he paused momentarily, "interesting to meet you." He and Erik turned to go back upstairs.

"Boy," Nyx called out, twisting around in her seat.

"Excuse me?" Erik laughed. "May I help you with something?" He didn't want to appear rude. Nyx had caught him off guard with her choice in salutation. He was, after all, quite old. But he recognized her name and realized to her, he wasn't.

Nyx turned her head back toward Grace, pointing at Erik. "Is this one of yours with the lower immortal, Ben, as you call him? One of The Three?"

"Yes. This is Erik. You could say he's the middle one."

"Hmm, quaint." She turned back to Erik. "Erik, do you have a basic understanding of the dynamic relationship between universes?" She wanted to see if there were any lower immortals who understood the workings of multidimensional space or if it was just the fact that Grace was uneducated in these matters.

"Yes." Erik was concise with his answer to the question. He had learned that rarely did anyone want an explanation. Nyx apparently was not one of those who expected a simple answer.

"Well then. Explain it."

Erik worked with quantum physics and energy transfer routinely. He didn't know how in-depth an answer she was looking for. "Oh, so this is a test. With the time constraint I'm currently under, I will give you the simplest explanation I normally pass on to my apprentices until they have the capacity to grasp deeper concepts. Will that be sufficient?"

"Proceed." She nodded, raising her eyebrows in approval.

"Utilizing a physical aspect of multidimensional space, I explain it as a stack of sheets contained in a pool of negative-energy superfluid. Each sheet in the stack becomes more porous as it ages. It loses mass, which allows it to float to the top of the stack. Once enough mass is lost, it will tend to collapse on itself, simultaneously creating a new heavy sheet at the bottom of the stack due to the vast amount of disintegrated mass particles spilling to the bottom. Did I pass your test?"

Nyx nodded approvingly. "Yes. As rudimentary as the explanation was, it shows you have the required understanding. Do your brothers also possess this type of knowledge?"

Erik scoffed. "Not likely. They are both tacticians. I am the only one who took an interest in science and technology. Learning is a process that I hope to continue."

"Do you understand the process of fusion?"

"Conventional or cold?" Erik tapped a small spot behind his ear, allowing him to see the time discreetly. He would normally be quite eager to engage in this conversation, but Asta was waiting for him upstairs. She was the first woman he had developed feelings for, and he didn't want to leave her waiting alone and give Mikkel the chance to move in.

"Either."

Grace had lost interest in the direction Erik and Nyx's conversation had gone. She was tuning in to some of the party conversation upstairs.

"Grace!" Nyx snapped her fingers toward her. Erik had already left.

"What?"

"Did you understand any of that?" Nyx seemed exasperated.

"Understand any of what?"

"After I leave today, Erik is going to teach you and Ivan about the process of fusion. You will need to practice creating small fusion reactions in your immediate area of space." Nyx had originally thought it would only take a few years of their time to get them to the point of creating a dwarf star. Now she thought it may take decades. And that was without considering also teaching them how to harness negative energy to fold space and shift. But first, they had to get that thing from around her neck. Nyx's head was aching again just thinking about it. These damned shells were so diminishing.

Grace had a thought come to her. She didn't understand the scientific aspects of what she needed to learn, but she wanted to know some other basic things.

"What happens to our shells when we are outside of them? I mean, do they sit vulnerable to outside influence? How do we protect them, so we know it's safe to come back to them? I only ask because of my current situation with my amulet. What if someone were to lock it down while we were away? Would they have control of us when we came back?"

"Those are important questions to which we need to find answers. My shell is manifested, and I have a safe place where I send it when I rise. I think your situation with your current shell is unique because of how it was constructed. The fact is, I have seen nothing that could lock us in before now." Nyx would need more information before she could give an adequate response.

"One thing I must emphasize is you need to ensure the Council can never have the means to control you. I don't trust them, and you shouldn't either. Their intentions in finding a solution to the balance issues were purely for their own self-interest, and I think them having the ability to control you would be dangerous to all Primordials. I would hazard a guess Frigg saw that. I'm not sure who you should trust to bring those questions to. Once you rise from your current shell, it may be better to simply create another without the restriction of using Ben's blood. I'm not certain who would have adequate knowledge about creating a seal to control you. Maybe Apollo, but he doesn't seem to have any allegiance to the Council, but Thoth's mate is on the Council, so I don't think we can say the same of him."

Grace's eyes darted toward the doorway, signaling Nyx to be quiet. "Leo's coming."

Both women sat quietly, waiting for him to appear. Once he did, Grace waited for him to speak first.

"There you are. I saw you burned through your nanites, but I didn't know where you were. Erik told me. I thought you'd need them replenished to get through the next ceremony."

Nyx turned to see a familiar face. "Asclepius! It's been forever! I am happy to see a friendly face. What did she call you? Leo?"

Leo glowed with a broad smile of respect and adoration. "It's simpler. I prefer Leo. It's been too long." He leaned down, giving Nyx a kiss on the hand.

She turned toward Grace, clasping Leo's hand firmly. "Now this one you can trust. He's taken the brutal wrath of other immortals frequently, divulging none of his secrets. He even got himself killed once because he couldn't stop saving things. I trust him completely."

Leo smirked. "Nyx, you trust no one completely. And they were people, not things."

"True, but you are as close to trust as I can manage." She addressed Grace next. "He respects all life no matter what form it takes, which seems to be a priority for you."

Nyx pulled Leo around the chair. "Come, sit with us."

"I wish I had the time. Grace will need to leave soon, and I must replenish her nanites for the next ceremony. I promise I'll come see you when this is all over so we can catch up." Leo was normally very professional around Grace. This was the first time in all the time she had known him that she had seen him as charming.

Nyx had a thought. "Grace, we should bring him to the chamber. He could work on a solution for you."

Leo hadn't realized Nyx was planning on being in the death chamber with Grace and Jack. "I'm already going to be in the chamber. I'm monitoring Jack's turning."

Nyx was very pleased to hear that. "Excellent. We'll all go together then."

Leo looked as if he had an epiphany. "Grace, I didn't realize you spoke Primor."

"Spoke what?" Grace appeared disoriented.

"Primor. The language of the Primordials. That's what we're speaking." Leo and Nyx exchanged a quizzical glance. "How could she not know she was speaking a different language?"

"I thought I was speaking English." Grace really didn't know she was speaking another language. She had never even thought about it.

"We've been speaking it the entire time. That's the main reason I was so surprised you didn't understand the concepts of our race. The only time we spoke English was when Erik was here. How could you not know?" Nyx regarded her quizzically.

"I didn't think about it." Grace shrugged. "I understood you and I answered you. There wasn't any difference to me."

"Ivan spoke it too," Nyx said factually.

"Hmmm. Apollo and Beivve told us we were a unique race. How is that possible that we could know a language we've not known existed?"

"The lower immortals have no concept of what we are. We came before all of them, including the Titans and the Leviathans. No offense meant, Leo." Nyx rubbed his arm apologetically as one would a pet.

"No offense taken. I know where I am on the food chain." He chuckled, then cast his eyes down, showing his contrition.

"Don't be sad, darling. I hold you in the highest regard." Nyx didn't like it when Leo was sad. She earnestly cared for him.

Leo tilted his face up slightly, half smiling. "I know you do. Let's get to it then so we can get off this depressing planet and onto Rasa. You'll find it much more comfortable than this place. I'll never understand the necessity for most mortals to consistently spread sadness and bring others down when they should be raising each other up. It's probably why they have never evolved. I'm seldom relaxed on this planet. They bring so much harm to each other. I can't help but want to save them."

"I'll never understand what you think you're saving them from," Nyx replied.

"Themselves, of course. The first reaction they usually have is to fear what they don't understand. Their second reaction is to kill what they fear. It's just such a waste of life."

Grace had thought that was an odd statement for Leo to make. Leo and Nyx seemed to be amused by his remark. Grace had always tried to see the light and the effort in mortals. Maybe that's why she didn't share their criticism of the species.

Leo moved over to Grace. "I've upped the amount of nanites in this dose. Hopefully, they'll last longer than the last batch."

Grace moved her amulet, giving Leo access to the sensor he had placed on her earlier.

Nyx added, "That was my fault, Ascle—Leo. I tried to get Grace to rise. That's what burned out her nanites."

"Oh Nyx! Not here! Whatever is consuming the light will see her as a beacon. Rasa has blockers covering the planet. It will be much safer there. You can rise there, too, but not in the chamber with Jack. I don't know how it will affect his turning." Leo was glad Grace hadn't been able to rise.

Nyx appeared to take the admonishment well. "Sorry about that. The amulet wouldn't let her rise, anyway. You need to figure that out."

Leo's mind caught up to what Nyx had said a few seconds ago. "Wait, did you say rise? Since when have the Æsir been able to rise? I don't think the Vanir can even rise, can they?"

"She's developed past that, Leo. I'll explain later. For now, let's just keep it between us, agreed?" Nyx lifted her chin, tilting her face to the side.

"I agree it's for the best," he said, placing the nanites on Grace's monitor, which gave off the same green glow it had before. He leaned back and scrutinized Grace for a few seconds. "I've been thinking about the blood seal. Maybe once we've broken it, I will be able to get more data from her scans." He turned back to look at Nyx.

"I am confident I'll be able to replicate the lock without the seal so she can take off the amulet when she wants. Breaking the seal will end the hold."

"We've already gotten past that conversation, Leo," Grace said.

"Oh, sorry. I should have figured. Did you tell her you needed Ben's blood to break the seal, then?"

Nyx rubbed Leo's shoulder. "Yes, Leo. We've been through all that."

"So, she's also told you she's the only one who can get Ben's blood, then? Well, her and Ivan. The only time he has bled was when she phased a sword into his leg."

"And where is that blood?" Nyx was internally panicking.

Grace didn't hesitate to ease that thought. "Ida, the facility AI, saw it as a biohazard and destroyed it. It doesn't matter even if it is here. What matters is that I have some."

"What do you mean, you have some?" Nyx narrowed her eyes.

Grace added, "I also took a small vial of his blood from his arm later. So, there were two times I've broken through his skin." She scrunched her face momentarily. "Three if you count the time I reached into his chest and threatened to rip out his heart. Anyway, I have it back in my quarters on Rasa. I can use it later to remove the amulet."

They both were slack jawed with astonishment.

"You did what?" Leo asked.

"Who knows you have that vial?" Nyx asked.

Grace ignored Leo's question, understanding he was referring to the heart comment. "I was going to take off the amulet so the Council would know who I was and stop screwing with me and Ivan. I stuck my finger into his arm and squeezed out a small vial of his blood. Ivan, Kali, Ma'at, and Thoth were there. Maybe Beivve and Apollo, too, but I can't remember if they had already left or not. And, of course, Ben. But Ivan is the only one who knows where it is besides me." Grace hadn't thought it was such a big deal at the time. She was rethinking that decision now.

"The second we port over, you need to get that vial and make sure every tiny particle of that blood is accounted for. Bring it to the chamber. That's where we will remove the amulet. I'll work on the closure as soon as you have it off." Leo seemed troubled over the revelation anyone else may be able to access the blood and amulet before he could study it. He believed it wasn't only the key to unlocking the amulet; it was the key to controlling her.

"Aren't you worried about how it might affect Jack?" Grace asked.

"Oh, right, Jack. I'll need to think about that," Leo answered, rubbing his chin.

Nyx rolled her eyes. "Her light will not affect anyone negatively."

"Well, we can make that decision later. The important part is that you get the blood," he said to Grace.

"I'll bring it straight to you after the ceremony." Grace hoped she hadn't made the wrong decision about keeping it.

"Good. How do you feel? Are the nanites working?" he asked.

"Yes. Normal. Thank you."

"The scans look good. Your hormone levels are even in a readable range now." Leo was making some adjustments to his device.

Nyx thought this was a good time to add her opinion. "And when the festivities are over, you and Ivan should mate and get through all of this."

Grace watched her with trepidation. She fumbled with her ring. "I'm still not sure if this is a good time. I don't know if I'm ready to bring another being into this with all the uncertainty surrounding us."

Nyx sighed. "Grace, you may never feel it will be the right time. I can promise you, though, it will strengthen you. And it will make Ivan stronger. You are bonded in ways you can't understand until you rise together."

Leo walked toward the door to usher the women upstairs. "It's time to leave."

CHAPTER FIVE

The ceremony was set to take place in the great hall. Grace stood with Nyx in the main doorway, taking in the architecture's beauty. Vivienne had outdone herself styling the event. It was the grandest place Grace had ever laid eyes on, which was saying a lot.

The room seemed to be a thousand feet long and half as wide. They had set the ceiling to be transparent, bringing in light from the four moons and billions of stars. It was lit at ground level by what appeared to be tiny flames, which were holographic floor lights. It felt like the warm outdoor spaces of old Earth.

The seating was circular, representing the infinity of immortal life. There was a raised round platform in the center covered in crimson, while the rest of the hall was the deep, rich warmth of midnight. It was scented lightly with honeysuckle and jasmine.

A few guests had taken seats near the outer rings of the circle. Everyone was formally dressed in black with crimson or scarlet accoutrements. Nyx had changed into an amazingly gorgeous heavily beaded floor-length black dress with crimson crystals that resembled drops of blood. It was more fitting to who Grace imagined her to be.

The feel of the room was thick and heavy but also warm and welcoming. The mood was as reverent as any place of worship Grace had been to. Soft string music played as more guests slowly made their way in. Grace was the only one still dressed in white, befitting the sacrifice.

Grace had already retrieved and given the vial of Ben's blood to Leo, who was performing a final check of the sensors in the chamber. This event was not only a turning; it would signify the acceptance of the new immortals into the vast interdimensional community. It also signified the blending of the old and new races into one people of Rasa. Every pantheon from this universe would be represented tonight. They were curious to see a mortal forever changed into an immortal being. At the reception, CB would be offered to anyone wanting to consume Grace's light. It would be a landmark step to bringing everything back into balance. Every race in attendance understood the gravity of the event. There would be no conflicts here. No one would be so bold with both Grace and Nyx standing side by side. This was a neutral sanctuary.

Vivienne had become excited to learn of Nyx's attendance. She placed a black seat resembling a throne on the platform, mirroring Grace's white one. She wanted everyone to see them united in their blessing of her daughter's union.

Primordials were, after all, the royalty of the multiverse as Vivienne understood it. The Council could no longer subvert Grace with Nyx by her side. Many of the Council members still had little understanding of what Frigg and Freya were able to create. Vivienne also believed they were responsible for creating the vampires themselves, giving Ivan the means to merge as Grace's equal.

Grace intended to ask the Fates about that if they came. They had sent an acceptance to the invitation, but it was rare anyone ever saw them in public because too often they were approached with questions about someone's future.

The hall was filling faster now. There would be thousands in attendance. Grace had been asking Nyx about several of the attendees whose race she didn't recognize. She was learning many things she hadn't understood about the inhabitants of worlds she never knew existed. There were so many humanoid and non-humanoid races of all colors. The eclectic rainbow of species that she had never encountered before impressed her.

"We should take our places. The ceremony will start soon." Grace had explained the sequence of events to Nyx earlier.

They walked side by side up the long aisle. The room quieted as they took their seats on the platform. As they scanned the crowd, their audience erupted in whispers. They heard bells chime as everyone stood expectantly, focused on the back of the hall. Grace and Nyx were the only ones to remain seated as the High Council entered, taking their places in the front section to the right of the platform. They nodded to Grace and Nyx, who acknowledged them with a reciprocating nod before watching them sit.

The remaining Council members and their partners filed in quietly, taking their seats behind the senior members. Grace smiled, seeing many faces she had come to know as friends. They shared unsure glances among themselves upon seeing Nyx by her side. Nyx smiled wryly, seeing their eyes widen. The realization of Grace's status was overcoming their thoughts as Nyx placed her hand on Grace's. In that moment, they seemed to understand what she was as tendrils of nearly imperceptible energy flowed between the women.

Grace was torn. She had wanted the Council to stop trying to control her these last few years, but she also didn't want her friends to see her differently. She was still the same Grace she had always been. The last thing she wanted was for their new perception of her to overshadow Violet and Jack's ceremony. She was never so happy as she was when she heard the music announcing the arrival of the ceremony's participants.

All again stood, apart from Grace and Nyx. Ivan came in first, dressed in black from head to toe, followed by Violet and Jack holding hands. Jack wore a black tux with a scarlet shirt to match Violet's dress. He finished with a black tie, a ruby tie clip, and cufflinks.

Violet's scarlet dress was daring. The top was strapless, deep cut, and corseted in intricately cut stiff black material melting into a scarlet skirt and long train. It was covered with clusters of black crystals that trailed into sequined vines. Her black tiara, earrings, and necklace dripped with rubies. Together, they were the picture of perfection.

They were followed by Asta and Erik, then Mikkel and Alex, who would carry Jack's body to the chamber. He wanted his brothers to be the ones to take him, but with that being impossible, he chose the only other two who could take their place as family. The Three, looking the same to most, had become the perfect backdrop for Jack. They melted together, none standing out over the others. Jack was remarkably calm, with what was coming.

They took their places on the stage at the center of the hall. Asta spread Violet's scarlet train over the darker crimson floor. It sparkled beautifully from the warm, dim light that seemed to emanate from nowhere.

Ivan began his speech about the deep, eternal bond the couple was entering. It brought tears to many eyes, including Vivienne's and Galin's, who were seated in the center front row of the gallery. Grace stepped forward as Ivan bound Violet's and Jack's hands with a scarlet silk cord. She carried the chalice adorned with rubies. She lifted the cord, exposing Violet's wrist, punctured it with a silver blade, and collected her blood until the cup was half filled. Then she placed her hand over the wound to heal the incision faster. When the dim green light glowed under her hand, gasps and murmurs could be heard throughout the hall.

Jack and Violet shared a long kiss before Violet slowly descended her mouth to his pulsating neck vein. She had never bitten a human on purpose before, but the warmth and scent of Jack's blood drew her in. Her lip quivered slightly as her tongue brushed against Jack's neck. She punctured his artery with her canis, injecting venom into him. She kissed him once again, allowing her venom to course through his body.

Grace placed the chalice into their bound hands, and Violet guided him to drink. He drained the cup, which Grace took from them. Ivan unbound their hands. Violet kissed him once again. With tears in her eyes, she placed her hands on each side of his face, whispering, "Return to me, my love." With a single swift movement, she snapped his neck.

Erik caught his lifeless body before it collapsed to the floor. Alex and Mikkel rushed to lift him over their heads for all to see. The audience was silent. Ivan requested the guests remain silent as they took Jack to the chamber.

Violet, eyes welled with tears, bound Grace's wrists through the loops on her bracelets with a black cord. She and Asta led Grace behind Violet's mate to his death chamber. Violet's shoulders dropped; her chin trembled ever so slightly while she cast her eyes down. Nyx rose and followed at the end of the procession.

Once they were clear of the platform, Ivan announced, "Rejoice and let the celebration proceed."

With the announcement, hundreds of service units massed on the hall, quickly turning it into a celebration space. They brought in tables laden heavily with food and drink. Dim lights were placed on tables and around the hall. The mood turned from somber to joyous as guests mingled and celebrated. They would remain for many hours until Jack arose immortal.

As the seven members of the procession entered the chamber with Jack, Leo was waiting for them. The room was small. Muted. Dimly lit and warm. It was a comforting space that would be gentle for Jack to wake up in. They laid Jack on a soft platform at the back of the room, removing his jacket, tie, and shoes.

Erik activated a dome that would soften any outside noise and light. It would be easier on his transition as he awoke with exponentially increased senses. Violet unbound Grace's hands.

"Take care of him for me," she whispered to Grace before hugging her tightly. She smiled through her tears, running her hand over the dome before leaving with Asta. Violet knew he would come back to her, but she couldn't bear to see him this way with his skin drained of color. She had never seen anyone die before. She certainly had never been the one responsible for taking a human life. It was more difficult than she thought it was going to be. The next hours would be excruciating for her.

The Three followed the women out quietly. They had all seen their share of death. It was still a somber moment for them. Jack was the only friend Erik had outside of his brothers. Unlike the other two, Erik was very introverted and friendships took a substantial amount of effort for him to maintain.

Leo checked his device. Jack's cells were beginning to deteriorate, as he had expected. He was very invested in the entire process. It would be several hours before enough of the human cells died and the fresh blood and venom would mix. He set an alert to let him know when that segment of the process started.

Grace and Nyx moved to the seating area that had been set up for them. They were also left with food, Shurian nectar, and wine. Grace filled three glasses with a nice red that Vivienne had picked for them. Nyx accepted a glass from Grace and sat down in a deep chair.

"That was unexpectedly emotional. I never thought about how hard it must be to kill someone you love more than anything. Violet was visibly devastated," Nyx noted.

Grace nodded in agreement at the statement.

Leo broke the awkward silence. "Are you ready to get that thing off of you so I can work on a proper closure, Grace?"

"What about Jack? I thought you said I couldn't take it off in here."

"That would be why I added the dome. It's sealed. He isn't exposed to the environment in this room."

She nodded in agreement. "I'm ready." She held out her hand. "Give me the vial."

He pulled it out of his pocket and handed it to her. She was nervous. There had never been a time when she didn't have something holding her in her shell, cloaking her energy. Before the amulet, she had a bracelet, and when she was dead, Frigg had her essence in a containment jar. She realized there wasn't any time she could remember being free.

Before she took off the amulet, Leo added, "Remember, no matter what you feel, you can't rise in here. I don't know how it might affect Jack, even with the protection of the containment, or maybe even me."

"Well, should I do it then? How will I know if I can control it? I don't want to hurt anyone."

Nyx responded, "Rising takes effort to release yourself from your shell. Especially the first few times. You must force it to happen. You won't be able to do it accidentally."

"And the nanites seem to be working to help control your emotions better now," Leo added.

Grace took an internal inventory. "True. They seem to be much stronger than the last batch. I didn't feel an above-average pull to Ivan during the ceremony. Then again, I was nervous standing in front of thousands of guests, and I had a lot to concentrate on." She unconsciously twirled a strand of hair. "Let's go ahead then."

Grace slowly opened the vial so she wouldn't spill any of the contents. She spun the closure of the amulet to the front where she could see it. "Here goes nothing." She placed a drop of blood on the closure. As she did, it sparked and glowed. After a few seconds, the glow disappeared, along with the blood she had placed on it.

She stuck her finger in her mouth, subconsciously removing the remainder of the blood. Neither Leo nor Nyx seemed to think this was odd behavior. It wasn't unusual for any of them to partake in blood sacrifices from time to time. She looked up nervously. The taste was enticing. She hadn't tasted blood since the merge. She had a mild urge to drink the rest of the vial.

Nyx reached out, taking the vial from her. "We should destroy this, just in case." As she held it, a dark mask covered it, collapsing it into nothing in the palm of her hand. It merely dissipated away.

Grace stared in awe.

Nyx peered back. "What? You've never dissipated mass into energy with your light? You have an entire bag of tricks in there you don't know about yet."

"Go ahead. Take it off," Leo encouraged.

Grace inspected the closure, carefully spinning it in her fingers. She saw it differently now that the seal was gone. There was a latch that hadn't been there before under a pin. Under that was a split barrel with a bezel in the center. She flipped the latch open, then twisted the barrel, pausing momentarily before pulling the loosened end back, revealing a flat spring inserted into the other side of the barrel. This moment had been a frequent thought for her in the last centuries. She took a deep breath, then pulled it open, dropping both ends.

The amulet slid off her neck into her lap. There was an intense rush of calm over her. She felt an incredible rush of power come over her. Time had slowed so that each second felt like several minutes to her. She felt an intense heat as the nanites burned away. Everything was different. She was different. She felt suddenly too big to be inside her shell. That must be the urge to rise, she thought. It took her full concentration to overcome the feeling of wanting to push outward.

Ivan felt it too. He had been talking to Ami, and he halted mid-sentence. Everything in his view appeared to grind down to slow motion. He looked past Ami into the room. He could see the core of each being swirling inside of them. Everything and everyone was made of countless particles that became visible to him. He had felt particles since merging with Grace, but he had never seen them in this way before.

He saw himself glowing as if he was seeing through a high-exposure camera lens. He saw light trails coming off everything in motion. It felt like he had taken a handful of psychotropic drugs. It felt like several minutes before he could regain normal speed. In real time, it had happened so quickly even Ami hadn't noticed. She figured he had just lost his train of thought. It wasn't odd. It happened to her all the time.

"Excuse me, Ami. I need to take care of something. I'll be back." He needed to find a more secluded place where he could have a conversation with Grace about what had happened.

Ami shrugged. "Okay." She continued to stand, looking blankly at the spot where Ivan had been standing as he moved toward the back entrance of the hall out to the courtyard.

Grace! Did you see that? What just happened? he asked telepathically.

Ivan! Did you feel it too? Isn't it amazing? she answered. She had never felt such a sensation of power and control.

I thought I was having an acid flashback, but different. It's … I don't know what it is. Better. Intense. Peaceful? What's happened? He felt weightless, like every burden he ever had had lifted. Like gravity no longer existed.

We removed the amulet. It feels like we're free from everything that has ever held us back. I don't know how to explain it either. We need to discuss this with Nyx and Leo. You need to come to the chamber. Grace knew he had to be part of the conversation. She wouldn't be able to explain it like Nyx could. He was better with technical things than she was. He would understand what they were saying.

Grace, we can't be close to each other now. You know that. He was concerned about the effects of being too close while she was still in estrus.

Ivan, I'm fine. I can control it now. I can control everything. Push into my mind. You can feel me. You know I'm right.

He didn't need to push. He felt her without doing it. She had full control. He had full control. Without additional thought, he appeared in the chamber. He hadn't opened a port. He had appeared with only the image of wanting to be with her.

"How did that happen?" he asked, looking around the room.

"Welcome to the Primordial race," Nyx beamed.

"Thank you?" Ivan remembered Nyx saying he and Grace were primordial beings, but he hadn't been part of the entire earlier conversation, so he wasn't sure what was going on.

Nyx approached him. "Here, this will be easier. May I?" She lifted her hand toward his temple.

"Sure," he answered hesitantly.

She touched his temple, imparting the remaining pieces instantly.

"There now. Understand?" she asked, taking a seat on the sofa across from Grace instead of the chair she had been in previously. "Come, sit." She slid over, opening a seat between her and Leo, who had moved to the chair between the sofas. He had taken the amulet from Grace's lap, but she seemed not to have noticed. Nyx patted the cushion beside her.

Ivan obliged, walking in front of Leo, who had become oblivious to what was going on around him. He had become enthralled by the amulet. After Ivan took his seat, he slapped Leo's thigh.

"What's so interesting, Leo?"

"I'm not sure yet. Since the blood seal has been removed, it seems like a simple linking closure that activates the properties of the amulet. What I don't yet know is what those properties are. We already know it's a cloak. It also subverts Grace's, and jointly, your higher abilities. I need a while longer to figure out the how. This is a magnificent piece of crafting." He turned the amulet over, giving it a closer visual inspection. "Grace, did you say Frigg crafted this? By herself? It seems to have some Elven qualities to it. Maybe dwarven?"

"As far as I know, it was Frigg alone, although she and Freya belonged to a group involved with energy manipulation. She could have had some help, but I don't think she would have taken that type of risk given the way she always protected me."

"Hmm. Do you mind if I disassemble it? My scans aren't showing me the inner workings for some reason. Odd," Leo stated, mostly to himself.

Grace began to answer when Ivan interrupted, "Grace has no other cloak. It would be better to create something else first, in case you destroy it."

"Good point," Leo agreed. "We have plenty of time to figure it out as long as Grace stays on Rasa." He went back to his concentrated study.

While still facing Leo, Ivan reached out toward the table between him and Grace, pouring himself a glass of nectar before realizing he hadn't seen it. He inexplicably knew it was there. It was immediately apparent to him, and he knew exactly what it was. The only thing he had thought about was he was grateful for something stronger than wine. He didn't even care how Vivienne had come across it as such a last-minute addition. When he looked up, Nyx was staring at him.

"Ivan, take off your watch. I need to see you clearly," Nyx commanded him with authority.

He wasn't certain why he trusted her, but he did. He unlatched the watch, sliding it off his wrist onto the table in front of him without hesitation. As he did, both he and Grace experienced another rush of euphoria. He sucked in a breath deeply, then let out a slow, controlled stream of air. The room swirled again to a more heightened level than it had been when Grace removed her amulet. Colors beyond their imagination became visible to them.

"That's better," Nyx said, taking them both in. There was a connection that formed among the three of them that was previously nonexistent. Leo was oblivious to it, but Ivan, Grace, and Nyx all understood their connection to each other and the weight of it.

She glanced between the two of them. "You can't understand it now, but what you feel will grow when you rise."

Nyx looked entirely new to Ivan. He saw her full essence swirling inside of her shell, under her skin. He reached out, lightly touching her arm. Her darkness felt like a comforting warmth to him. She smiled at them, and they accepted the vastness of their being.

They were one with everything. In this room, on this planet, and in every crevasse of every universe in all times at once, they were a singular being, even though they were separate individuals. It was unlike anything that could be explained. They had access to all matter and all time in one instance. It was as if time didn't exist, while simultaneously existing everywhere. He could peer back through a thick mist to a time before he was born, to places when there was only Chaos. It felt familiar, in a way. Intangible, in another.

He could look forward, too, but it was hazy, shrouded. And there were so many paths. It overwhelmed him. He pulled back into this moment. Grace was experiencing the same things with him. He could feel her beside him, no, within him, and he was within her simultaneously. He could see all her memories and she could see his. They were two halves of one living thing. Yet, still distinct consciousnesses. Their heads swam.

Grace had become motionless, taking it all in. They were on an immeasurable precipice of the line between The Everything and The Nothing. Nyx felt their need to rise beyond their biological restrictions. They needed to combine their light. She picked up Ivan's watch and placed it back on his wrist, locking the clasp. It was like being slammed back into a cage. They were both overcome by a sense of desolation. The release had forever changed their reality. Nyx had dug deeply and clearly into them both when she touched Ivan's arm.

"It's clear to me how you were brought together."

Neither Grace nor Ivan had seen what she had. They understood everything and nothing. They both focused their attention on her.

Nyx continued, "Ivan was born a child of Chaos. He is both light and dark and the only possible being that could bind with your light, Grace. He was created for you by the first consciousness.

"He was already a Primordial when he was turned, giving him the ability to bond with you. The two of you together *are* balance. You are *anti-chaos.*" Nyx slumped back into the cushion behind her with the amazing clarity that their union was the answer to every question she had ever wondered about how anything was able to exist. They wouldn't just bring balance; they *were* balance against Chaos.

Even if they did nothing, their very existence was the answer. Chaos had brought them forth as the solution. She may have used Frigg to do it, but they were clearly her work. It was brilliant. Nyx hadn't seen this coming. She had a clear imperative to bring them to Chaos. But she didn't know how. She didn't know if she could. She didn't know in what time or dimension to begin her search. Chaos existed everywhere and nowhere. They were looking to Nyx for answers she didn't know if she had. How could she teach them what she couldn't fathom herself? Chaos had created no beings since the beginning that Nyx knew of. Why did there need to be two of them? Why wouldn't Chaos have only created one if the purpose was to bring balance forward? Millenia had passed. A second had passed. How could she explain any of this to them? They weren't ready to comprehend it. She wasn't ready to comprehend it.

She tipped back her glass, swallowing hard. Grace and Ivan exchanged glances. They weren't sure what to think. Nyx appeared … unsettled, frozen in her own thought.

They were startled by Leo's alarm. It had been over five hours but seemed only an instant to the three of them. Time was different for them now. Reality was different now.

"Ah, excellent!" Leo exclaimed as he picked up his device, checking on Jack's progression. "The venom is mixing with Violet's blood. It won't be long now."

He leapt to his feet, placing the amulet on the table in front of him. "Oh, and I've figured it out," he said as an afterthought as he made his way over to where Jack lay. "It's the overlay. That's what's keeping me from reading the sapphire. She was brilliant, by the way. These runic symbols on the back aren't all Æsir. Some of them are Ljósálfar, and it's a riddle referring to the mixing of light and dark. I don't understand it all yet, but I'm close."

There must be answers in the amulet. Had it been protecting her, or had she been protecting it all along? She picked it up. It was warm to her touch. It felt alive. She felt connected to it in a way she hadn't before it was unsealed. She was more confused than ever, yet strangely clear that this path she was on was uniquely her and Ivan's together. It was comforting and irresistible.

She needed a distraction. She needed time to come to terms with this new information. It had to germinate in her mind. Perhaps it would make better sense when she rose. She made a conscious decision to move it out of the forefront of her thoughts and let it percolate on its own. Jack would wake soon. She would put her energy into that for now.

Grace placed the amulet back on the table. Standing purposefully, she walked to Leo's side. Nyx and Ivan watched her move away from them, exchanging a concerned look. As Grace and Leo conversed about Jack's progress, Nyx seemed to snap back to herself.

"Ivan, what's she doing?"

"Processing." Ivan had also decided the previous conversation needed to be paused for the moment.

"What do you mean, processing?"

"She needs time to let what you said marinate. She's not like us, Nyx. Since her creation, she has been sheltered, protected, and lied to. She doesn't easily trust what people tell her. She needs a little time to make sense of it all."

Nyx was relieved. She poured herself a glass of the nectar. Wine wouldn't be strong enough to allow her to absorb the revelation of these early morning hours.

"She's not the only one who needs some time to make sense of it all. And what do you mean by 'like us'? How are you so unfazed by all of this, anyway?"

"I'm not unfazed. I deal with what is in front of me. There's no changing it. All I can do is move forward. And by 'like us,' I mean pragmatic, deductive. Somewhat detached, sanitized in our assessment of a situation. I can see it in you as clearly as I can see my reflection in a mirror."

"You're right. We are more alike than I thought, brother," Nyx replied gently.

She was clearly right when she called him brother. He accepted it without further thought. They were connected. They had both been born of Chaos, but not Grace. No, Grace was something else altogether. With the clarity of looking back over time, some things made sense to him now, being an only child in the days when families were large.

Ivan stood, extending his hand to Nyx. "Let's get some air, shall we?"

She reached out, accepting his offer. "Yes, thank you. Some air would be lovely."

They left the chamber with no acknowledgment from either Grace or Leo. The evening air was refreshing and cool. They easily controlled the weather on Rasa. Despite the planet's size, the band containing the city was continually washed in spring or summer. Rains were scheduled to produce the optimal amount of lush foliage all year long. Vivienne made sure perfect weather would be forthcoming for the duration of the ceremony. Leo had been correct in his prediction that Nyx would find the atmosphere here much more comfortable in her physical form. The pair strolled slowly toward the festivities. Ivan saw everything around him through a new lens. He ran his fingers over foliage as they walked. Textures of things familiar to him were heightened. Vegetation seemed to stretch up from the ground, offering their energy as tiny slivers of it detached and wafted toward him.

"I hope you don't mind making our way over to the celebration hall for a moment. I need to announce that the second stage of Jack's turning is beginning. It will be a relief to Violet. I'd like her to know as soon as possible." Ivan was both diplomatic and considerate, even with everything else that was going on.

"I don't mind at all. I would like to find Apollo and see if there's anything he knows about the amulet or Grace's creation that he hasn't already revealed."

Ivan furrowed his brow. "Are you certain he'll even tell you if he knows anything?"

"Ivan, he doesn't have to tell me anything. I can see his thoughts clearly, much in the same way you can alter them when you are entrancing someone."

Ivan was surprised by her comment. He had never mentioned that ability to her. She smiled slyly at him. Then it dawned on him. He had let her in when she recounted the evening's conversation he wasn't in attendance for. And she had seen him again when she placed the watch back on his wrist.

He gave her a scornful glance. "I don't appreciate you rummaging around in my thoughts."

"You gave me permission, remember? Besides, I have the same ability you and Grace do to see gifts in others, only mine is by touch. Grace told me you two don't need to make physical contact. You perceive by feeling, by just being in proximity to others. That alone is a powerful gift. I didn't investigate your personal thoughts or memories, if that's what you're concerned about. I respect privacy."

Ivan scoffed, amused. "You *just* told me you were going to do that exact thing to Apollo."

Nyx rolled her neck. "That's different. We need that information, and it's not like I'm planning on digging around for anything personal. You know I cannot ask him straight out about it in this crowd, either." She motioned toward the celebration.

"I guess I can do the same with Thoth to find out about the blood seal. I don't enjoy doing it though. It's better we don't raise suspicions. No one knows Grace took off the amulet, anyway."

"It's not like anyone could get another one on her either."

"Good point. I'd still rather know," Ivan said.

When they reached the hall, the few who were outside followed them in. Nyx moved around to the outskirts of the room to begin her search for Apollo while Ivan took a path to the platform in the center of the room. Violet met him at the base of the stage, anticipating his announcement. He offered her his arm, assisting her up the stairs. Ivan nodded to her with a slight smile. Relief washed over her. A suspenseful hush fell over the room as all eyes focused on them. Ivan took position behind a small transparent floating podium with Violet at his side. His announcement would be short and simple.

"I am delighted to announce that the latest addition to our immortal family, Jackson Kelly, has begun the second phase of his transition. We are expecting the remainder of the process to continue as expected. He should be ready for presentation sometime within the next two to three hours. Please continue to enjoy the festivities. If you have questions about the rest of the transition, you may address your queries to any service unit or any interface throughout the hall. Thank you all for your patience and attendance."

Ivan did not wait to address questions. He and Violet left the podium, moving toward the stairs.

"You could have called out to me to let me know what was going on," Violet told Ivan.

"Where's the fun in that, Violet? We can't disappoint your guests. They were expecting a formal announcement."

Before they landed on the bottom step, Vivienne and a crowd of family, friends, and well-wishers swept Violet away. Ivan had caught sight of Thoth and Ma'at at a table on the far side of the platform. He also saw Nyx had found Apollo. She had taken his arm as a gesture of long-dead chivalry that still held a place in this crowd of ancients. She had likely already found the information she was searching for. It was Ivan's turn to do the same with Thoth. Before he had made it halfway to their table, Thoth approached him. They exchanged greetings. Ivan expected Thoth to have a few questions of his own, which made it easy to access his memories without suspicion.

"No one expected Nyx to be here. It was a startling surprise. What exactly is her connection to Grace?"

Ivan pressed in like he used to do when he was entrancing someone; only now, with practice, he was able to see their thoughts and memories, not only where they were contained. Ivan could see Thoth had a theory that was very close to the truth. Ivan found no reason not to confirm it. Everyone would know soon enough, anyway.

Ivan answered Thoth, simultaneously projecting the conversation to Nyx. "I'm sure you are already aware Grace wasn't only a child of light created by Frigg. Frigg somehow managed to create a Primordial. As for Nyx, it seems her connection is closer to me." He paused, then continued speaking once Thoth presented a quizzical appearance, furrowing his eyebrows.

"She's my sister. I learned only a few hours ago that I am a son of Chaos."
Saying it out loud made it more permanent in Ivan's mind. He heard Nyx erupt in
laughter inside his mind, while leaving Thoth stunned.

You're quite the imp, aren't you, little brother? That was on the verge of being mean, Nyx
said between bursts of laughter.

He looked over, giving her a nod. *Sometimes.* He turned back, digging deep
into Thoth's thoughts while Thoth was struggling to acquire the seriousness of
the information he had received. Ivan wanted to catch him off guard. It was
easier to pinpoint what he was trying to find that way. Ivan decided to ask him so
he could see if Thoth would try to hide anything.

"How could you not know that Frigg created a primordial being?" Ivan
queried.

Thoth shook his head. "The four groups did all the initial research and
planning together. After that, they all went back to their respective home worlds,
creating each subject on their own. None of the groups had a hand in the process
the others used. None of Frigg's reports indicated that's what she created. She
reported Grace didn't live. Since the other female subject didn't either, and
the males weren't viable, no one questioned the outcome. No one within the
community had any idea. Except for Apollo, as we came to find out later."

Ivan saw all of it before Thoth had finished speaking. He also saw Thoth
knew nothing about the amulet or the blood seal. He had no reason to, without
knowing Grace had lived.

"What are your thoughts on how she could have been created, then?" Ivan
asked.

"Given your own revelation, I would have to deduce that Chaos was somehow
involved. Wouldn't you?"

Ivan had come to the same conclusion. "I would have to agree."

Thoth's mind was catching up. "Wait, how could you have become a vampire
if you were already a Primordial?"

"I haven't quite figured that out yet. I always thought I was a regular human.
None of my abilities manifested until I was turned. Nyx thinks it's all part of a
somewhat grander plan we don't yet understand."

"If Nyx was the one who told you that you were born of Chaos, what makes
you think she's not lying to you? How would you not know you were different

than an average human?" Thoth was suspicious of Nyx's motives. Then again, Thoth was suspicious of most things. It was in his nature.

Ma'at and Thoth had regularly discussed the true motivations behind the Council's actions. He didn't believe some of them were as concerned about the descent back into The Nothing as they should be.

"I grew up on a feudal tract outside a tiny village on the eastern side of medieval Europe. Apart from my family, I hardly saw anyone. I can't explain it, but I know Nyx isn't lying to me. What she said about my creation explains a lot about the connection I have always had to Grace and how we were able to merge."

Ivan was working within his own thought process. No wonder his father seemed to worship him for being alive. Ivan had always thought it was because his parents weren't able to have more children. Thinking about it, his parents didn't have any children. It also explained how he survived in excellent health well into his thirties when most of the lower class in that time were dead or infirmed by then.

Thoth bit the inside of his cheek. "It makes sense. I just don't understand how it all came together. This is perplexing."

Ivan heard Ben and Ami approaching. "Let's keep my part between us for now, shall we?"

"Agreed," Thoth nodded.

Ivan could already see that he was going to tell Ma'at as he was walking away. Ivan continued to flow through the hall, making small talk with guests while keeping Nyx in his view. She had left Apollo smiling, going next into the gathering of the High Council near the center of the space. Ivan continued to read the mood of the room as he checked in with Grace. It wouldn't be much longer until Jack would be ready, allowing Ivan to escape the festivities.

~~~~

Jack sat on the side of the slab with his legs dangling above the stone floor. He rubbed his eyes, shaking off the disorientation from being dead. Leo went
~~~~

back and forth between the data HUD and physical examination of Jack. Grace leaned against the back of the chair in the seating area, watching them.

"Everything shows the results I expected. How do you feel, Jack?" Leo waited for an answer.

Jack looked around the dim room. "Thirsty," he said, his voice cracking above a whisper.

He jumped off the table, moving quickly toward Grace. She braced herself, closing her eyes without moving. She told herself not to phase. If he needed to drink, let him drink.

As remote as it was, she knew there was a possibility he would need to drink to complete his transition. The setback disappointed her. She felt the air swirl as he passed her, picking up a large pitcher of water from the table. He took several huge gulps, breathing heavily.

"You should have seen the look on your face, Grace," he chuckled. "Not that your blood doesn't smell enticing. I really did just want some water. Ooh, and an apple." He tossed a red apple into the air about six feet away and zipped across the room to catch it. "Wow! I'm fast."

He gave her a side smirk, biting into the apple as she smirked back, shaking her head at him. She was noticeably relieved.

"Are you done?" she asked as condescendingly as she could muster.

"C'mon, Grace. You know I couldn't pass that up," he replied sheepishly.

"I know. I probably wouldn't have either. Now let Leo look at you so we can get you out of here."

Jack leapt over the arm of the chair, landing with his feet propped up on the table. "All right then, doc. Ready when you are. How long was I out?"

Leo strode over to Jack, swiping his feet off the table and forcing him to sit up, and then sat where his feet had been. He made a tossing motion, throwing the HUD up to the left side of Jack.

"You were dead five hours and twenty-six minutes. Total transition time was seven hours and five minutes," Leo stated flatly, without taking his eyes off the data.

"Oh. Is that normal?" Jack asked.

"A little longer than I expected with no damage to your body prior to Violet killing you," Leo said, smirking at him. "You weren't drained, so the first phase took a bit longer than I thought it was going to. How do you feel? Headache, physical pain, powerful urge to bite anyone?" Leo asked the last part with sarcasm.

Jack's demeanor became more serious. "I've got a mild headache, a little dehydration. Everything is loud and bright, but nothing I hadn't expected. Lukkas prepared me for what would happen. He said he couldn't explain the urge to drink, but I'd know it if I had it. I don't, so at least we're safe there."

"Good, then. I'm not seeing any cell deterioration or abnormalities. I want to keep the monitor on you for a couple of days to make sure. Your transition looks complete. Be sure to let me know if you feel a blood thirst or if anything seems unusual," Leo ordered.

"Everything feels unusual, Leo."

"You know what I mean, Jack."

"I'll make sure you're the first to know if I have any murderous urges."

"I'd appreciate that."

"Anything else, doc?"

"Let's check your canis. Can you control them?" Leo examined Jack's mouth. Jack rolled back his upper lip, allowing his canis to descend.

"Good. Any urges with them descended?"

"No."

"Retract them." Leo watched closely as Jack's fangs retracted smoothly into his gums.

"No problem." It surprised Jack how painlessly they slid back into his upper jaw.

"Last thing I need is a venom sample." Leo was interested in monitoring how venom flowed as much as he was in comparing Jack's venom to a known sample to see if there were any differences.

"Right here? That's kind of personal, isn't it, doc?" Jack's eyes were wide as he glanced at Grace.

She stifled a laugh. He had clearly misunderstood.

Leo didn't stifle his laugh. "I said venom sample, *not* semen."

"Oh," Jack said, embarrassed, "I'm not sure how."

Leo tossed him a small round container similar to what was used in milking snake venom. "Sink your fangs into this and see if you can press out any venom. I have no idea how to give direction on doing that. We might have to get Ivan back here to show you how if you can't figure it out."

Jack shrugged, biting into the container. He closed his eyes and concentrated, feeling a tingling sensation producing several drops from each descended tooth. Leo watched the HUD as the venom sacs in the back of his throat pulsated. He was satisfied with the sample and the process.

"That's enough, Jack. Go ahead and retract."

As he pulled back his canis, Jack felt the last drop fall into his mouth, giving his tongue a numbing sensation on the left side. He made a *tsk* sound.

"The thide of my thung ith numb," he lisped.

"Venom contains a mild numbing agent. It only lasts a few minutes. The aim is to prevent the victim from feeling any pain. It's part of that vampire seduction," Grace replied, amused.

"I non't plan on theducing any vithims," Jack slurred.

"I didn't make the rules, Jack," Grace replied. "Is he done, Leo?"

"He's done. Get dressed, Jack."

Jack put his jacket and shoes back on. Leo spun around on the table and picked up Grace's amulet. "You should put this back on, so no one asks any questions."

"No one has the balls to ask me questions, except maybe Ben. Besides, I burned off your last set of nanites. I don't know if I'll be able to control myself if I put it back on. You hold on to it."

"Okay," Leo replied with some trepidation as he slid the amulet into his pants pocket.

Grace watched Jack struggle with his tie.

"Here, let me do that." She reached out, taking it from him.

"Thank you. I never could thy one of these." Jack's speech was almost back to normal.

She quickly set it right. "There. All done. Let's get you presented, shall we?"

She took Jack's arm as the three of them walked to the door. As Jack reached forward to open it, Grace opened a port, and they walked out into the center of the stage.

She whispered, "A whole bag of new tricks to learn, Jack."

CHAPTER SIX

Sunrise had been quite the display through the transparent ceiling. Vivienne had decorations in the center of each table that bloomed into spectacular white floral arrangements the moment they were grazed by the sun. The celebration would continue throughout the day. Grace wanted to get back to Ivan and Nyx to see what they found out. She could have reached out to them if the celebration hadn't gotten so noisy. Crowds were still difficult for her to filter out. She made a note to herself she would need to work on that.

Just because she had power didn't mean she understood how to use it. There was a significant learning curve ahead of her. She wished Frigg were here. She felt Ivan's presence across the room. As she turned toward him, she nearly ran smack into Ami. It seemed like an eternity since they had been together, although it had only been a few days.

Ami spent most days on Rasa now. It was new and interesting. Ami reveled in interacting with a new group of beings who hadn't grown weary of her unyielding curiosity. Grace embraced Ami tightly in a physical display that was unusual for her. Grace was grateful for the familial bond. Ami had been a constant source of stability throughout most of Grace's life and was the closest thing she had to a sibling.

Ami was startled by Grace's uncommon display of affection in public.

"You're crushing me," Ami whispered.

Grace was much stronger than she had been before. She let up, but still held on for a few more seconds.

"I'm so happy to see you. It's been a difficult day."

Her conversation with Ivan and Nyx could wait. She needed to spend some time with Ami to get a little perspective. She wanted to feel normal again, even if it was only for a few minutes.

"You're different. Why are you different? Where is your amulet?" Ami asked in her wide-eyed childlike way. There was never any pretense with Ami. No filter either. Grace loved that, even if it irritated her sometimes.

"Come on. I'll tell you everything. Let's get out of this crowd." Grace grabbed Ami by the hand, pulling her toward the side exit. She didn't want to make a spectacle of herself by rudely porting out.

Once they were outside the hall, Grace wanted to go somewhere quiet. She thought of her quarters. They instantaneously appeared in her kitchen. It had happened so easily. Grace didn't know what to call this type of transportation. It wasn't porting. She never opened a port. There was no squeezing through. There was no disorientation either. They were there, then they were here. It was an unfamiliar process altogether.

"How did you do that?" Ami asked.

"Not a clue. I thought about it, then it happened." Grace shrugged, letting go of Ami's hand. "You've been around longer than I have. What would you call it?"

"I think it's location shifting. My father does that. He can shift through space *and* time."

Ami seemed to suddenly recognize where they were. "Oh, can I make coffee?"

"Ami, you know we don't have a coffee maker here."

Ami looked disappointed. When Grace had her quarters fitted, she opted for some standard kitchen equipment like a stove and sink, but many of the apartments had none of these. The service panels could produce food, but with Ivan's love of cooking, she wanted to keep some familiar routines for him. She had designed this kitchen to be as similar to the one in their cabin as she could.

"You can order from the service panel if you want," Grace said, pointing to the counter unit.

"I can do that. Cinnamon cappuccino?"

"Yes, please." Grace would have preferred another glass of wine, but she didn't want to disappoint Ami again, so she took the coffee.

They sat at the far end of the island closest to the French doors that opened onto a much smaller deck than the one at the cabin. The view was of the community gardens. Beyond those, the great hall and an outdoor courtyard and cultural center. They could hear a low din from the celebration, which Grace was more than relieved to be away from.

"What's going on, Grace? I don't understand what's happened to you. Your light has changed. It's brighter, and it's also, I don't know how to describe it. Thick? No. Alive. Yeah, I guess that's a good enough way to describe it." Ami was thinking hard about a different way to phrase that last bit. Nothing that fit was coming to mind. It reminded her of her father's light.

Grace decided it would be too long and difficult to recount the last day of events. She wanted to try sharing her memories with Ami. She had no idea how to start that process, but something made her feel it was possible.

"Ami, can you show me how to share a memory?"

"Don't be silly, Grace. You can't share a memory. I can go in and get it if you want."

"I can do a lot of things I couldn't do yesterday. Show me how."

Ami stared back warily. "I can try. Close your eyes." Ami reached out and touched Grace on the temple. Ami shook at the touch as though she had contacted a live electrical wire. Grace instantly understood the process. Ami pulled her hand back quickly, nearly falling off the barstool.

"Grace! Your power is overwhelming. I … I've never felt anything like that."

"I'm sorry, Ami. Did I hurt you?"

"No. It shocked me a little. Like electricity shocked me, not like surprise shocked me. I mean, that way too, but mostly the other way. Not touching your skin, touching your light." Ami was rambling quickly.

"Ami, calm down. You'll understand in a second. I don't have to touch you. Is that okay?"

Ami nodded her head. "Uh-huh."

Grace watched Ami's face passing her thoughts in the same way she used her telepathy to speak to someone. Ami's eyes got bigger and bigger. Ami sat frozen, quietly staring at her cup for a short time before looking up.

"So, you have to stop The Everything from collapsing into The Nothing? It's not a 'who' coming after you but a cataclysmic event you have to stop?"

"That sums it up pretty well. Although I'm sure there's a 'who' out there who has learned to flourish in The Nothing and would love to see The Everything blown to oblivion." She paused. "Are you okay?" Grace was more concerned that the normally inquisitive Ami had gone mute. Grace sat patiently, giving Ami the space to process the information.

"How do you fix it?" Ami finally asked, ignoring the question.

"I don't know," Grace replied.

Ami's brow scrunched, concentrating harder. "How are you what you are, Grace? I mean, how do you even exist?"

"I don't know that either, Ami. I need to find Chaos."

"Nobody finds Chaos. Chaos finds you," Ami stated without expression, still trying to assemble all the pieces.

"Well then, Chaos better find me quick before I fuck this all up," Grace said, deprecating herself.

There were several more moments of silence.

"If Ivan is Nyx's brother, that makes him my father's brother, too. Which makes him my uncle. Which makes you my aunt. I don't have to call you Aunt Grace, do I? That would be weird."

And Ami's back, Grace thought to herself. "No! You're like a *billion* years older than me."

"More like five, but who's counting?" Ami snorted, making Grace feel an immense sense of relief. Grace couldn't help but giggle.

"What do we do now?" Ami asked.

"Want a drink?"

"Yes. Absolutely, yes."

Grace forwent the wine and headed straight for Ivan's scotch. She poured two glasses, sliding one to Ami across the counter as the sky darkened.

"That's odd. Vivienne requested no rain for today," Grace said.

It didn't look like clouds. It couldn't be an eclipse. Rasa was close enough to the next galaxy to receive light from their sun, too. Even if one was in eclipse, they couldn't both be in eclipse on the same day with no one expecting it.

Ami went to the open doors. "Grace, you better come over here." Her voice pitched lower than normal.

Grace went through the island over to Ami. They looked at each other, speaking in unison, "Nyx."

Grace grabbed Ami's arm, instantly appearing in the courtyard, where a large crowd had gathered. Ivan was having difficulty physically restraining Nyx as she and Zeus were exchanging heated words. There had been bad blood between them going way back. Nyx was livid.

Grace assessed the situation quickly. Without knowing what had started it all, Grace had decided she had two choices: drop Zeus like a wet rag by inflicting pain, rendering him unconscious, or help Ivan restrain Nyx. In the split second it took Grace to weigh her options, Ami ripped off Ivan's watch, allowing him to overpower Nyx with relative ease.

The action also gave a blast of power to Grace, letting her push back the darkness in what seemed like slow motion to her, without the slightest challenge. It was an unconscious decision. Grace's and Ivan's eyes were still glowing with light while the crowd fell dead silent. Her light was still green, but Ivan's light was gold. Maybe it was only a reflection of their eye color. She'd have to verify that when she rose. It was so quiet; you could hear the birds singing in the distance.

As Ivan and Grace powered down, Nyx roared with laughter. Grace could see she had planned the entire altercation, and it irritated her. Whispers and shocked muttering overtook the sounds of the birds chirping.

"Nyx, what have you done?" Ivan grimaced harshly at Nyx, slowly letting go of her arms.

"They needed to see Ivan! They all needed to see your combined power is enough to save them." She placed her hands on either side of Ivan's head, showing him her entire plan as his eyes widened.

They had to be smart about the next steps. He quickly passed all of it on to Grace.

"You have to save it all. You can save *everything*," Nyx said loudly for everyone to hear.

"There had to be another way." Ivan tried to sound disappointed that their hand had been forced.

Nyx released Ivan's face. One hand remained on his shoulder. She pointed directly at the Council.

"They knew, Ivan. When I spoke with Apollo, I could see they all knew." She pointed toward the Council members. "Go ahead, Grace. Look for yourself. They're using you. They intentionally kept it from you for over a year. Your so-called friends knew about The Everything descending back into The Nothing, and they lied to you."

Ivan and Grace dug into the Council members' thoughts. It was true. Apart from Ben, everyone on the Council knew. They had private discussions about it, and they conspired to lie to everyone, keeping them in the dark. Their friends, Kali, Apollo, and Beivve, even Zeus and all the High Council understood exactly what was happening.

They had known all the way back to the beginning, from the first time Grace, Lukkas, and Ivan had seen Ma'at in the Council chambers. There were scanners in the room. Beivve had detected the Primordial signature in both Ivan and Grace. They orchestrated the entire situation to push Grace and Ivan together and they crafted it so well that Ben thought it was his idea. They played them from the beginning. Even Apollo's spontaneous revelation at the lab was planned.

Grace was tortured to see it. She was heartbroken and disappointed. At least Ben and Ami didn't know. Neither had Ma'at, thankfully. As an appointed judiciary, her position didn't allow access to closed meetings. That would surely have brought her to her knees. She passed Nyx's plan to Thoth and Ma'at while the Council members glanced uncomfortably at each other.

Kali indignantly stepped forward in front of the others. "She's trying to drive a wedge between us, Grace. You know she enjoys creating turmoil."

Grace's gaze swept over them. She could see as clearly as if they had painted it on their foreheads. Grace lowered her head, stepping toe-to-toe with Kali. She placed her hand on Kali's shoulder, in what Kali thought was a gesture of trust and sympathy. She leaned forward, whispering into Kali's ear.

"I know," she said as she squeezed Kali's shoulder. She lifted her head, revealing a cold, hard stare directly into Kali's eyes. "I can see all of it. I know you were the ones who lied. It's clear your fear is controlling you, but we're going to save you anyway," she stated in a low, controlled tone. "I believe it's time for you to leave our planet."

Kali's knees went visibly weak. She swallowed hard when Grace lifted her hand. This was the first time Kali had ever felt intimidated by anyone.

"Ben, Leo, Ami, and Thoth. We would like a private meeting in the administration chambers, if you please." Grace raised her head to address the remaining guests. Her tone became apologetic as she smiled. "My apologies for the disruption of the festivities. You are welcome to continue in the celebration of Violet and Jack's special day."

Thoth stepped forward, away from Ma'at. She grabbed at his arm, which he quickly snatched away. She pled with him, and he raised his hand to silence her. He shook his head, turned, and walked away. He was afraid to let her go back with the Council. It wasn't his choice; it was hers.

Grace turned sharply, heading directly to the meeting chambers, followed closely by the few she had named, trailed by Ivan and Nyx. The Council members scrambled quickly in the opposite direction toward the exit port. The remaining guests were stunned. Most stayed to discuss the unusual events and speculate on the impending situation. Vivienne nodded to Grace before stepping in to encourage the celebratory atmosphere and move guests back into the hall.

Ivan wasn't pleased with the events that had taken place. He still couldn't be angry with Nyx. He saw her logic. It had to be an ambush. The Council had to be caught off guard and the rest of the delegations needed to witness it with their own eyes. Her plan was tactical. If Ivan had known about it beforehand, it wouldn't have worked.

It didn't make him any less bothered that it happened at Jack and Violet's celebration, but there may never be another time where so many were assembled on a controlled playing field. It was instinctive and intelligent. She had been planning it since she spoke with Apollo, which is why she had avoided Ivan. She approached the Council, knowing full well she could bait Zeus into a confrontation. Nyx was cunning and loyal to her cause.

Nyx said quietly to Ivan, "I didn't come here to hurt anyone. I came to see if Grace was what I thought she was. I had no idea I'd find you. I didn't know you even existed. I'm sorry for not letting you in on it sooner. I wasn't certain you could keep it from Grace. We both know she couldn't have pulled it off if she had known."

Ivan offered his arm to her, knowing what she was capable of. "I see that. We're good. I'm just trying to figure out how we use this to our advantage. We're not the ones taking the greatest risk."

Grace opened the door to the meeting room. It was rectangular, painted in a light blue gray. The long side walls were floor-to-ceiling viewing panels set to a daytime view of what was outside the building. A large oblong white conference table sat in the center, topped with clear crystal. Twelve blue chairs with shiny silver-colored wheeled bases surrounded it.

On the table, in front of each seat, was a TAC. Grace touched a panel at the side of the door, enabling a dampening field for privacy. The viewing panels changed to opaque back lighting. She took the seat farthest from the door, followed by Ivan, Nyx, and Leo to her right. Ami, Ben, and Thoth took seats to her left, leaving five empty chairs across from her closest to the door.

She swiped at her TAC, locking the exit, after which she pulled off her shoes and tossed them aside. Ivan, Ben, and Leo stripped off their jackets and ties and unbuttoned their collars. Ben rolled up his sleeves. Thoth didn't move once he was seated.

Grace leaned forward, placing her elbows on the table. She looked around at each of them.

"Who can we trust?" she asked warily.

"Apparently not my wife," Thoth replied defeatedly. He wasn't certain who, aside from Grace, knew about this plan, and he had no intention of placing Ma'at in additional danger.

"Sorry about that," Nyx replied with an uncharacteristic sound of empathy.

"I can't believe she lied to me all this time. My job is to weigh souls and yet I couldn't see the woman lying next to me held one heavy with deceit." Thoth appeared betrayed and disappointed. He was angry at Ma'at for what she was doing. He only hoped it was worth the risk she was taking.

Ivan read him. He was really selling the anger part. It was apparent to everyone. "Are you with us, Thoth? Can we trust you?" It was a harsh question but necessary for him to ask in front of the others.

"Yes," Thoth replied simply. Ivan could see the truth in his words. He was with them, perhaps more than anyone.

"What about you, Leo? I have to ask you the same because of your father and all." Ivan was reluctant to question him. Leo had been drug into this by Grace. She had an off feeling about Apollo from the start. She wanted someone who had given up everything to do what was right, but that didn't mean someone else hadn't placed him in that position.

"There's not much love lost there. He let Artemis kill my mother and sent me to be raised in a cave by a cyclops. Then he let Zeus kill me, although he got me resurrected later. I think that was more out of guilt than any kind of love for me." Leo was deep inside his own head, letting it all spew out.

"Leo!" Ivan raised his voice.

"What?"

"You're rambling. Are you with us or not?" Ivan repeated.

"Oh, yes. Of course. I absolutely want to save The Everything," he finally replied.

Ivan saw his heart was true to saving as much life as he had the capacity for. He also saw Leo had a fierce loyalty to Nyx.

"Nyx." He paused.

She scoffed defensively.

"You know I have to ask you the same. Are you with us?"

"What an idiotic question. If it weren't for me, all of you would still be in the dark."

"That was not an answer to the question."

"Yes," Nyx huffed back.

He didn't need to ask Ben or Ami. He knew their hearts to be true. Ben had given his entire life to protect what he knew about Grace's secret, and Ami could never betray Grace.

"So, what do we do now?" Ben asked.

Grace shifted in her chair. "First thing we need to do is catch everyone up."

Ivan fidgeted with his TAC, producing a bottle of scotch with seven glasses on a tray in the center of the table.

"That could take a while. Drink, anyone?" he asked, pulling the tray toward him.

"Not the way I'm going to do it," Grace replied ominously.

Ivan could see what she was planning and continued to pass drinks around.

"Ready?" Grace asked.

Ben took one large swig, draining his glass. He exchanged a glance with Thoth, who appeared confused. Ben had learned a long time ago not to be surprised by anything Grace could do.

"Ready now," he replied.

Thoth nodded, looking up from the table.

Grace dug into Ben's and Thoth's consciousnesses. She also included Leo, who had been present for most of the events of the day but had remained oblivious to what had gone on around him. She quickly made the transfer to the three of them. It had been a smooth transition. Easier than she thought it would be, doing three at one time. Ivan felt how she did it, accepting he could do the same when he wanted.

Leo was the first to speak. "Seriously? Right under my nose? I've got to start paying more attention."

Ben was deep in thought.

Nyx grinned at Grace with pride. "Well, aren't you catching on splendidly?"

Thoth questioned, "And the Council knows *all* of this?"

"With the exception of Ivan being a child of Chaos. They don't know the details of how he was created, but yes, they know the rest of it," Grace said.

Leo redirected, "Not the amulet. They don't know anything about that. Even if they scanned it directly, they couldn't have gotten anything from it while it was still sealed." He pulled it out of his pocket, placing it on the table in front of him.

"Let me see that." Ben reached out toward Leo.

Leo slid the amulet across the table.

"There's something inside of it, but we can't open it unless we decipher the riddle on the fretwork. Can you read it?" Leo asked.

Ben picked it up. "It is different." He remembered discussing it with his mother when she made it.

Ami peered over his shoulder. Her eyes narrowed, and she snatched it out of his hand, startling everyone.

"It does look different." Ami turned it over. "Grace, this is an allure."

"A what?" Grace had never heard of an allure.

"That's it!" Ben exclaimed, grabbing it back from Ami. "She said she put her entire essence into making this piece. She told me I should remember that."

"What are you two talking about? What is an allure?" Grace hadn't caught on yet.

Ami was exasperated. "It's a containment that draws your essence to it after your body dies. Frigg is *in* there!" She snatched the amulet back again.

They were all trying to talk at once.

Ami yelled, "Shush! Would all of you idiots SHUT UP?! I can hear her! Can't any of you hear her?"

They all shrugged bewilderedly at each other. No one could hear her but Ami.

Ami was talking to her. "Okay." Ami paused. "Okay. Slow down. Yes ma'am. I missed you, too. Oh, I mean … yes ma'am. I miss being able to hear you too. Let me tell them."

"Okay. First, she's a little miffed it took you so long. She realized her mistake using Ben's blood also meant she couldn't communicate with you once it drew her in, since he's her son and all."

Ami turned back to the amulet. "Okay, okay."

Ami continued to the others, "She needs a shell made with the genetic material contained behind the fret. She said she'll tell me how to get it out and the design specifications she wants in the shell."

Ami looked around the table. "She said to stop gawking and get to it."

Leo and Thoth immediately sprang to their feet.

Ben was unexpectedly emotional. He wasn't thinking clearly. His voice quivered. "Follow me. I'll take you to the lab." He unlocked the door from his TAC.

Ivan shook his head. "No. Stop. There are too many people out there. Ben, you and I need to port over first to secure the lab, then the rest can port over."

"Agreed," Ben said.

Everyone nodded. "Agreed," they said in unison.

Grace restored the lock on the door.

"Ivan, you'll need to shift Ben over like you did earlier. The dampening field won't let you open a port. Contact me when you're clear and I'll bring the others," Grace stated firmly.

"Okay," he answered. He understood the shifting process better now from sharing Grace's thoughts. He placed his hand on Ben's shoulder.

As soon as he touched Ben, they were gone. Leo and Thoth took one of the TACs at the far side of the table to build the specifications for the pod they would need to grow Frigg's shell in.

"Never a dull moment around here, is there?" Nyx asked, amused.

"I'm not repeating *that*," Ami said to the amulet.

"Oh no. Go ahead. I'm sure I've got it coming," Nyx laughed.

"Ooookaaayyy," Ami drew the word out, grinning. "She said, 'Fuck off, Nyx.' All this drama could have been avoided if you had come as she requested nearly two thousand years ago. She wouldn't have been locked up inside of this thing for the last thousand years," Ami said, referring to the amulet.

"How was I supposed to know what that was about? I thought it was another dreary funeral invitation when Balder died. I don't do funerals anymore. Especially those long, drawn-out Asgardian ones. They're so depressing," Nyx stated defensively.

"That's enough from both of you," Grace said. "There's nothing we can do about it now. Let's concentrate on getting you out of there." She directed her comment toward Frigg.

"Ivan just gave me the all clear. They have the dampening field up. Nyx, you shift, don't you?"

"Of course. But I don't know where I'm going."

"Leo does. You take him. I'll take Thoth and Ami," Grace directed.

"Let's go, pretty boy." Nyx addressed Leo, motioning him closer.

CHAPTER SEVEN

Grace knew where the lab was, but she had never been inside it before. It was a large, empty square room. There was nothing in it at all. Not even a door she could see. The only way in was by porting or shifting. The walls, floor, and ceiling were bright polished stone with white surfaces. Light was everywhere, emanating from nowhere.

"We didn't know what you would need, so we reset the room," Ivan said, explaining the reason it was devoid of anything.

"Perfect," Leo said. "Where's the panel?"

"Here." Ben placed his hand on the wall, activating the interface, then stepped out of the way.

Leo held his TAC up to the interface. He glanced at the TAC, then around the room, then back at the TAC.

"Everyone, stand over there," he said, motioning behind him to an area at the far end of the room and to his left. He made a few more gestures. Panels in the wall and floor moved. Tables and equipment slid out. Display panels lit all around.

An adult-sized gestation pod rose in the center of the room with a built-in STAG used for accelerating gestation time.

Leo took off his shirt, donning a lab coat over his undershirt. Thoth took a lab coat and replicated Leo's actions. They worked silently, tapping against a dimly lit digital display, getting everything set up.

"This is going to take a few hours. Ami, sit there," Leo said, pointing to a stool between him and Thoth. "The rest of you may want to get some sleep."

Nyx shrugged. "We don't need sleep," she said, pointing to Grace and Ivan.

They hadn't realized. Since the amulet and watch were gone, they weren't physically tired. Mentally, yes, but their bodies weren't.

"I don't either," added Ami.

"Well, yay for you," Ben said wearily. He pressed a panel close to where he was standing, producing a reclining lounge chair. "I can sleep here."

"You can go back to your quarters where you'll be more comfortable. We'll stay here. I can come get you when it's time," Grace told Ben.

"I'm not leaving my mother," he replied.

"At least take a shower and get out of that monkey suit," Ivan suggested. "We can be back in twenty minutes, tops."

"Yeah, I can do that." Ben moved beside Ivan, who didn't waste a moment shifting them out to Ben's quarters.

"We'll go when they get back. I'm sure I have something to fit you," Grace said to Nyx.

Nyx scoffed. "Why? All you have to do is this."

Nyx seemed to disappear and reappear at the same moment. Only now she was freshly washed. Her hair was newly trimmed, pinned up and perfect. She wore a lightly flowing deep-purple dress bound at her waist with a silver belt.

"That's better," she said, brushing imaginary wrinkles out of her skirt.

Grace was curious but unflustered, tilting her head as she scanned Nyx from head to toe.

"Shifting isn't only about location, Grace. It's about time, too. You can go forward into any timeline you please, but you must always go back to your exact point of origin. Otherwise, it disturbs the balance. One specific rule you can never break is to go back and change anything that has happened. No matter how much you want to. That mistake can produce dire consequences. Shifting time is the ultimate test of responsibility. Change one tiny little thing and the descent into Chaos can be immediate. Do you understand?"

"So, you've already seen how this all turns out?" Grace asked.

"I've seen thousands of ways this *could* turn out. What I don't know is which one is our path and what choices in this time will lead us there. Can you not see that yourself?" Nyx's words sounded more like a warning than an answer.

"I can't sort out *what* I see. Are there any paths where The Everything is in balance?"

"A few. There are also many paths that lead us back into The Nothing." Nyx's expression was heavy.

"What happens to the other timelines?" Grace wondered.

"They melt away. There is one timeline past to present, but there are infinite timelines forward from each present moment."

"What helps us choose a timeline with an outcome we want?"

"We don't choose a timeline. Something as insignificant as someone setting their drink on the wrong control station, in a galaxy or dimension we've never heard of, could launch the entirety of The Everything down a path that can't be corrected to our favor. We have no control," Nyx answered.

Nyx's demeanor changed from heavy to light. "Now, let's get you cleaned up, shall we? I'll take you to my home in Tartarus so we don't disturb the time in your apartment where Ivan is."

"How long can we stay there without causing a disruption?" Grace was trying to grasp the concept.

"As much time as you want. Minutes, years, millennia. It doesn't matter as long as we come back to this place in the same exact moment as the one we left. And it's better if you limit your contact with others."

"Your invitation to your home is gracious. If it's all the same, I'd prefer to go back to my cabin on Earth. I'd be more comfortable having my things if that's not too much trouble. Is distance an issue?" Grace wanted to take small bites of this apple.

"Earth?"

"The other planet we were on for the wedding."

"Oh, actually, what you refer to as Earth or Midgard, we call T28-66," Nyx corrected.

"That'll take a little getting used to," Grace said.

"Call it what you want," Nyx said, flippantly waving her hand in a smooth sweeping motion. "Tartarus is much farther from here than T28-66. Distance doesn't matter. All you need to do is think of the place, and I'll get us there. You may want to start reading me now. As soon as I touch you, we're gone."

Nyx extended her hand with her palm up and fingers extended as if she were expecting a tribute to be placed in it. Grace grasped it, and they were in the living room of the cabin. Nyx looked around.

"Hmm. Charming," she said snidely, moving her eyes over the room. "You'll have to pay closer attention on the way back because we'll be going through time as well. Don't want to foul that all up now, do we?"

"Certainly not," Grace replied. "Make yourself at home. I won't be long."

"Take your time," Nyx snickered. It doesn't matter anyway, she thought.

Grace went upstairs, showered, then changed into a pair of khaki cargo shorts, a white gauze shirt tucked in at the front, and a pair of soft-sole hiking boots. Her hair was still wet when she pulled it back into a ponytail. It was long and straight as the weight of the water pulled it taut, leaving a wet patch down the middle of her back. She didn't much care about her appearance as long as she was finally out of that dress and comfortable. She was back downstairs in under thirty minutes.

"What are all of these? They're attached to everything." Nyx was holding a lamp cord in her hand, sneering as if she had found a dead, decaying animal behind the chair.

"It's a power cord. Electricity is wired here." Grace hid a smirk.

"That's barbaric. Why would they use these?"

"Earth, I mean T28-66, doesn't have the technology to utilize wireless electricity yet," Grace replied.

"Well, that's just ridiculous. The first humans on this awful little rock were given the technology. It was rudimentary, but it was still far more advanced than this. No wonder the species is doomed."

"I'm sure they'll figure it out. Are you ready to go back?" Grace had faith humanity would survive.

"That depends. Are you wearing that?" Nyx glared disapprovingly at Grace's clothing choice.

"Yes. It's comfortable," Grace defended.

"What I'm wearing is comfortable. What you're wearing is hideous." Nyx got up, wasting no time getting to Grace. She didn't like this place at all. Disgust was all over her face.

"All right then. Pay attention," she said as she grabbed Grace's arm.

They were back exactly where they had been, less than a millisecond later than when they had left. Ami looked up at them, unbothered by their return. Leo and Thoth were facing away, noticing nothing.

Ivan, on the other hand, had a severe but momentary pang of loss. He had stepped into the shower when he suddenly began violently vomiting. It was a millionth of a second. At the same time, it was almost half an hour. He felt ripped in two. Grace was gone. He couldn't feel her at all.

As suddenly as she was gone, she was back. He was completely disoriented as he slid down the wall onto the wet floor, and then, just as suddenly, he was completely fine. He wondered if it was a side effect from shifting. Had he done something incorrectly? He'd make sure to ask Nyx when he got back.

A short time later, Ivan and Ben appeared back in the lab. They were surprised to see Nyx and Grace dressed differently, and Grace's hair was wet.

"Where did you two go? I thought you were going to wait until we got back," Ivan asked.

"Nyx showed me how to time shift. We went back to the cabin," Grace answered.

It clicked for Ivan. "Let me guess, twenty-eight minutes?"

"Yeah. How'd you know?" Grace was curious about how he had pinpointed the time so precisely.

"Because when you left this timeline, you ripped out half of my essence. It was only a fraction of a second and twenty-eight minutes all at once. I puked my guts out in the shower. A warning would be nice next time." At least he had his explanation.

Nyx reached over, touching his hand. "Oh. Oh, that was awful. I didn't expect that. You two ought to not do that separately, then, should you?" She pulled back her hand.

"No. My preference would be no." Ivan sat down on a sofa that hadn't been there when he left. He leaned back, covering his eyes with the jacket from his navy tracksuit. He was slightly nauseous thinking about it.

Grace and Nyx shot each other a jointly felt we-screwed-that-one-up glance.

Ben took the awkward silence as his opportunity to change the subject.

"Where are we at, Leo?"

"Growth specifications are in and appearance specifications are set. All we need now is Frigg's genetic sample."

Ami listened to the amulet. "On the back?" she asked. "My right with the back facing me or the front?" she asked, squinting at the writing on the amulet.

Ami tapped the symbols as instructed. When she twisted the back plate, a tiny panel popped off, flinging itself into the air, and she stumbled off the stool, fumbling to catch it. "Got it!" she exclaimed, holding the disk up triumphantly. "Oh," she said, frowning, placing the piece of metal onto the counter. She held the amulet up and pulled out a tiny bead from inside and handed it to Thoth.

He placed the bead holding Frigg's sample into a slot on the pod. "Ready to start the STAG. We're estimating time at about six hours."

Ben dropped into the lounger he had set up earlier. "Good. Wake me up after she has clothes on. I don't need that picture swimming around in my head."

Ami added, "She'd prefer you not see that either."

Ben dropped off to sleep. Leo and Thoth both seemed exhausted. Ivan pulled the jacket off his face and sat up.

"Is there anything we need to do now?" he asked.

"No. All we can do is wait," Leo replied.

"If you want, I can take you over to the guest quarters to get cleaned up. Then you can come back here and grab some shut-eye too," Ivan offered.

"I, for one, would appreciate a shower and a nap. You coming, Leo?" Thoth asked, accepting the offer.

"We can't do anything else here." Leo turned to Grace. "If that thing beeps, come get us immediately," Leo added.

"We will, Leo."

Ivan shifted them out, and Grace set up two more loungers for when they returned.

Nyx stood over the pod, watching the nanites reproduce Frigg's genetic material, creating her new shell. She thought she probably could have created a shell from the material. She had never done one for another essence to inhabit. Only one for hers. She wondered how different the process would have been, but she certainly didn't want to experiment with the only sample Frigg had left. Frigg was already pissed at her.

She regretted not coming when Frigg had asked. She was one of the few lowers Nyx liked and respected, even though she would never let her know it.

Ami paced the room, chatting with Frigg and occasionally making odd gestures or laughing. Grace took a seat on the sofa, waiting for Ivan to return with Leo and Thoth. She was making a mental list of others she felt she would be able to trust. The Three for sure. Galin, Vivienne, Violet, Jack, and Asta.

Lukkas she could certainly trust, although she would feel guilty about having him involved in all of this. All the turned could be trusted. She didn't know many of them well enough to understand their strengths and weaknesses. Better to keep it as a small group for now until they had an idea of what they needed to do. They would share the information with the community once they had things a bit more figured out.

She mulled it over and over. Was that really it? Could there be anyone else outside of this small group? Then she thought about Vaeweth. She wondered if she could trust Vaeweth. Sure, he was a mercenary. He sold his services to the highest bidder most times, but he had never pledged his loyalty. He never took jobs that reduced his integrity. And he was retired. He finished his contract with the Council. And toward the end, he told her he didn't like or agree with some things they were doing.

She wondered if he knew. She wondered if he was trying to warn her without saying anything that would violate his contract with them. He had been at the celebration earlier. He and his wife had left during Nyx's performance. It was worth a shot to at least talk to him. He would be quite an asset to have on their team. More importantly, he would be an asset she didn't want the Council to have.

Her thoughts were interrupted when Ivan, Leo, and Thoth shifted back. Thoth dropped straight into one lounger, but Leo seemed distracted, inspecting his clothing. She wasn't sure if he even knew where he was yet. Nyx lifted her head, momentarily acknowledging they were back. Ami ignored them completely.

The two men wore the same tactical clothing as Ben: black pants, long sleeved T-shirts, and black soft boots.

Leo approached Grace. "Look at this, Grace. It's impact absorbing. There are injury sensors woven into it. Thermal regulating. And the boots! I feel like I'm walking on air. And they don't leave shoe impressions. How impressive is that? And it's comfortable. No wonder that's all he wears," he added, nodding toward a lightly snoring Ben.

"Oh, shut up, Leo!" Thoth grumbled. "Get some sleep. He's been going on like that since he got dressed." Thoth rolled over, facing the wall, covering his face with his arm.

Ivan sat on the sofa beside Grace.

"Vaeweth, huh? Do you think it's worth talking to him?" Ivan asked.

Leo climbed onto the lounger on the other side of Ben, closest to the sofa. He had closed his eyes, still rubbing his hands over the shirt he was wearing, looking pleased.

"I think I should at least try. He's got skills and a small army. They follow him anywhere he leads."

"You should go then. Take Nyx with you. I'll stay here and watch over Frigg." Ivan put his arm around Grace.

When he kissed her on top of the head, she felt a pull to him. Not as strong as it had been the day before, but enough to remind her she was still in estrus. She snuggled into his chest for a moment before getting up.

"You know you can always entrance him into joining," Ivan said, half joking.

"With our power, that would make him a slave. I don't want to become that type of person, do you?"

"No, you're right. It must be his choice. If it doesn't go your way, though, you need to at least make him forget you came to see him."

"I don't know if that's possible. The Jur are near impenetrable to mind probing," Grace replied. "Nyx. How do you shift to a person when you don't know where they are?"

"Same way you shift to a place," Nyx answered offhandedly, still hovering over the pod.

Grace turned back to Ivan. "Can you let The Three know what's going on while we're gone?"

"Already took care of it while those two were getting cleaned up. Erik wasn't too happy about leaving Asta. Once I caught them up, he was okay with it. They're back in their quarters getting some sleep. That thought transfer thing's slick. With their shared ability, it was like I was only transferring to one."

"I knew I kept you around for a reason." She winked at him, crossed the room to Nyx, touched her arm, and shifted out.

Vaeweth was standing on a pier next to a green ocean, fishing.

"I've been expecting you," he said without turning around. "Kali was here with a job offer. I told her to shove it. I didn't like one bit of what they were doing to you. She thought I didn't know. She thought paying us didn't make us chattel while they held our families at their mercy."

Grace saw he was telling the truth. She saw their conversation. She still couldn't help feeling something was off. Seeing his thoughts shouldn't have been that easy.

"And?" she asked.

He turned around. His gold-trimmed eyes lit from behind, matching the sunset sky. "All I need to know is where, when, and what. I'll be waiting."

"And how much?"

"Freedom, Grace. We want to be free from Council rule. You're our only hope, and my bet is on you." He extended his arm with an open hand.

They grasped forearms and leaned forward to meet foreheads. They grasped the back of each other's necks with their free hands. That was the Jur pledge of loyalty. It was till death. The pledge was their agreement. As they stood there, Vaeweth's army appeared up over the sides of the pier.

Nyx hadn't seen them or felt them, but Grace had. Their signature was faint. She remembered what it felt like from the raid. And she could smell them, which was something she hadn't been able to do before the merge. One by one, they all pledged to her. Over one hundred of the most elite soldiers in The Everything, it seemed. With each pledge, Grace's stomach churned a little more.

When they finished pledging, each Jur returned to where they came from.

"The Council thinks they can carve out their own dimension and stabilize it. They're working out a way to speed up the collapse of the rest into The Nothing. Their plan involved using you and Ivan. They were trying to trick you into creating a permanent balance in one dimension while letting you think you were saving them all. They didn't count on her showing up." He nodded to Nyx. "When I saw her, I left as soon as it wouldn't raise suspicion, got my army together, then went fishing.

"You scared the crap out of them, Nyx. When they saw you up on that platform with Grace, they didn't know what to do. You never attend any of these things. They didn't think you had any interest in saving The Everything. Your lot can survive in The Nothing just fine. I don't know what they're going to do now."

"How many more do you think they have?" Grace asked.

"Don't know how many. Don't know what species."

"I'd suggest you start cleaning up your ocean. You have a lot of Zinna bodies down there. Guess Kali was stupid enough to think you'd be out here fishing on a pier alone." Grace raised her eyebrow.

"Guess she was." He smiled back.

"We changed our port codes after they left. I suggest you change yours too. I'll have Ivan message ours over to you shortly," Grace suggested.

"Already ahead of you on that one. We've fortified our blockers and defense systems as well." He assumed Nyx was the one who got them past their blockers. He didn't know Grace had her powers enhanced.

"Good. Let us know if you need us." Grace turned back to Nyx to shift out.

"Grace. One more thing."

She turned back to face him.

"It was the Council. They killed Tyr and then manipulated the lower realms to riot, taking out Asgard. They made a big mistake not killing me when my contract ended."

Grace felt her anger well. "Yes, it was an incredibly big mistake."

Grace knew the story of the riot was something the remaining Æsir had made up while they searched for who was responsible. Ben had told her they didn't know who attacked the planet, but it hadn't been the lower realms. Vaeweth didn't have to add that last part. It was like he was begging her to kill him.

Grace grabbed Nyx harder than she intended when she shifted.

"Ow! Don't take it out on me!" she snapped, jerking her arm out of Grace's grasp.

"I take it didn't go as well as you had hoped?" Ivan asked.

"No. It didn't," Grace snapped.

"I thought they pledged their loyalty to you. Didn't you read him?" Nyx didn't understand.

"Jur are trained to be impenetrable to mind probes. From a distance, even to me. He showed me what he wanted me to believe. What he didn't expect was that when I touched him, I could read him clearly. He's loyal all right, just not to us. What he said was true. He told Kali to shove it until she offered him a choice: for her to take their families with her to their hidden dimension or spread her death and kill them all in slow agony. She used their families against him. What he said about their plan was also true. He was trying to gain my trust or warn me, I'm not sure which. As soon as we send over the port codes, they're coming for us. And when he said they made a mistake not killing him, he was right. Now we know what they're planning. His soldiers were the ones who destroyed Asgard. They killed our people."

"What about the pledge, Grace? I thought their pledge was till death," Nyx added.

"The first one is. By the time we got there, they were already pledged to Kali. Their pledge to me meant nothing."

Ivan woke the others. He shoved the information into their heads. Before they were even out of their chairs, Ivan had shifted out to get The Three. Grace sent Nyx to get information to the Zinna delegation leader. Her people couldn't have died fighting on the pier. The blood spatter was all wrong for a battlefield. Some bodies still had on parts of their cruise ship uniforms. Grace thought she would be interested to know the Council had ambushed one of their recreational cruisers to stage an attack. The dead had Kali's stench all over them.

This all had to happen fast.

"Ben, come with me. You three stay here and make sure Frigg gets into that shell," Grace ordered Leo, Thoth, and Ami.

She had a plan.

Ami protested, "Why do I have to stay here?"

"You expect those two to protect her? If anyone gets in here, you take care of them." Grace turned, grabbed Ben, and shifted out to the cargo port.

"What are we doing here?" Ben asked.

"We're moving this port to an open field on the other side of the planet. Grab four of the containment field generators and put them on the platform." Grace began disengaging the lock down stabilizers to release it from the floor.

"I see where you're going with this. Wait. Can you shift this whole thing?" The port was massive. It was the largest-sized equipment port they had on the planet. It was designated as a 20p, which could hold a medium-sized personnel carrier.

"I'm not sure. I can get Ivan to help if I have to."

Grace contacted Ivan. She told him to bring Erik with him and to send Mikkel and Alex to get their squads armed and staged in the open field. She then called to Nyx and instructed her to keep everyone inside the hall. Nyx needed to find Galin and have him set the planet's defense mode in case they also brought an aerial attack. It was up to her to defend that position.

"We're here," Erik said. "What are we doing?"

"Erik, Ben, get on the platform. Ivan, I need you on the other side. We're shifting this to the field with the rock face we climb. I want the back to the rock so there's only one way out," Grace directed.

"Got it." He moved to the other side of the port. Ben and Erik got on the platform.

"You ready?" she asked Ivan.

"Ready." They felt each other pulling. It took so little effort shifting something that size, Grace thought she could have done it herself. It would have been harder, but she could have. The placement was perfect. They backed it up against the flat rock face.

Ben grabbed the containment generators. He tossed two to Ivan. Ben went right, and Ivan went left.

"Erik, set the port with a remote lock. If they send a scout, we'll leave it open. If they come in force, we'll lock it down. I want you up on the top of the cliff so you have a view of the field. I'll signal you when to lock it down and turn on the containment field," Grace instructed.

Mikkel and Alex ran up.

"Troops are in place on the perimeter," Alex announced.

"Ivan, scan the perimeter through all light spectrums. We don't know what the Jur can see. Make adjustments," Grace ordered.

The squads contained both species of Rasans. It was impossible to see the vampires with their gear, but Ivan could barely make out a few Æsir even with their concealment equipment.

"Mikkel, positions at twelve degrees, twenty-nine degrees, and one hundred sixteen degrees are visible."

Mikkel tapped his comm, relaying those positions to conceal. Ivan scanned again, tapping Mikkel on the shoulder twice. "Good. Hold there."

Mikkel and Alex went back to their squads.

"Send him a random six-digit code and tell him it's for the small ports in the main hall. I guarantee he'll ask for the equipment port," Grace told Ivan.

He wrote, "Vaeweth, Grace asked me to send you our port code in case you need to evacuate your planet. This is our personnel port in the community center. Code sent encrypted xxx-xxx. Use decryption key 296."

Vaeweth responded, "Thanks, Ivan. I hate to ask, but if we need to evacuate, there are going to be a lot of us. Can we get the code to your equipment port?"

"You were right," he said to Grace.

Ivan typed his response: "It's on the other side of the planet where we're building the new city. There's nothing out there. We haven't even broken ground yet. We wouldn't be able to get to you quickly. Are you sure?"

Vaeweth wrote back, "We understand. That's fine. We want to make sure we can get our families out if we need to. The larger, the better."

Ivan replied, "We have a 20p at the end of a cleared field. Code sent encrypted xxx-xxx. Same decryption key. Will that work?"

Vaeweth sent his last reply: "That works. We appreciate the help, Ivan."

Ivan sent his last reply: "No problem. Let us know if you need anything else. We're here for you."

"Okay, it's done." Ivan grimaced to himself at that last sentence. They really were here for them.

Ivan grabbed Ben and Erik, shifting them to the top of the cliff. Grace took a position at the control panel of the port platform. They didn't have to wait long before the port activated.

Vaeweth came through alone. Grace pretended to be surprised.

"What in all hells, Vaeweth! You startled me. What are you doing here?"

"Testing the port code. What are you doing here?"

"Checking to see if the pad accepted the code. Some idiots set it in front of the cliff. It's blocking the signal, so we never got a report back that it acquired the new code."

She could see he was scanning the perimeter, but he didn't show he saw anything.

"Why didn't you send a service unit?" he asked.

She couldn't tell if he was suspicious or curious. "They're all still at the party. These ceremonial things can go on for days. We don't want the guests to think anything is going on yet." She tried to sound as irritated as possible without overdoing it.

"I've got to get back. I haven't slept in two days, and I'm exhausted." She knew from what she saw in him earlier that Kali hadn't told him about Grace's power being enhanced.

"I've got to get back to my side too and let them know the code worked. I'll see you soon, Grace."

She turned and started walking into the field. When he thought she was far enough away, she heard him say the word "clear."

"Hey, Grace, I almost forgot." He ran up quickly behind her. She spun around to see what he wanted. He slammed down a set of shackles on her wrists. And she let him.

"Vaeweth! What are you doing?" Lights flashed on the port pad, and she heard the hum of it powering up. He moved out of her way so she could see the soldiers appear on the platform.

Disable the port, Erik, she communicated.

"Are you kidding me?" she yelled at him. "You pledged your loyalty to me!"

"That was one pledge too late, Grace. We'd already given our loyalty to Kali," he growled.

That's just what she had been waiting to hear. *Raise the containment field, Erik.*

The Jur soldiers began shooting as the containment field went up. The blasts were bouncing off the field back into their ranks. They tried to port out, unsuccessfully. The unit was locked down. They were trapped.

"Yeah, I know. Surprise," Grace said while Mikkel and Alex signaled their squads to step out of their concealment.

Vaeweth held his blaster up to Grace's head. "Get back!" he commanded. "These shackles are frequency modulating. She can't phase while she's in them. I'll kill her."

Grace chuckled.

"What are you laughing at?" he yelled at her.

"Kali didn't tell you, did she?" Grace taunted.

"Stop laughing!" He took a swing at her. She easily phased as his hand went through where the back of her head had been. His confused look was priceless to her as she held up the shackles on the end of one finger.

"It's all about the jewelry, isn't it?" she said smugly.

How could he have missed it? Her amulet was gone. Kali intentionally kept it from him. He knew she would lie to him. He was a loose end. If he had succeeded, Kali would have commended him for his skill. Otherwise, all he was to her was a sacrifice, a board piece in her game. Something to slow them down while she escaped. He believed from the start this might happen.

Ivan shifted Ben and Erik down.

"Immobilize them, Ivan," Ben ordered much too calmly.

Ivan was more than happy to comply. He applied increasing amounts of pain until they were all close to unconscious and held them there.

Alex took the blaster from Vaeweth and shackled him. Grace applied enough pain to drop him to his knees.

"Now, you get to feel what my people felt." She grabbed him under his chin, turning his face toward his soldiers.

Erik dropped the containment field, moving out of the way. Ben raised his blaster.

"Release them, Ivan," Ben said. Ivan let them go. They were sluggish, shaking off the pain. Ben began firing emotionlessly. It was no more to him than shooting practice in the field. He sneered as the cold comfort of vengeance embraced him. The Three began firing next. Less than half of the Jur were able to get their wits back and return fire. The squads stepped up and finished the remaining soldiers. It was brutal, bloody, and finished.

Grace hadn't wanted this. She had wanted no part of this fight. They brought it to her door. She would do anything to protect her people, even if it meant sending a message as vile as this.

Anger ebbed inside her for what she was doing to the Jur and for what the Council had forced the Jur to do to her people. There were no winners here.

"You know what we're going to do now, Vaeweth?" She paused. "No? Can you guess?" She paused again. When she spoke this time, her voice dripped with bitterness. "We're going to go back to your planet. We're going to tell your people the truth. The Council sent you into an unwinnable massacre. We're going to tell them the Council had no intention of taking them to their safe little hidden dimension. The Council used their husbands and wives and sons and daughters to buy them enough time to get their own people out safely. They sacrificed all of you for them. And then you know what we're going to do?"

She squeezed his face harder, moving close, glaring directly into his eyes. "No, we're not going to kill them. And yes, I can read your thoughts. Surprise again." She wanted so badly to snap his neck, but that wasn't going to be enough. He was bound by his oath. As much as she detested him in this moment, she realized he was a victim in Kali's game. These weren't actions he had wanted to take.

"We're going to leave your families alone. With their anger. With their hate. And if they go after the Council, we won't do anything. But if they come after us? Guess. Oh no, not that, worse than that. Come on. What's worse than that?" She gave him a second to think.

"Wrong answer. What we are going to do is lock out their ports so they can't escape. Then we're going to blow up one of their suns. That will decimate their entire solar system. Maybe even their entire galaxy. So, you better hope they're not as stupid as you are."

He shut his eyes. He tried to scream. Grace was holding his face too tightly for screams to come out. All he could produce was a gurgling, choking sound.

"You bet on the wrong side, Vaeweth." She shoved him hard backward.

"Let me die with them, Grace! Kill me, Grace! If I get out of this, I'll come back for you! Grace! They'll make me come back for you!"

"Get him away from me," she commanded harshly. "And incinerate these bodies. We're taking the ashes back to their families. Make sure they're properly marked. And none of those crappy synthetic containers. They deserve stone burial jars. They were warriors. Treat them like warriors."

She was upset at the senselessness of all of this. She had been right about all of them. They followed Vaeweth to their deaths, as she knew they would. Why had it been so easy? It was a slaughter. She was angry it had been by her hand. She may not have pulled the trigger, but it was her responsibility all the same. This was the only way to stop them once they had been pledged. It could have only ended in death. Either theirs or Kali's. Grace would have preferred if it had been Kali's, but that wasn't a choice she got to make.

Grace couldn't go back to the city. She was too angry. To eliminate some of the rage, she had to burn it. She started running the trail up into the mountains. It was steep and rocky. It would have been a hard trail for most to even hike.

"Where's she going?" Mikkel questioned Ivan and Ben.

"Nowhere. She's just running," Ben answered first. Grace had always worked out her anger with hard physical activity. Ben remembered her sparring well into the night with warriors twice her size. Axe, sword, it never mattered as long as there was something she could hit.

"She shouldn't be out there alone. We have a buddy system for a reason," Mikkel protested.

"I'll let you tell her that," Ben quipped. He turned back to supervise the scanning and disposal of the bodies. Just because they were on the other side didn't mean they weren't worthy of a proper, respectful ending. Grace was wrong about one thing. They weren't warriors, they were fodder. He would still ensure they were treated appropriately. Even Ben had difficulty hating the dead.

Nyx tried to contact Grace, who was ignoring everyone. After the third time, Grace snapped at her to call Ivan. She wasn't ready to deal with anyone yet.

Ivan! Grace won't talk to me. You need to get back here. There's something you need to see, Nyx demanded.

He didn't like the tone in her voice. She sounded not worried, but perplexed, maybe?

On my way, Ivan answered.

"Ben!" He raised his voice enough to be heard over the commotion. Not loud enough to draw undue attention.

Ben came over to his position. "Yeah."

"Nyx needs me in the hall. You good to finish up here?" Ivan asked.

"Yeah. We're almost done. It's not about my mother, is it?"

"I don't think so. I'll let you know."

"Okay. See you back there soon," Ben responded uneasily. He wanted to finish so he could get back to check on Frigg. He also wanted to make sure this task was completed correctly.

Ivan shifted out.

"What's going on?" he asked Nyx.

"Over here. By the personnel port." She led him around the corner to a small hallway with three two-person ports on either side. There was a single Jur flanked by two Rasan guards. He was dressed for the celebration, not in typical Jur gear. He was young. Likely a soldier. Not old enough to be a Commander. Ivan studied him. The young man was afraid. Ivan could smell it on him. It didn't matter what species they were; fear always had the same pungent stench.

Ivan spoke to the guards. "Get him down to interview room three. I'll be there in a minute."

"Wait," the man exclaimed. "I was told I had to find Grace. I have a message for her. It's urgent."

"If it's urgent, tell me," Ivan demanded.

"I can't. I'm only allowed to tell Grace."

Ivan leered at him. His fear heightened.

"Take him."

As the guards were taking him, he didn't resist. He yelled over his shoulder, "She knows me! Tell her Paneth has a message for her! She knows me!"

Ivan didn't recognize his name. Even with sharing her memories, he couldn't place the man. He didn't want to bother Grace while she was in her current mood. He could feel her anger, frustration, and guilt. It was her decision if she would talk to the man or not. He didn't have much choice other than to tell her.

Grace, he said cautiously.

Not now, Ivan, she snapped.

He didn't want to push too hard. He thought for a second before simply uttering, *Paneth.*

She stopped in her tracks. *What?* She knew the name. She thought back momentarily before she placed the young Jur on Vaeweth's team. He was the tech kid. The one who coded the port back at Ben's facility during the raid.

What about him? she said in a much less hostile way.

He's here. He's been here the whole time. He has a message, and he said he can only speak to you.

"Where is he?" She startled Ivan by appearing suddenly behind him. She had started speaking mid-shift.

Nyx smirked. He'll get used to it, she thought to herself.

"Downstairs. Interview three," he managed to say calmly.

"Where's Ben? Are they finished?" she asked, breathing a little heavier than normal.

"Almost," he replied.

"Good." She walked to the stairs at the end of the hall, disappearing into the staircase.

Nyx and Ivan stood watching her.

"Shall we?" Ivan extended his arm toward the end of the hall.

"Shall we what?" she asked.

"Go watch the interview?" It was blatantly obvious to him what he had meant.

"Don't talk to me like that. I'm not a child. You could have meant to go check on Frigg, couldn't you have?" she huffed back.

"Sorry. Not looking for an argument here. Yes or no?"

"Yes," she replied, walking past him with her nose in the air.

Ivan rolled his eyes.

"I saw that."

"No, you didn't."

"Well, I felt it then."

Ivan could tell she wanted the last word and decided not to disappoint her.

They entered the viewing room behind room three. Grace was already inside. She was pacing. She hadn't spoken to Paneth yet. He was staring at her uncomfortably as she looked at her feet. The room was small and brightly lit. It took Grace ten steps from end to end. Paneth was sitting unbound in a cold metal chair. The only other thing in the room was a second chair a few feet in front of him. She stopped behind it, placing her hands on the back.

Ivan could smell his fear even through the wall. The man was terrified but didn't show any outward signs of it.

"What's the message, Paneth?" She finally broke the tense silence, walking back around the table.

"There are more of us. A lot more of us," he said.

"Is that a threat?" She narrowed her eyes at him.

"No! No. Just the opposite," he stammered.

She leaned forward, folding her arms on top of the chair back. "Explain. And choose your words carefully," she warned.

"He knew they would come. The Council, not Kali specifically. He hoped you would get there first, but you didn't. She did. The soldiers he had with him weren't his regular ones. They were volunteers. Mostly prisoners who wanted to clear their names. For their families. On Jur, prisoners' families are outcasts," he spoke nervously.

"Keep going," she directed.

"We don't have much crime, so when someone breaks an oath or steals or kills another Jur, their entire family pays the price," he continued.

"How do you even know any of this if you were here the whole time? We have blockers over the entire planet. You couldn't have been communicating with him after he left."

He lowered his head. "I hacked your system. I turned one of the blockers into a relay. But I didn't disable it. I just hijacked the signal so I could get an outbound channel." He looked at her nervously, then dropped his head down, waiting for repercussions.

"Look at me," Grace commanded. Paneth did as he was told, meeting her eyes.

"What is your message for me?" she asked again.

"The Council thinks our army is small. They had only ever seen a few freelance mercenaries. Two hundred or so. But we're not small. We have over two thousand soldiers they don't know about ready to pledge to you. He knew if he had to pledge to the Council to save our people, he would have to try to kill you. He knew they would lie to him. They always lied to him. So, he went back to set up his plan. I haven't spoken to him since he pledged. He's loyal to them now, so he won't ever speak to me again. He also won't ever betray the rest of our people to the Council. If he's not dead, he's stuck." He swallowed uncomfortably. "Is he dead?"

Grace ignored his question. "Vaeweth is the Commander of your entire army."

Paneth didn't see it as a question. "Yes," he said anyway.

"Aren't they all pledged to him?" She was suspicious this was another trap.

"It doesn't work like that." He thought that was a ridiculous assessment. The way she was glaring at him made him squirm, so he continued. "It's tiered. His Vice Commanders are pledged to him. Their Captains pledge to them, and so forth. The only way for someone to get promoted is if their direct superior dies. At that point, all of their soldiers have the option to pledge to the new superior or move to another unit."

"Tactical … smart," Grace muttered mindlessly, more to herself than to Paneth. She turned her attention back to him.

"He went back and killed his Vice Commanders to release the army from their pledge to him." She formed it as a statement, not a question.

"He gave them an option. They opted to commit Q'kt. It was the honorable way," Paneth stated.

She had to phrase her next statement very carefully.

"Who are you pledged to? How are you free? Or are you free?"

"I'm free. I was pledged to my mother," Paneth said, recoiling at the words.

Grace felt a knot tighten in her stomach. She understood what phrasing his statement in the past meant for his mother.

"Is he alive?" Paneth asked again.

Grace let the question linger. He was nervous. She walked behind him again. He closed his eyes, bracing for his inevitable death. She placed her hands on either side of his head and felt his body shudder. She read him. It was getting easier for her. She could read him before her skin contacted his. It wouldn't be long before she didn't need physical contact with them anymore. She saw he believed what he said. She saw he believed it all to be true. In addition, she saw other things.

She moved in front of him, spun the chair around, and sat down. He opened his eyes. Confusion swept over his face.

She leaned in toward him. He didn't move. The pit in her stomach had grown to the size of a boulder.

"Your father's not dead, Paneth. The others are. All of them. We haven't decided what to do with him yet. We haven't decided what to do with you yet either."

Grace rose, leaving him in the room alone as he sat in the chair, lowering his head to stare at his hands.

The door to the viewing room swung open.

"What do you think?" Grace asked Ivan.

"I knew it was too easy. They couldn't have been soldiers. Real soldiers wouldn't have made the mistake of shooting inside of a containment field. They would know the blasts would come back at them." Ivan didn't know if it was worse that all these people knew they were walking into a certain death, or better, knowing they sacrificed themselves to save the rest of their people.

Nyx looked at the floor, shaking her head. "This is senseless! Maybe we should let it all descend back into The Nothing. Are these creatures even worth saving? This is exactly why I hate being around lower beings. Their word is more precious than their lives? More precious than doing what they know is right? They would be loyal to ones they knew were corrupt just to save face. I don't understand them at all! Needless sacrifice and death when they have such short lives anyway. What is wrong with these broken things? Chaos didn't create life to be like this. It's supposed to be beautiful and precious! NOT LIKE THIS!"

Grace didn't know if Nyx was angry at the situation or having a complete breakdown. She didn't know what to think. The last thing she needed right now was an unstable Primordial with the ability to go back and break the timeline. The room started trembling.

Ivan grabbed Nyx by the shoulders, shaking her to get her attention. That's when time stopped for what seemed an eternity and a partial second at once. Nyx had time shifted and taken Ivan with her. Grace felt a rush of pain. Not as bad as Ivan had described it, although she had been absorbing pain from others for centuries. Maybe she had a higher tolerance.

As soon as they were gone, they were back. Their clothing was different. Ivan had about a week's worth of facial hair. It looked good on him, she thought, before quickly dismissing it as ridiculous. They were both dressed in black. He wore pants and a loose, casual button-down. She was in a dark jumpsuit with wide legs.

"Apologies, Grace," Nyx said as if it were only a courtesy. "We've got a solution to your little problem." She took a seat on the edge of the small table at the back of the room, watching Ivan and Grace.

"What kind of solution?" Grace asked hesitantly.

"You're probably not going to like it," Ivan warned.

"Not going to like what?" she said with suspicion and a slight edge of bitterness.

Ivan continued cautiously. "Vaeweth mounted a huge tactical plan to get most of his forces away from the Council and onto our side. And he did it in minutes. We can't have that kind of mind working against us now. If the only way for him to be released from his pledge to Kali is death, we give him death."

"That's what you came up with for the entire week you were gone? Kill him? I thought you said you had a solution?" Grace waved her hands in irritation.

"Nobody said he has to stay dead, Grace. Can you imagine a Jur-vampire hybrid sired to you? Now that's an unbreakable bond that only begins with death." He gave her a sly look.

The wheels inside her head spun fast. The thought had never even crossed her mind. They had dismissed turning other immortals as unnecessary. On the other hand, Jur were a long-lived species, but they weren't immortal. She had to admit, it was a solid solution. With one caveat.

"I can't do it, Ivan."

"But Grace, it's the perfect solution. Wh—" She cut him off.

"I can't do it. And neither can you. He needs to be bonded to someone with unquestionable loyalty to us that the Council will never suspect. We can't be bonded to him directly. There is no way to determine what would happen if one of us sired. There's no telling what a sire bond will do to us, either. Not only that, but you and I can't have any kind of connection to him that will compromise him doing his job or compromise us in order to save him. It needs to be someone who won't be on the front lines." Grace continued to think.

"Ben will not like this. He will not like working with them after finding out they were responsible for killing off most of his people. We'll have to think about how to handle breaking that news. Think I should probably let you handle it." Ivan said. He didn't normally shy away from delivering unpleasant news. This time, he didn't want any part of it.

"I'll take care of Ben. He'll see the logic. And after I explain everything, he'll see it's an advantage we can't pass on." She was dreading that conversation already.

"I know who should do it," Nyx added in.

"Who?" Grace and Ivan said in unison.

"The boy. Erik," Nyx proceeded matter-of-factly.

"But he's not, he can't." Ivan's voice trailed off when he realized what she meant for him.

"That little blonde one. The one he's so smitten with can turn him. You saw them at the party. They couldn't take their eyes off each other." Nyx saw no problem with her suggestion.

"Asta?" Ivan questioned. "We've never turned an immortal before. It's uncertain if it's even viable. We don't know what the repercussions may be. It's too risky."

"Don't be daft," Nyx admonished. "You were immortal when you were turned. Even if you didn't know it yet. And Grace, she was turned when she merged with you. Can you imagine the mind that one will have? He's already far more intelligent than most of the lowers."

Neither of them answered her.

"Do you have a better choice?" Nyx stood up. "If you do, I'd certainly like to hear it." It offended her they didn't see her solution was exceptional.

It has to be Erik's choice, Grace thought to herself.

"Ivan. Ask Erik if he is willing. Explain everything. And Asta. She needs to be part of the decision too. If she's reluctant to take responsibility for him, there's no point in entertaining this as a solution."

"Grace! I can't believe you're even considering this. He's your son!" Ivan was taken aback.

"You're right. He is my son! And he's a warrior. And a tactician. And it's his decision to make. *Not* yours and *not* mine. You forget because of the way he appears that he's ten times your age. He can decide for himself." She was stern in her statement.

"You should be the one to ask him," Ivan replied.

"I have something else I need to do." She shifted back over to the room where Paneth was sitting. He jerked back hard enough to have toppled the chair if it hadn't been secured to the floor.

"Paneth, can you contact the new commander?" Grace asked without hesitating.

Paneth wasn't sure how to respond. "You don't understand, Grace. *You* are supposed to be the new commander."

"But I'm not Jur."

"No, you're more. You're our salvation." He paused, gazing hopefully at her. When she didn't respond, he continued. "I need my device back. That is, if they haven't disabled it yet," he added.

Grace opened the door and said something to the guards.

"I want you to have the Vice Commanders come here. All of them. I'll provide you with the port code for the secured platform on the guard deck." One of the guards brought in Paneth's device and the code. "Make sure they understand if we see even a single blade, they will be disintegrated where they stand."

He nodded in agreement. She handed him the device. He tapped out a message, which she read before letting him send it. They agreed. She took back the device without speaking to him and left the room through the door.

She stood on the platform as the four of them arrived. Three males and a female. They were hesitant but appeared relieved to see her standing in front of them. One stepped forward. The guards moved toward them. Grace held up her hand, signaling the guards to stop.

"Come forward," she said, examining them.

The security port scanned them. They had no weapons. The man proceeded toward her, dropping to one knee.

"Commander. I am Yaden. We are at your service."

She stepped forward, placing her hand on his shoulder.

"Are you pledged or are you free?" she asked while she read him. What Paneth had told her was truthful. The events had unfolded as he had described. Reading Jur through their blocking capabilities was much easier. She no longer needed physical contact, although she could still see more with it.

"I am free," Yaden stated.

She directed the others forward, asking each the same. They were all free. They were all newly anointed Vice Commanders. And they each had hundreds pledged through them.

They had taken post on the second moon of Jur, waiting to be called. Their families were drifting in a fleet of ships outside scan range behind Sierra Alpha four in the ninth quadrant. It had been a huge risk for them because of what they had done to her people. Yet they felt no guilt in doing so. They were following their commander as their people were born to do.

They were The Everything's perfect soldiers, following orders without hesitation or conscience. They were an asset she could not allow to fall under control of the Council. She didn't want to see an entire race exterminated because of their unwavering loyalty to the wrong cause.

She had the guards take them to a large, comfortable holding lounge. It could be quite some time before she was ready for them.

CHAPTER EIGHT

Ivan didn't know where Erik was located, so he made the decision to shift to him instead of trying to find him and port there. He wished he hadn't. When Ivan popped in, he found Erik and Asta in a compromising position. None of them was too pleased. Once they got their composure back, Ivan transferred the information from the last hour. He left out the part where he and Nyx had time shifted, but Erik had already figured something like that had happened, given Ivan didn't have any facial hair earlier that day in the field.

Ivan left to wait in the other room for the two of them to discuss what he had proposed.

"I thought my family was screwed up," Asta said, sitting on the edge of the bed, sliding on a pair of Erik's shorts that were too big for her. She pulled the drawstring as tight as it would go. When she stood up, they slipped down, resting on her hips over her tank top. Erik stood in front of her in his tac pants and bare feet. He pulled a sweatshirt over her head, lifting out a mass of tangled blonde hair.

"At least it was Ivan and not your dad," she said.

"Or yours," he chuckled.

"Can you imagine? That would be mortifying." She ducked down, searching for her sandals. "Where's the other one? Do you see it?"

"Here," he said, tossing it to her. She snatched it out of the air with quick, exacting measure, as a hawk would pick running prey from the ground.

"Thanks." She sat back down, sliding the strap over her ankle.

Erik pulled a T-shirt over his head and sat on the bed next to her.

"Do you think you would?" he asked.

"What? Turn you? Mate with you without a ceremony?" she sighed. She had only known him for six months. They hadn't had any counseling. There were rules about these things. At least there were rules … before. But it was Ivan asking, and he was the one who had made the rule to begin with.

"Is that what you want? You're already immortal. It will change you in ways you may not like." She seemed troubled.

"I know I love you. I've never loved anyone before. All hells considered, I've never even wanted to date anyone before you. I want this to happen, eventually. And me siring Vaeweth makes sense."

"I love you too," she replied with a sarcastic edge to her voice. It was the first time she had said it out loud. The derisive tone didn't make it any less true or real for her. Feelings for him had come quickly, hitting her the first time she had a conversation alone with him at the vineyard. "That's not the question, though, is it? You're already ten times smarter than me. Will I still be enough for you when you're a hundred times smarter than me?"

Asta had always had self-esteem issues. Growing up with Violet, she had always felt like the silver medalist. Violet was smarter. Violet was prettier. Violet was better at hunting and sports. Asta couldn't imagine why Erik would want to stay with her.

"I," Erik said.

"I, what?" she questioned.

"Smarter than I," he corrected without considering he may be condescending.

"See what I mean! NOT HELPING!" She smacked him on the leg hard enough to break most men's bones, then stood in a huff.

He grabbed her wrist, gently pulling her onto his lap.

"Asta, you *are* smart. You speak seven languages. You're kind and you're beautiful. You have the biggest heart I've ever seen. And I will always love you." Erik thought she was far too good for him. He had his own self-esteem issues, being the middle born of the trio. Who wouldn't, growing up with brothers like Alex and Mikkel? They were better at everything than he was. At least, he thought they were.

"Eight. I speak eight languages," she said with a contrived smug attitude, sitting up a little straighter.

"My point is, you're perfect and I couldn't imagine being with anyone else." He loved her with his entire being. Ironic, seeing as he only met her at Jack's insistence.

"My mother does think you're the catch of a lifetime," she joked.

"And my grandmother is going to adore you. You'll never want for anything once she gets her hands on you." He smiled at her. He couldn't wait until she was back. Out of the three grandsons, he was the closest to her.

"Wait, I thought your grandmother was dead." Ivan hadn't given her that information, and Erik hadn't had the time to discuss it with her yet, either.

"We thought so too until a few hours ago. Turns out her essence was in my mother's amulet the whole time. Leo's growing a shell for her. We should have her back with us anytime now." The thought delighted him.

"Well, that's it then." She stood back up. "Come on." She took his arm, pulling him swiftly off the bed and placing him on his feet. Sometimes he forgot how much strength she had packed into her slight frame.

"Come on where?"

"To see your grandmother. If she doesn't approve, I'm not doing this," she stated adamantly.

"What about your parents?"

"They'll forgive me. I'm impetuous." She resumed pulling him toward the door, flinging it open a little too hard. She didn't expect it to slam into the wall, lodging the handle into a fresh indentation.

The noise startled Ivan.

"Ivan, take us to see Frigg," Asta demanded, planting her feet in a determined stance in front of him.

She had never spoken to him like that before. She was always respectful and somewhat timid around him when he had been Regent. He deferred to Erik.

"As the lady says, please."

"As you wish," he smirked, placing his hands on their shoulders.

Ivan, Erik, and Asta instantly appeared inside the lab. Asta was momentarily lost. She spun around, seeing Frigg's shell sitting on the edge of the open pod. The older woman was enchanting, even if she looked younger than Asta had imagined. Her light auburn hair was loosely swept up on top of her head, with a few well-placed curls dripping down. She was dressed, to Erik's relief, in a flowing light-blue and silver dress that appeared to be a hundred layers of silk so fine a single touch would melt it away.

"Is that her? She's so pretty!" Asta gushed.

"Thank you, little one," Ami said.

"I didn't mean you, Ami," Asta retorted.

Erik explained gently, "That's only her shell, Asta. Queenie's still in the crystal. Ami is the only one who can hear her."

"Oh," she said, a little embarrassed. "Wait, you call your grandmother Queenie?" Asta snorted.

Now Erik was the one who was embarrassed. "Yeah, it's kind of an inside joke." He shuffled his still-bare feet and blushed.

"You're back." Leo raised his head toward Ivan. "Where's Ben? He wanted to be here for this. We're ready to install her essence."

Ivan did a quick search for Ben. He was with Grace. Their conversation had gotten heated. She was yelling. He was brooding. Ben could see the logic in what she was saying, but he wasn't ready to let go of his rage yet. It would be a while before that conversation concluded.

"He's a bit tied up right now. You should go ahead," Ivan explained.

Leo raised his eyebrow before he turned toward Ami. "Ask her how we're supposed to open the crystal."

Ami replied to Frigg, "You sure? That's it? Okay." Ami placed the crystal between the palms of her hands, squeezing until it shattered, exploding into dust. A stream of light rose from the dust, gliding toward the shell, entering through the mouth and nose. She tilted her head back, took a slow deep breath, and then exhaled, opening her eyes, which shined blue when she twisted and stretched.

"Mmmm … finally. You have no idea how good it feels to be out of that prison," Frigg said to everyone. Her eyes were a normal blue now. She turned to face Erik and Asta.

"Where are your shoes, little man?" she asked, emphasizing the t's in "little." The way Frigg emphasized each consonant made her speech pattern sound regal to Asta.

Frigg smiled broadly, embracing Erik, rubbing his back.

"Welcome back. I've missed you," Erik said, hugging her tightly without answering her question.

She released him, moving on to Asta.

"Asta, my sweet little one. It's lovely to finally see you." She touched Asta's hair. "You're much more delicate than I imagined you'd be. Delightful."

She slid in front of Ivan next. "Ivan, I feel I know you so well. I can't imagine how difficult life has been for you. After that missed opportunity seven hundred years ago, I never thought you and Grace would come together. You broke her heart when you left her there. She loves you deeply, even if she will never say it to you." She hugged him gently.

"It's better to have happened when it did. We wouldn't have understood what was going on back then. I'm glad to have her now." He took Frigg's hand, clasping it to his chest.

She squeezed his hand lightly, holding it for a few seconds before letting her grasp slip away. His eyes followed her as she glided across the room to Ami. She was quite possibly the most refined creature he had ever laid eyes on.

Ami jumped up from the stool, grabbing onto Frigg tightly. Frigg laughed delicately, stroking Ami's back.

She lifted her hand toward Leo. Ami wasn't letting go, so Leo took her outstretched hand.

"My dearest Leo. Thank you for this divine shell. It is just as exquisite as I expected it to be." He kissed her hand, releasing it gracefully.

She next reached out to Thoth. She had slipped out of Ami's grasp by easing her back onto the stool. Frigg took both of Thoth's hands into hers.

"Thoth, you're going to be fine. It's painful and raw at this moment; however, it does get easier."

"Thank you for your kind words, Frigg. Anything of that magnitude is difficult to overcome," he replied and kissed her lightly on the cheek.

"We all do unexpected things out of fear. Immortals fear death far more than mortals do. A mortal expects their life to end at some point. They at least have the resolve that they will someday have an end. Immortals have more difficulty aligning themselves to that fate. Try not to judge her too harshly for succumbing to that fear." She released his hands and swung round.

"Now, catch me up on what I've missed." She floated over dramatically, lowering herself onto the sofa.

"Doesn't seem like you've missed much," Ivan said.

"I could hear everything from inside the crystal. I was, however, unable to communicate because of my own misjudgment of the blood seal."

Ivan's embarrassment flashed across his face. Frigg had witnessed every intimate moment of Grace's life with him.

She continued, "With the exception of the last bit since all of you flew out of here. I understand there was a brief episode with the Jur? You know, you can hardly blame them. They were under contract, then bound by pledge. That's how they work."

Ivan thought her overly forgiving, given the situation.

"That's quite magnanimous of you. Forgiving the Jur so easily," Ivan noted.

"Not at all. I won't forget. I also don't have the luxury of dwelling on the past. None of us do, really." Her voice was cool. "Now, proceed with your thought transfer so we can all be on the same page."

They wouldn't all be on the same page. Frigg had a great deal of information the others didn't. He transferred the events to her, Leo, Ami, and Thoth at the same time.

Frigg addressed Erik, "Seems you have a life-altering decision in front of you, little man. And you, Asta dear. What are you willing to sacrifice for the continuance of The Everything?"

Asta straightened herself. "That's why we came to you. I told Erik I would only turn him if you approved. I can't bear the thought of you hating me for doing something so drastic to your grandson. And what if he doesn't make it? How could I live with myself then?" Her voice was small.

"Come here, child. Sit beside me."

Asta slowly sat, gently sliding Frigg's dress out of the way so she didn't crush it. Frigg took her hands, holding them in her lap.

"No one can make this choice for you, Asta. There are some things that are bigger than all of us. If you're reluctant to sire him, I am certain someone else will. Ivan or his mother, for instance. No one is forcing you to do anything. You must decide if you are willing to be responsible for Erik. They came to you first because you are invested in him. You were the logical choice. No one would find it unusual if it were you who sired him after being caught up in the romance of your sister's ceremonies. And no one would logically connect him as a sire for Vaeweth. The strategy is sound."

"Are you saying you think this is a good plan? Are you saying you think I should sire him?" Asta was still seeking her approval.

"I'm not saying anything of the kind. I'm saying it is not my decision to make. You can't concern yourself with the approval of others. You can only do what your conscience will allow you to survive. Your decision requires a discussion with Erik. Then he can come to a decision about how he is willing to move forward." Frigg's position was firm. It would not be up to her. She would neither approve nor disapprove.

"Go. Discuss." With that, she released Asta's hands, ushering her away.

Asta got up and moved to Erik's side. She and Erik went to the far corner of the room, and Frigg transferred her attention to Ivan.

"Ivan, come sit. I believe you have questions about your origins?"

"Yes, I'd—" Nyx appeared in the room, interrupting Ivan's statement. She had grown tired of watching Paneth sitting alone in the interview room.

Frigg sighed. "Nyx." She acknowledged her presence coolly.

"Frigg." Nyx mirrored her tone.

"I suppose you have some interest in this conversation as well," Frigg stated flippantly.

"I certainly do." Nyx had no idea what they were currently discussing. She didn't care. She had questions of her own.

"Would you care to join us, then?" Frigg invited.

Nyx didn't reply. She sat in the chair at the end of the sofa.

"Leo," Frigg called. "Would you be a dear and see about the most efficient particulars of turning Erik if he so chooses?"

Leo motioned to Thoth to assist him. He was glad for something to do that would keep him out of the way.

"Thank you," Frigg replied. It seemed to be her agenda, too.

Ami remained seated, studying everything going on around the room. She preferred observing to interacting most of the time.

Ivan sat where Frigg had indicated, and she began.

"When we were attempting to create the child of light, I called out to Chaos. Chaos answered, taking the form of a female. Probably because the feminine form is less overtly threatening than the male form to most. Henceforth, I explained what we were attempting to accomplish, including my perspective on why we hoped to perform such a task. Chaos enlightened me on what was truly happening to The Everything."

She shifted in her seat. "You've heard the phrase 'from ashes to ashes, from dust to dust'?"

"Yes," Ivan replied.

Nyx rolled her eyes while she propped her elbow on the arm of the chair and leaned her cheek into her open palm, appearing bored already, while Frigg did her best to ignore her.

"Chaos created the outward burst that brought forth The Everything from The Nothing."

Frigg changed her tone to instructional. "'She' will be the pronoun I choose to address Chaos with proceeding forward."

She shifted back to a storytelling demeanor. "She hadn't had the experience to realize that it would all slowly disintegrate back into chaos without intervention. Chaos is not only a place; it is also her consciousness and an action. She, being an extension of original Chaos, was unable to provide the necessary balance to alleviate the disintegration of The Everything. She, too, had been searching for a way to bring a consciousness that could equal hers, preventing the slide back. She was unable to create a single being to be her equivalent, providing order. The fabric or mesh of space that held the matter in a state of suspension was crumbling.

"She had created other beings of consciousness. The Primordials. Her children." She extended her hand in presentation toward Nyx.

"Even they could not counter her, no matter how many she created. She created both positive and negative matter beings, but nothing was working as she had expected. Once the Primordials began creating their own beings, the power was too diluted to have much effect in countering the slide. The descent was slowing, but not enough. She graced me with the gift of shifting time with her. Together, we planned for centuries. Ultimately, we landed on a plan to create two beings that, when combined, could directly oppose Chaos, with order forming balance.

"The first being, Nanna—Grace, as you know her—would be constructed from pure energy instead of matter. Her container needed to be strong enough to keep her energy from bursting through. The second being would be created by Chaos from positive and negative matter. She took me back and we, together with Freya, created Grace. Over time, without having a being she could merge with, her energy began to leak out. We created her current shell and then locked it down with the amulet. Your creation, however, was a more arduous task, Ivan.

"Chaos was unable to produce an equal that was capable of merging with Grace. The blending of matter and energy was delicate. She had to devise another plan. You had to be a being of mass to compress and contain Grace's energy. She believed she had succeeded when she created the first vampire. She had not. The negative matter was forcing an acceleration with the positive matter, canceling out to zero."

Ivan raised an eyebrow at her. That statement had caught his attention.

She continued, "He had the ability to pass the appropriate control measures through blood and venom. He was able to create immortals from non-immortal beings of several species, but he and all his descendants were incompatible with Grace. They could not contain her energy. Chaos concluded you must come directly from her composition of matter and antimatter before being combined with the enhanced mass of the vampire species. She concluded she would need to physically give birth to you.

"You were the third attempt she had any success with. The other two did not complete their process with their intended requirements. One devolved into an ordinary vampire. The other rejected his biological shell and rose, becoming drawn into and absorbed by The Nothing. You bonded to your shell, showing the ability to ascend perfectly."

"I can't say I understand the different types of matter and energy. How is it supposed to affect us or our abilities? How can we alter the decline?" Ivan found Frigg's information far too elevated for him to grasp. Grace would have even less comprehension of it.

"In short, you can recharge inert matter into stars, providing a positive energy flow, reducing the amounts of negative energy until there is a balance. It's not specifically about light the way you've been thinking, it's about energy. Over time, I've additionally come to believe that it's not about being able to stop the decay. It's about harnessing the ability to regenerate it when it can no longer expend energy." Frigg still wasn't certain he could comprehend.

"But how can changing one star at a time make any difference? Is it all we'd be able to do? Is that how we're meant to spend our entire existence? Can't Chaos already do that? She created The Everything by herself. How can she not have the ability to stabilize it?" Ivan was becoming frustrated.

"No, of course not. Stars will be nothing for the two of you. You will be creating entirely new galaxies at once. When The Everything is in balance with The Nothing, all you need to do is maintenance. Your shells are constrictors that keep you contained. Once you rise, your joint power will only be equal to Chaos's. Since The Everything exists, she can no longer harness enough power to create from The Nothing. It is her power base, while your power base is The Everything." Frigg made it sound like such a simple task.

"Wouldn't she be able to recreate The Everything again after it descends back into The Nothing?" He was still not completely clear on the subject.

"She doesn't think she could do that again. It will never be exactly The Nothing it began as. You would still exist. She isn't even completely sure how she managed it the first time."

Frigg stopped momentarily.

"Not to add insensitivity, but you must be aware Nyx is incorrect." Frigg was trying to be as delicate as possible, for Ivan's sake.

"Excuse me!" Nyx exclaimed indignantly, sitting straight and grasping the arms of the chair. "How dare you!"

"Wrong about what?" Ivan questioned somberly as he tightly folded his hands together. He already knew what she was going to say.

"Having children with Grace. The two of your combined essences will provide delicate balance to the imbalance of Chaos once you are able to rise. Adding a child would cause the exact thing you were created to prevent. I am sorry to be the one to tell you, but it had to be said."

She reached over, placing her hand on Ivan's folded ones. He thought he had braced himself against her words. He hadn't braced enough and had become utterly overcome with grief. Until Grace, he had never even considered wanting anything. Now, a child was the one thing he wanted for himself. Frigg had swept it away from him in seconds. His eyes stung hot as he tried to hold back tears. His cheeks flushed and burned. Hearing he could never have children was too much. He had already assumed it. The words made it real. He unconsciously pushed his emotions out into the room. Everyone could feel how completely distressed he had become.

Grace felt his unmitigated despair. She appeared in the room with a still-angry Ben in tow. He was the only one immune to the disturbing shift of mood. He only became aware something wasn't right when he saw Ivan. Though unsure why, Ben felt an intense sense of compassion for his friend.

"Mother? What did you do to him?" Ben asked as Grace rushed to Ivan's side. That was not the way Ben had pictured the reunion with his mother.

"I simply told him the truth," Frigg defended.

"Ivan. Ivan, what's wrong?" Grace was concerned with Ivan's lack of response. "What's going on?"

Ivan couldn't speak. He couldn't think. His thoughts were too muddled for Grace to read.

Nyx reached over, touching Grace's arm. She passed on the conversation that had taken place. Grace tried to console Ivan as best she could. Her own sadness was strong as she attempted to suffocate her emotions and pull Ivan's back from the room. Nyx rose to pass the same conversation on to Ben. He was sullen. If faced with a similar situation, he was unsure of how he'd respond. He had his sons. He couldn't imagine his life without them. The latest information made it even more difficult for Ben to accept that Erik may consider what Nyx had suggested.

Grace shifted Ivan to their apartment to stop his effect on the others. The atmosphere of the room they departed from was eased.

Ben would try to lighten the atmosphere. For his own alleviation, if nothing else.

"Mother." He nodded to her. "You always did know how to make an entrance. I see you've made a few improvements to your shell."

"Thank you. I'm surprised you noticed. I'm glad to see you, too," Frigg replied before sighing heavily.

Asta and Erik nervously approached the group, holding hands. Frigg was the only one remaining seated. She pulled herself up straight as if she had been installed on her throne. Back to business, it appeared.

"Do you have your decision, then?" Frigg addressed Erik, forcing a stern face.

"Yes," Erik replied hesitantly.

"What shall it be?" Frigg asked.

"We'll do it," he said, locking eyes with Asta.

Ben felt his anger well again. "Why are we still considering any of this? When Grace and Ivan rise, won't that solve the entire issue?" he protested loudly.

"No, it doesn't," Nyx answered. "The Council still has plans to isolate and stabilize a single dimension, flooding the others with enough negative energy to force a collapse. We don't know how far along they are in their plan. They don't understand it won't work. Their ineptitude will cause a total collapse of The Everything, including their own dimension, before Grace and Ivan understand how to do anything about it. They need to be stopped. We need to remove as many of their resources as possible. There is still a war coming."

"Fuck!" Ben exclaimed, slamming his fist down onto the table beside him, shattering it. He dropped into a lounge chair, resigning himself to the bitter loss.

Erik cleared his throat. "We were going to get to this point eventually, anyway. The two of us together have decided it's time to step up and do our part. We don't have the luxury of being selfish." Erik tried to sound conciliatory.

Asta cowered at Ben's display, although she tried not to. She could smell the sharpness of Ben's anger oozing off him. It was a nauseating scent.

Ben was holding onto a great deal of hatred for the Jur and specifically Vaeweth himself. He didn't want him to be saved. He didn't understand how

Vaeweth could have exterminated an entire race of innocent people without question. Ben was better at doing what was right than he was at doing what he was told for someone else's agenda. He was not as good at forgiving as his mother apparently was.

CHAPTER NINE

Ivan went from extreme depression to uncontrolled laughter. He couldn't stop himself. He had been bottling his emotions up for fifteen hundred years. He had been adamant after his children had been murdered. He would never bring anything innocent and defenseless into this world again.

Until the morning of the wedding, he didn't even want to consider children. But things had changed. When he found having a child was possible with Grace, it had become an obsession. A child of theirs wouldn't be vulnerable. It had become his greatest desire. It was ironic that the one thing he now couldn't have was the only thing he desperately wanted.

His swift turn frightened Grace. Was he now the one becoming unstable? She couldn't think of anything that had ever frightened her more. She wasn't scared *of* him; she was scared *for* him.

"Ivan?" She approached him cautiously.

He didn't meet her eyes. He mumbled incoherently, "Why does it always have to be? In order to do the right thing for everyone else, we always have to sacrifice what we want the most?"

"I wish I knew," she whispered. She sat down beside him, staring at her own hands, hoping not to give away the part of her that was secretly relieved. It took everything she had to block that thought from him.

They sat in stillness, letting the feeling of loss wash over them. It was odd to her. Feeling loss over something they never had. Feeling loss over something she didn't want in the first place.

"I guess we'll just have to be enough for each other," she whispered.

"I guess we will." He mirrored her volume, placing his hand on her knee. "I'm sorry, Grace. It overwhelmed me. I didn't see it coming. My reaction, I mean. I hadn't expected I'd be so distressed about it. We'd never even discussed it until yesterday. Once the idea had taken root, it's all I could think about. What life would be like having a family with you." His voice was disconnected as he regained a somewhat even temperament.

It was harder for him. Grace had three living children. She had no idea what to say or how to comfort him. This wasn't a pain she could take from him. All she could do was sit there, useless. He had to work through it on his own. She despised herself for not being able to set aside her own mixed feelings of guilt and relief to help him. Guilt consumed her for not admitting to him earlier that she didn't want more children. She would have done anything not to have given him hope.

"Ivan."

"Hm?" he grunted back.

"Ivan, I need to get back. Erik has decided to take the turn." She tried to be gentle with her words and tone.

"Go. Take care of your son. He needs you," he uttered in a monotone voice.

He hadn't meant for the words to sting her, but he felt her wince.

"I don't have to, Ivan. I can stay if you need me." From one situation where she could do nothing to another. She guessed it didn't matter. She would feel inadequate in either place.

He looked at her sympathetically. "No, it's fine. You need to go. I'll be all right. Let me wallow in my self-pity a little longer." He flashed her a faltering smile, went to the bar, and poured himself a scotch.

Grace smiled wistfully to herself.

Scotch had always been his thinking companion. His metabolism was far too high to get drunk from it. He liked the smooth feel of the glass in his hand, the tingling in his throat, and the taste. It was a signal to his reasoning mind to take over, putting away the emotional side. It was a crutch he used to reconcile himself. The second he took the first sip, Grace felt him calm. It was for him the same as a warm hug and a sympathetic ear would be to most. It created an internal therapy session between his id and ego. She watched as he settled into his favorite chair before quietly shifting away.

Erik was sitting on the side of the pod, naked, with only a nanite-infused sheet covering his lap. Asta was in front of him, leaning with her back against his chest. He buried his face deep in the wild tangle of her hair. Frigg and Nyx retained their former places, having a cool but cordial discussion. Leo and Thoth were quietly arguing in the far corner, intermittently changing each other's entries on the control panel. Ami still sat on the stool, watching everyone, and Ben was at the far end of the room, leaning against the wall. He respected Erik's decision. He didn't agree with it. All he could do was stand by and watch it unfold.

"What are you arguing about?" Grace addressed Thoth and Leo.

"Calculations," Thoth replied.

"More specifically, we are concerned about the timing of his essence leaving his shell. With no Valkyrie to collect and transport his essence, we have no way to know how long his shell will retain it after his body is deceased. We can't be sure the process will allow his essence to come back to his shell once the transition has begun. With his physiology, we cannot determine which strand ties the essence to the shell. And we have no containment to hold his essence if it departs the shell so we can reinstall it manually, if necessary. We're programming the STAG to minimize the time between death and the turn," Leo explained.

"Can't you use the information you collected from Jack's transition to determine that?" Grace did not even pretend to understand the science behind the process.

Thoth shook his head. "No. Human biology is completely different. It's nowhere near as complex as Erik's."

The conversation drew Frigg's attention. "You only needed to ask. Did you forget? I have more than a little experience in designing shells for my people and Grace. Bring me your device." She held out her hand.

Leo and Thoth appeared as school children would after being admonished by their teacher. Thoth took the TAC across the room, handing it to Frigg. She opened a diagram into a three-dimensional model, tapping and pulling until a single bit of code was revealed.

"There. If this specific sequence remains intact, his essence will be drawn back to the shell if it departs." She handed the TAC back dismissively before returning to her conversation with Nyx.

Thoth stood frozen, calculations swirling in his mind. "I still think we should take time to assemble a containment jar."

"I can hold it." Everyone except for Frigg and Nyx spun around to see Ami standing. "Valkyries aren't the only ones who can transport souls."

"Ami, how is it you can still surprise me?" Grace asked.

"I'm not stupid, you know. I'm usually just not interested enough in what all of you are discussing to engage in the conversation." Ami had always been honest to the point of awkwardness.

"That solves everything then, doesn't it?" Leo broke the silence.

"Erik, we're going to drain about half of your blood volume before we begin the process. That will reduce the amount of time it will take you to begin the transition. Your shell won't survive exsanguination for long, so we will need to move quickly when it's done."

Erik nodded in agreement.

"Once you go into the STAG, the change will be complete within thirty minutes. Are you ready to begin?" Leo pulled out a needle attached to a tube hooked up to the pod.

Erik sat up straight, holding out his arm, nodding to Leo while Thoth transferred calculations from the TAC to the pod. Asta turned, then backed up in a sweep of panic.

"Now? We're starting now?" Her voice cracked. She raised a hand to her mouth, chewing on the inside of her lip.

"Asta?" Erik reached out his free hand to her. "Look at me."

She shook her head, concentrating on the floor as if she believed it would open and swallow her at any moment if she took her eyes off it.

Erik held steady. "Asta, do you trust me?"

Her eyes landed on his, fixing on his gaze. "Yes," she replied nervously.

He nodded without breaking eye contact. She reached forward, taking his hand. He decided it was best to give her a distraction.

"Tell me something. How would someone be able to kill me after I turn? I'm immortal now, but I can still be killed. I like to know my weaknesses."

She knew he was distracting her. All the same, she was glad for it. She inhaled deeply, exhaling fast, taking a step toward him.

"Complete exsanguination and fire." She paused. "And decapitation, I guess. As long as the head isn't reunited with the body before it decays."

"What about drowning or suffocation?"

"We don't process oxygen in the same way as humans do. They will die if the oxygen levels are below six percent. Our cells continue to regenerate faster than a lack of oxygen kills them off. It's uncomfortable, but we can survive it."

"Oh." He feigned surprise. "So, no stake to the heart or holy water or garlic? I shouldn't be afraid of those things?" he mocked lightly.

"Now that's just insulting. How have you even heard those ridiculous stories?" She was regaining herself. Defensive and ready to debate.

"Jack, of course. Although I'm sure he knows better now." Jack had never believed any of the old lore. He had only told Erik so they could have a laugh.

"I'm sure he knew better when he told you." She narrowed her eyes at him. "A stake through the heart is a temporary measure. And it doesn't have to be wood, either. I have no idea where that came from. Anything that stops the heart from pumping blood can immobilize us briefly. As soon as it's removed, the body repairs itself. It's more of a suspension than anything else. For the rest of it, I'm not even going to lower myself to address that with you." Bias against her species was something she was always ready to climb on a soapbox for.

Erik had easily found the appropriate trigger. The blood loss was causing him to become tired. Disoriented. The room was spinning. He slumped forward near unconsciousness. Asta caught him before he slid off the table. Leo pulled out the needle, allowing Asta to lay Erik out on the slab. Leo reached out to help her, but she grabbed his wrist hard enough to crack the bones.

"Don't touch him," she hissed, instantly regretting her harshness.

She contemplated all the ways this could go wrong. He was so helpless. So vulnerable. So weak. This was far more painful than she had expected. She wanted him back. At this point in the process, she knew what she was expected to do to bring him back. She would have to kill him, as her kind had done for centuries. She raised his wrist to her mouth, hesitating momentarily, then sinking her canis into his soft flesh. Drinking blood directly from flesh was an unfamiliar experience for her. She had been nursed by a bottle with Grace's blood as an infant and from her refrigerated blood later. She had transitioned to CB with everyone else once it was available.

Erik's blood was sweet and metallic. The thickness of it coated the inside of her mouth in warmth. She found herself enjoying it. As quickly as the blood flowed out, her venom was filling his veins. She hoped it was enough. No one explained to her how much would be enough. Grace placed her hand on Asta's shoulder, signaling her to stop. She pulled away, licking the remaining deep-red drops from her lips. Asta extended her arm, taking the scalpel from Leo's timid hand to slice her own wrist. She tilted Erik's head back, letting his mouth drop open. Her wrist hovered above him, filling his mouth with her blood. Was it too late? Was he already gone? Should she have done this part before he went unconscious? Doubt knitted her brows together, painting her face in worry.

"Swallow it." She drew in close, whispering to him while she ran her fingers through his thick dark hair. "You need to drink it." Her body was shaking with fear.

Erik's eyes fluttered momentarily, and he arched his back as a cough emanated from his throat, spewing her precious blood. She pressed his mouth shut, and he finally swallowed. Asta's eyes closed, and she sighed with relief, resting her forehead on his. The slit in her wrist healed over quickly. Her blood covered Erik's face and chest and had spattered into her hair. It was done. Grace rubbed her back. Asta quickly turned, burying her head in Grace's chest, smearing tiny specs of blood onto her shirt.

"I can't kill him, Grace. I can't."

Grace felt the depth of Asta's emotions. She had never killed anything, even when she hunted. Asta had always caught and released her prey. Everyone thought her a terrible hunter. Little did they see she was excellent at catching. It was the killing part she was unable to stomach.

"It's okay. You don't have to. I'll do it." Grace was no keener on the idea of killing her child than she was on killing herself. It had to be done swiftly before Asta's blood healed him. She knew she couldn't force Asta to do it. It would break her. Grace had to take responsibility for her son. She gave Asta one last squeeze. As she stepped away, she heard the familiar sound of bones breaking.

"It's done." Ben was standing over his son, holding his head. He leaned over, pressing his forehead to Erik's with a gentleness Grace had rarely seen in Ben. He stepped back, allowing Leo and Thoth to seal the pod.

Once they finished, Ben grabbed Leo's wrist. It was the same one Asta had cracked, extracting a wince from Leo.

"This better work," he warned.

Leo stepped back carefully, rubbing his wrist without responding. He turned away, grabbing a medical device to heal the bones in his wrist for the second time in the last ten minutes.

The only thing to be done now was wait. The next half hour would be agonizing.

"Why is it taking so long, Leo? It's been over thirty minutes. You said it wouldn't take longer than half an hour." Ben was not a very patient man on his best day. Tolerant, yes, patient, no. He hadn't moved from the side of the pod since Erik was closed in.

"Phase one went as quickly as we had anticipated. All his readings are appropriate. He has made the transition, but it's taking longer to replenish his blood than we had expected. Otherwise, there's nothing unexpected. It shouldn't be much longer." Leo was failing at reassuring Ben.

Ivan had shown up with Alex and Mikkel in tow a few minutes earlier. They were sitting at a table on the other side of the room, teaching Ami to play poker. Ivan had recovered his normal, calm demeanor. That was, as far as everyone else could tell. Grace saw he was still disappointed.

"His soul didn't discharge. That's a good thing, isn't it?" Ami added.

"Essence, Ami. We call it our essence," Ben corrected loudly, thumping his chest.

"It's the same thing. Whatever you want to call it, it didn't flee." Ami was trying to be sympathetic. He hadn't needed to be so rude when she was only trying to help.

Grace was sitting on the edge of the sofa braiding Asta's hair. Grace and Asta had sat through several turnings, although none previously held the same personal significance as this one. They were much more patient in this situation. Erik was breathing and hadn't had a seizure or any other signs of rejection. Those were all favorable signs.

Nyx seemed entertained by the whole thing.

Frigg was patient and pragmatic. "Dear, if the procedure doesn't take as expected, we can always grow another shell from his reserved blood, install his essence, and try again. It's not difficult." She turned to address Ben. "I had to grow a half-dozen shells before I got Grace's right after you had her killed. And that was before we had a STAG."

"I don't think you're helping," Grace replied with a warning tone to the edge of her voice.

Frigg shrugged, continuing her conversation with Nyx. They were getting along better than anyone had predicted, given the animosity of their first conversations.

"He's fine," Alex added calmly, without looking up from his cards.

"*Fine?*" Ben snapped. "How would you even know what *fine* is for him now?"

"We'd be the first ones to know, wouldn't we?" Mikkel snapped back, shooting Ben an irritated glance.

"Are you sure about that? We don't know *what* he is now," Ben snapped back just as hard.

"Enough!" Grace glowered at both of them. "He is *fine*," she growled through gritted teeth. The entire room tremored as she spoke the word "fine."

Everyone went back to what they had been doing before, pretending that the room quaking hadn't happened.

Nyx opened a thought conversation with Frigg. *Their power is growing quickly.*

Frigg replied, *These things are difficult to calculate. That display, however, was certainly spiked by her anger. She wasn't controlling it.*

They shared a thoughtful, although equally concerned, glance.

"Nyx, may I ask you a question?" Asta had found her nerve somewhere.

Nyx studied her for a moment, curious as to what an insignificant lower such as Asta would want to ask her. She found it amusing. "I have nothing better to do. What's on your mind, girl?"

"Why are you helping us?"

"I'm not. I'm helping myself. When the original Primordials were created, Chaos told us about The Nothing. We have been searching for our entire existence to find a solution to strengthen and expand The Everything. Does that answer your question?"

"No. I don't understand why. Erik said Primordials can live in The Nothing. Why do you care if *we* live or not?" Asta questioned further.

"Aside from your entertainment value, I don't. Erik is not entirely correct either. We can exist in The Nothing. We can't live. Not like this." She raised her arms out from her sides. "You don't seem to understand. The Nothing is literally that. *Nothing*," she emphasized. "No light. No dark. No sight, no smell, no hearing, no taste, no touch, no time. No physical presence. No senses at all. Each consciousness that remains in existence is alone with only their own thoughts for all eternity. No external input. I'd be mad as a hatter. That isn't living. Your lot would at least have the respite of ceasing to exist. And those blind fools on the Council think they can create a bubble inside a single universe that could withstand the collapse. They have no understanding of the power of Chaos. It's everything or nothing. There is no between."

Asta could only stare at her. The room was silent again.

"Finally!" Ben exclaimed. Erik was stirring. "Open it."

"Not yet," Leo said. "The pod will open itself. It must complete the shutdown process. Keep an eye on these lights. When all six are blue, it will open."

"Readings are excellent." Thoth showed Leo the TAC screen.

"Ida, dim the lights to twenty-five percent." Ivan noticed the bright lighting and believed it would be uncomfortable for Erik to awaken with. His senses were already more acute than a human's. Ivan theorized his waking would be exponentially more painful for him than it had been for Jack the day before. Ivan was prepared to restrain him if necessary. Among the group, Ivan, Grace, Nyx, and Ami were all capable of overpowering Erik if anything got out of control. It was a low-risk situation in his assessment.

The pod slid open. Erik sat up slowly, rubbing the back of his neck. When he opened his eyes, everyone was staring at him.

"Why's it so dark in here?"

Leo stepped in front of him, scanning his TAC. "How are you feeling? Any headache? Audio or visual issues? Tremors? Blood thirst?"

Erik contemplated rubbing his neck again. He felt strong. He had the strength of at least ten humans before the turn, but that strength was miniscule compared to what he felt now. Things around him seemed to be moving far more slowly than they had before. He theorized he would be faster than he had been.

His senses were extremely heightened. He saw colors he never knew existed. He heard every heartbeat and breath in the room. And the scents were nearly overwhelming. Disinfectant, soap, perspiration, even the vanilla chai Ami had on the other side of the room. It was all so overpowering. No wonder Ivan's people didn't wear much perfume or cologne. He supposed he'd get used to it; however, it was a lot to take in.

"Neck's a little stiff. Other than that, I feel pretty great." He reached his hand out to Asta without looking. He sensed where she was. She took his hand, moving to his side.

"No urge to rip out anyone's throat and drink them, then?" Leo mused.

"Not anyone in this room, anyway," Erik answered. "How long did the transition take?"

"Slightly over forty minutes."

"Not bad. I'm starving. Anything to eat in here?" He jumped off the pod table, letting the small nanite sheet drop to the floor.

Grace reconfigured the setup of the room with a table so they could plan while everyone ate.

"Do you mind?" Erik motioned toward the TAC.

Ben shoved Erik's clothes at his chest. "Pants first." His relief processed quickly upon seeing his son alive, no matter what form that life took. He resumed his normally stoic demeanor as one would don their favorite sweater.

Leo handed Erik the TAC after he had dressed. "It's a lot of medical and genetic coding. Not sure how much you'll understand."

"I'm only investigating the math," Erik said, panning through the numbers. "If you increase the nanites by eight percent per cube of body mass, and adjust this setting," Erik pointed out the reference to Leo, "by plus zero five, you can cut the transition time by thirty percent." Erik handed the TAC back.

"The nanite increase is practical. The setting increase wouldn't work. It would multiply the decay ratio, causing additional damage to the tissues. Thus, the process time for the second stage would increase instead of decrease." Leo pulled up a calculation diagram.

"This is the variable limitation table. Plus, zero two five would be a more optimal setting. The time would be decreased by about twenty percent with those two changes. We were being cautious with the calculations for your process. Wouldn't want to lose our first patient, would we?"

"I appreciate your caution."

"Ida, turn the lights back up," Leo ordered.

"Voice authorization denied in current security level," Ida answered.

"Sorry, Leo. The room's set to tier one. You don't have clearance to override Ivan's commands." Erik shrugged at Leo. "Ida, return lighting to work mode." The lighting returned to the previous setting.

"How'd you know it was Ivan who set the lighting? You shouldn't have had any auditory input from outside the pod."

Erik shrugged. "I don't know."

Grace interrupted, "Through me, maybe? I'm linked to them both. Asta has fed from my blood from the time she was born, which connects me through her as well. Additionally, dampening fields no longer prevent me from communicating."

"It's not that. I hadn't realized your bond would still be intact. I thought the sire bond would sever previous connections and enslave him to Asta." Leo hadn't let that thought pass through his filter. He had just blurted it right out.

Thoth sighed, rubbed his forehead, and moved quickly back to his workstation as far away from Leo as possible.

Asta was extremely offended by his remark. She had been advocating for turned education, dispelling exactly this type of misinformation for her entire life.

"Wow, from enlightened demigod to bigoted Neanderthal in less than two seconds. That *must* be a record. You've been working with us for nearly a year, and you think a sire bond is enslavement?" She took a step toward Leo. He took a step back, bumping into the stool Ami had been sitting on earlier.

Nyx perked up. This is going to be entertaining, she thought to herself.

"Well, well, no," Leo stammered, stepping sideways. "I don't think I said that correctly. I just thought the sire bond overrode familial bonds, that's all. It's not like I have any real data on that. Jack's the only one I've seen turned, and none of the rest of your sired populations on Rasa have any living, natural families. What was I supposed to presume?"

"You weren't supposed to presume anything. You were supposed to observe and ask. Since you didn't, I'm going to explain it to you." She paused. "Sit," she commanded, pointing at the stool. Her previous lack of confidence diminished with Erik's resurrection.

Leo took the seat, eager to listen to what Asta had to say on the subject. She was oblivious to the fact that she had everyone's attention.

"A sire bond creates an unbreakable connection between both parties involved. It does not create a relationship of subservience or enslavement. It creates a relationship of equals. Both parties giving and receiving life. They become connected on both a physical level and a level of consciousness. Say, if you cut him, I wouldn't feel it, but I would know he felt it. We are highly aware of each other."

Leo nodded and began taking notes as Asta resumed her diatribe.

"If more than one is sired, they all share the same connection. The entire sired lineage becomes connected. In turn, they all become connected throughout the whole community. If I walk into a crowded room, I can tell who is turned and who is not. A sire connection is deeper than that of a natural family bond. It does not negate the natural family bond. They have less in common with them and they eventually need to hide their immortality. The turned family replaces the original family in a slow, natural progression. Our children will maintain the same parental bond as any other family. Sired individuals will be bonded more closely to us than even our own children will be. That's how sire bonding works, and why we now use it very sparingly. Love can fade over time. Our bond never will. Do you understand?"

"Does that mean your bond overpowers your emotions?" Leo asked hesitantly.

Asta reflected on this question before answering.

"Somewhat. I'm sure we'll still clash over some things. The bond doesn't subvert our emotions or opinions. My parents once fought for an entire decade. It does mean that no matter what divides us, we can't be wedged apart for long. We will always be drawn together. We don't take this lightly."

"How do you consider Erik siring Vaeweth will work without complications, then? He's mortal. Granted, his mortality is far greater than an average human. Won't he have difficulty? Will he even be able to consent to such an endeavor?"

Asta and Erik exchanged a concerned look as Ivan interceded.

"It will be much the same as an old turn. A thousand years ago, we didn't understand the implications of siring as we do now. Vaeweth is different in many aspects. His people already understand given loyalty. His death, will break his verbal bond with Kali. His new rising will compel his loyalty to Erik. We don't anticipate an adverse reaction from him, given his people's natural longevity. Not to say there may not be complications, and, no, he will not be able to give consent because he doesn't currently have the free will to do so. That does go against our current principles, which is why we will need to call for a vote from all the citizens of Rasa. We will also consider input from his son and his Vice Commanders."

Grace and Ben both nodded in agreement. This would be the first major vote they had from their newly formed government. They needed to present this delicately without revealing who would be sire to him. The turned population was certain to support them, but they were unsure about the support from the minority of the former Æsir population. They would need to be careful not to reveal, to anyone who didn't already know, how the Jur were involved in the demise of their world.

Grace continued Ivan's thoughts, "Ivan will draft the proposal going out for voting within the hour. I will speak with Paneth and the other Jur."

"Why is saving this one Jur so important? The two of you are the ones meant to save The Everything. Why do you need Vaeweth at all?" Leo didn't see the bigger picture.

Grace didn't think she would need to explain her motivation to anyone in this room. She had obviously overestimated their grasp on the situation.

"We don't need them. They need us. We are trying to save them. All of them. The Council will certainly send anyone they can against us to their deaths if we don't bring them under our protection. They will be used as pawns. We don't want them involved in the war with the Council, and we don't want to kill the Jur or anyone else. This is the best option for their survival."

Ivan added, "That's how I'm drafting my proposal for the vote. We need to incite compassion for all forms of life. We want to save as many species as possible, and if we must turn a few, then that is what we should do. It's the right thing."

CHAPTER TEN

The vote had been nearly unanimous. Surprisingly, the opposition had come from a small percentage of the pure born. A few had seen turning Vaeweth as an invitation to confrontation from the Council. The very young didn't see a problem with a few deaths. There were some that thought little of sacrificing some, innocent or otherwise, to save The Everything, even if it wasn't necessary.

The draft for the vote couldn't explain the entire extent of the situation. Some believed that the pledge of the Vice Commanders was enough to save the Jur. Some didn't have enough life experience to see how the gain of respect would weigh heavily for other species in The Everything in the coming battle. They didn't understand that all life was precious, and it was important to save everyone, if it was possible. Fortunately, that was the minority opinion. Less than two percent had voted against the siring of Vaeweth.

"It's time, Paneth. Do you want to be there or not?" Grace asked with as much coldness as she could muster. It would need to be his decision.

Paneth seemed hesitant. "As the head of my family, I should participate," he said, thoughtfully furrowing his brow. "For the safety of everyone involved, I shouldn't have knowledge of who will sire him."

She watched closely as he weighed his options. She hoped not to expose her own son any further than necessary. In the end, it wasn't her decision to make. It was his father's death and rising. He had the right to be involved.

"I shall sit Shata'ak with the Vice Commanders," Paneth stated firmly, staring hard into Grace's eyes. Shata'ak was the Jur mourning ritual. Grace was relieved at his decision. She realized how difficult the sacrifice was for him. He hadn't even been able to properly mourn his mother, yet now she was also asking him to mourn his father if things didn't go well.

She gave him a firm nod before turning to the guard. "Take him to the others. Ensure they have whatever they require for their rites."

As he rose to follow the guard, Grace placed a hand on his shoulder. "You'll see him soon, Paneth. I realize how hard this is for you."

"It would have been safer for you to kill him. I am forever in your debt for trying to save him." Paneth walked forward, eyes straight ahead. She could feel his emotions overtaking him as she watched him disappear down the corridor.

She shifted to the room where Vaeweth was being held.

Vaeweth stared at her silently.

"You're getting your wish, Vaeweth. I'm taking you to your death."

He said nothing as he rose to his feet. He seemed resigned to his fate, almost welcoming of it. Grace placed a hand on his shoulder, shifting them back to the lab.

He appeared confused to have an audience. She placed him in front of the pod. He didn't resist as Leo and Thoth stripped him. Thoth released him from his shackles, forcing him to sit on the side of the pod. He placed the nanite sheet over Vaeweth's lap, inserting the needle into his arm to drain his blood. Grace sensed the revelation in him that his death wasn't intended to be final. It wasn't what he expected. They weren't injecting him with anything. They were draining him. She had found a way out of the situation he had created for himself.

The room was embedded with silent curiosity. As Vaeweth began to lose consciousness, Erik stepped up to the side of the pod. He mimicked Asta's earlier actions, lifting Vaeweth's wrist to drink from his flesh and replace the blood with venom. He could feel the warmth of the blood in his mouth. It was bitter and cooler than he had expected. Not at all like what Asta had described to him. He found it both repulsive and enticing to drink blood from a living being. The feeling of life draining out from another was exhilarating as it had never been before.

Erik had taken many lives in his time. He had killed warriors only a short time ago that very day, but no kill had ever been as intimate as this one was. He could hear Vaeweth's heart slowing. Grace signaled Erik to stop, taking a scalpel to silently cut her son's wrist. She forcibly held Vaeweth's mouth open as Erik's blood drained into it. Then she roughly held his nose and mouth shut, forcing Vaeweth to swallow. As Erik's wrist healed, Grace sunk the scalpel into Vaeweth's chest, cutting through both of his hearts. She drew her face close to his to watch as the life left his eyes, sliding them closed with her free hand.

Leo had to pull her away from his body to close the pod. It had been more than a century since she had watched death so closely. She was angry at Vaeweth for making her responsible for the slaughter earlier that morning. Then, to find out they weren't even warriors. The fact that they were martyrs only made it worse. She was also relieved that she had a chance to save him. She had grown to care for him over the last few years. At that moment, she also hated him.

This turning was different. No one was upset. No one was nervous. There was a lack of investment in this procedure. It was clinical to them. It didn't seem to matter much to the rest of them whether he completed the turn or not. Even Erik seemed to appear sanitized to the process. Grace was the only one who could see that he felt it deeply. It was remarkable that Asta didn't feel his connection as much as Grace did.

The group waited while disconnectedly engaged in conversations. Ivan, Alex, Mikkel, and Ami continued their card game, oblivious to the rest of the audience. Nyx and Frigg continued their passive-aggressive one-upping of each other. Grace finished cleaning the remainder of blood from Asta's hair and then neatly re-braided it into a different style. Erik stood watch over his sired while Leo and Thoth monitored uninterestedly.

Jur physiology was less complicated than Erik's had been. The species was bred for battle. Aside from two hearts and a much denser skin layer, they were only slightly more complex than humans. They had no gifts aside from multispectrum eyes, and certainly no complex parentage, as Erik did. Their resistance to mind probes was learned, not inherent. They were unremarkable compared to other species.

The process went quickly. When the pod opened, Vaeweth sat up. They were all looking at him. He didn't know what to say. He was grateful to have been spared, but he was also ashamed. His plan was to die in the invasion. It would have been wise for them to have killed him. Leo moved forward to begin his assessment. Erik stepped in between Leo and Vaeweth. If something was off, it would be his responsibility to kill him and protect the others. Ivan moved behind the pod, placing his hand on Vaeweth's shoulder. He would read him as Erik verified his allegiances.

"Do you know who I am?" Erik asked.

Vaeweth was disoriented. He recognized him as one of Grace's sons. He vaguely remembered drinking his blood. However, he felt connected to him. It was a stronger connection than any he had shared with his own brothers. He felt bound somehow. This man's existence was important to him. He was drawn to him more deeply than he could be by any pledge he would ever speak, but he didn't know him.

"No. And yes. You killed me and yet I believe you gave me life."

"Actually, my mother killed you. I sired you. Do you know what that means?" Erik glanced up at Ivan, who nodded back.

"Yes."

"Your pledge to Kali was broken with your death. Is that true?" Erik scrutinized Vaeweth's face.

"Yes. Death is the end of any pledge. It has been broken."

Ivan nodded again. It wasn't necessary. Erik felt his words were true. The bond between the men worked both ways.

"You've likely realized our bond will have no end, even in death. We are eternally linked. No pledge you make will be greater."

"Yes. I am bonded to you both." He turned his head to look at Asta. "I don't have words for it. I feel your blood in my veins, your existence in my mind. Who are you?"

Asta rose, moving halfway across the room toward Erik.

"I am Erik. And this is Asta, my sire, and mate. We'll explain the rest after Leo has had a look at you." Erik began to walk away.

"Saving me was a mistake. No one goes against the Council without consequences. They will slaughter my people."

"Like you slaughtered my people?" Ben spat from across the room. His people weren't only biologically killed. Their essences had been dissipated back into The Everything. They would not be returning. It was as permanent as his resentment.

"Yes. Exactly like that," Vaeweth stated gravely.

"You'll have to figure out a way to make sure they believe you're still on their side then, won't you? We don't believe in killing pawns. The Council used you and you still found a way to go against them and save your people. You were smart enough to do that. Now you can help us save everyone else." Erik motioned to Leo to begin while he and Ivan went back to the others.

Asta walked ahead of the men back to Grace's side. Erik certainly wasn't happy about Vaeweth's part in the demise of his people. Unlike his father, he had a more critical mind. He understood Vaeweth's position in what had taken place. He also saw what an asset he could be to them now. They would need to continue hiding the role of the Jur from their remaining population. That information could never leave this room.

When they got back to the group, Ivan whispered, "And how exactly do we protect them from Kali? She *is* death. Once she finds out the Jur have betrayed her, she will spread death among them like a virus. Her wrath will be inescapable."

"Let's hope we can keep her distracted long enough to come up with a plan. We're not equipped to turn them all, even with a STAG," Erik answered.

"I'm not convinced turning them would be in their best interest anyway," Grace added.

"What about sending them to Hel? I mean your Hel, not my hell. It's empty now, isn't it? Kali wouldn't think of searching for them there, would she?" Ami asked.

"They have to be dead, Ami. And there's no one to take them there anyway," Ben answered.

"Why do they have to be dead? Your brother wasn't dead when he visited you. He paid a toll to cross the bridge, didn't he? And with it being empty and all, would anyone even care?" Ami shrugged.

"I'm not following this. Wasn't Hel destroyed with Valhalla and Fólkvangr?" Grace questioned.

"No. The other places were destroyed when the essences of the warriors were released. To fight in the great war, they released the other essences in Hel, but since I was still there, it was never emptied. The gates unlocked to release me after it was over when Hel was killed, but it still stands. Nobody would voluntarily go back there, and with Hel—my cousin, not the place—dissipated, there isn't anyone to claim an essence," Ben explained. "How did you know that, Ami?"

"Alex told Frigg and Nyx how you said you got out while you were fighting with Grace that day at the facility," Ami replied.

"Oh." He paused, thinking for a moment. "I did leave the gates open when I was released. And it's concealed. It's completely cloaked, so you need to know how to find it. I don't think you can port over the river, though. I'm not sure if you can even shift around it. If the bridge is still being guarded, Morgud takes her toll in blood, not gold. It may be worth a trip to see if she's still there and if we can negotiate a toll with her. It's an interesting idea, Ami."

Ben contemplated the complexity of guiding thousands of Jur families on the arduous journey. As much contempt as he held for the soldiers, he still knew protecting their families was the responsible thing to do. He would have wanted the same for his people. He was bitter, but he knew he had to swallow it to save the innocent. It was something he needed to do to rise above the resentment he held. He also needed to consider some people of Rasa would need the safety of Hel too if things got dangerous enough.

"If only we knew someone who had been there and remembered the way," Nyx added sarcastically, flashing Ben a coy smile.

Ben rolled his eyes contemptuously back at her. Nyx smirked. This was all a game to her. She was as brilliantly devious as she was stunning. That mix was lethal, and he didn't trust her.

Grace smirked back at Nyx. "Nyx, since Ben knows where it is and all, maybe you'd like to shift him there. It would save quite a bit of time, and Hel's your kind of place. It's dark and cold. Lovely this time of year. I think you should go."

It was more than a suggestion, and Nyx knew it. She also knew Grace was, to her dismay, superior in power. It wouldn't do her any good in the long run to be on Grace's bad side. Even Nyx wouldn't risk Chaos's anger from going against Grace, but there was no way she was about to show her diminished position to anyone.

Frigg raised her hand to her mouth, covering her smile. She relished the idea of Nyx being forced into doing something she didn't want to do, even if it meant putting her son into an uncomfortable situation.

Nyx huffed, "I guess I asked for that one. Anything for the cause," she replied, plastering on a feigned smile. "I'll take him."

In the next instant, Nyx was standing in the same place, wrapped in a long light thermal cloak woven with an intricate metallic thread pattern. She also had a complementary hat and glove set with pants tucked into medium-heeled riding boots. Nyx accepted nothing less than warmth and elegance.

"Where's your coat?" she asked Ben, feigning mild irritation.

Hel really was the type of place she would like. Dark. Cold was fine too if it wasn't damp. She disliked dampness.

Ben was mildly surprised she had any concern for his comfort. Alex tossed Ben his jacket over his shoulder. It was thin and thermal regulating like the rest of his clothing.

"Let's get on with it, then." He was less than enthusiastic about going back to Hel, even if it was only for a short time. Especially with her.

CHAPTER ELEVEN

It was the type of cold that sunk into the bones. Deep darkness shielded by ancient footings squirming with night creatures. Climbing the slope brought into view the bridge, emanating its own eerie glow spun from diffracted light and hanging by a single thread for the entire span. It seemed impossible the way it hovered over the vast expanse of fast-moving water, as if physics held no influence here. It was certainly an illusion.

The only other light radiated from a single lantern at the bridge's entrance, allowing them to see that they were standing on a thick layer of ice. A few steps forward and the crush of a fresh snow layer yielded under their feet. The river rushed unnaturally silent in front of them. Thick clouds and layers of trees shrouded the moon. It was wickedly beautiful. Out of the darkness came a chilling, low voice.

"You're the last person I expected to see again. And you're so ... *alive*," Morgud said, curling what remained of her lip back over her teeth. "What do you want, Balder?" Disgust at his name showed on the grizzled bones of her face.

"We've come to negotiate terms, Morgud," Ben growled back through gritted teeth.

"Terms? What makes you think you have anything I want? You and your delicate little companion here. On *my* bridge? I could kill you both, piss on your dead flesh, and imprison you inside for all eternity!" Morgud was deftly upon them, towering above.

She was seven feet tall. A terrifying skeleton with rotting flesh dripping off her bones. She wore a tattered black shift that barely covered her ossein torso.

"Mind your tongue, Morgud, lest it be ripped out of your putrid skull!" he shouted back at her with a reddened face.

"Ha!" she exclaimed, inching closer to his face so he could smell her rotting flesh. "By who? *You*? You're a soft, pretty girl, aren't you, Balder? Standing there with your long curly hair and manicured fingernails. Do you think I am afraid of you? You're a pathetic little nothing of a man!"

"Well, at least we can agree on something," Nyx interceded, stepping forward.

She placed her hand in the center of Ben's chest, creating a space between them. She slid in front of him with the back of her shoulder against him. He could feel the warmth of her body pressed against his. The clean honeysuckle scent of her hair cut through Morgud's decayed odor. Ben shot Morgud the dangerous smile of a man holding a nuclear weapon.

"But no, he meant your tongue would be ripped from your skull by me, dear."

Morgud had been stunned silent. She stepped awkwardly backward.

Nyx continued. "Now let's be civil about things and discuss the reason for our visit. I assume you haven't had visitors in quite some time, have you? Oh, and where are my manners? Let me introduce myself."

Nyx extended her hand, not in a way to be shaken but in a way to be kissed. "You may call me Nyx." Her tone was sickeningly sweet.

Upon her introduction, Nyx's eyes grew large, filling black with darkness. Her hair turned the deep red of old blood. Wafts of dark smoke drifted off her, encircling her and Ben as if they were a living extension of her body sent out to protect them. The grander the show, the better.

Morgud scrambled, unsettled, dropping to her knees in front of Nyx. She was as close to cowering as someone of her size was capable.

"Mother of dark gods, forgive me! I am but your humble servant. I didn't mean to offend you!" She bowed her head, taking Nyx's tiny hand in her enormous bony fingers.

Nyx returned to the appearance she had held previously. She pulled her hand back, brushing over her coat, excising the remaining tendrils of smoke. She craned her neck, winking at Ben as Morgud bowed in front of her. Ben shifted uncomfortably, stepping up to Nyx's side. He had no idea what she was going to do next.

"It's an honest mistake, dear. You could never imagine I would arrive in *his* company, could you? Now please, get up. We have some business to discuss." Nyx was relishing the recognition. She so enjoyed adoration.

"Yes. Of course." Morgud clambered awkwardly to her feet, pushing herself between Nyx and Ben as she spoke. "I am so honored to meet you. Your darkness is legendary, even in my tiny realm. Tell me how I could possibly be of service to you."

"I'd like to lease Hel," Nyx stated seriously.

Morgud was taken aback. "That's not possible. It's *Hel.*"

Nyx looked around theatrically. "Yes. It is. Is there someone else here I should be speaking to about this? It's empty, isn't it? No one living or dead for years."

"Well, that's true, I guess. I hadn't thought about it in those terms. I mean, it's Hel," Morgud replied.

"Technically, it was Hel. It's no longer a prison for souls of the dead. There's no owner. Or is there?"

She thoughtfully turned back to Ben. "It was your cousin's place, wasn't it? Who inherits from her?"

"Not sure. I'd have to go through the family books. There is a strong possibility it is mine," he said, cluing in on her inquiry. "I'm certain I'm the closest living relative. If that's the case, you're welcome to it free of charge." What started as a way to leverage acceptance wasn't just supposition on Nyx's part. It was most likely he did own Hel. At least he would if there were any laws left.

Morgud looked worried, as if she suddenly believed she was missing out on a huge opportunity.

"That is excellent," Nyx exclaimed, tapping Ben's chest. "I accept your offer. But you still need a caretaker, don't you? Wouldn't it make sense to keep Morgud on? She does know the place." Nyx was flippant.

"I don't know. She's insolent. I'm sure she'd try to kill me in my sleep," Ben added.

"Well then, it's a good thing you're not sleeping here. Personally, I'd feel very comfortable having someone with her experience watching over my things."

"People aren't things," Ben retorted.

"Maybe not to you," Nyx replied while eyeing him from head to toe with a sideways glance.

"Fine, she can stay. But you're paying her." At this point Ben and Nyx had Morgud bewildered and afraid of losing her home. Where else could a half-dead giantess skeleton find a home?

Nyx turned back to Morgud. "I'd like to keep you on as caretaker and guardian of Hel if you'd like to stay."

Morgud scratched at the back of her skull with a bare finger. "I don't have anywhere else to go. I've been here nearly all my life."

"Can you guarantee my anonymity in this matter and afford the location with all the protections it previously held?" Nyx queried Morgud.

"I can. No one has ever passed the bridge without my permission. And we all know what happens to anyone trying to cross the river." She signaled with a slashing gesture across her throat.

Nyx wasn't sure what that was supposed to signify since those who came through were already dead. Dissipation, maybe? Or did she mean an end for any living who tried to pass? She wasn't interested enough to ask.

"At any rate, I'll need to make some renovations for the living. Creature comforts and such. We should only have a few thousand. There's plenty of space for such a small group. What's your price then, Morgud? I've been told you prefer to be paid in blood. Any type in particular? I have access to some very exotic species." Nyx smiled deviously.

Morgud was unsure of what had just happened. One minute she was ruler of the kingdom, the next, a mere employee who could be ousted at the whim of a man for whom she had requited hatred.

"I've only ever been paid in the blood of those condemned to this place. I'm not sure what I should ask for or what would be fair for so few living beings. We don't usually get live ones here."

"Well, what do you need it for?" Nyx asked.

"It restores my flesh," Morgud answered, holding out her hands.

"What if I could get you an exotic type that would allow you to never need more? Would you be interested in that?"

Morgud's dark eye sockets widened. She had never heard of such a thing. She was skeptical something like that would exist.

"Wait here." Nyx shifted out in a dramatic trail of smoke, leaving Ben behind.

It was a lengthy and uncomfortable few minutes for both of them before Nyx reappeared holding a tiny vial of blood.

Morgud scoffed, "What do you expect me to do with that amount? I require many casks to soak in to be restored. What are you two playing at?"

"This is the most powerful blood in all the worlds, carried by only two beings. Do you want it or not?" Nyx was stern.

"What if I accept and it doesn't work?"

"Then you owe me nothing. We will leave and never return. But if it does work, you uphold our deal and protect anything I choose to bring here. Do you accept the terms of the agreement?"

"What if it kills me?"

"You're already dead."

"What if it dissipates me?"

Ben sighed loudly, taking the vial from Nyx. He opened it, leaned his head back, and let a single drop fall into his mouth. He felt a rush of energy and calmness. His eyes glowed for a moment. It had to be Ivan's blood. He didn't taste Grace in it. He held the vial out to Morgud. She took it from him, astonished at what she had witnessed.

"Deal," she said without hesitation.

She moved the top of her dress, landing on a patch of flesh still attached to her rib. She carefully watched the two of them as she coated it with what remained of the blood in the vial. It was Ivan's blood enhanced by Leo with nanites to speed the process. The skin began to stretch and spread painfully over her chest, shoulders, and torso. She fell writhing on the ground for several minutes.

When she rose, she had an appearance more akin to an Amazonian beauty than an ugly giantess. She had deep dark eyes, nearly black. Her frame held the muscular femininity of an athlete. Her skin was deep brown, taut but also holding the soft, supple appearance of someone young. She wasn't anything at all like Ben had expected. The only remaining sign she was even the same being was the tattered rag she wore. Her presence was truly astonishing.

She inspected herself in disbelief at what had occurred. Her cursed existence was over. Strength accompanied her youthful appearance. She was once again restored to the way she had been before she was damned to this place eons ago by Loki for refusing his advances. She was at a loss for words.

The thing she wanted most was to see her face. It had been so long; would she even recognize it as her own? She ran her fingers over her high cheekbones and full lips, feeling the warm, tight skin she remembered having. All the blood she had ever collected and soaked herself in had never brought her back to her former beauty. She had been seeking an end to her curse ever since she had been banished to this place. She was utterly joyful. Her heart pounded in her chest. She was alive.

She dropped to one knee, bold and proud. She wasn't cowering as she had before.

"Nyx, my gratitude is eternal. I am indebted to you." Morgud's voice was thick and powerful. It was pleasant to hear her speak. Nyx touched her shoulder, urging her to rise to her feet.

"And you, Balder. I hated you the most. The adoration you received made me envious, as I had once been adored for my beauty and kindness as you were. I shall serve you guarding your realm for as long as you will have me. I beg your forgiveness."

"Balder has been dead for a very long time. It's Ben now. You'll have to earn your forgiveness with loyalty." Ben peered at her wryly.

"Is the bridge the only way in?" Nyx asked, breaking the tension. She wasn't one who enjoyed sentimental dribble or overly dramatic unease. Weak emotions were for weak beings.

"Yes," Morgud answered.

"Can the river be passed over?" Ben questioned.

Morgud bent down, picking up a large chunk of ice. She threw it high into the air over the water. The river itself appeared to sense the disturbance above it, sending a stream gushing upward, smashing the ice into a fine powder.

"Nothing can pass over the boundary. Only the bridge."

"How high does the boundary go?"

"As high as the birds can fly."

Ben narrowed his eyes toward the sky, attempting to see signs of a limit to the boundary. It was too dark for him to see anything. It would need to be tested.

"Can the bridge be raised or drawn?" Nyx queried further.

"I can control the frequency of the light so it no longer supports passage. Anyone on it will fall through and be swallowed by the water. There is also a control on the other side that can do the same if the need arises." She pointed to something on the other side of the river they couldn't see. "The support can also be broken, crashing down the entire bridge, but anyone on the other side will likely never be able to pass back to this side."

Nyx wondered if she could shift over. It was something she wasn't ready to attempt. Not that she was concerned about surviving. She thought it could get messy and Nyx most definitely did not like messy. She would let Ivan deal with that experiment. He didn't mind messy.

Ben had once been told that porting didn't work in the vast forest surrounding Hel. It was a three-day ride from the entrance if you could find it and manage the tormenting journey. He wondered if physical ports would work.

"Can anyone port in or out?" Ben continued.

"Not as far as I know. I don't think it's been tried. You are the first ones I've seen appear as you did. I didn't see how you had gotten here until she left and came back. I wondered why you had no horses and how I hadn't heard you approach. What you did, didn't look like porting," Morgud answered.

Nyx ignored Morgud's observation.

Ben thought Erik would be a fit candidate to figure out that puzzle. He didn't want to give too many of his thoughts away. They should examine the control areas of the hall first. All the time he had spent there gave him little knowledge of the real workings or defenses of the place.

CHAPTER TWELVE

"That was strange even for Nyx," Ivan said.

"Your blood heals everything. It makes sense to use it." Leo didn't see what Ivan found peculiar about the request.

"Not sure it's something I'll get used to. People asking for my blood."

"You have always had the ability to heal through your blood. Haven't you ever healed anyone before?" Leo inquired.

"I only tried once, but it didn't work," Ivan answered.

"Well, the nanites alone probably would have cured her. But Nyx asked for blood. It'll spread your light signature, anyway." Leo wasn't sure what he meant when he said it hadn't worked. Maybe it had just been too late for him to save them.

"I don't know if that's such a good idea in this case. Can't the Council track it? It shouldn't be so close to where we are hiding anyone." Ivan was worried.

"Trackers don't work in Hel," Thoth offered. "Whatever they are blocking the location with is substantial. No one has ever been able to find it without guidance from Asgard. I don't think there's anyone left aside from Ben who even knows where the entrance is. And even that isn't much help if you don't know how to navigate the forest. There are some nasty things in there, from what I've heard."

That alleviated most of Ivan's concerns for the time being.

It was morning now. The ceremonies were over. The guests had all gone back to their home worlds. Everyone would be getting up soon. Ivan had stayed back in the lab, waiting for Ben and Nyx to return. Mikkel and Alex had gone to assess the equipment available for the required renovations and move. Grace took Ami and Vaeweth to meet with the Jur in the cargo hold. Frigg had been taken to her new quarters to get some rest. And Erik and Asta went to break the news to her parents.

Erik was the one Ivan was the most concerned about. Facing an angry Viv was not going to be a healthy situation. At least, facing the old Viv wouldn't have been. He wasn't sure about this new Vivienne. She seemed somewhat … demure.

<center>~~~~</center>

"But Mommy I *had* to. I thought you liked Erik." Asta pleaded with her mother not to be angry.

Erik and Galin stood in the corner of the room as far away as they could physically be from Vivienne and Asta. They were silent and uncomfortable. Vivienne was fuming.

"Liking him has nothing to do with it! There are rules. Your father is Regent now. Do you not understand how embarrassing this is going to be for him when everyone finds out his own daughter broke the law?" Vivienne was shouting uncharacteristically. She was normally quite calm and refined. It wasn't a completely foreign behavior to her, although she didn't normally do it in front of guests.

"That's back there. Those rules don't exist here!" Asta shouted back at her.

"But you live there. Not here! Those laws *do* apply to you!" Viv retorted loudly.

"No, they don't! Uncle Lukkas is taking over the transition. We decided on it weeks ago. I'm staying here." Asta stomped her foot, crossing her arms.

"That is *not* up to you." Vivienne took a stern stance, pointing at Asta. "Your father and I never agreed to that. You didn't even have a mating ceremony. This isn't right."

"Mother, I am over fifty years old. You don't get to decide that for me anymore. I am staying here with Erik." Asta dropped her arms, balling her hands into fists at her sides.

As they continued to argue, Galin leaned sideways toward Erik, keeping his eyes on the women. "Sorry about all this, Erik. Viv has some … control issues. She just gave away one child and now the other is flying off unexpectedly. She'll get over it."

"We never meant to cause such a problem. We just couldn't wait, with the war coming and all." Erik would rather they think it was more of an impetuous elopement of a sort than what it really was.

Galin was more intuitive than that. He had already seen through their story. Erik was older than his entire race by ten times. The man was anything but impetuous. Ivan had come to see Galin before the vote, so Galin knew the generalities of the plan. It hadn't been difficult for him to deduct the "who" of it all once Erik and Asta showed up. Even with everything going on around them, he didn't doubt Erik's love for his daughter. He had seen it long before either of them had.

"I understand. It had to be you. It makes sense. I'll make sure everyone knows you had our blessing so it doesn't appear suspicious." Galin wasn't upset about it. It was unexpected and, in his mind, somewhat rash, but it was sound strategy.

"Of course, it had to be me. I love her." Erik understood what he meant. They didn't need to say the words.

"That's what matters, isn't it?" Galin slapped Erik on the back. "Let's put an end to this, shall we?"

The two sighed in unison and stepped forward together.

"Vivienne," Galin said firmly, distracting the women from their argument. "We never had a ceremony, did we?"

"But …" Viv was surprised and embarrassed. Her eyes widened; her cheeks blushed hot.

"We turned out fine, didn't we?"

"Galin! That is not the point!" she exclaimed back at him.

"Then what exactly is the point? They love each other. And there's a war coming. How can we possibly deny them a little happiness?" he said calmly.

Vivienne screeched in exasperation and stormed out of the room, nearly knocking down Violet and Jack, who were coming to see what all the commotion was about.

"What in the hell is going on in here? I've never seen her that upset." Violet's surprise turned into puzzlement. She flew up within inches of Erik's face, taking his scent in deeply.

"What? How? When? There wasn't enough time. Asta, how did this happen?" She clamped down hard on Erik's arm, dragging him over to Asta. "Explain!"

Jack hadn't caught up yet. "Explain what? Violet, what's wrong with you?"

Erik and Asta couldn't help but be amused. Even Galin saw the humor in Violet's reaction.

"Come here, Jack. Smell him!" Violet demanded.

"I'm not smelling him! Why would I do that?" Jack was still in the doorway. He hadn't picked up the scent. He may not have been capable yet of distinguishing the differences in species scents from that distance.

"Just do it, Jack," Violet demanded loudly.

Erik shrugged. Jack stepped closer. Not as close as Violet was, but close enough.

"I don't smell any difference. What are you saying?" Jack answered.

"Exactly that. You don't smell *any* difference. We all smell the same," Violet stated.

"Oh. OHHHH! I didn't know he was turned. Erik, why didn't you tell me you were turned?" Jack questioned excitedly. He was a little insulted that his best friend wouldn't have told him he was turned. He would have been much more comfortable asking Erik about the turn than being coached by Lukkas.

"Because he wasn't yesterday!" Violet exclaimed.

"I am really confused here. How could you have turned since we saw you last night? How does that even work? You were already immortal. What's the point?

You didn't even have to go through counseling." Jack was a little ticked about the counseling part. It had been excruciating for him. More than a year of being assessed for mental instability was enough to make even a sane man doubt his sanity.

"That's a lot of questions, Jack," Erik said lightly.

"Why don't we discuss this over breakfast?" Galin interceded diplomatically. "A full stomach always makes things clearer." Galin stretched out his arm, directing everyone into the dining room. It gave Erik a little time to put together answers.

Jack looped his arm over Erik's neck playfully, pulling him forward.

"Best friends and now brothers. Could this day get any better?" Jack was elated.

"That depends. You want to go to Hel with me?" Erik asked low, so the others couldn't hear. Erik had been itching to try out the new drones that he and Jack had been working on.

"I would absolutely walk through fire with you." Jack pulled harder on Erik's neck.

"Wrong end of the temperature spectrum, buddy. I mean my Hel," Erik replied. "We'll talk about it later." Erik slapped him on the back while unwrapping Jack's arm from his neck in one swift move as everyone took their seats at the table.

As the service units brought in the food, Erik was lost in his own thoughts. He was worried about this young community. *Galin was one of only a handful who had survived a war of any kind, much less something of the magnitude that could be coming. The Council was certain to be amassing a force if for no other reason than distraction while they implemented their plan.*

These people had become civilized, which wasn't a bad thing given that they were living among humans. They didn't need to be prepared for battle. They were stronger and more intelligent. For the last few centuries, they had been able to dominate their weaker counterparts through the use of technology, as opposed to brute force. They were covert, subtle. Again, those were all valuable traits in a peaceful living situation.

The problem is, it isn't going to work much longer. We all must be prepared for battle. The Council has had ages to plan. Our people have only had hours since we found out their true agenda. We are so far behind. Mother and Ivan don't even know how to use their abilities yet. Who knows how long it will take for them to be able to have any kind of control?

His thoughts were interrupted. *Turn the volume down, Erik! I can't hear my own thoughts over yours.* It was Mikkel.

I guess I have to try a little harder to block you two out now. Didn't mean to interrupt, he answered.

It's all right. I agree with you. They're physically stronger than we are. We need to be able to make that an asset. We need to teach them how to fight differently than they're used to, Mikkel added.

We need to do more than that. They're so immature, and we have very little time. We need to gain an advantage. Our warriors' skills paired with their strength, instincts, and abilities. Alex made a covert suggestion.

It appalled Erik that Alex would propose what he was thinking. Their people had been through so much already. How could he even think of asking them to consider something like that? *I'm not having this discussion with you.*

You made your choice. It isn't up to you to decide for everyone else, Mikkel replied.

And it's not up to you either. He blocked the rest of his brothers' thoughts. He needed to get through this meal first. It's not like he hadn't had that thought on his own since he had turned. He just didn't have the audacity to think it was an acceptable idea.

Galin tapped his glass to get the attention of the room. He raised a toast as the rest of the group emulated his position. "Even though your mating was hasty and unexpected, I am quite pleased with my youngest daughter's choice. I am delighted to welcome you, Erik, to our family. Your mother has always been a very important and respected part of our community. I am proud to have your line merge into ours." Galin was diplomatic, as always.

Erik replied to his toast, "Thank you, Galin, for your warm welcome. I am happy to be part of such a distinguished family. I hope I am only the first of many to strengthen the bond of our community." Erik reflected on the conversation he had with his brothers.

They each voiced their approval and drank. As they proceeded, Vivienne entered the room in a much more controlled and contrite manner, taking her seat at the foot of the table. The group pretended not to notice her entrance, waiting for her to acknowledge them first. The room fell silent as they ate until Vivienne finally felt she had enough control of the room to speak.

She treaded lightly, avoiding the topic of their impulsive mating that had caused her such an emotional and embarrassing display.

"Erik. This war is imminent. The Council appears resolute in bringing it to us. How do you propose we prepare for it?"

Erik loathed being put on the spot. He expected it would happen. At least it wasn't personal.

"Well, Vivienne, we're not altogether certain about that yet. We've had only hours to assess the situation, whereas the Council has had eons to plan. In all honesty, being caught on the back foot, so to speak, we need more information. How would you assess the situation?" He wanted to throw the ball back into her court. He needed to make her feel important, even if she didn't have any answers.

She calmly and unexpectedly rose to the occasion. "In my humble opinion, we need a four-part strategy. The first thing we need to do is spread the word through all the dimensions and find out who steps up. We need to know who our allies are and, among them, those who can actually be trusted."

Erik leaned toward her end of the table, showing interest, as Vivienne continued.

"Nyx's little dramatic display received the attention it required, but now we need to inform the other species of the actual threat. Secondly, we need to remove the non-combatants from the line of fallout. The vulnerable need to be moved to a safe location. Third, we need to turn as many of the Æsir warriors as are willing. They have the experience of time in battle and the multiple dimensions, but neither the strength nor astuteness of ours."

At those words, Erik raised his eyebrows. Had she somehow heard the conversation with his brothers?

"And fourth, we need to train all our people to defend themselves. None of our community has previously faced anything on this scale. Grace and Ivan undoubtedly have the potential to be assets, but at this specific moment, they are raw, reckless, and untrained. They are currently of little use to us. Ivan has always had a great ability to control his circumstances. Your mother, on the other hand, has always been impulsive. She's more the fly-by-the-seat-of-her-pants type, and that could be catastrophic. They could become a greater liability than an asset unless they learn to harness and control their power."

Erik thought her assessment was spot on, and she didn't even know the entirety of it all. He suddenly saw much more depth to her than he previously had.

Everyone except Erik stared at her with their mouths gaping open.

"I am exceptionally impressed by your complete grasp on the situation. I couldn't agree with you more."

He was almost stunned that she had offered the same conclusion Alex had, but he wasn't ready to address that part of her four-pronged plan. "It's difficult for me to properly address my mother and Ivan because I am likely too emotionally tethered to them. I am completely refreshed by your candor. Each of your points is competent and valid. I think it is important we should convene a committee to address each of these issues. I had no idea you were so well versed in this type of strategy."

"We don't need a committee to sit around pontificating strategy. We need leaders," Vivienne retorted.

Galin had a broad, proud smile. "Viv was quite the revolutionary in pre-industrialized Italy. And she was the first woman to join the resistance to Mussolini. She has survived things most of our people can't imagine."

Erik turned back to Vivienne. He never imagined by looking at her that she was a hardened survivor. "Would you consider staying on here? Instead of going back? I think my mother needs someone to ground her a bit. Someone she will listen to."

"What would make you believe she would listen to me?" Vivienne asked. "I've known her for a long time, but I really don't know her well. She must certainly have others whose opinions she would value more."

"Would you mind if we had a private word?" Erik asked, standing.

He wasn't supposed to know about the memory changes that his mother and Ivan were given. He knew they had been done, but he wasn't supposed to know the content. That hadn't lasted long, though. Anything Alex knew, Erik and Mikkel eventually knew, too. They had all the backstory from both timelines. Vivienne was important to Grace. Very important.

Vivienne had always thought there was more to Grace's story. There was no way she would ever pass on the chance to find out, no matter how angry she was at this man.

"Certainly," she replied. "Excuse us, please." She stood and led Erik out of the room to the study.

The others, with the exception of Galin, were perplexed by the conversation that had taken place. Ivan had addressed part of the background with Galin earlier when he had come to discuss the vote. There was no need to abide by the Council's directive any longer, and Galin would need the information to address some domestic issues while Ivan's group forged a plan to deal with the impending situation.

Asta was simply relieved that they were being publicly civil, while also being afraid of what her mother might say to Erik in a private setting.

When they got to the study, he asked for a moment. He contacted Ivan, who was still waiting in the lab for Nyx and Ben to return. Ivan arrived, wondering what situation he had been summoned to.

Erik asked Ivan to read his thoughts from the breakfast conversation. He complied. He agreed Vivienne had a commanding grasp on her assessment, including her assessment of him and Grace. They had been reckless. They were also nowhere near ready.

"Now give her the old memories. The real ones." Erik stunned Ivan with the request. He wasn't supposed to know. "She needs to understand why my mother will trust her."

After a brief discussion, Ivan begrudgingly agreed. "Viv, when you see this, it will be like you are watching a movie of someone else's life. But this is the true timeline. The memories you have of your life since you met Grace are false. They have all been implanted by the Council. You need to understand that you can't tell anyone. Galin isn't aware of everything yet, and you especially cannot mention anything to Lukkas. It would skew their entire perspective and likely cause severe repercussions for everyone involved. Do you understand? You must keep this a secret until we can figure out a less traumatizing way to let this information out."

Vivienne contemplated for a few moments. "I understand. If I am going to be of any help, I need to know." She could see the gravity of the information she was about to receive on Ivan's face.

"You'll need to sit down for this." He directed her toward one of the reading chairs.

Ivan pulled another chair close, sitting with their knees almost touching.

"Relax. Put your head back. Tell me when you want me to start," he instructed.

She was more interested than nervous. She rolled her neck in a circular motion a few times before letting her head rest on the back of the chair, taking in a few deep breaths.

"I'm ready," she uttered. She was open, relaxed, and prepared.

Ivan started slowly. Viv had only known Grace for a little more than a century. He didn't need to go back to the beginning. He only needed to pass forward from the time she met Galin, Lukkas, and Grace. But since she had heard the story, he also wanted to give her the memory of the village. The memory of how Grace came to be with Lukkas in the first place.

Vivienne started to tense a little. Ivan kept a steady pace. He didn't want to overwhelm her. He included the part with the Council that she had never been privy to, including Grace's tribunal. All the guilt and angst they had felt was passed to her. He gave her both his and Grace's perspectives of the hospital and the cabin. He gave her the confrontation with Ben.

Then he gave her the good memories. He gave her Grace and Violet's backward sunset ritual. Memories of Lukkas. Viv and Grace shopping, sailing, and vacationing with the girls at the best resorts. Finding the vineyard and decorating it together. Ivan, The Three, and the car. He gave her Grace's memories of Ami finally finding her and restoring her old memories.

He gave her simple memories of Grace teaching Viv English, German, and Spanish. Funny memories of Viv disastrously trying to teach Grace to bake and getting caught by Mrs. B., nearly setting the kitchen on fire.

Desperate memories of Galin carrying Viv's near-lifeless body to Grace to take away her pain as she lay dying in a back alley. Grace encouraging Galin to face his feelings and turn her or at least heal her.

He gave her exciting memories of Grace's first time seeing Ben and the times she went to the facility. Seshet and her betrayal. He gave her sad memories of Josh and Molly when she died.

Frightening memories of Ben and the broadsword incident were part of the package too. He wanted her to understand not just *what* had happened, but *why* it had happened. Why she made the choices she made and who she was protecting. When he finished, Vivienne didn't open her eyes right away. It was a lot to absorb. She blinked rapidly before sitting upright.

She stared hard into Ivan's eyes, searching for the connection they had. He had been Lukkas's best friend. Ivan had also been her friend, not just the Regent she had come to see him as. The choices he and Grace had to make were brutal. Viv was even angrier at the Council than she had been before. They forced them both into horrible choices just so they could further the Council's agenda. They made their entire communities' lives a lie. She was sad and happy and livid all at the same time. She was on the verge of tears and rage all at once.

"Ivan, I could have been there for her this whole time. Instead, I was so distant when she needed me most. I treated her as nothing more than the Regent's wife. Not the true friend she had always been to me. If it weren't for her, I wouldn't even be alive. If it weren't for her doing what she did, he would never have turned me. He would have let me die gutted in an alley for a few lira. I owe her everything and I haven't been there for her when she needed me most." She placed her hand on her throat, clearly saddened by the memory.

"Does she remember all of this too? What you gave me?" She was almost pleading with him to say no.

"Those are her memories. We share them now," he replied softly.

She turned suddenly vengeful. "How do we hurt them the most? I want them to suffer. I want them to pay." She pushed herself out of the chair, leaning over Ivan. "How do we make them pay, Ivan?"

"We win. We stop them," Erik injected in a cold tone.

Vivienne looked up at Erik. Her eyes were callous, her mouth rigid. "Then let's win," she said in a cold, dry tone that mirrored his.

CHAPTER THIRTEEN

When Grace arrived back at her apartment, it was dark. The windows were blacked out. The control panels were dim, and she smelled a light scent of lavender. When she turned around, she saw Viv sitting in the chair by the sofa. They didn't need light. They could both see in the dark.

"Vivienne," Grace feigned surprise.

"Cut the crap, Grace. I know. And I know you know. You're trying to do too much on your own and it's affecting your judgment. You're lucky your son is smarter than you are."

"Don't hold back. Tell me what you really mean." Grace was relieved that Viv knew. She was more relieved that Viv was Viv again. She needed her more than she understood until that very second. Viv always had a way of putting her in check.

"You can't run a campaign and learn to harness your abilities at the same time. You need someone you trust to take part of that burden off your shoulders while you and Ivan figure out what you need to do. Stop acting like you're alone in this, because you're not. You have a whole team. An entire community. And now you have me. So, get off your ass, learn what you need to learn from Nyx and her devil spawn, and rise."

"You don't know how much I've missed you, Viv." Grace was mentally stretched. So much had happened in such a short time.

"I know exactly how much you've missed me. I didn't know how much I've missed you. And if it weren't for Ivan and your boy, I'd never know." Vivienne dramatically overstated the "I" parts. She got up out of her chair, embracing Grace. The hug ended with Vivienne tugging hard at Grace's hair, momentarily immobilizing her.

"OW!" Grace exclaimed.

"You deserved that. I swear I could kick your ass for leaving me out of this."

This was not the new, overly cultured, refined Vivienne. This was the old, hard-ass, take-charge, street-smart Viv that Grace had come to love. This was the Viv that Grace needed.

"We found out we were played in the middle of the ceremony. It's not like I could tell you then."

"You had no intention of telling me at all. But you had time to have your son mate with my daughter and sire him so he could sire Vaeweth," she stated sarcastically. "That's the first thing we need to fix. We need to turn your other two sons and as many other Æsir who want to take the step so no one else figures out who Vaeweth's sire is. That was a colossal mistake. You should have had more turned first," Viv stated as an evaluation more than a critique.

"I'm not so certain turning others is a road we should go down here, Viv. Besides, why would anyone else need to know he wasn't turned by a regular vampire? What does Galin think of all of this, anyway? What have you told him?" Grace was attempting to get her off the subject.

Viv shook her head in disappointment. "If you wanted them to think he had been turned by someone else, you either shouldn't have had Erik turned at all, or you should have turned more first. And as for what Galin thinks, I'm helping you and Ivan. That's all. Ivan already gave him the broad strokes, and I didn't need to tell him anything else. What exactly is it that you're thinking, Grace?" Viv questioned back, knowing full well what Grace was trying to do.

"I don't think the Æsir need to change who they are to win this. That's the first thing I think."

"They don't have to change *who* they are. They have to change *what* they are. They will always be who they are. Only … more. The people you come from are intelligent, Grace, but they don't have the capacity for knowledge we do. They have experiences of time that we don't have yet, but their memories fade as new experiences replace them. Their biggest flaws are that they are weaker than we are, and they can't spread your light. They're not tied to you in the ways that tie us together. You've been reacting. Looking at what's in front of you. You need to expand your perspective. We need to get in front of this. We can't engage and win by only having an acceptable defense."

"Obviously you think I made other mistakes, too." Grace had thought she had done the best she could with the given situation. She thought she was good at seeing all sides. Perhaps Viv was right. She couldn't see outside the box she had been placed in.

"Yes. We need to move the vulnerable. Quickly. I understand Ben has been considering Hel as a safe haven. If that's not ironic, I don't know what is."

"Erik and Jack should be surveying the place now. We have to make some renovations before it can be fit for the living," Grace replied.

"That's not good enough. They need protection now. You don't know when the Council is going to make their move," Viv added.

"We can't do that. It was set up to house the dead. There are no facilities. No creature comforts at all. No beds, no showers, no toilets, no food. We need to set up greenhouse space and supply feeding stations. Plus, we need to make sure it's safe for the living. We don't know what kind of little traps were left behind. It needs to be cleared. We also need to decide the best way to get people in. It's protected and impossible to find except by Ben and now Nyx." Grace wholeheartedly defended the decision to wait to move the families in.

"That. Right there. Is exactly what I am talking about." Viv pointed at her.

"What?"

"You have an entirely capable group of scientists at your disposal. Look around you at what we've done with this whole planet in under a year. We stabilized the atmosphere, built a city and an ecosystem, created a new government. We moved upwards of fifteen thousand people. All that while explaining to many that something outside of their small world existed. What's a little renovation to something that already exists after all of that? And you don't have to place anyone in danger to do it. That's what you use service units for. You're expecting weeks or months doing it your way. We could do this in days. Use your resources, Grace. Delegate. That's what good leaders do."

Viv was right. She and Ivan had been making all the big decisions themselves. She didn't know who she could trust, so she didn't completely trust anyone, including herself. In order for this to work, she had to relinquish something. She had to let others take part of the burden.

"Fine," Grace shuddered slightly at the word.

"Fine, what?" Viv was going to make her say the words.

"You do it then," Grace stated dejectedly.

"Fine. And you go figure out how to control yourself."

"Fine."

"Now pour me a drink," Viv ordered, turning her back to Grace with the confidence of someone who had won. "Then, get a shower and get out of that hideous outfit. And that hair of yours. Either put it up or cut it off." Viv sat back in the chair she had been in when Grace got there.

"I am not cutting my hair." Grace was indignant at the suggestion. That was going too far. She handed Viv a glass of Ivan's scotch, then retreated toward her room.

Viv yelled after her, "Put on some tac gear and look like a leader."

Viv waited for Grace to shower and change. She had already begun making her plans for Hel. She needed to get a briefing from Erik about whatever obstacles they may encounter.

While she waited, she mulled over the situation regarding Erik. He really was the perfect choice for Asta, and Asta did like him considerably. Maybe even loved him if she really understood what that was yet. He was intelligent, thoughtful, anything but rash. It didn't hurt that he was also Grace's son. And now he was turned. Viv would still make life a little uncomfortable for the two of them because of the situation they put her in. They shouldn't expect anything less from her.

Another thought strolled through her mind, making her shudder. Mikkel! At least Asta hadn't chosen him. Mikkel was far too brash and daring for her liking. He would have been a terrible choice for Asta. Alex would have also been a horrible choice. He didn't take women seriously enough. He wouldn't be one to readily see his mate as his equal. No, neither of the other two would have been right. Erik had been the right choice all along.

"Viv." Grace was standing a few feet in front of her.

"That's better," Viv smiled.

Grace was dressed in tac pants, boots, and the signature black uniform shirt. Her hair was given a fierce styling. Four braids on each side pulled back from her face into another mass of small braids hanging nearly to her waist.

"You look … commanding," Viv complimented.

"Thanks?"

The uniform was comfortable. Far more comfortable than Grace had expected. Even if it was lacking in style. It was utilitarian.

"Grace," Viv huffed. "You must play the part. It's not for you. It's for them. Stand up straight. Have confidence in yourself. You're the baddest bitch in The Everything. Act like it."

"Fine," Grace replied arrogantly. She straightened herself, giving Viv a smug side-eye.

"Fine," Viv said back. "Now, let's go see that command center."

Grace shifted Viv back to the lab. Leo, Thoth, Mikkel, and Alex were already there. Ivan, Ben, Jack, and Erik had communicated their return from surveying Hel would come shortly. Ami was with Nyx and Frigg scouting a location outside the city where she could instruct Ivan and Grace without causing any harm.

Viv looked around, unimpressed, to put it mildly. She rolled her eyes. Her mouth hung half open. She finally shook her head, throwing up her hands, then bringing them down on her hips forcefully.

"This won't do. It won't do at all. You need a proper command space. Somewhere to display the current operations with phases and completion data. An area for mass briefings and a SCIF. This is completely inadequate. We need someplace bigger."

"Bigger? Like the cargo bay?" Alex asked.

"No, that can't be secured easily. Too many people need to have access to it. We need a place where access can be restricted. It needs to be secured. Have you not thought about this before?" Viv asked.

"Well, Mikkel and I are field operatives. We don't have any flag command experience." Alex wasn't used to being out of his element.

"Lucky for you, I do. Where else?"

Alex took a moment.

"Guard deck section six is vacant," Alex replied with authority.

"Now you're talking." Viv scanned him from head to toe. "You'll be a good candidate for the turn. You considering it?"

Alex glanced at Grace, who was clenching her jaw. She wasn't happy Viv had thrown it out there like she was asking how his morning was. She also wasn't debating it.

"Ever since we found it was possible. We need every advantage we can get."

"Good. It should happen sooner rather than later." She spun away from him to approach Thoth. Alex followed, curious to see what else she had to say.

"Thoth, tell me about the technology in these uniforms."

He had no idea who Viv was aside from being the bride's mother and the new Regent's wife. He knew she had been Grace's friend from before and looked to Grace for direction.

"Go ahead, Thoth. Viv is my problem solver. She's going to be assisting with general operations while Ivan and I are figuring out how we're supposed to control our abilities. She and Ben will have joint operational control. He'll be heading up strategy, she'll oversee risk assessment and asset implementation. Everyone else works for them." Grace directed with a confidence she had been lacking the past few days. Inside, she was anything but confident, wondering how she was going to explain to Ben that he was going to be sharing responsibilities and control.

"So, they're your generals. If we're using rank, that is." It was a statement, not a question. Thoth preferred having a ranking structure. It made it easier to see who was in charge of what when you needed something to be done. He didn't like the disorganization they were currently experiencing.

"Why not? While we're settling on rank, you can be the Captain in charge of R&D. Leo, you're the medical officer."

"Am I a Captain too?" Leo asked with a hint of a mocking tone.

"Sure," Grace replied. "And to round it all out, The Three are my field commanders. How's that sound? Great? Great. Now, answer her question, Thoth."

"Okay then," he said uncomfortably before turning to face Viv. "Each uniform is thermal regulating. They absorb and diffuse impact, thereby reducing most damage to the body. They have a sensor grid that assesses damage, which reports back the viability and strength percentage of the wearer. The fabric is infused with medical nanites that heal minor injuries and accelerate the healing of more advanced injuries. The nanites additionally repel and deactivate liquid and dry chemicals." He stopped, feeling he had completed his assessment.

"What about fire? Is it resistant to fire?"

Their species didn't require the healing aspects. They did require fire resistance.

"Not direct fire. At least not for more than a few moments. They regulate body temperature inside. Fire would eventually burn through."

"What about the head, face, and neck? What protection is there for those parts?"

"We do have helmets that can be worn with the uniform," Thoth answered.

"But those must be physically donned by the wearer, correct?" she asked.

"Yes."

"That won't be sufficient. The Council knows our only real weakness is fire. They will use that against us. May I see your TAC please?" Viv reached forward with her palm up.

He distrustfully handed it to Viv, uncertain why she wanted it. She tapped out a message and opened the room to porting, while keeping up the remainder of the security. A short time later, a port opened, allowing a girl to step through.

She was young, seventeen or eighteen, or so she appeared. Short height, average size. She had Indonesian and Mediterranean features. Her skin was caramel with yellow undertones and lighter than his; a mixture of something Thoth couldn't place. She had an exotic air to her. The girl had bright blue and purple streaked hair with small braids in the front and black and shorter hair in the back. She wore lip, nose, and eyebrow rings, with multiple piercings in both ears.

Her attire was even stranger, consisting of a pair of worn skinny jeans topped with a dark-pink anime T-shirt and cropped jacket. A pair of pink-and-black board shoes finished her odd attire. She was quite unexpected to the rest of the group. Grace had seen her before. She didn't know her very well. Only well enough to know she wasn't what she appeared to be.

Viv reactivated the port block, handing the TAC back to Thoth.

"Lilly, thank you for coming. I need your assistance with something."

"Other than the apartment?" she shrugged. "Sure."

"Excellent." Viv led Lilly over to Thoth.

"Lilly, this is Thoth. We need to design new uniforms with all the current specs, plus the addition of fire and heat shielding, as well as adding some type of head covering that is activated by heat. Thoth has the specs for the existing garments. Lilly, I need you to ensure that it is comfortable and allows for unrestricted movement as well as unencumbered vision when the hood is activated. Is that possible?"

Lilly answered, "Sure. Kinetically powered with secondary manual triggers for the helmet and visor portions too?"

Viv turned back to Thoth. "That seems reasonable, doesn't it?"

"Well, yes. But you want me to work with a child? I could do this on my own." He resented Viv bringing in an outsider for this project when he had a perfectly capable department.

"Thoth, she's not a child. She's nine hundred years old. While that may seem young to you, it isn't to us. She is extremely good at design and fabrication. Your designs are technologically good. They are also utilitarian and restrict movement somewhat. Her designs are sleek, modern, and highly technical. We need teams, not egos." Viv would make sure they were going to collaborate on the uniforms whether he liked it or not.

"My apologies, Lilly. I didn't mean to insult you," Thoth apologized.

"Yes, you did. I've been insulted before. Whatever." Lilly let it roll off her back. "Just don't think you can order me around." She walked to the service panel, grabbing the TAC out of Thoth's hand, leaving him dumbfounded.

Viv turned away, looking smug. Taking Alex's arm, she said, "Alex, is it? How about you and I go find our command headquarters?"

Alex pulled his TAC out of his pocket. "Ida, allow port opening to level six, section six." He proceeded to open a port. Grace stopped them before they could walk through.

"Alex, she needs a BAT first."

"I always forget about those. Probably because I don't need one," he answered irreverently.

"What's a BAT?" Viv asked.

"It's a little biometric device to enhance your telepathic abilities so you can communicate with the team. It's coded for your genetic material. Goes behind your ear," Alex answered.

"I saw Erik with one of those at the facility." She didn't know any of his people were telepathic.

"My brothers and I were born telepathic. It didn't take much tweaking to learn to communicate with others. We only needed them at the facility because we hadn't figured out how yet. We must have gotten it from her," he said, nodding toward Grace.

"And here I thought it was going to be a weapon," she replied sarcastically.

Alex chuckled at that.

It took Leo less than a minute to fit her for the device. Grace also raised her security level to command one.

"Now you're ready," Grace told her. "Go have some fun."

Viv took Alex by the arm again, walking through the open port.

"Ida, lock out porting," Grace ordered.

Viv looked around, shaking her head. This place was a hot mess. It was time for her to roll up her sleeves and get to work. The first thing she did was call for a dozen service units to empty and clean out the space.

They installed two viewing walls, enhanced security walls, and added dampening fields, scanners, a briefing area, and a SCIF. She also decided to add an independent atmosphere that was off grid from the rest of the facility. The entire thing had been built around a new, secure AI. All that was left was to finish the locker room and a quiet area where those who needed it could get some sleep at times when returning to their quarters wouldn't be practical.

Six hours it had taken her to complete the command headquarters she had begun referring to as The Six. To her, six seemed to be an appropriate number. It was also easier to communicate than "command headquarters" or "level six, sector six." It was also a fun metaphor for having your back. She thought it to be quite appropriate.

While supervising the project, she had also gotten Hel's layout from Erik. She already had a working model for those renovations. They had decided on renovating only one quarter of the place. Enough room for two thousand families, up to eight thousand residents. There were living quarters, two dining halls, a market, public shop spaces, a greenhouse, daylight emulators, a school, a medical facility, two community centers, two indoor sports fields, and a large gym and training center.

The plan rivaled that of any small town. They didn't have anywhere for livestock, but they could grow their meat like they did on Rasa. She didn't think the Jur would mind that. Her people were used to it already. If they needed more room, it would be easy enough to add later. She thought this was an excellent start.

She had the plans pulled up into a three-dimensional model on the enormous planning table in front of viewing wall one when Erik came in. They had found a few surprises in Hel. He and Jack had been able to deactivate everything in the area they had planned to renovate.

Morgud had assisted them in testing the equipment ports. They worked going to and from the foot of the bridge to other ports. When they had tried to use them over the river, they would get bounced back to the originating port. Ivan had been able to shift over. When he crossed, the river erupted in an attempt to rip him to shreds, but the assault had been ineffective. When he stood at the base of the bridge, he could shift to the other side without a disturbance.

It had to be something about the bridge's frequency that kept the water calm. Jack took on the task of finding a solution to crossing. At least Ivan, Grace, or Nyx would be able to shift the larger equipment in. Everything else would need to be carried over the bridge.

"Looks like someone's been busy." Erik was impressed by her progress. "Where's Alex?"

"Quiet room." She pointed to a door behind her at the far corner of the bay.

"You put him in time out?" Erik chuckled.

She turned around to smirk at him. "Well, he looks like you ... so, you know."

"Yeah." He figured he was still going to get a hard time from her for a while.

"He's finishing the sleeping bays," she stated in a monotone voice.

"I came to see if you needed any help on the room. Looks like you have it under control." Erik surveyed the space.

"I'm quite capable of handling a project of this size."

"I can see that." Erik found the conversation to be uncomfortable. He was sure that was her intention. "Can I see the tech specs? I'd like to familiarize myself with the security features."

Viv turned, sweeping aside the plans laid out on the table.

"Sadie," she started.

"Sadie?" he queried.

"New AI the boys in the tech department have been working on. Enhanced security."

"Boggs and Ramirez?"

"No, Harmon and Ruzzio."

"Huh. I always thought they were slackers. Guess they're not useless after all." He was surprised they had this going and hadn't boasted about it to everyone.

"They had been working on it for a few years before we came here. Getting access to Ida's code pushed the project forward by a decade or so. Ida was designed to be more domestically oriented. Sadie interfaces with Ida to utilize sensors already in place. It will be deployed through the entirety of the existing system by the end of today. In this space, though, it's exclusively Sadie. It's quite elegant. It can tell the difference between a live voice modulation and a recorded or synthesized one. The system performs real-time scanning of everything within a designated area. Access is biometric. It can even tell if you're lying," she explained, turning to leer directly into his eyes.

He shifted his weight to the other foot, largely ignoring the accusation.

"What about targeting capabilities? Any of those?" He wondered if it was a security protocol system or a full defense system.

"There are. Direct electrical charge targeting from the atmospheric electrical network is what they have so far. They're working on a paralyzing dart but are having some difficulty setting up origination points to cover the entire room. They'll get there." She was confident in their abilities.

"May I?"

"Sure. Go ahead," she replied with a broad smile.

"Sadie, pull up the tech specs for the command headquarters."

"On the plan table or the viewing screen, *Erik*?" Sadie said his name in a mocking tone.

"You programmed it to be pissed at me?"

"No. I think it picked that up all on its own." Viv smiled much too sweetly for it to be real.

He rolled his eyes. "Sadie, *please* pull up the tech specs for the command headquarters on the plan table."

Sadie didn't reply this time, but the plans appeared on the table.

"Thank you, Sadie." Erik would have to work to get on favorable terms with this AI. That would be an odd situation.

Sadie ignored him.

Viv found it humorous.

Erik studied the model. "What are these white flashes?"

"Domestic porting events. Sadie monitors all porting activity. External natural porting in either direction is set to flash yellow; internal, white; porting platform activation, green. Unauthorized porting of any kind will flash red and issue a visual and audio alert on the top right screen on wall two for now," Viv explained.

"What about communications?"

"Sadie monitors all internal and external communications for the planet."

"But not telepathic," he said as a statement.

"That's a little more nuanced. Natural ones like yours can't be monitored. It can monitor telepathic communications of any of us using a BAT." Viv saw this as a flaw they may not be able to overcome.

"So, my communication with Alex would be private, but my communication with you would be monitored and recorded. Hmmm."

"Yes. Harmon and Ruzzio don't have a solution for that. Each individual telepath uses a different frequency given their level of ability. Sadie can see when they communicate, and with whom, but it can't determine what they are communicating." Viv was a bit dismayed by that.

"Why don't we give Boggs and Ramirez a shot at it? They designed the BATs. I'm sure they could manage a telepathic link to Sadie. I imagine something like that would be useful. We would be able to communicate with her directly," Erik suggested.

"You're assigning Sadie a gender? It's artificial." Viv didn't get why men always assigned feminine genders to things. Cars, guns, machines. Anything that served them.

"Harmon and Ruzzio assigned her a gender. She has a feminine voice and name. She is just as capable of rational thought as we are. By your own words, she's 'quite elegant.'" Erik thought sucking up to Sadie wouldn't hurt. He was impressed with her capabilities. More impressed that Harmon and Ruzzio were the ones to design her.

"Thank you, Erik. It's nice to see someone appreciates my potential. You appear to be a somewhat intelligent biological life form as well."

Erik was pleased with Sadie's response. Point one: Erik. Viv seemed less than pleased.

Viv decided it was time for a few tests.

"Sadie, what life forms are in The Six?"

Erik wasn't familiar with that designation. He waited to see what Sadie's response was before questioning.

"In The Six there are three biological life forms: Vivienne Eliassen, Aleksander Odinson, and Erik Odinson. There are additionally twelve synthetic level one–secured life forms."

"What species are the biological life forms?" This was something Viv was curious about.

"There is one pure humanoid Vampirus species, one humanoid containing biological signatures of Vanir and Æsir with an energy signature of Protogenoi, and one humanoid containing biological signatures of Vanir and Æsir with a dominant base signature of Vampirus and an energy signature of Protogenoi."

Erik had an additional question. "Sadie, what is the biological signature of Grace Novak?"

Viv looked at him suspiciously.

"Grace Novak's biological signature can no longer be determined from information I possess. The energy signature is undiluted."

Viv held eye contact with Erik. "Sadie, what is the biological signature of Ivan Novak?"

"Ivan Novak's biological signature can no longer be determined from the information I possess. The energy signature is undiluted."

Erik asked, further holding eye contact with Viv, "Sadie, explain the response of an undiluted energy signature."

"An undiluted energy signature matches no species. It is the combined energy signature of all wavelengths and polarities."

Viv had one last question. "What is the biological signature of Nyx?"

Sadie replied, "Nyx's current humanoid shell is synthetic with no biological signature. It has a pure energy signature of Protogenoi."

"It?" Erik asked.

"Nyx has no assigned gender. Most often, Nyx takes the form of a female; however, that is not an assigned gender," Sadie answered.

Viv gave her first command-level instruction. "Sadie, restrict information on Grace and Ivan Novak's biological determination to command level one personnel only. Set a notification to alert Erik and me if anyone attempts access."

"Restrictions are in place, Vivienne," Sadie replied.

"Sadie," Erik added, "set further restrictions for Grace and Ivan Novak's information to disallow any changes in access level unless placed by me or Vivienne."

"Good thinking. We don't need this getting out to anyone, even your mother and Ivan, for now." Viv seemed to have forgotten her vendetta against him for the time being.

"Additional restrictions are in place, Erik," Sadie replied.

The door to the quiet room opened suddenly, startling Erik and Viv.

"Whew! Those neural hoods are fantastic. They give you a full sleep cycle in twenty minutes. We should put those in the troop quarters," Alex shouted, full of energy.

"Even a blind squirrel finds a nut on occasion," Viv joked about Alex's idea. Erik found it humorous.

"Sadie, install a bank of fifty restoration stations in each of the troop barracks and one in each of the command-level quarters. Additionally, install enough stations for twenty-five percent of the personnel capacity in each transport ship."

"On the smaller cruisers, restoration stations would take over fifty percent of the available floor space in the cargo hold," Sadie replied.

Viv was thinking.

Erik suggested, "Sadie, would they fit stacked on the upper level of the aft deck spaced four high along the walls?"

"Yes, Erik. They would take up twelve point five percent of useable floor space if installed in that manner."

"Install them stacked in all the ships," Erik further directed.

"I'll have to assume you hadn't realized troop transports have stacked berthing. It helps fit more in," he offered.

"I've never been on any type of space transportation," Viv replied.

"Not even a shuttle?" Erik asked.

Viv shook her head.

"We've got two hours until the first official briefing. Would you like to see one? We have a cruiser in orbit."

"I'd like that." It seemed her coldness toward him was melting.

"Let's do it old style, then. Shuttle to cruiser." Erik would give her the full treatment.

"Where do we keep the shuttles?" Viv had gotten so used to porting she hadn't thought about other types of transportation. They headed toward the door.

"Up in the mountains. The bay openings are cloaked. It makes it more difficult to tell where the shuttles originate from. We can port over. By land vehicle, it would take three days."

"Okay then. You two go ahead," Alex called out as they walked away. "I'll stay here and finish up the facilities. No trouble at all. You can count on me."

Alex sat down at the briefing table, unsure of how to react to being ignored.

CHAPTER FOURTEEN

"I want to get down there a few minutes early to have a look around before everyone arrives," Grace told Ivan.

"I need to change first," he replied, mildly irritated. "This is my favorite shirt."

"I didn't mean to burn it. Who knew a tiny little energy ball would have that effect?" She sounded apologetic.

"I'm more curious to know how it burned the shirt. I haven't had any trouble phasing my clothing with me before." He pulled his shirt over his head, inspecting the large hole in the back of it.

Grace rubbed her hand over his back. "But your T-shirt didn't burn. Maybe it was too fast. You can't say you were expecting it. It got away from me."

"Maybe if it hadn't surprised you, it wouldn't have surprised me." Ivan thought it could have had something to do with the shirt coming from Tartarus. The energy ball had been converted from negative energy. He'd save it for Jack to look at.

"I don't know. I'll see you there in a few minutes." She kissed him on the cheek before shifting out.

She appeared a few feet inside the door to the main briefing room.

"Welcome to The Six, Grace," Sadie greeted her.

That wasn't Ida's voice, and she didn't know what The Six was.

"Where's Vivienne?" she asked the AI.

"Vivienne is in the quiet room. Her sleep cycle will end in twenty-nine seconds. Would you care for anything while you wait?"

Grace didn't think alcohol would be appropriate for their first official briefing, and she was in the mood for something sweet. "Vanilla cappuccino, please."

"Your body temperature is slightly elevated. Are you sure you wouldn't care for a cold beverage?" Sadie inquired.

Most definitely not Ida.

"No, thank you. Coffee will be fine." Grace made an internal evaluation before realizing the elevated temperature readings were due to her still being in estrus. She had simply forgotten about that over the last few days. Three more days and it would be over.

"As you like. You will find it in front of your seat at the planning table," Sadie replied.

Grace looked to her left, seeing a cup appear in front of the leftmost chair at the top end of the massive table. The table was elliptical in shape. Narrow on the two ends, thicker across the middle. There were twelve chairs running down each side. The table sat perpendicular to her with twenty-by-twenty-foot monitoring walls fanning outward forty-five degrees from a narrower center wall at the far end. Clear side walls came parallel to the table on either side, extending about six feet beyond.

The screen walls could be seen from any point in the room. There was a slot in the floor at the end of the clear walls. Grace assumed another wall could be raised or lowered to isolate the planning area. The screens were filled with data and camera runs of the planet. There was a third screen area on the far center wall, which was set to a rotating view of the space surrounding the planet.

Further away, adjacent to the clear wall farthest from her, was a smaller room with clear walls. That was most likely the SCIF Viv had alluded to. Directly in front of her, at the other end of the bay, was the locker room. To the right of that, a door marked "Quiet Room." To her right, running the length of the bay, was a solid quartz wall. When Grace touched it, she could feel that it was a series of walls. Five layers of alternating quartz and graphene. All the outer walls, floors, and ceiling were constructed in the same manner. The room didn't just house the new AI, it was the new AI, vibrating with energy.

She went to the table, picking up her coffee, when Viv emerged from the quiet room.

"This is impressive," she said to Viv, scanning the room.

"Oh, The Six? It was nothing. All in a day's work. What have you been up to? Any progress?"

"Nyx tossing balls of negative energy at us for hours on end. We managed to convert most of them toward the latter part of the session. I can't say it was pretty. We had a lot of difficulty controlling them. Well, I had a lot of difficulty controlling them. Ivan was perfect, as usual. I'd say it was more humbling than anything. What did you call this place? The Six?" Grace wondered about the name.

"Am I the only one who gets it? Got your back. Got your six. This is The Six. The back, backbone? Oh, never mind." Viv was exasperated. She had thought it was brilliant.

"No, Viv. I get it. I like it." Grace didn't keep up with military slang. She kind of got it after Viv explained it. "What's up with the new AI? She's not Ida. She's different," Grace asked, wanting to change the subject.

"That is Sadie. It, I mean she, is an autonomous security-enhanced quantum-based system capable of independent learning. Our tech department did some excellent work with her."

Ben and Mikkel entered through the door.

"Welcome to The Six, Ben, Mikkel. Would either of you care for a beverage?"

"That's new. The Six, huh? I like it," Ben said.

"Finally! Somebody gets it," exclaimed Viv.

"Can I get a beer?" asked Mikkel.

"No," replied Ben and Grace in unison.

"I'm sorry, Mikkel. Your request has been denied," Sadie replied. "Would you care for something else?"

"Water then, I guess," Mikkel requested with disappointment.

"Your beverage will appear in front of your assigned seating at the planning table," Sadie said.

"Thank you, Sadie," Grace responded.

"This place is awesome, Viv. Much better than that cramped little lab," Mikkel said, scanning the room as he headed toward the clear cylinder of water that appeared on the table.

"I agree. It's a proper war room," Ben added. "New AI?"

"Yes. I'll explain when everyone arrives," Viv replied.

The meeting began promptly at sixteen hundred hours. The entire screen wall was visible from every seat. On the left side of the table were Grace, Viv, Ami, Leo, Thoth, and Frigg. The right side seated Ivan, Ben, Erik, Alex, Mikkel, and Nyx. They proceeded with minor business, first explaining Sadie, her interface, the restoration stations, and the workings of The Six. They all agreed to deploy Sadie to all the battleships, cruisers, transport ships, and shuttles. Ida would be utilized for domestic service in residential quarters and public spaces throughout the home planet.

Next, they reviewed everyone's new roles. Ben was running command strategy; Viv, operations; Erik, domestic security and the reserve division. He would have preferred engineering, where his strength lay, although he wasn't too disappointed. There were many technical opportunities in security. Alex and Mikkel would each head a troop division. Ami would assist with interdimensional communications and recruitment; Leo, medical level two access; and Thoth, R&D, also level two access. Nyx and Frigg would serve as consultants only with level three access. Grace and Ivan would largely take supervisory roles until they had better command of their abilities. Everyone was satisfied understanding their part.

The next item on the agenda was Hel.

"Sadie, open Hel model one on the plan table," Viv commanded. "This is only a rough plan that I drafted up this morning. Feel free to suggest any changes. I'd like to get started tomorrow if no one has objections."

Everyone surveyed the plan.

"Excuse me, Vivienne, is it? I don't see my apartments on your plan. You can't possibly expect me to stay in one of those tiny little residences, can you?" Nyx was intent on making something about her today.

Viv side-eyed Grace. "My apologies, Nyx. I hadn't been informed you'd be staying there."

"Well, I paid the lease," she continued.

"With his blood," Ben said, directing his thumb at Ivan. "And it was free."

"Nonetheless. It was leased. That forest is loaded with dark energy. It will make a perfect training site for Ivan and Grace. Besides, you'll need someone who can shift in and out at will. And I have a good rapport with Morgud. And if someone runs into any little leftover surprises, wouldn't you rather have a Primordial in residence who can deal with it? The best part of the whole thing for me is I don't need to constantly be restricted to this shell there," Nyx argued her case.

Ben had a feeling she just wanted to be Queen of Hel. Fine with him. She'd be out of his hair.

Viv searched the others' faces for any objections. It seemed they had none.

"Well, what about the throne room over here?" She pointed out an area away from the common areas and residences. "It's close enough if you're needed, but far enough away that you won't be bothered."

"That's an excellent suggestion. I've always loved a good throne room." Nyx seemed content with the compromise. "I'll send you my requirements," she finished.

Viv quickly carried on, "Since that's settled. The next item on the agenda goes to Thoth. Are you ready with your presentation?"

"Yes." He stood up, moving to the foot of the table near the screen wall with the view of exterior space.

"Ida—excuse me, I meant Sadie. Allow Lilly to port in next to me."

He next contacted Lilly using his BAT. *We're ready for you.*

Lilly appeared next to Thoth. She was wearing a prototype of the new uniform. The bottom half was very similar to the current uniform. There was a discernible difference in the boots' structural integrity, as evidenced by a thicker sole and a one-inch increase in height on the leg. The pants were still a cargo style. They were more closely fitted and the pockets were not as bulky. The top was where the majority of changes appeared to be. It resembled racing leathers, but thinner and longer in the back. Somewhat like a thick button-down shirt without buttons. It had a front closure with the center flap flattened. The collar was band style with a blue tab closure. There was a cluster of three overlapping blue triangles, hollow in the center.

It reminded Grace of the Valknut, the symbol for balance. Only this was a more modern version. There were also two small metallic dots on either side of the center tab, in line with the neck arteries. The collar was slightly thicker in the back and on the sides, stopping approximately a third of the way up the neck. There was a slightly darkened visor across her eyes that looped over her ears the way sunglasses would, tethered loosely to the collar.

It was sleek and unisex. It fit well. The aesthetics seemed to meet everyone's approval.

"Lilly, set surveillance mode."

Lilly tapped the pinky of her left hand to her thumb once.

"Sadie, put Lilly's panel on the center screen," Thoth requested.

Lilly's panel was divided into two parts, with a blue band across the top. The left side of the screen was her life support readings, including an impact diagram for her uniform and remaining life percentage level. The right side was split into top and bottom. The top was a view from her collar cameras, the bottom from inside her visor. A dim white silhouette was visible around each person seated at the table through the visor.

"Lilly, set battle mode," Thoth directed.

She tapped her left pinky finger on her thumb two times. The visor display changed to show targeting distance across the center of each outlined figure with morbidity percentages in targeted areas. Grace and Ivan's readings were all a series of three dots occasionally flashing "unable to calculate." The others were covered with varying percentages.

The collar rose to cover her throat and came to a point at the base of her skull. The covering resembled black metal. Even though the appearance was rigid, it moved with her unrestricted. Her hair was short in the back, which enabled everyone to see it. If she had longer hair, it would push up underneath unseen. The top of the collar band and the edges of the skull piece glowed faintly. From the sleeves extended the same type of metal material, covering the backs of her hands through the first knuckle.

Erik asked the first question. "What's the illumination around the neckband?"

The wave of confusion made it apparent that the light was outside of the normal sight spectrum for those who hadn't taken the turn.

Thoth answered, "Personally, I can't see it without assistance. It's a range high in the UV band. The light is cast from the face shielding. Would you like a closer look?"

Erik didn't hesitate. He scrutinized Lilly's face as closely as he could. He didn't see a face shield, only the very slight glow emanating from her collar.

"May I?" he addressed Lilly, lifting his hand toward her face.

She nodded her head, keeping her gaze forward. Erik touched her face. He didn't feel a barrier.

"Strike her face," Thoth encouraged.

Lilly shrugged. Erik slapped her with a medium-velocity open hand across the face. Only he never contacted her face. Lilly didn't even blink. Her injury status never wavered. He could see a blue static charge dissipate the force from the point of impact. It showed on her screen as well. It hurt his hand far greater than a slap of that magnitude should have.

Thoth pronounced, "That is a resistive force shield. Increase the impact, increase the resistance. It covers the entire head and neck region."

"What about fire resistance?" Viv asked. It had been the main priority of the redesign.

"Yes, just getting to that. We've successfully tested subjects for fire resistance at high temperatures from one to seven minutes. Species specific down to seventy-five percent mortality rate. Anything over seventy-five percent, the subject is unable to remain conscious. The suit sustains integrity. The problem we have is the thermal regulation inside the suit is unable to counter very high temperatures. She can walk for a nearly unrestricted amount of time in a standard wood fire. High-temperature chemical fires is where we run into issues. On the battlefield or in space, the most likely types of fires will be chemical in nature. Most likely after an explosion or from a flame-producing weapon. One to seven minutes in that type of fire is the current limit, depending on the species." Thoth and Lilly had accomplished a major amount of work in a very short period.

Viv nodded. "I believe that is quite adequate. It's one to seven minutes we didn't have before. And I can't reasonably see anyone standing around in a fire for that long without attempting to escape from it. I'll assume the one-minute marker is for an unturned subject and the seven minutes is for a turned subject?"

"A non-turned individual is on the lowest end of the time spectrum. A turned subject, while at the higher range, would only last until around the five-and-a-half-minute mark. An unturned Jur subject was at the topmost end of the spectrum because of their thicker dermal layer. We performed both simulated and live subject testing." Thoth completed his answer.

Viv wasn't quite satisfied yet. "What about the results for a turned Jur subject?"

"With only having one, we were unable to complete any live testing." Thoth felt his work was incomplete. Vaeweth had gone back to Jur to recruit volunteers into taking the turn. Paneth stayed behind and tested the uniform.

"Where is your simulation data? You performed simulations, did you not?" Frigg added in.

"We did. However, I believe the results were highly inaccurate. Limits came back at more than double the non-turned Jur rate. We didn't find that plausible." Thoth was dismissive.

Lilly shifted her body language, showing she did not agree with him.

Viv wasn't finished with the subject yet. "I'm sure Vaeweth will make himself available for testing in the near future." She had concluded speaking.

"Excellent work with the new uniform design, Thoth, Lilly. Is that top piece a shirt or a jacket?" Grace asked.

This time Lilly replied, "It's an overshirt. Underneath is the same long-sleeved T-shirt you're wearing now. The overshirt can be worn open or closed and interfaces with the sensors of the one underneath. If the shirt is open when entering battle mode, it will retract and seal itself."

"Why's it blue?" Alex wasn't sure he wanted any color in a uniform.

Lilly continued, as the color coding was a design choice. "Color coding gives a simple visual cue for the field of service. This is my uniform. The blue signifies SET. A combination of the science, engineering, and technology fields. Command is green; emergency response, red; communications and navigation, yellow; transport, orange; and ground forces, black. If you don't like the colors, we can change them. I just thought it would be easier for identification."

"What about the insignia? Is that a rank structure?" Alex furthered his questioning, satisfied that at least his uniform wouldn't have any color. He hadn't deduced that, even though he oversaw troops, he was, in actuality, part of the command group.

Lilly took that question also. "Not rank, access level. I have level three access, so all three of my triangles are open. Level twos would have the outside triangles filled, leaving the center open. Level ones have everything filled in with open lines."

"What about lower-level access?" Alex wasn't certain about levels instead of rank. Grace seemed to like it much better than a standard rank structure.

"Same idea with circles instead of triangles. Both symbolize balance. I just like the way they look, personally. Thought the uniform was a bit too plain. If you're out among civilians, the center flap folds back, covering the rank and the field designator for a more covert look," Lilly answered again.

"What about the visor?" Mikkel asked.

"I get used to having it on. If you are working with a piece of technology or equipment, it interfaces with Sadie, giving you access to a diagram overlay. It can be used like a normal sunshield or activated. The interface is operated by touching your little finger and thumb on your right hand. Squeezing for two seconds activates or deactivates them. Squeeze a few seconds longer, they stow away. Tap once for surveillance mode, twice for battle mode. You can also remove them manually and let them hang from the tether.

"The uniform is controlled by the left hand. Engaging the uniform also engages the visor. On the monitor, you can see now that all of you are outlined in white. If any of you had on a uniform, that data would update to correspond with your organization's color and stats. Targeting would be disengaged."

"What about if someone steals your uniform?" She wasn't sure if Mikkel was trying to catch her out or if he was really interested.

"Your uniform is bio-coded to you. If anyone else tries to wear it in the presence of another uniformed person, the visor will flash red around the target. All the technological capabilities will disengage. Any other questions?" Lilly had concluded her part of the presentation.

"One more question." It was Mikkel, again. "How does the suit know you are tapping your little finger and not any of your other fingers?"

Lilly wanted this to be her final question. She thought he was intent on irritating her.

"Sensors in the sleeves of the overshirt detect muscle movements necessary to engage the thumb and little finger. Any additional feature questions can be answered during uniform fitting at the supply station tomorrow. If the uniforms are approved without any changes, that is."

Ivan nodded to Lilly. "I think a vote is in order on the uniform issue. I am transferring to your TACs now." Ivan made a few gestures over his device, then set it down on the table. It was a blind vote, but he could tell who disagreed.

Ben was against the uniform. He was predictably old school. He wasn't fond of wearing the green accent color. Alex wasn't comfortable with the level structure. He preferred a rigid rank structure. Once he took the turn, he would come to realize the clan mentality was much more tightly knit than a loosely tethered military unit. They didn't need to be dominated or intimidated into working together. Each was already invested in the greater good of their community. Each one would sacrifice themselves for another to survive. It was a different kind of bond. They could certainly fight among themselves, but inject an outsider into the mix, and they would all turn on them. It didn't matter much, though. Majority wins.

Ivan picked up his TAC once the others finished voting.

"On item one—new uniform. The ayes have it. Item one passed. On item two—level insignia and color-coding structure. The ayes have it. Item two passed.

"Lilly, you may begin fittings tomorrow in the supply sector on level five. Have Sadie work out a schedule based on personnel availability."

"I'm all over it." Lilly was excited about this project. She had never created a design that would be worn by so many. She was proud of what she had produced. And she supposed Thoth had helped too. He had mostly only given her the old design specs, letting her run with it. She had done all the real designing. Except for the resistance shield. He did deserve credit for that.

She got back to the lab to transfer the specs for mass fabrication. She was so irritated by Mikkel's ridiculous questions, she had forgotten to tell them about the boots. That'd have to be a surprise for the fittings.

They had gotten through a lot of business in two hours. The next order of business would be the most controversial by far. The turn.

"Leo. Where do we stand on pods for those ready to take the turn?" Ivan asked.

"We have twenty-two medical-grade pods with active STAG units," he replied.

"Twenty-two? Why so few?" Viv asked.

"We have five hundred medical pods. The problem is we don't have enough STAGs to fit them with. We are building more, only not as quickly as I had hoped. It takes time to build them. They are complicated and delicate. One tiny thing done incorrectly could have damaging effects," Leo explained further.

"I can't think that would be too few. How many have elected to take the turn, anyway?" Ben asked. He certainly wouldn't be one of them, and he couldn't imagine many others were willing to do it.

"Sadie, pull up the current volunteer list for the turn on the center screen," Grace requested.

"Yes, Grace. Pulling the list now," Sadie replied.

The list had grown much longer than he had thought it would. It had only been a few hours since they had begun it. He glared at Mikkel and Alex, whose names were in the first two slots. Nearly everyone of consent age on the planet was on the list. All two thousand Jur soldiers and many of their family members, a few dwarves whose names he recognized. There were several names he knew from other pantheons. Nearly three thousand in all. And the biggest surprise for him was Morgud.

"Why is Morgud on that list? What reason would she have to take the turn?" Ben was bewildered by her reasoning.

"Ben. We spent the better part of a day with her. Did you not listen to her at all? She has been shunned by her entire race. She has no one. She wants to be connected to something. Her desire is to join a community. This community," Nyx admonished. "I'd consider it if I wasn't, well ... *me*."

Frigg rolled her eyes at Nyx's conceit.

Grace added, "Remember the day at the cabin when you made the offer to bring us here? Wasn't it you who said we can't be only one species anymore? We can't survive alone. A lot of people are taking that to heart. They've made their choice. No one is asking you to agree with them or take the turn yourself. We're only asking you not to hold it against them."

"I'm not holding it against them. I'm having difficulty understanding why some of them would want to," Ben retorted sourly.

"Because we're outsiders. Our people barely survived the destruction of our entire world. I never want to feel that helpless again. We were stuck half a universe away. All we could do was watch the feeds," Alex stated plainly. "Since Erik has turned, Mikkel and I feel his connection to the community. We feel how he has bonded to them. We see them through his eyes. He's the one who's connected. We're merely watching from outside the window. It's hard for us to see that and not want to be a part of it. I can't speak for the others. I only know what it is for us."

Mikkel was nodding in agreement as Alex stated their case. The Three had always had each other. Erik was bound to something bigger now. They felt drawn through him, although not as much to him anymore. They wanted to have that for themselves.

Ben wondered if the draw was to them or to Grace through them. If that was the case, Ben would never feel it. He was immune to her while she was in her current shell. It was designed so he would be immune to it. It was designed so he couldn't be tempted or swayed by her. Maybe that would change after she and Ivan rose. He didn't know.

What he knew for certain was it would hurt more if he were drawn to her. It was hard enough to live and work this close to her and not want more from her. He often wondered if he would have had a happier life if he had never met Grace. He felt isolated. Even his own mother seemed drawn to their kind. She was too pragmatic to take the turn right away. He could see her considering it after she studied others that had turned more closely. He was beginning to see how hard it must be for others not to be drawn to them.

"We should set sire lines," Ivan suggested, as much because he wanted to rescue Ben from his thoughts as because it was a good idea. Deaths were difficult enough for their community without having any singular one that resonated through the entire population at once.

Viv seconded the motion. "What would be an ideal minimum to start with, do you think?"

"I think we should set some parameters before we start thinking about lines," Ivan replied. "We should set a sire limit per individual. Maybe five direct sires per individual?" he added.

Erik spoke next. "I don't think it would be a good idea for Alex or Mikkel to have Asta as a sire. She doesn't have the emotional hardness to withstand the number of potential deaths that could take place in their troop divisions. With what they're already feeling from their bond to me, I think it could be too much for her."

"While I appreciate your concern for my daughter, she's far stronger than you think. But you're right. They should have different sires. I'll sire one. We'll need someone else for the other. Does that work for everyone?" Viv surveyed the room. It was agreed. Ben abstained from commenting.

"What about the elder families? Do you think any of them would be willing to extend their lines?" Ivan already knew the answer. He wanted to see what Viv's opinion was on the matter.

"Come on, Ivan. They've been given a lot already. I don't think any of the elders would even consider siring most of the species on that list. Until a few days ago, they weren't aware so many others existed. We don't want to chance anything that may push them to go back to Earth. Besides, we can't tell them everything yet."

"I think that's a lot to put on your family, Viv. Violet, Asta, and you, all with individual sire lines? Are you sure that's a good idea?" Grace asked, concerned.

"What other choice do we have? It's already started with Asta. My sire line is Galin's sire line through me. We all need to step up, and the top lines need to be people who know what's going on. I think you should, at least, consider sharing the information with Galin, and he can decide for himself. It's not like I suggested Lukkas. He shouldn't be exposed to the truth about the past. At least not yet. You do understand it will eventually need to come out? People need to see the lengths the Council will go to manipulate them." She directed the last bit to Grace and Ivan.

Grace opened her mouth to object before closing it again. She knew Viv was right. Anything she said against it wouldn't even make sense to her.

"What about Ty? He's not sired anyone." Ami suggested. She enjoyed her lengthy discussions with him. She didn't get to see him very often since he hadn't moved here yet.

Ivan hadn't considered Ty. On the positive side, none of the elders could fault him for not expanding the species if he accepted. He already had suspicions about Ivan and Grace's history, so the truth wouldn't be a far stretch for him to believe. He had asked Ivan some odd questions in the last year. Ivan wasn't sure if it was because he was incredibly good at scrutinizing evidence or if Ami had let something slip during one of their conversations. He wasn't sure it mattered, anyway. Ty still had another semester to teach. The last thing a doctoral student needed was a new professor in the last semester, especially one who was already grading thesis papers.

"He doesn't even live here, Ami," Ivan finally said.

"Why does he have to live here? He only needs to come for a few hours. It wouldn't be odd at all for him to come here. He already visits sometimes. He's on the education committee," Ami objected.

Ivan saw Ty as a suitable candidate. He had no other sires. And if he did already know something, he knew how to keep his mouth shut. Then again, if he didn't already know anything, he was good enough at deduction that he would figure it out when he moved here.

"I'll ask him. Go ahead and put him on the short list. That would make four. I think we should start with five, seeing how many we have who want to take the turn. Is there another suggestion for the fifth?"

Viv was thinking hard. Who else was indebted to Grace or Ivan? Who could possibly realize the genuine memories were real once they received them?

"What about that girl, Grace? The one you rescued from Seshet's little torture test?" Viv suggested.

"Olivia? What even made you think of her?" Grace asked.

Ben sighed, laid his head back, and rolled his eyes. His body was tense. He definitely did not look forward to seeing her again. Seshet was supposed to be doing research, not torturing innocent people.

"Sorry, Ben. I forgot you were involved in that," Viv apologized.

"I wasn't involved in that. I was preoccupied with finding Grace when I should have been paying more attention to what was going on in my own facility," he defended.

Nyx perked up. Anything that made Ben this uncomfortable was entertaining.

"Why did you think of her, Viv?" Ivan repeated Grace's question.

"Because she's been places she never should have been: the facility, the Council headquarters. The memories will trigger something in her like they did in me. She will see they are real," Viv explained.

Ivan and Grace weren't sure that was the kind of thing they wanted her to remember. Ben was certainly against it.

"The only other person who was traumatized enough by the changes to have a grasp on the reality of the original timeline would be Lukkas, and you don't want him involved. You and Ivan weren't great at making close friends. As far as I can see, it's Lukkas or Olivia," she ended sternly.

Ami thought they were all missing someone right under their noses.

"What's wrong with Lilly? She's already working with us and she wouldn't even have to know."

They all looked at Ami. Nyx sniggered. An alternative really had been right under their noses.

"She can turn me," Mikkel said suggestively. He immediately appeared a little embarrassed at his overly excited support of the idea.

"If that's okay with her, that is." He liked Lilly. She had a sense of humor, and she didn't give a shit what anyone thought. They were a lot alike.

"Well," Viv pondered, "she has no sires. She doesn't even know who her own sire is. Thank you for the suggestion, Ami. I think that resolves the argument. If she'll do it, that is." She looked at an uncomfortable Mikkel, echoing his words.

"Who could possibly convince the antisocial little urchin?" Nyx added, casually tilting her head toward Mikkel.

"This isn't the mating game, Mikkel. You are looking for someone who would be a compatible sire," Grace admonished.

"I most definitely don't want a mate. Don't worry about that. I think she's fun," Mikkel said.

"Fine. But you are going to ask her. And if she says no, let it go." Grace seriously doubted Lilly would take him up on whatever proposition he had for her. The alternatives were far less appealing.

They discussed the tiering awhile longer. Viv consented to siring her full allotment of five, starting with Alex. She also stipulated that he would be her only male direct sire. She preferred mentoring females, especially those that needed a bit more confidence and guidance. Viv had always felt inclined to helping orphans and broken things like she had helped Lilly, but that was a memory for another time.

If Lilly agreed, she could sire others if she wished, but they didn't factor her into anything after that. Mikkel was willing to extend her sire line. Erik and Viv agreed Asta would most likely agree to one or two of the women on the list that she had already become friends with. They were single and had no potential mates. Viv would ask Violet if she was willing. If not, Erik believed Jack wouldn't pass on the chance to have a sire line.

After a bit more discussion, Ivan believed it would be better if Ami would ask Ty. They had become friends. She said she wouldn't have put his name into consideration unless she was certain he would agree. Ivan didn't feel it was appropriate for him to ask Ty. He may feel pressured, seeing it more as a voluntold than a volunteer.

The chart was drawn. They further agreed they should have everyone sign an agreement to sire no more than five each. They also added that all turns must be done under supervision on Rasa. Every candidate would be thoroughly evaluated for suitability and stability before undergoing the procedure. It was up to Leo to get more pods set up, or this would take a very long time. Frigg agreed to oversee each turning procedure while Thoth and his team assisted Leo with the STAGs.

Once the meeting ended, Grace pulled Ben aside.

"I'm sorry about Viv bringing up that whole mess with Seshet and Olivia. Those were not some of your best memories."

"It wasn't your fault. It made me think I owe that girl an apology. At least for not stopping what was being done to her." Ben felt horrible about the situation. He hadn't thought about it in a long time.

"She doesn't remember it, Ben. As far as she's concerned, it never happened. You can't apologize to her," Grace said.

That was great. One more thing he had to live with. Like he didn't have enough guilt already.

CHAPTER FIFTEEN

Three days weren't supposed to feel like three years. The renovations took longer than Viv had planned, thanks to Nyx and her extravagant demands. Both sports fields, the market area, and all the common areas now had "natural" emulated sunlight with a time-appropriate sunrise, sunset, and shadowing for whatever planet she had dreamed up in her mind. Nyx's quarters were fit for an actual queen, although even Frigg found them over the top. And she had taken credit for all of it, even though she had done nothing to help execute her rigorous demands. Viv had no problem being a team player as long as there was an actual team.

Other than that, things had been quiet. Too quiet for Ben's taste. He had fully expected the Council to have made a move by now. It was unsettling. They had been monitoring the other dimensions, collecting allies, spreading the word, checking for energy shifts. There was nothing. There had to be something going on. He had a sense there was something more.

Grace had other things on her mind.

"I don't understand how you have the ability to control it and I can't, that's all. I can feel what you're doing. I can see exactly how you're doing it. I simply can't."

"You're trying too hard, Grace. Let go. Let it take over. It's like shifting. I see it doing what I want, and it does it. I'm not concentrating on it." Ivan was trying to be supportive. He didn't know how he could do something she couldn't.

Grace sat on the ground. She was frustrated. He was not only able to convert the energy Nyx was throwing at him, he could control it and send it back. Make it dance, send it on a path looping around the forest and back again. When she changed it, if she could change it, the best she had been able to do was deflect it to move on a sporadic path in an uncontrollable direction, like striking a ball with a warped bat. She picked at a chunk of ice and chucked it so hard into a tree behind Ivan, the trunk exploded into a shower of splinters. Ivan had to phase to keep from being pelted.

"Sorry," she said sullenly.

"What's the real problem, Grace? You've had something else on your mind for days. I can see you're blocking it from me. What are you afraid of?" he questioned sympathetically.

"I'm not afraid of anything. I'm worried."

"Worried about what?" he asked.

She shook her head, unwilling to answer him. He may not want to know the answer.

"Grace. We can't figure out a way to get past this if you don't tell me."

"You killed her, Ivan. What's going to stop the others from doing the same? From turning against the community. I'm worried that we're going to turn a traitor, and everything we've built will decay from the inside," she said meekly.

"Going to? Or already have?"

"Not you. You know I don't mean you. But if you could kill your sire, what's stopping the others from doing it?"

"You know that was different. For a lot of reasons."

"I know." She sunk lower. It had been weighing on her.

"Okay. Let's talk about why it was different." He sat on the ground next to her. "I never wanted to be turned. Everyone on that list wants to take the turn or they wouldn't be on the list."

"Not Vaeweth," she interjected.

"Oh, so it's Vaeweth you don't trust?"

Grace sighed. "No. I know he was desperate for a way to get out of the situation Kali had him in."

"Then who? Anybody?" he asked.

Grace shrugged and threw another piece of ice.

"The second way my turn was different was I woke up to something horrific. I didn't have anyone to help me. She made sure I would be isolated. None of these people will be forced to go through that."

"I know that too," she said.

"The last thing is I was different. The hatred I had for her was greater than the love I previously held or the draw I had to her as my sire. She didn't turn me because she cared for me or was concerned for me or wanted to bring me into her clan. I was turned as an act of revenge. Her hatred fueled me. I felt the loathing she had felt for me. That isn't going to happen here either."

"I know all of that. I felt it in your nightmares. It doesn't explain why or how it could happen." Grace had been floundering in her own anxiety.

"No. It doesn't. I don't have an explanation. What I can say is, we are only turning those who want to take the turn. We're doing the best we can to evaluate and support them. Once they take the turn, the whole community will be able to feel their emotions, especially their sires. I don't know what else we can do to make this safer for everyone."

"Deep down, I know what you're saying is true. Maybe because my turn wasn't like everyone else's. It was gradual for me. I didn't have to die for it. I didn't lose my connections to the outside and instantly become connected to everyone else."

"How am I supposed to stop your obsession with the worst-case scenario?" This was one situation he couldn't talk her down from. If she couldn't resolve it on her own, she wouldn't be able to move forward. He only had one idea, and it was really going to suck for him.

She saw what it was the moment he thought about it.

"No. I can't do that to you again," she said pityingly.

"I don't think you have another choice," he said, a little dismayed. "I'll be fine. Go. Take Ty with you. He's the most observant person I know. He'll be able to see things you can't." Ivan delivered his words with the heaviness of dread they deserved for him.

"Are you sure? We can wait until after dinner. You could come with me," she suggested.

"No, I need to keep my perspective. I don't want to know what's going to happen. I don't want to be constantly second-guessing myself if the choices I make will change what should take place. It's better you do it now. It'll be worse for me on a full stomach." He was already feeling nauseous remembering the last time.

Grace placed her head on his shoulder. She didn't want to hurt him. He was right, though. She had to see. If she didn't see, she may never be able to get over what was holding her back.

He rubbed her back and kissed the top of her head.

"Go. Before I come to my senses and tell you it's a bad idea." He pushed her to get up.

"I'm going. I'll bring Ty back and we'll shift from here so no one else sees."

He nodded at her, then leaned back against the tree behind him to prepare himself for what would be coming.

About ten minutes later, they were back.

"Are you certain this is an appropriate journey? Is it safe?" Ty asked.

"I need to see, Ty."

"Yes, but two of you in a future timeline? Is it wise? Where will we go that you won't be recognized? Where you won't run into yourself?" He thought that was the most appropriate question.

"The way I figure, it doesn't matter where I go. I'll already know I've done it. Either I'll make sure I stay away from myself, or I'll seek myself out, won't I?" She had put a lot of thought into time shifting since she had first done it with Nyx.

He pondered that for nearly a full minute. She could see him debating the statement within himself.

"Then when are you proposing we go to? A month, a year, five years? How far will be far enough to rest your mind?" His question was reasonable.

She glanced back at Ivan sitting against the tree. "Any suggestions?"

He had his eyes closed. He spoke without opening them. "I think a year should be enough. Don't stay too long. Find out what you need to know and get back. Do you remember how to come back to this exact time and place?"

"Yes. I remember."

"Now, you should decide where," Ty said. "What would be the best place to get information without raising suspicion?"

Grace already knew where she was going. She had decided the moment Ivan had suggested it. "Chaos."

"You mean The Nothing? Grace, I can't survive there." Ty was jittery.

"No, I mean the consciousness. We're going to find Chaos." She was adamant that was where she needed to go.

Ty gasped, "Grace! I can't. I shan't. What if Chaos is in *Chaos*? Ivan, you should be the one to go." He couldn't have ever imagined she would suggest something so ludicrous. So dangerous. He was completely unnerved.

"No, no, no. No! I'm not doing that." Ty shook his head. "I'll stay back here and wait. I'll wait right here." He was prattling.

Ivan glanced up at Grace. "I think you've broken him."

"I think you're right. Well, how do you feel about meeting your mother?" Grace offered weakly.

"On the fence. But I guess it's as good a time as any." Ivan had no idea she was thinking about seeing Chaos. He had his own reasons to see Chaos, and it had nothing to do with the future. Ivan got up. He wasn't sure he wanted to find out what would happen on this trip any more than he had been looking forward to being ripped in half again. But Grace was determined to go. Once she had resolved on an idea, there was no talking her out of it.

"Ty." Grace snapped her fingers in front of his face. He was still shaking his head, repeating no to himself under his breath with his eyes closed. He was terrified of the possibility of meeting the strongest being ever imagined.

She snapped her fingers again. "Ty! I'm taking Ivan!" she yelled at him.

He stopped, opened his eyes, and grabbed her arms. "Thank you, Grace. Thank you. I'm sorry. I just can't."

"I know. It was too much to ask. Sit under the tree. We'll be right back." She lowered him down to where Ivan had been sitting.

"Yes. Yes, of course. I'll wait right here," Ty muttered.

"Some great adventurer you got there, honey," she chided Ivan.

"Yeah," he responded in disappointment.

"Shall we?" she asked.

"Lead the way."

Grace took a deep breath, relaxing herself. She concentrated on Chaos and took Ivan's hand.

It was bright enough that Grace saw red through her closed eyelids. When she opened them, the sun shone brilliantly, spilling warmth over her exposed skin.

They were outside on a grassy hill, standing in damp, soft grass a few feet in front of a stream. The field on the other side was filled with wildflowers. Birds chirped softly. Colors were more vivid than either of them had seen anywhere before. Greens, blues, yellows, purples, pinks, and reds. It was more like they had stepped into a crisp, pristine movie set than traveled to the depths of The Everything. They hadn't expected it to be so stunning. They could smell the sweetness of the flowers. Hear the trickling of the water. They heard children giggling and screaming playfully in the distance. It was the most perfect place they could imagine.

They turned to see a woman behind them. She appeared ancient, but young at the same time. Her hair was glistening white with silver streaks, adorned with flowers. She had light wrinkles around her eyes and mouth from an eternity of pleasant thoughts. Her presence projected serenity.

"I wasn't sure you'd be able to find me. No one ever has. How did you do it?"

"I thought of you and when I took Ivan's hand, we shifted here. What is this place?" Grace asked.

"It isn't a place. You're inside my consciousness. This is where I keep all the things I love most. You're inside and outside your shells while inside my thoughts," she observed.

"You didn't shift here. Your shells are here and also still in Hel. But you didn't rise, either. Hmm. Curious," Chaos revealed, raising her eyebrow.

"Then how are we here?" Ivan asked.

"That is not a question I can answer. It is also not your real question, my son. Your real question is *why* are you here?" she replied with a soft smile, touching his shoulder. "You've grown strong," she said proudly.

Ivan felt a warmth spread over him from her hand. It was calming, caring, motherly. It was a sensation he had never expected to have felt again.

"Our path seems to be unclear. We don't know how to do what you created us to do. We need to know how it turns out. That's why we came to see you in our future," Grace pleaded for guidance.

"Oh, Grace," Chaos said with a soft laugh.

It wasn't condescending. It was comforting in an odd way.

She continued, "Time isn't always linear. And it's often not written. You can change it as you wish. You can create the future you hope for. To fully embrace it, you must be open to it. You need to rise together to see what you are capable of."

"But Nyx …" Grace started.

"Doesn't know as much as she thinks she does," Chaos said.

"Then what about the Fates?" Grace was grasping now. Her beliefs about what was real and what wasn't were melting away.

"The Fates are merely record keepers. They track each being's past and present. They have learned how to access thousands of futures for each all at once. Their desire is to persuade others into believing they know the future, but they don't any more than you do. They only see the possibilities. They calculate the probabilities based on your past decisions. Your choices create your timeline. This is only one of them. If you were to go backward from here, you may not have the same past you previously had, as this time hasn't been written into your story yet. I'm sorry, I have no answers for you here. This may not be your path."

"If this is true, how do we save everyone?" Grace wanted to understand how they were supposed to win.

"You can't. You will triumph and you will fail, and you will triumph again, and you will fail again. That's what all life is," Chaos replied. "Your very existence brings balance to mine. I know you feel it here. You will create from what has already fallen. You'll create stars that will fail into black holes. From those, you will create new stars and solar systems, and galaxies. It is a cycle without end as we are a cycle with no end, ever dancing about each other. Everything has a purpose. This is ours. To ensure it all continues in balance."

Grace's head was swimming. This wasn't what she wanted to hear. Ivan was absorbing it much better than she was. He understood his role. While loss affected her emotionally within, he remained undisturbed. He found peace with a balance that she couldn't yet accept.

"What about the Council? They're building a device to flood The Everything with negative energy, to collapse it back into The Nothing. How do we stop them?" Grace was losing her hope that they could fix it.

"You may or may not be able to stop what they are doing. You don't need to. It's not your role. Regardless of what you think you know, what they're doing won't collapse The Everything. Many dimensions would need to be collapsed to make any difference. But you …" She studied them in awe at what she had accomplished with them.

"You are here to create. You're the only ones who can create a scale that would correct the balance. If they collapse a dimension, you will create a new one. But you're not ready yet. You have a very long road to prepare and unlimited time to do it." Chaos now touched Grace's shoulder, giving her a sense of peace she didn't have within.

"Rise. Create. Let the others find a way to come to terms with their enemies. Let them spread your balance, your energy. That isn't your war. War isn't meant for us. We must be the balance, or it will all become The Nothing and we will never be able to move outside of that."

Grace understood the words. She was so torn. How could she possibly abandon her people for another purpose? Even if it was the only way to save The Everything? She didn't know if she could. She didn't feel ready. Moreover, she didn't feel worthy of such a task.

"You must accept your lives will not be the same as in the past. The others will need to save themselves. You have a long road ahead of you, but without you, they have no road at all. Do you understand?"

"Yes, I understand," Ivan replied.

Grace was still unsure. She needed longer to process. Processing information had always taken her a longer time. She wanted to run. When she looked up, they were watching her.

Chaos leaned in toward Ivan, whispering, "I'm proud of you, Ivan. Don't think I love you any less than I love my other children. I created all of you with a purpose. It wasn't their fault they were unable to fulfill it. I love you more because you could. Don't tell Nyx I said that last part." She smiled playfully. "My first children are very jealous." Her tone was still light, although the edge of it contained a warning.

She looked back at Grace. "You'll have to help her understand, Ivan. She's fragile. Her vulnerability is her strength. Her bottomless capacity for love is her strength."

"I know it is." He smiled at Grace in a melancholy way.

"One thing I can tell you: Ker is somehow involved. Nyx will be furious about that. Use that fury to help your people. Let Nyx take on that fight," Chaos said to them both.

"You need to stay on your path. You need to go back. If you stay too long, you won't be able to leave. I will see you both again. But not soon."

They were back exactly where they had been. Their bodies hadn't moved. They hadn't even been gone for a millisecond. No time had passed. Chaos had pushed them back to the exact moment they had left.

"I'll wait right here. Go ahead," Ty said, still staring at them. He had no perception of their journey.

Ivan looked down at him. He thought better of telling him what had happened.

"I think we've decided it's better not to go. Knowing the future may be the thing that changes it in a way we don't want." He gave Grace a quick glance.

Even in her mildly incapacitated state, she had caught on to what Ivan was saying.

"I think I'll go for a run instead. Try to shake it off in my own way," she replied in a monotone, disconnected voice.

Ivan placed his forehead against hers, grasping the back of her neck. He kissed her quickly on the lips.

"I'll get Ty back. I think we traumatized him enough for one day."

Grace didn't reply. She backed away slowly, then turned and ran. With so much to process, she felt like she'd be running in this dark forest for days. Her mind drifted. She preferred running in the sunny mountain trails on Rasa. After a few minutes, she realized her mind had brought her where she yearned to be. She stopped at the top of a cliffside to take in the view before she began to run again.

This was her home. These people were her people. Why was she constantly being forced to leave the things she cared for? Why did she need to choose? She could shift anywhere she wanted, any time she wanted. Why couldn't she and Ivan live here and still do what they were being asked? They needed to live somewhere, didn't they? This was as good a place as any she could think of. Chaos hadn't told her she had to leave here. Chaos only really said they couldn't take on the fight and save The Everything simultaneously.

Grace had run well into the night convincing herself she was right. She made every argument to justify her ideas. She didn't want Ivan to have a single objection she couldn't counter. It was imperative for her to stay and remain connected to these people. To remember who they were doing all of this for. Even if she couldn't fight alongside them, she couldn't leave them either.

Ivan was waiting for her when she got home. It was three in the morning. All she could think about was a shower. She would talk to him after. He was in the living room reading. He didn't come into the bedroom when he felt her shift in. She took off her uniform, placing it into the sanitizer. Wonderful little device, that was. Hang the clothes inside. Two minutes later, they were as fresh as you would get from any dry cleaner. Laundry was one horrible chore she would never miss.

She asked Ida to play some loud bluesy rock as she made her way to the shower. She turned the water on as hot as she could stand it. The steaming drops smelled like rain as they poured over her hair and skin. She allowed her mind to drift as she wondered how they made it smell like that. The water reclamation they had in place recycled every drop with no hint of chemicals or minerals. It was soft and relaxing, taking her back to the hot springs she would visit in Saturnia, without all the sulfur odors. She must have stood there for at least thirty minutes, losing track of time, before finally emerging refreshed.

She walked back into the bedroom to find Ivan had turned the lights on low. He had taken her uniform out of the sanitizer and hung it in her closet. Her favorite sleeping outfit, flannel shorts and one of his oversized T-shirts, was lying on the bottom corner of the bed.

They didn't need to sleep, but they still liked the ritual of getting into pjs, lying in bed, and catching up on the events of the day. Rasa had their own version of information and entertainment on demand. Anything you wanted produced in a holographic projection whenever you liked. Scheduled weather for the month, community center events, your child's education criteria and results, upcoming votes, and even off-world transport schedules and arrivals were seamlessly delivered for easy consumption.

They also had secure news reports created by Sadie to be informative and entertaining, for those who had access to her. She was doing well in such a short time at figuring out how much each person wanted or needed to see.

Ivan was already under the blankets reading something on his TAC. He didn't look up or say anything to her. Reclining patiently, he waited, giving her time to come to him. He knew it wouldn't do any good to push her or come to her before she was ready.

Grace climbed into bed. She was swiping through reports. After a short time, she had gotten to the list. Ivan started listening in as Sadie reported that only a handful had already taken the turn. Alex had been the first of about one hundred. There were four more pods tested and placed into rotation late the previous night. They had six more in testing and another twenty in various stages of production.

Grace noticed Mikkel hadn't taken the turn yet. Lilly must not be as receptive to his charm and wit as he thought she would be. Mikkel never had much luck with smart women. He somehow managed to come across far shallower than he was. If he couldn't convince her soon, they would need to find another to begin the sire line. Grace paused Sadie's holographic interface. She stared up at the ceiling, which she had painted to reproduce a soothing Monet.

"Have you spoken to Nyx yet?"

"No," he replied without taking his eyes off his TAC display.

"Why not?"

"I'm considering my approach. I want to find the one most likely to result in me leaving without carrying my head in my hands." Ivan was only half joking.

"The direct approach might be best. She'll know if you're lying to her." Grace turned on her side to face him.

He looked down at her.

"And how do you think that conversation is going to go? Grace and I went to visit Chaos without you. And, hey Nyx, by the way, your most horrible child, the one who takes untold pleasure in unbridled destruction and violent death, is helping the Council."

"I see your point. I think today would be a good time to visit Thoth. Having a secondary source may not be a bad idea. Chaos said when we were there that this may not be our path. Maybe Ker isn't helping them yet." Grace had nearly come to terms with what she had been told. Almost.

"That's another thing I've put off long enough. I dislike putting Thoth in this position and not telling the others. If she gets caught, it will destroy him."

"The information has been accurate so far. It will be better for Nyx to think it came through him," Grace added.

"Um," he grunted, only partially agreeing with her. "I think you should talk to Lilly. If she doesn't agree soon, we have to figure out another sire line."

Grace knew what he meant by that. They would need to choose one of the other two options, and she didn't like either choice. She needed Lilly to work out.

CHAPTER SIXTEEN

Moving day. Viv and Nyx were making a last walk through. Viv had renamed Hel. It was now designated The Desert. It was better. No one would think of Hel as a desert. It had a sentimental ring for her. Biblical roots of a people wandering, waiting to be welcomed home.

Viv viewed the word differently now. The stories were inspiring. The lessons were important. They molded morality. The view was different, knowing why they had been written the way they were. They were a guidebook on how people should treat each other. Love, peace, consequences.

If taken in their purest form, they showed people how to evolve. Remove the singular, all-knowing deity and the lessons still worked. Remove the manipulated translations by humans vying for power, wanting to control others, and the ideas should have led to prosperous futures for all. Viv preferred the pure meaning of the original texts. Not the unyielding, muddled interpretations used to hold others down. Not how the churches used them to show how they were right and every other religion was wrong. It wasn't meant to be about one group being right. It was meant to show people how to live together in peaceful harmony. How all humans should accept others and work out their differences.

Viv's mind had strayed. She realized she was romanticizing the ability of humans to accept anything different. She was glad her people had a chance to start fresh. It was time to give others the same chance.

"Everything pass your inspection?" she asked Nyx dryly. She didn't want an answer. She didn't think anything would be good enough.

"It will work for now."

The comment had a hint of approval Viv hadn't expected. She barreled on, deciding not to acknowledge the comment.

"The service units are setting up orientation and quarters assignments in the community centers. We can do two groups at a time, starting on the Tenora cruiser in one hour. Do you need to see the schedule?" Viv asked.

"I have it. I'll meet you back here in an hour."

Nyx shifted out before Viv could say anything.

"Sure, I'll stay right here. I didn't need to go back to Rasa for anything," she said out loud to the empty room.

Viv walked across the bridge to check on Morgud and brief her on the schedule. Morgud was conversing with one of the service units. She seemed to enjoy conversation with them. Greater intelligence and none of the emotion to be offended if she said something wrong. Viv thought it good practice for her after being isolated for so long.

She still had the awareness of her surroundings to acknowledge Viv before she had placed the first foot on the bridge. Morgud had made a fine addition to the community. She had a purpose to protect this place now, not simply a fear of consequences for making a mistake.

Viv had asked to be her sire for two reasons. First, Morgud wouldn't extend the line, which took some pressure off Galin. Second, she was strong and proud and completely alone. She had lost everything and had lived in fear most of her days. Morgud reminded Viv of how she had been before she was turned. She had empathy for her, a soft spot for broken things. Viv didn't feel sorry for her or look down on her as some of the others did. She saw a strong woman who needed someone to provide unconditional support.

"Ready for your lesson?" Morgud asked.

She had begun giving Viv self-defense lessons. Viv had not been interested before now. She hadn't had the need, being stronger and faster than humans. This was a different playing field. She wouldn't always be able to run anymore. She wasn't interested in hurting anyone. None of the turned were. They were interested in stopping the Council from hurting others. She only wanted to be able to protect herself. The uniform gave her an advantage, but it may not always be enough. Those coming after them were skilled in matters of war she couldn't comprehend.

"If you don't mind listening to the briefing while we do it," Viv replied.

"You sure it won't be too distracting?"

"I'll manage."

Viv put her uniform into training mode. She had insisted it be added to all uniforms after her first training session with Morgud. It highlighted nonlethal strike zones only, showing moving diagrams of the best forms to use for each probable attack. It also scored how well each strike was delivered or countered and tracked defense postures and blocks.

Morgud put down her spear, leaving her uniform in rest mode. This was early training. Hand to hand only. She was already a skilled warrior before the turn. She was more interested in testing her elevated abilities than testing what the uniform could do for her.

They had been sparring long enough that Viv was out of breath when Grace shifted in, looking for some information on Lilly.

"She's different. Hard to pin down. Twelfth-century Sumatra. Her family was in the spice trade. She was a Buddhist before the turn. Now, not so much," Viv indicated offhandedly.

"How's that supposed to help me?" Grace asked.

"She'll do it. She's dedicated to the community. I'm sure she's enjoying making Mikkel suffer. Buddhists love their suffering. That, and he's being a shit about it. A smug, arrogant little shit." Viv expressed amusement.

"So, he's being himself. Great," Grace snorted.

"What else did you expect?"

"For him to finally take something seriously maybe?" She shook her head. "When do you need me back here?"

"On the hour," Viv replied.

Viv briefed her on the rest of the schedule. Next stop, Lilly, Grace thought to herself before she shifted out.

The lab looked empty. She was sure she had shifted to Lilly. She could feel her standing barely beyond an arm's distance in front of her, but she saw nothing, not even a distortion.

"Put your visor up." Lilly's voice came from exactly where Grace had expected it to.

Grace tapped into surveillance mode. The visor showed Lilly in front of her, with a blue outline flashing around her.

"I couldn't see you in any light range. How are you doing that?"

"Refraction. It's a new camouflage I'm working on. I've set Sadie with an algorithm to detect the refracted light, displaying an image in the visor. She already has the coordinates to where each of us is, which makes it easy for her to detect the patterns. Neat, right?"

"Amazing. I know you're there." She lifted her visor. Now that she understood what she was seeking, she could make out a very slight blurred edge around where Lilly was standing.

"I see a minor distortion." She dropped her visor back down.

"That's only because of your ability. To everyone else, I'm totally invisible. I mean, the turned can feel me, but that's all." She was satisfied with her progress, turning the camouflage off.

"I know why you're here, Grace." Lilly turned her back, making notes on her TAC. "I was wondering how long it would take him to bring out the big guns."

"You honestly think he sends me anywhere?" Grace was amused at the inference.

"I think you'd do anything for your children," Lilly replied, still facing her back to Grace.

"This is to strengthen the community. If you're reluctant to sire one of the lines, we need to look for someone else." Grace didn't address her comment.

Lilly turned, appearing exasperated. "Did you not pay any attention to my report? I didn't say I wouldn't do it. We don't have enough pods to support five lines. We need a minimum of ten per line. My preference would be twenty. We currently have twenty-six active and six in testing to go online today. That is thirty-two. We need eighteen more before we can move forward in earnest. Ty sired his five before he went back. Those are trickling through. Erik and Asta's line takes precedence currently because it includes the remainder of security and the rear guard. Our safety is paramount. If we don't have a secure home world, we can't perform to the level we need. We can't risk bringing outsiders in to take the turn. The other two lines are on hold as well. It wouldn't be responsible for me to start a new line before we can accommodate the others."

"I understand your reasoning, but there wasn't a report from you in Sadie's system this morning," Grace stated adamantly.

Lilly looked smug. "Sadie, where is my report from last night?"

"Your report is in draft. It has not been finalized for release," stated Sadie.

Lilly's confidence deflated. She opened her mouth to speak, then shut it again. She squirmed before finally saying, "Sadie, finalize and release my draft report."

Grace restrained herself from saying "I told you so." Her look, however, betrayed her thought.

"When are you going to tell him?"

"When he stops thinking he can get me to give in by flirting with me," Lilly retorted.

"You haven't shut him down, which you easily could have," Grace countered. She saw Lilly was taking enjoyment in the process. She couldn't be certain if Lilly liked the flirting or liked seeing him suffer more.

"Not the point. You don't ask to be sired by someone you don't know by flirting. It's disrespectful. I'm not one of his conquests. I deserve more respect than that. He needs to treat me as an equal and take it seriously. This isn't a game, and I am not now, nor will ever be, his mate," Lilly defended.

"He uses humor when he can't face the seriousness of a situation. You'll see that side of him after he's turned. I suggest you have it out with him. Make sure he understands you won't tolerate him being flippant with you. I'm not going to interfere. I needed to make sure you were on board and we didn't need to start this process over." Grace's words were more than a suggestion. She had bigger things to deal with than playing peacemaker between Lilly and Mikkel.

Ivan and Nyx were already waiting when Grace shifted into the community center. They would be transporting nearly four thousand family members today into groups. They would use both community centers for orientation and assigning quarters. Each community center held five hundred. Orientation would be roughly thirty minutes. If everything went as planned, their part would be over in half a day.

They shifted the groups directly into Hel's main hall. No reason they should see what was outside of this place. It was safer if they didn't know where they were. They weren't prisoners. They could leave if they wanted. Leaving needed to be controlled for everyone's safety. If they chose to leave, they needed to be entranced into forgetting this place, which they had agreed to before coming here.

Things were going smoothly. Grace and Ivan sat in the back of the third group of the day.

"Did you talk to her yet?"

"Thoth was testing the pods earlier. I haven't been able to see him yet. I can't talk to her until after," Ivan replied.

Grace concentrated on locating Thoth. "He's in the dining hall. Why don't you go now? Nyx and I can finish up here. There are only a few hundred left. I'll catch up with you after."

"Let me know if you run into any trouble."

"You mean other than the Queen of Hel?" Grace nodded toward Nyx.

Ivan smiled and walked out the door before shifting into the hallway outside the dining hall.

CHAPTER SEVENTEEN

Ivan sat at the table across from Thoth.

"I think it's time we had that talk," he said, signaling for Thoth to turn off his BAT.

Thoth complied. The dining hall was close to empty. Ivan estimated two dozen without looking. Maybe another half dozen service units. Not too crowded to have the conversation without looking suspicious. He had thought about going to a secure area, but he didn't want to chance Sadie would record the conversation. Common areas' audio wasn't recorded unless there was suspicious activity. There was always video. He pulled out his TAC, then ordered a sandwich and a dark ale so he wouldn't appear out of place.

"I was wondering when you would come." Thoth was ready.

"It's only been a few days. The fewer times we do this, the better for her," Ivan replied.

"I still can't believe she's in there with them. I'd feel better if we had a way to get her out." Thoth was still angry at her.

"It was her idea. When she's ready, we can get her out. I can get her out." Ivan didn't think that made Thoth any less concerned. Ivan could shift to her and snatch her out at a moment's notice. The only problem was, how could she let them know? Grace had given her the perfect cover, branding her with the same betrayal as the others. The words Grace spoke to Kali made sure the Council thought Ma'at was still on their side, not even telling her husband what she knew.

When Ivan and Grace had investigated the Council members' thoughts, Ma'at told them to turn her away with the others. She could do more for them on the inside. Nyx saw it because she was touching Ivan. Thoth had been caught off guard but immediately understood what she was doing. When she grabbed his arm, he read her soul. His anger that day had been real. His apparent disappointment was worry. He had been terrified of her being caught.

Ivan connected with Thoth first. Then he called out to her.

Can you talk?

Ma'at nearly spit her tea on Osiris. She made a display of coughing, motioning to him it was hotter than she expected, as she answered Ivan telepathically.

I'm not alone. Hold on so I can excuse myself.

"I am so sorry, Osiris," she coughed. "Drinking and breathing are two activities one should never indulge in simultaneously." She continued coughing. She had intentionally spilled a small amount on her shirt. They had been having lunch when Ivan interrupted.

"Are you all right?" he asked.

She held up her hand and coughed a bit more and wiped at her shirt with a napkin. "Please excuse me for a moment. I should get this before the stain sets."

"Of course. Take your time," Osiris answered.

Ma'at proceeded slowly to the restroom as she walked and blotted at her shirt. She understood the information flow needed to be one way. She wouldn't ask any questions of her own. If she didn't know, she couldn't tell.

I'm alone. I only have a few minutes.

We're getting nervous waiting for an attack. We need to know what's going on there, Thoth spoke through Ivan's connection. Ivan let him take the lead.

Ma'at started to tear up at the sound of his voice. She coughed to cover her reaction.

There's a lot of discord here. The tension is palpable. Several Council members are questioning their plan after seeing Ivan and Grace's display of abilities. They are earnestly discussing giving them a chance. She stepped through the restroom door. There were three people in the room. She grabbed a small cloth from a tray on the counter and stood at the sink, daubing at her shirt.

And the others? Ivan asked.

Terribly angry. Grace did call Kali out in front of all the pantheon leaders. She has all the most heinous, vile members on her side calling for an all-out war. The only thing stopping her is that she doesn't have the votes. She can't afford to make her move without them. If she did, the rest of the Council would throw their loyalties over to you, Ma'at finished, wiping at her shirt.

She stepped into one of the stalls, sitting on the seat lid. After removing her shirt, she examined it meticulously for any stains she may have missed. She needed to make certain she didn't look suspicious if anyone was watching her.

When you say most vile, who are we talking about? Anyone we can persuade? Ivan wanted her to say it without him prodding too much or raising Thoth's suspicion.

I doubt it. Mostly the expected warmongers. Anhur, Moloch, Ares, Toci, Sekhmet, Irkalla, Oro, a handful of others, and Zeus, of course. After what a fool Nyx made of him, even Hera can't talk sense into him now. There are whispers of Ker being here too, but I haven't seen her. I hope to never see her. She's not part of any pantheon, so that may only be rumor to create fear since Nyx has come against them. Ma'at stayed inside the stall until the others left the restroom. She moved back to the sink to wash her hands, taking an extra minute to touch up her makeup.

Where are you? Thoth asked.

I don't know. We're given different port codes every time we leave. Coming back, we go through three separate port stations and are given different codes at each one for the next. Ma'at dried her hands.

What about the energy weapon? Are they making any progress? Thoth continued his questioning.

I don't think so. And I can't afford to draw attention by asking about anything. They're watching everyone. They're afraid of something big. She made a final check in the mirror, turned, and walked out the door. She smiled at Osiris, looking apologetic as she walked back to the table.

I'll try to get more when I can. Give me a few days. I have to go.

"Osiris, I am incredibly embarrassed. I hope I didn't get any tea on you." She hadn't skipped a beat, bouncing between the two conversations.

Stay safe, Thoth concluded.

Ma'at smiled just a bit wider at Osiris before she sat to continue their lunch conversation.

Ivan ended the link with Ma'at. He scrolled through Lilly's report that had posted since he looked this morning. As he read it, he continued the conversation with Thoth.

I recognized most of the names Ma'at said, but who's Ker? Ivan wanted to bring it up specifically so Thoth would remember Ma'at providing the information.

She's an especially nasty thing. She revels in destruction of any kind. The more violent and cruel the death, the happier she is. She is feral and vicious. And she's Nyx's daughter. Thoth made fleeting eye contact with Ivan.

Ivan sighed, finished his lunch, finished reading the report, and folded his TAC. He motioned to Thoth to turn his BAT back on before he left. Today's conversation gave Thoth some sense of relief.

For Ivan, the conversation had led to exactly what he had needed it to. All he had left was to reveal the information to Nyx. She wasn't going to take it well. He couldn't be sure Nyx wouldn't go off half-cocked, hanging Ma'at out in the process. He needed to be careful about how he presented it.

A few minutes later, Ivan stood in front of Nyx, who did not take the accusation well at all. Ivan saw the anger welling in the way she tightened her posture. Her temper was quick. Her eyes blackened. The hue of her hair transformed into a deep shade of blood red. She was oozing black. He wasn't altogether sure she wouldn't explode. He grabbed her arm hard as she tried to shift away. Ivan pulled back. She tried harder until the two became a blurred tug of war. Blinking back and forth, half in and half out. The power struggle began to shake the room. She didn't have the ability to slide away from him, making her even angrier.

Sadie had had enough. She sent a high voltage shock through them, giving Ivan the upper hand. He pulled hard, sending them both tumbling to the floor. He had thought about phasing, letting her pass through him and hit the quartz floor hard. Ultimately, he decided that would only make her disposition worse. Instead, he braced his back to hit the stone. He was relieved to find the impact absorbed by his uniform. The fall wouldn't have done any actual damage to him, but he was glad to have not felt the pain, nonetheless. Nyx's small frame impacted lightly on top of him, facing away. He wrapped his arms around her arms and waist the way you would a small child throwing a temper tantrum. To her disappointment, she wasn't going anywhere.

"Calm down!" he said forcefully, squeezing her.

She shook, breathing heavily. Her appearance changed back.

"Get off me!" she shouted at him, squirming.

"No. I'm not letting you out of here like this."

Ivan somehow managed to get to his feet while holding on to her. She was strong. She slammed the back of her head into his face. His blood dripped into her hair before his broken nose and the gash in his lip healed. He released his right arm from her waist, pulling her into a modified choke hold. With his left arm, he wiped the remaining blood from his face while she dangled like a rag doll, her feet several inches off the floor. That was much better. He could hold her like this for days if necessary.

"I can do this forever," he said to her.

"How can you treat me this way? Please! Let me go." She sobbed hard. Her body had gone limp.

"Not buying it. Crocodile tears don't work on me. I see what you're thinking. As soon as I loosen my grip, you'll try to shift again," Ivan stated calmly.

Immediately, she began kicking at him again. She reached up to scratch his face. He phased his head, letting her hands flail in the air as she let out a guttural scream.

"If you saw what I was thinking so clearly, I wouldn't have blood in my hair!" She spat at him.

"Think about that. I could have let you hit me, or I could have phased out and let you snap your own neck, or I could have phased solid and let you hurt yourself. Only one of these options made you slightly less angry."

She stopped kicking him, hanging off his arm. He let her hang until he felt her rage drop to a simmer. Neither said anything. Time passed until her mood reduced to merely angry. They were both too stubborn to speak first. The first one who speaks has lost the argument. Nyx crossed her arms, hanging for nearly an hour. Ivan had flipped out his TAC and began reading in silence.

To an outsider, it looked like every sibling argument that had ever taken place anywhere in The Everything. One sibling dominating the other. Neither was ready to admit defeat. It was a standoff. Another hour passed. Nothing moved except Ivan's eyes as he read. Nyx's rage had softened into irritation at being rendered ineffective.

It was no longer about being angry. It was about who could outlast the other. Nyx had never lost. Ivan never had a sibling to torment. They were both stubborn.

"How long has this been going on?" Grace asked Frigg as she entered The Six.

"I don't know. They were already at it when I got here."

She was sitting at the planning table with the list pulled up. It had become far larger than it had been only a few days ago. Ami was working diligently at getting the word out. The response was tremendous. There were more than thirty humanoid species on the list, totaling close to one hundred thousand individuals. It was a relatively small sample of each of their populations. No group was going all in, but they wanted representation within the community. It showed they wanted to support the cause and be remembered as ones who stepped up to help once The Everything was safe.

"This isn't sustainable. We need a solution." Frigg slumped back in her chair.

"I'd give it a couple more hours," Grace replied.

"What?"

"I don't see any harm in letting them stay like that for a while." Grace watched Ivan and Nyx frozen in mutual determination.

"I don't care about them. The list. We need another way to turn. I've been pushing them through as fast as possible, and this list is only growing. Even if we had all five hundred pods fit with STAG units, we could have difficulty keeping up." Frigg was frustrated.

"Lilly said they would have six more online today. That will bring you up to thirty-two. How many can you turn in a day with thirty-two pods?" Grace asked.

"We have the process down to twenty-three minutes for most species. Cleaning and prep time for each pod, twelve minutes. Thirty minutes of diagnostics twice a day." Frigg did the calculations in her head.

"One thousand three hundred sixteen per day, given no issues arise. That's running twenty-five/five. Just to get through this list would take seventy-six days.

That's three months here. And for each one we turn from the list, another two are added. I can't keep up this pace. Twenty minutes in a restoration pod, ten-minute showers. It's harrowing."

"Can one STAG run more than one pod?" The question made sense to Grace. It was basically just an accelerator, wasn't it?

"I'm more skilled in the biological side of things. That's a question for engineering." Frigg took a few more swipes at the data in front of her. "But maybe …" she trailed off. "Huh. Maybe," she continued to herself.

"That's it!" Frigg exclaimed. She quickly folded her TAC, shutting off the data stream in front of her. She immediately instructed Sadie to allow her to port out and disappeared.

Once Frigg was gone, Grace turned back to Ivan and Nyx. She decided their little standoff was unproductive. Neither would give in.

"Both of you stop behaving like children. It's time to rise and give the Council a proper show. If they have members on the fence about our ability to save The Everything, we need to knock them off." Grace had made up her mind. They were going to do it their own way. They could do what they were created for and win this one. Chaos said victories and losses. Grace had decided this would be a victory.

They both looked at her. Neither budging. Grace strode over to them, grabbing Nyx by the wrist. She phased her, yanking her straight through Ivan's arm.

"I win. Now apologize to each other." Grace leered at them, raising one eyebrow. Challenging them to say something smart to her. It was time to move forward.

Ivan and Nyx both glanced down at their feet, then at each other. The corners of their mouths were downturned. Nyx scrunched her nose. Ivan rolled his eyes. "Sorry," they said in unison to each other.

"How do we do this?" Grace cocked her head to the left, raising her eyebrows.

Nyx straightened her back, taking a commanding posture. She had been trying to get them to rise for days. Suddenly, now they thought it was important. She wondered what had changed.

"The first few times, it will be easier if you sit." She took three chairs from the table, lining them up. She sat in the center one. Grace sat to her left, Ivan to her right.

"Close your eyes and relax."

They did as she said.

"Reach inside. Deep down in the center of your chest. That need to expand, the one you have been surrounding with fear, holding in. You feel it?"

"Yes," they answered.

"Good. Let it burn. Let it grow and fill you until you feel your insides will burst through your skin," she said, slowly building her own need to rise.

"When the pressure is so great you can no longer hold it in, push, hard." Nyx pushed outward, streaming from her shell.

Grace and Ivan felt her doing the same. The euphoria was exhilarating. They were untethered from their shells. They were unrestricted, floating above themselves. It was neither hot nor cold, bright nor dark, loud nor quiet. They felt nothing and everything.

When they rose, tendrils of their essences reached for each other, pulling them together as one. They saw each other as white smoky figures inside of an unseen membrane that held them loosely together. One being, two consciousnesses. Their forms were ghostly shapes, shifting, gliding, not quite holding any form. They could see each other clearly, but not as physical shapes. They each swung their view outward.

Another translucent shape appeared before them. It was Nyx. Her essence wasn't dark as they had expected. It was bright. Dimmer than they were. Still, on its own, bright. It had smoky tendrils swirling around it. It was the way Ivan had seen her, swirling under her skin, after he had taken off the watch the first time.

They drifted higher as though they were floating out to sea, letting the tide determine their path. They saw their shells beneath them, disconnected as though they were viewing strangers. Unseen strings pulled them higher upward through the ceiling. They passed through the layers of quartz and graphene, absorbing Sadie's knowledge as they rose.

They passed slowly through the remaining floors between their bodies and the sky. It mesmerized those who saw them, bathed in their warm glow. People were overcome with peace and comfort. Even with Nyx beside them, their presence affected everyone. Their calm spread through walls and floors. Their entire population felt them whether they saw them or not. All the turned felt them more deeply than the others. Even Ben, who had been immune to them in their shells, was overcome with contentment, reprieving him from his lifetime of torturous thoughts.

They rose out into the open common area. Their brightness rivaled the sun in ways. In other ways, it was soft. It could be looked upon by everyone and absorbed. They continued upward through the daytime sky, through the blockers that covered the planet. From the space above, they could look back down at their lovely, pristine planet and out into the deepest parts of their universe. They understood everything surrounding them. They were at peace within themselves and with each other.

Movement was effortless as they traveled through the universe, feeling where they needed to go. The flow of energy took on the principles of a river current. They saw flows of light and dark. They saw the mesh that held it all in place. With only a thought, they could heal a black hole or restore a dying star. Little by little, they could mend tiny bits. Reverse the damage that had been done through eons of decay. It was small. It was a beginning.

Now you understand. It was Nyx's voice. It was a whisper and an echo. Muted and thunderous. There and not there.

They didn't answer. It hadn't been a question. Nyx knew what they would feel. She couldn't have begun to explain what they were experiencing now. They had to rise to truly understand.

Time didn't matter here. Nothing mattered here, and at the same time, everything mattered. The need to create took them over. They absorbed negative energy, changing it. Pushing it back out. Small bits at once. It was enough. They had done what they came to do. Every living entity in this universe having the capability had taken notice of them. They had changed enough to make a marked difference to anyone looking, one tiny bit at a time.

It's time to go back. Remember what you've learned. They heard Nyx's there-and-not-there voice again.

They didn't want to stop, but they needed to. They would learn how to do more, and they would come back.

CHAPTER EIGHTEEN

"What are you doing, Ami?" Ben asked.

Ami was sitting on the center of the plan table with her legs crossed, facing him. There was a multilevel board game in front of her, partially blocking her face.

"Watching," she replied.

She reached out, moving a game piece from the bottom tier edge to one of the center tiers. Ben sat in a chair close to her, facing the three shells of Ivan, Nyx, and Grace.

"How are they?" He wrinkled his forehead, scrutinizing the empty bodies in front of him more closely.

"The same as yesterday." She didn't look up from her game. She sucked in her lower lip, squinting at the move Sadie had made.

Ben could feel the residual calmness that had planted itself inside of him. It had grown into what he could only imagine was contentment. He wondered if it would last after they were back. He missed their presence, missed talking to them. Despite the situation, he remained unconcerned. Grace didn't need his protection anymore. She had become what she needed to be. What they needed her to be. He was clear now. Grace and Ivan had their part to play: balancing The Everything. The rest of them had another task: protecting those who lived in The Everything. It seemed Ben wasn't done being a protector. He smirked as his gaze glazed over. He guessed he would never be done being a protector. It was what he had been born for.

He shook it off, spinning the chair to face Ami.

"Where do you think they are?"

"Everywhere," she responded, simply searching for her next move in the game.

"I guess they are," he contemplated, as he spun back slowly to watch the empty shells.

"Have you considered taking the turn, Ami?" Ben swung his chair around to view her reaction.

"I can't." Ami was blank. Her body language was relaxed. Her facial expression hadn't changed.

"Why not?" He was curious.

"This body isn't mine. The woman who used to live in here traded me. She got to go to Heaven so I could use her form. If I took the turn, I couldn't stay in it. It would be empty. No soul at all." Ami made another board move, then grinned broadly.

"It doesn't have a soul now, does it?" Ben's eyes narrowed.

Ami leaned over, resting on her elbow to see Ben around the board. It was simple. She thought everyone knew how it worked.

"No, but if this body dies, even for a second, it revokes my permission to live in her. She would get to stay in Heaven because I broke the agreement, and I wouldn't be allowed back in her body." She shrugged, sat back up, and tried to decipher the move Sadie had made while she had been distracted.

Ben frowned, furrowing his brow. He tried to estimate how dangerous a turned individual without an essence would be. The havoc and potential devastation it could cause the community would be difficult to deal with. It was only a guess, though. He wasn't even sure a biological shell could be animated without an essence.

The knowledge didn't help with his own decision. The small taste of what he was feeling from the rise was enough to make him want more of a connection to the turned community. He was also worried it would leave him too vulnerable to their persuasion. He had historically been able to make the hard decisions because of his ability to remain disconnected. It was an impossible decision for him. He had spent his life doing what was right. When would what he wanted matter? Even the times when he was the center of attention, he was the outsider. His only real solid connection was with his sons. Soon, that would pale for them against the connection they had to the community.

After Mikkel took the turn, he wouldn't have anything left that was wholly his. He felt the other two beginning to drift away already. It was subtle. It would be slow. He would eventually be alone. He was beginning to see why Mikkel was so desperate to make the turn. It was hard enough for Ben. Mikkel hadn't spent a single second of his existence without his brothers. Now that they were becoming distant, it had to be agonizing for him.

~~~~

Mikkel awoke in a cold, panicked sweat. His mind was quiet, and it terrified him. He had to concentrate on connecting to Erik and Alex. What had always been natural for him was something he now needed to force into happening. He could feel that he would be entirely disconnected from them soon. The feeling of his loss overrode the feeling of soothing from Grace and Ivan's rise. He was being pulled toward the community in general. And he was being pulled away from his brothers in the way they had been connected before.

He hadn't had a proper night of sleep in over a week. He forced himself out of bed. His head ached; his muscles ached. He couldn't concentrate on anything. Dark circles surrounded his sunken eyes. There was only one thing he could think to do.

Mikkel staggered down the long hallway to a small lab at the end of the R&D floor. He couldn't even concentrate enough to open a port. He was barefoot, wearing the same sweatpants and T-shirt he had been wearing for the last three
~~~~

days. Before he had gotten to the end, he heard a loud thumping beat. As he got closer, it became some horrible noise that he believed in no way passed for music.

Mikkel opened the door, fending off an attack on his senses. The room was smaller than the others he had been in. The walls were brightly colored in shades that normally shouldn't go together but somehow worked. Half the open floor space was taken over by holograms and calculation tables and diagrams he couldn't decipher. Lilly had her back to him as she interacted with the data, appearing oblivious to the auditory antagonist that accosted him. Any other day, he would have found the scene entertaining. Today, it was an assault on what senses he had left. She spun around, almost colliding with him, came to a dead stop, and cut off the music. Her face shifted from surprise to anger, finally resting on concern.

"You look like shit." She swiped at the hologram, pushing it into a jumbled mess in the corner of the room.

"Yeah, I feel like shit." He crossed the room and sat on a stool at one of the counters.

"Why are you here and not in medical?"

"It's not a medical issue, Lilly. I need to turn. I'm losing them." His voice cracked.

She could see how much more difficult the effects of his brothers' turns were for him. As a scientist, it was an interesting dynamic. As the friend he was becoming, it was hard to watch. She was also cynical that he may be perpetrating a maneuver to get what he wanted.

"Mikkel, if this is another one of your games, I'm not interested. I have work to do. If you're not going to take this seriously, you shouldn't do it at all." She placed her hand on her hip, shifting her weight to her left foot.

"No, Lilly, it's not a game. I can't hear them anymore. It's too quiet. I feel empty." His posture sunk. He looked defeated. It had been hard for him to confess it to her, but he had to trust someone.

"Mikkel, we've discussed this already. It wouldn't be responsible to start another line yet. Frigg is working on a way to turn larger groups at once, but right now we don't have enough pods to turn more," Lilly explained.

Mikkel reached out, grabbing Lilly's forearm firmly but not hard.

"I'm not asking to start the line. I know I can be an ass sometimes. I am aware you think everything's a joke to me. This isn't a joke, Lilly. I am taking this seriously. I need your help. The quiet is driving me crazy."

Lilly saw his desperation. She tightened her mouth. "This is against my better judgment."

Mikkel sprang to his feet. "Thank you, Lilly!" He grabbed her, hugging her tightly. She broke away from him, holding him back at arm's length. He threw up his hands, stepping back.

"Whoa. Back off. There are ground rules!" she exclaimed.

"Anything you want."

"Rule one. I will not now nor at any time in the future be your mate. Is that clear?"

"Crystal, I see you like a sister."

"Rule two. Don't ever lie to me. EVER." Lilly had heard enough lies to last her a lifetime.

"I swear," Mikkel agreed.

"Okay. Last one. Stop being such a dick all the time." She narrowed her eyes. This was the rule he was least likely to be able to keep.

"To you or to everyone?" he questioned.

"To me."

"Agreed. I will stop being such a dick to you," he answered hastily.

Lilly sighed. "Why do I feel like I just sold my soul?" She understood how difficult it was to be alone even when you're surrounded by people. She was skeptical if being tied to him for eternity was the best idea. Trouble followed him like a clingy ex-girlfriend.

"What's next? Do we go up to medical now?"

"What's next is I get us moved up the list." She scrunched up her nose. "You get a shower."

"Yes, ma'am."

"Be back here in twenty minutes. I'll give you a crash course on the turn."

"I already know what to expect. I've sat through Erik's and Alex's turns," Mikkel argued.

"Hey! My rules, remember? I'm not shortcutting this. You get the same information as everyone else. You're lucky I'm not testing your mental stability."

"Understood. We do it your way. Be right back." With a renewed sense of hope, Mikkel was able to open a port back to his room.

After Mikkel left, Lilly ported up to Frigg's office next to the med lab they were using for turning.

"It's time. He's getting worse." Lilly dropped into a chair across from Frigg's workstation.

"He lasted longer than I thought he would," Frigg replied without moving. "Is Ami still in The Six?"

"Yes. Is it ready?" Lilly asked.

"It's ready. Give me an hour to get set up."

When Lilly and Mikkel arrived at The Six, Frigg was already there. Ami was still playing her game with Sadie, and Ben had left before Frigg had begun setting up.

"Gram? Why are we here? I thought we were going to medical." Mikkel shifted his focus between Frigg and Lilly.

Frigg reached out, waving them over to an elevated table. It wasn't one of the STAG pods. He couldn't figure out what was going on.

"We're going to try something a little different."

"How different? And why is Ami here?" He frowned, rubbing the back of his neck.

"Just a precaution." Frigg waved her hands slowly in front of her. "Ami was at Erik's and Alex's turns, too. Your biology is different, like theirs. I want to monitor you individually, not with a group." She tried to soothe him.

"Nice try, Gram. How different?" Mikkel asked again.

Frigg sighed. "We're not using a STAG. We have programmed the nanites to use the same properties, and Sadie will be monitoring and adjusting their core properties throughout the process."

"So, I'm a guinea pig." He began to sweat.

Frigg squinted at him. "I don't understand that reference."

"Lab rat. I'm a lab rat," he retorted, rubbing his throat. He was clearly uncomfortable.

She still didn't get it. She shook her head quickly. "This is a new procedure. We've run hundreds of simulations. I have no concerns at all. You know I'd never do anything to put you at risk."

"Uh-huh," he replied cynically.

He turned to Lilly, glaring at her. As soon as he started to open his mouth, she cut him off.

"Rule three." She smiled halfheartedly.

"Yeah, rule three." He tapped his foot, sucking his teeth. "What do you want me to do?" he finally acquiesced.

"Strip down to your shorts and lie on the table, please." Frigg directed with a soft smile.

"I'm not wearing any," Mikkel replied.

"There are some pink ones in the locker room." Lilly pointed toward the door, looking smug.

"Thanks," he replied sarcastically, walking toward the locker room. "Rule three should apply to you, too," he called back over his shoulder.

"It should, but that wasn't part of the deal," Lilly yelled after him.

When Mikkel came out of the locker room, he was wearing very tight gray boxer briefs. Lilly admired the artwork on his torso. She had seen the ones on his arms. She hadn't considered he would have a full torso piece. He must certainly have a full back piece, too. He met her gaze as she stared. Lilly looked away, embarrassed, until he had settled himself on the table. She hadn't meant to ogle him. She found his tattoos extraordinary. Frigg laid the nanite sheet over him, covering him from mid-thigh to waist.

"Whenever you're ready, Lilly."

"You're not draining him first?" The previous procedure included draining half of the blood for a quicker transition time. Lilly wasn't aware that would change.

"No need. The nanites will eliminate all the necessary cells at once. The turn will begin immediately upon activation. It shortens the first phase to under a minute and the second to under two," Frigg explained.

Lilly approached Mikkel cautiously. She didn't show any outward signs of being nervous. As she got closer, Mikkel felt her anxiety. When she was leaning over him, she saw he had many scars both over and under the ink. She found herself wondering how many battles he had been in. How many times had he been close to death? Some of the scars were thick, newer than the others. The deeper injuries must have been near fatal.

"You've been telling me all week about how much you want to kill me. Now's your chance." Mikkel grinned up at her.

"Rule three, asshole." She smiled back at him.

Lilly placed her hand gently on the side of his face. Mikkel thought it was a touching moment until she shoved his face hard to the side, exposing a very thick artery pulsating fast. Lilly was old school. She bit hard, letting him feel her canis rip into his flesh before she began letting her venom flow in, numbing his throat. She drank a little longer than she needed to, feeling the ecstasy of draining the life from someone. It had been many years since she last tasted blood from the tap. She didn't have the thirst. What she had was blood lust. She enjoyed it.

She broke off, licking her lips and wiping the last few drops away from the corner of her mouth with her thumb. She peered down with a satisfied, smug face.

"Your turn." Lilly bit into her own wrist, ripping it open with a rough, jagged edge. Blood spewed over Mikkel's face and chest as she shoved her wrist forcefully against his mouth. He reached out, pulling it down harder, biting into it.

Her blood was hot and sweet. Not gamy, like animal blood. The slight metallic bitterness balanced against the sweetness. He liked it more than he wanted to admit. She pulled back her wrist, which started healing immediately.

"Now for the fun part." She winked at him.

"Wait!" He put his hands up in front of him.

"You're not chickening out now, are you?" Lilly looked disappointed.

"No. But if we're doing this old school, we should go full old school. A warrior has to die with a weapon in his hand." He wasn't planning on his death being permanent, but if things went wrong, he wanted to die Æsir, the way he had lived.

"I like that idea." Lilly reached down to her boot, pulling out a long dagger. She placed it in his hand, wrapping both of hers around it. They exchanged satisfied looks. With a quick, hard stroke, she plunged the knife into his heart, twisting it. The sound of his sternum cracking followed by the suctioning sound when she twisted the knife made Frigg want to gag.

His shocked look turned calm. He reached up, squeezing her shoulder with his free hand, pulling her toward him. He wanted to see his death reflected in her eyes. It was a good death, he thought to himself as the light went out of his eyes.

Lilly reached over to close them. She raised her head to see Frigg staring at her with her mouth open.

"That was a tad brutal, don't you think?" Frigg saw no necessity for that level of violence.

"It was the death he wanted," Lilly countered sternly.

She pulled the knife out of his heart, wiping his blood on her thigh before slipping the dagger back into her boot.

"Sadie, start the process." Frigg threw up the monitoring image over the side of his head.

Sadie replied, "Stage one will be complete in thirty seconds."

The seconds ticked off.

"Stage one complete. Reconfiguring programming. Stage two will begin in thirty seconds."

Frigg and Lilly were watching the data. Five seconds before stage two began, Ami flew through the data table, moving straight up over Mikkel's head. Neither Frigg nor Lilly had seen Ami's wings before. They were mesmerized by the breadth and luminescence of them. It took them a second to see what she was after. Mikkel's essence was fleeing. His body began convulsing on the table. He was vomiting Lilly's blood.

"Shit!" Lilly exclaimed, jumping on top of Mikkel.

She held him down. The open wound in his chest wasn't healing. He was vomiting everything he had drunk. She ripped open her wrist and plunged it into the gaping hole in his chest. The seizures subsided, and his chest began healing. Ami had caught his essence before it had gotten out of the room. The last few seconds had been an insane adrenaline rush. Lilly dropped her head onto Mikkel's chest, collapsing her tense muscles. Her hair soaked up their mixed blood. The remainder smeared over her face and his chest.

Sadie's voice proclaimed, "Stage two will be complete in thirty seconds."

No one paid attention as they recovered from the previous event. Fifteen seconds later, Mikkel opened his eyes. Only Mikkel wasn't in the shell.

What had been Mikkel was wild and feral. His eyes were dilated to the point the color had been overtaken by black. Lilly felt it. By the time she could raise her head, she had been slammed onto her back on the floor. She was pinned under his body's weight. He was suffocating her. She couldn't move. His strength was too much for her to break free from. She felt the emptiness inside of him. He was savage, running on instinct.

Lilly screamed an agonizing screech only a survivor of a traumatic event could be capable of understanding. Something tripped inside of her. She screamed, writhing underneath him. She fought with every ounce of strength she had. Ami shoved his essence back into the hollowed-out shell, giving Lilly a fraction of a second to arch her back before pushing him up. She slammed herself back to the floor, creating enough space between them to bring her knee up hard into his groin. He bore his fangs, hissing at her, then rolled to one side, regaining his senses as Lilly shot out from under him. He was horrified by what he had done to her. She fled to a far corner of the room, screaming hysterically, sobbing uncontrollably.

Mikkel felt Lilly's bottomless emotional trauma. Ignoring his own physical pain, he sprinted to her side. She tried to get away from him, kicking, sliding back further into the corner. Eyes wide, screaming until there was no sound. He grabbed her face with both hands, forcing her to look into his vibrant green eyes.

She saw him. She felt him, their connection and his need to protect her. She felt safe, rescued from her own intensely powerful memories. She collapsed forward onto him. He sat against the wall, pulling her into his lap. He rocked her gently as she sobbed. Instinctively, he positioned his wrist against her mouth, allowing her to drink. It calmed her, completing their bond. It wasn't a mating bond. There was nothing erotic about it for either of them. It was a bond of two damaged beings healing each other.

As Lilly lay in his lap, Mikkel could see that she was small and delicate. She was nowhere near as strong as she had wanted everyone to believe. She dressed and acted the way she did to keep others away. Mikkel could see her ever so clearly now.

Alex and Erik ported in, feeling Mikkel's connection to the community. They also felt his distress. He wouldn't speak to them. He didn't want to speak to any of them. It was imperative for him to concentrate on Lilly. She had shut down, staring straight ahead with her teeth in his wrist. He slid it away, holding her against him. As he held her tightly, he stood, opening a port and stepping through in one movement. He stepped into her room and tried laying her in her bed, but she wouldn't let him go. He pulled off her boots. They were both soaked in blood, but it didn't matter. He wrapped her in a blanket and laid next to her until they were both asleep.

"What in all hells happened here?" Alex demanded. He was angry, not just because something went wrong. He was angry because no one let them know Mikkel was turning. They should have been there.

"His soul fled when he died," Ami stated in her matter-of-fact way. Was it really so difficult for them to grasp the obvious?

Erik had Sadie pull up an analysis on the plan table.

"He didn't flee, he rose." Erik squinted, reading the data again.

"How is that even possible? He's only half, the same as us." Alex was sure Erik had to be wrong.

"Either way. It doesn't matter. What matters is, why did his essence leave his shell?" Erik stared Frigg down. He was irritated she had run an untested experiment on Mikkel without testing it on a less advanced species first. It had been irresponsible.

"The gap was too long between the stages," Frigg answered uncomfortably.

Erik scrutinized the data again. "About five times too long. You did this on purpose," he accused.

"No," she defended.

"Then you're incompetent," Erik continued. "He was physically exhausted, exhibiting isolation symptoms. His viability was below seventy-five percent because of mental stress. Factoring in those statistics, there should have been a maximum of six seconds between stage one and stage two. Why did you wait thirty seconds?"

"When I fed in the data, the program set a thirty-second break," Frigg defended.

Erik was not satisfied at all. She didn't check the math. It was obvious to him. She had been working with shells for thousands of years. She should have seen the calculations were wrong. He could tell she was hiding something.

"Sadie, why was there a thirty-second break between stage one and stage two?" Erik stared directly into Frigg's eyes as he asked his question.

Sadie replied, "Thirty seconds is the amount of time required to wipe stage one programming from the nanites, reset, and reprogram them for stage two."

That answer made matters worse in Erik's eyes. "Sadie, why were single command nanites used as opposed to multicommand nanites?"

"There are currently no available multicommand nanites. The supply has been depleted."

"When will more be available?" Erik still hadn't taken his eyes off Frigg. Nothing Sadie had said to this point appeared to surprise her.

"Three cycles."

Now Erik understood. Mikkel may not have been mentally stable enough in three days. Frigg only thought she had two poor choices. Use single commands and hope the gap wasn't too big or wait and maybe not be able to turn him at all.

"You should have consulted me first. We could have figured out a way to mitigate. Did you think of feeding two separate sets and waiting to activate the second set until the first ones complete their program?" Erik was disappointed. She had always been smarter than that. Maybe it only seemed that way before when she used to be smarter than he was.

She bowed her head. "I didn't think of it." She was disappointed in herself as well.

"Sadie, did you consider that option?" Erik wanted to prove a point.

"I was not consulted or requested to render any options."

"Sadie, what other options would you have considered?"

"The two separate streams of nanites would be an excellent option for single as well as simultaneous turns. A specific option for a single turn would be to implement a stasis field for the thirty seconds it would take to reprogram a single set of single-command nanites."

"Thank you, Sadie. Those are two excellent options which would have mitigated the risk of damage. That took how long to find out? Less than a minute, would you say?" He continued glaring at Frigg. "I expected you would have learned to utilize your resources better since you've been doing it for thousands of years. You not only rolled the dice with Mikkel's life, but he could also have killed that girl, and possibly even you. That would have been on your head." He pointed at Frigg angrily. "Sadie, revoke Frigg's live testing authorization without a level one approval."

"Your request has been implemented, Erik."

Erik and Alex ported out abruptly, leaving Frigg to her own humiliation.

CHAPTER NINETEEN

Mikkel woke up crusted in dried blood and stuck to the sheets. He had slept for almost fourteen hours. The lights were set low. Lilly was sitting cross-legged on a desk across from the bed, watching him. She was freshly showered. Her braids were gone. Her hair was wet. She wore soft pink shorts and a white T-shirt with a pink animated cat on the front. Her face was clean of makeup. Except for slight curves, she could pass for a twelve-year-old. She had a pained expression of sadness on her face.

"Hey," he whispered, sitting up.

"Hey," she whispered back with a halfhearted smile that didn't reach her eyes.

"I'm sorry, Lilly. I never meant to scare you." Mikkel bit the side of his lip.

"I know. You should shower. I think we need to talk."

"Yeah. I'll, um … be back in a few minutes." He stood up to go back to his room.

"No. I mean, you don't have to leave. I left you some clothes in my bathroom." She didn't want to be alone.

"They're not pink, are they?" he joked. He could feel her pain and wanted to make her feel better.

"No," she chuckled lightly. Her voice was strained and low. "They're not pink."

Mikkel came out of the shower feeling almost clean. What he had done to her weighed on him, twisting him up inside. When Ami pushed his essence back into his shell, he felt all the rage, the rawness. The carnage he wanted to inflict on Lilly. The things he wanted to do to her had made him feel sick. He pushed the thoughts away, dressing in the black cotton shorts and tank top she had left out for him. They were slightly smaller than he normally wore, but not too tight.

When he left the bathroom, he saw that Lilly had made the bed with clean sheets. Her room was large for a studio. Looking around, he noticed a thermal pot of coffee next to a small bowl of sweetener and plant-based cream close to where she was sitting on top of the counter. She was dangling her legs off the edge, leaning against the wall. He cautiously moved across the room to sit on a stool at the island across from her.

"I didn't know how you liked it." She half smiled again.

"Black is fine." He poured a cup and tasted it. It was slightly bitter, strong. It tasted nutty, earthy and acidic. He had been drinking the same coffee for a year. It tasted different to him now. He tasted things in it he hadn't before.

"You'll get used to it. You feel any better?"

"Physically, a lot better than this morning. Mentally, not doing great," he spoke candidly. She would know if he lied. "You?" he asked.

"Physically, same as yesterday. Mentally, pretty awful." She rolled her eyes slowly away from him. He felt her holding back.

"I'm sorry about what happened. I don't want you to think I would hurt you like that again." She could hear the remorse in his voice and felt the pain it caused him.

"It wasn't you. When you pinned me down, it brought up some really horrible stuff from a long time ago. I didn't mean to lose it like that." Her voice was strained.

"What happened?" He wanted to know what had hurt her so much.

"It's a long story. I haven't told anyone."

"I have as much time as you need. You don't have to say anything you don't want to," Mikkel said, chewing the inside of his cheek.

She leaned forward with her elbows on her knees, holding her coffee cup with both hands. She crossed her ankles, swinging her legs back and forth.

"You already know my family was in the spice trade. We had a fleet of ships."

"Viv told me."

"My father decided he had a few too many daughters. It seemed to him like a fine idea to trade us along with the spice."

"Lilly, no." Mikkel was horrified.

"No. Not like you're thinking. He sold us to families. I was a farm slave. Thirteen or fourteen, I think, I'm not sure. Manual labor, household chores. That kind of thing."

"Oh." He was slightly relieved.

"It could have been worse. For me, it was easier than ship life. On a ship it's all day, all night, any weather, no shelter. It's endless. At least on the farm, I did what was expected of me. I had chores to manage, I had a place to sleep. It wasn't as bad as you would think. The master was nice. He let me go to the village and the market. He took me when he went to sell his herd or grain. After my work was done for the day, he gave me time to myself. He didn't chain me up at night or lock me in after the first few weeks. He knew I had nowhere to go." Lilly shook her head as Mikkel continued to listen.

"His wife was nice too at first. She taught me to read and to cook and some other household skills. The first few years were almost pleasant. When I started filling out a bit, she started finding fault in my work. She decided to teach me lessons from her holy book, but I didn't believe in her god. That's when it started to get hard. She thought she could force me to be a Christian by beating it into me. Her husband felt sorry for me. He would intervene sometimes, but that only made it worse. She thought he was paying attention to me because she was aging while I was young."

Mikkel refilled his coffee. Lilly took the pot from him, refilling her own. He waited until she was ready to speak again. She smiled a sad, wry smile.

"She turned me over to the church, claiming I was a witch. I already had two strikes in their eyes. I was what they called pagan, and she had told them I cast a spell beguiling her husband into becoming my lover." She snorted nervously;

the distant look remained on her face as she stared into the corner of the room. Her eyes had begun to sting, and she felt she would likely burst into tears if she looked at him.

"So, they locked me in a small cage, taking me out to question me or beat me into confessing that I was a witch. They held me for half a year. I wouldn't confess. I didn't even know what a witch was. Since I wouldn't confess, they told me I had to face three trials that would prove me to be either innocent or a witch. I was more than ready to prove my innocence. How could they find me guilty? Right?"

She glanced in his direction, not making eye contact.

"The first trial was a water trial. Funny thing they don't tell you is if you don't drown, it proves you a witch. If you drown, you're vindicated as innocent. You're also dead. But you're innocent."

She made eye contact with him. Her posture straightened and her eyes widened.

"Mikkel, I grew up on a ship in the sea. My sisters and I would scrape barnacles off the hull constantly. I could hold my breath for well over five minutes. My oldest sister could hold hers for nearly twenty. I tried to explain, but nobody would listen. They strapped me to a chair weighed down with stone, plunging me into the water. I was under for less than three minutes. Of course, I was alive when they pulled me up! They declared me a witch, saying I had to stand two more trials to prove my innocence. It was insanity. The village wanted my blood. They wanted me dead."

She took a swig of her drink. Mikkel was dumbfounded by the insanity of what she had told him. It took her a few minutes of deep breathing before she was ready to continue.

"The next trial was hanging. I was certain I was going to die. The noose was tight around my neck. When they pushed me off the platform, the thick rope slipped up under my jaw. They had starved me for months, so I didn't weigh anything. My neck didn't snap. I could still breathe. It was hysterical and terrifying at the same time. Surviving a hanging convinced them at that point I was a witch. They had spun the entire village up into a mob. I was beaten and locked back in the tiny cage. My only thought was that they were planning on burning me alive.

I resolved myself to the idea that by the next day I'd be dead. I thought anything would be better than the things they were doing to me."

She closed her eyes. When she opened them again, she focused on something behind him in the corner of the room.

"I sometimes wish they had set me to burn. At least that would have been over quickly. What they had planned for me was something far worse. Far more horrible than I believed I would survive. Nightmares of it still torment me."

She rubbed her temple, trying to push something unseen away from her mind.

"The next morning, early, they took me out to a field on the edge of the village. I remember the grass was still wet with dew. I only had on a filthy linen chemise and no shoes. It was early sprint. The morning was still cold, and I could see my breath in the air. They staked me to the ground, splayed out. I was terrified of what they were planning. They thought me the vilest being they had ever encountered. Nothing would have been unjustified in their thoughts. It was worse than anything I had imagined. They called it pressing."

Her bottom lip quivered. Mikkel didn't know what pressing was. He didn't want to know. He wanted to stop her from saying it out loud. Her eyes welled with tears, filling him with a deep dread of the next words she would speak.

"They brought out a barn board and laid it on top of me. It was heavy. My head, hands, and feet were all that stuck out from under it. They laid a heavy stone on it in the center. It took my breath away. They watched and waited until I had recovered my breath before they placed another. When I close my eyes, I still see my mistress's face smiling wickedly down at me. It was slow, horrifying torture. They waited between each stone, gently placing them on top of the board. They made sure not to drop them. Wouldn't want me to have an easy, quick death now, would they? My bones began splintering under the weight. I could feel them stabbing through my skin from the inside." Lilly pulled her knees up to her chest, gently rocking herself as far as the space between the edge of the counter and wall would permit. Her bottom eyelid finally succumbed to the weight of liquid, allowing it to spill over and run down her cheek.

"My hands and feet turned black. After the sixth stone, my skin began to split open where the bones were poking through. Blood seeped into the ground all around me. I remember it feeling so warm against the cold. I lasted through the entire day. Nine stones. Then they left me there alone in the dark. The ground was so cold. Overnight, I had become numb to the pain." Lilly sucked in a breath that hitched in her throat.

"They came out the next morning, certain I would be dead. Finding me alive, they continued laying stones. My legs and arms were crushed. My pelvis snapped. I had blood pouring from every opening, even from my eyes. My muscles and bones pulverized into mealy, grizzled meat. I felt my ribs push through my lungs. My own blood was drowning me. I have no idea how I lived for so long. My world swirled black, and I just let go. There was nothing left to fight for. I don't even know why I was fighting so hard to live in the first place. I let myself slip away into the darkness. Peaceful darkness. Everything was gone. It was quiet. The pain was gone. They were gone. I was finally released from my torture."

Lilly's tears were now flowing unencumbered down her cheeks, dripping onto the floor. Mikkel felt his eyes stinging. He couldn't hold his own back any longer. He allowed them to stream down his face in silence. Lilly wiped hers away with her free hand, taking another swig of her coffee that had turned too cold to be drinkable. She let her feet dangle over the counter edge again, taking a deep breath, pushing it out slowly. She found a way to stabilize her quivering chin.

"And then I woke up. I thought I must have ascended to my next life. In a way, I guess I had. I was lying under a tree close to where I had been. It must have been the smell of my blood that drew them. Someone had smashed the stones and board into pieces. All the villagers, except for the mistress, were torn to shreds in pools of their own blood. But I was alive. I had no idea how it was possible at the time. I was alive. And I was still me. Sort of." She shrugged.

"They were all dead except for her. They had staked her to the ground in my place, splayed out as I had been. Left as a gift, I suppose. She screamed and begged. It was pathetic. How could she have thought I would feel sorry for her? After what she had caused, how could she think I would let her go? I took my torture in utter silence, while she screamed at the mere sight of me walking toward her. In my mind, she deserved everything she got. I broke her fingers first, then her arms and legs. I knelt on top of her, pressing her ribs until they snapped, stabbing into her lungs. The whole time she screamed, but I couldn't hear it over her pounding heart. The sound and the smell of her blood only made me want to hurt her more," she said, dropping her eyes to the floor.

"Finally, after what seemed like hours of taunting and torturing her, I fed. And I left her dead with the rest of them. I wasn't a witch. I had become something worse. And I was grateful for it. No one could ever hurt me like that again."

Mikkel lowered his head, choking back his sorrow and tears.

"But you were all alone?" All he could think was that she went through all of that and then was left alone to figure it out with no help.

"It wasn't for long." She smiled a genuine, but still sad, smile. "I found a clan within a few days. I was drawn to them. The one that turned me wasn't with them. I didn't find out what happened to them or where they had gone, but at least I wasn't alone. The clan taught me how to survive, and I stayed with them for a few hundred years until I felt I needed to set out on my own for a while. I traveled the world, going from clan to clan. Learning, teaching, trying to fit in. I think, somehow, I was always searching for the one who turned me."

"I'm so sorry I brought that back to you. I wish I could take it away. I wish I could take all of your pain away," Mikkel said.

"Mikkel, I know that wasn't you in The Six. I don't want you to take that experience away from me. If it hadn't happened, I'd still have all of this buried inside of me. I never would have told anyone. It's out now. Without you, that wouldn't have happened. It *will* get better for me. Just maybe not today. At least I don't feel alone anymore. Turning you helped me to not feel alone."

Lilly hopped off the counter, putting her coffee cup under the service panel and sending it back to wherever it had originated from. She took a bottle of spiced rum and two glasses out of the cabinet. She poured them both three fingers deep, sliding one to Mikkel. Lilly threw back her entire glass and poured herself another. She wiped the remaining tears and snot from her face with the tail of her T-shirt, collecting herself back into something that resembled a person in control of herself.

"Now, it's your turn. Deepest and darkest. How'd you get those scars?" Pointing at his chest, she sniffled. She needed someone else to speak for a while. She wanted to talk about anything else.

Mikkel lifted his shirt, examining his stomach and chest. He rubbed his hand over his now-smooth skin. "What scars?" Feigning ignorance. The scars had been healed by the turn. It was unusual for old scars to heal with the turn, but Mikkel didn't know that.

"Rule three, asshole. AND two. Actually, why don't we just start with why you're a dick all the time."

"Fair enough. But don't think I'm going to be able to top your story. I'm not that interesting." Mikkel knocked back his rum, grabbing the bottle from her hand to refill it.

"I already figured that out," she said, snatching the bottle back from him and leaning onto the counter.

"You've met my brothers. Alex was born to be a leader. He didn't have to try. People just followed him like they did our father. Erik was the smart one. Not regular smart either. Exceptionally smart. And me, I was plain Mikkel. Not exceptionally good at anything. Not like they were. So, I took to being funny. When they got too serious or too cocky, I'd knock them down a peg or two. They said I kept them grounded. What they really meant was it got me attention I couldn't get by being good at something. I was okay with it when we were kids. The older I got, the more I realized I was the one with a grasp on living. They were so serious. Always so caught up with war and science, they created a gap between themselves and our people. They were admired, sure. But they weren't one of them. I didn't have that problem. I could be as comfortable working in the fields alongside the farmers as I was at royal dinners. The two of them only had one lane. I had options. Or so I thought."

He took a sip of his drink, then swirled it around the glass.

"Go on," Lilly encouraged.

"Where things got harder for me." He met her gaze. "Where I started becoming a dick, as you put it, was when it came to war. I didn't see it the way they did. I had questions it wasn't my place to ask."

He stopped again, swirling his rum. He drank it and poured another.

"You see, we are good at it. More than good at it. We were born different. We can hear each other, see each other's moves before we make them. The three of us fighting back-to-back have not been defeated once in a hundred and fifty thousand years. The three of us against a thousand have won. Alone, we're each good. Together, we are indomitable. But should we be when it's not just? When it's not a war we should be fighting? Defending our people is one thing. I don't mind that fight. Being the shield is important. But when is it ever necessary to invade someone else's world and slaughter them? Because they opposed Odin?

Because they didn't want us for rulers? I hated doing it. I hated being the sword of oppression," Mikkel sneered at the memory.

He pointed at Lilly. "That's where I started getting into trouble. I questioned why we were fighting. Entire planets would know we were coming, and they would give up. Lie down like sheep. We dominated other worlds through fear where we had no business being." He took a sip of his drink, reflecting on a bitter memory.

"I believe our own realm's downfall was our fault. My brothers and I had become the talismans for our warriors. They believed if we were with them, they couldn't be defeated. Without us, they lacked the confidence they should have had in their own abilities. They were amazing on their own. There were some none of us could beat one on one. We weren't there when the forces attacked during the great war. We had been sent to cool our heels on your planet. It doesn't matter who attacked our people. They knew we weren't there. Our own people lost their confidence in their own skills because we weren't there. They defeated themselves because they didn't believe in their own ability to win without us. It's my fault there are only a hundred and ten left. We let them get to the point where they truly believed they needed us to win."

"You can't put that responsibility on yourself, Mikkel."

"I don't take all the blame. I put a lot on Odin too. He's the one who held us up as a talisman. He's the one who convinced them they could win any battle if they had The Three fighting alongside them. My grandfather was vain. He failed to consider that it would lead them to believe the opposite was also true. They believed they couldn't win if they didn't have us. Hundreds of thousands are dead because they didn't have their false idols, their good luck charms with them."

Lilly needed to ask him another question. She was getting a sick feeling because she already knew the answer. She hoped she was wrong.

"Where did you get the scars, Mikkel? Those wounds should have killed you."

He swallowed his entire glass in one gulp. Lilly poured him another. He picked it up to drink again. She stopped him, placing her hand over his glass.

"Where did you get the scars?"

"Those were lessons in how to be quiet and take orders. They were also the real reason we were on T28-66 when our people were slaughtered. We were in a time-out because of me."

She pulled away her hand, letting him take his drink. He set the glass on the counter.

"With Frigg thought dead and my father in Hel, Odin had become bitter. He wanted obedience without question. Questions undermined his authority. He had already driven our remaining uncles away with his iron-fisted ways."

Mikkel shook his head, quickly clearing out a thought he hadn't wanted to face yet.

"He wasn't always like that. He felt his power slipping away. His wisdom seemed to go with it. Before, he was smart, cunning, just. Don't get me wrong. He wasn't the benevolent leader he's made out to be. He always loved his wars. Leading warriors was something that made him feel powerful, alive. That was changing. The more he conquered, the more he had to rule. He didn't like ruling as much as winning. With no one standing by his side to temper him, all he wanted was to conquer," he scoffed.

"I dared to question him. Publicly. Not the smartest thing I ever did. So, he challenged me. And since no one was permitted to take him on in singular battle, he named his champion. He named Heimdall. No one, and I mean NO ONE, could beat Heimdall one on one. And I certainly didn't. He should have killed me. He nearly did. My guts were splayed all over the floor. Odin stopped him before the final strike. We were still a symbol of victory for him. He couldn't kill me and keep up his charade. Somehow, our father got word about the incident in Hel. I think it was Heimdall himself who told him. Anyway, he convinced Odin that to get his power back, he should make an example of us. He got us out so I could heal. We were sent away to set up the facility in case the coming war couldn't be won. It was always a war that was supposed to be the end of the realm. If it wasn't for me, we would have been there." Mikkel looked pointedly at Lilly. "It would have been a very different outcome if we had been."

"And it may not have been," Lilly replied, raising her eyebrows. "Looks like we both have some pretty screwed up baggage."

She refilled both their glasses, and they drank.

"See, I'm still not as interesting as you."

"No, but you're still a dick."

CHAPTER TWENTY

"Some of you have been trained your whole lives to fight. Some of you have never fought for anything. Some of you have killed hundreds or thousands. And some of you have never taken a life. Today is a new day for all of us. I'm asking you to put away your old ways. I'm asking you to embrace your new roles. We are not looking for warriors. We're not looking for war. What we need are protectors. Killing as a first instinct is no longer acceptable. Taking a life is no longer acceptable. Life must only be taken if it is to protect another. Only as a last resort. To protect an innocent. To protect those who are unable to protect themselves. Taking life is not to be taken lightly. Every one of you has lost one life already. Make the new one you were given mean something."

Vaeweth paused. There would be no cheers. No uproar. It was a training day.

"We will no longer idly sit by and let the weak be brutalized into submission. We will not seek out conflict. If it comes to our door, we will be ready. We will protect ourselves. We will protect those who seek our protection. We will create a peaceful existence in The Everything so the Risen can bring balance to it. Our community exists to spread the light, to spread the peace, to honor life."

"He gives an excellent speech, doesn't he?" Viv whispered to Ben from the side of the platform.

Vaeweth was addressing a group of newly turned. They would be trained in defense today. Tactics, defensive postures, and the utilization of their uniforms. Nonlethal training. Training to preserve life. Similar speeches were being given to four groups in different locations throughout Rasa. Each group of five hundred would have three training days before being assigned to units. They would be assigned to ships. These units would be trained and travel throughout The Everything, with most stationed on or near their home worlds. They would be bridges to their species. They were the turned. They were Rasans. They were part of the community, and they were also a symbol to their old communities that all were welcome and would be protected whether they turned or not.

"It's a speech," Ben replied, glancing sideways at her, unimpressed.

"Why are you so suspicious of everyone? Cynical of every motivation except your own."

"What? Now that he's turned, you suddenly trust him. You forgive and forget and live oblivious to all the atrocities so many of them have committed for the Council."

"We're not happy little oblivious drones here, Ben. We have tempers, we get angry, we have conflicts. The truth is, anger and war have never led to anything positive. We understand the benefits of peace and creating a world where species can get along and thrive. We understand the need to compromise to resolve conflicts like adults. Our capacity for empathy and compassion is significant. We cherish life. We don't want to kill someone because they don't see things our way. It's crucial to learn how to work with them for everyone's benefit."

Ben rolled his eyes at her diatribe. Viv grabbed his arm to refocus his attention back to her.

"You think there aren't people here who look at you the way you see him? You're not any better than he is. You've annihilated entire populations the same way he did to yours. You've enslaved entire planets." Ben was shocked to hear Viv saying these words to him. She was not finished with him yet, either.

"Don't look at me like that. You think it was fine for you to do it because you were in the right? Why would you think that? Who says you were right? Because daddy said so? Pull your head out of your ass, Ben. You're no better and no worse than Vaeweth is. You two are *exactly* the same. Maybe if you took the turn yourself, you'd figure out what empathy is."

Viv didn't wait for his reply. It was nothing she wanted to hear. Nothing that he had to say would help the situation. She walked away briskly.

She didn't understand why Grace would put him in charge of tactics. He had the mind for it, sure. He had the experience. She couldn't deny that. But he lacked compassion. He lacked the understanding of the community's connection. The basic principles needed for peaceful conflict resolution were absent from him. He didn't hold the same vision of a peaceful Everything. In her mind, he couldn't be the leader they needed.

Viv was headed back to her apartment when she felt it. She opened a port back to the hallway outside The Six. She felt their presence before they had gotten through the blockers. Everyone had felt them, even Ben, although not in the same way. Viv heard the others porting in behind her. When they walked through the doors, she saw Ami was still in place on the planning table. When Ami saw Viv, she ended her game, coming to Viv's side.

Alex, Erik, and Jack were training the other three groups. They would come only after their training was finished for the day. Mikkel ported in with Lilly. Viv had gotten the report on their episode, and she was planning to have a conversation with Leo about the incident. It was his department; therefore, his direct responsibility. Viv had already determined that anything involving new procedures for the turn would need to be evaluated by someone who had already been turned. She thought there were too many unturned in decision-making positions over the turned. The whole structure needed to be reevaluated.

Asta and Violet came next. Ben came in behind the small group that had gathered. He was still stung by the truth in Viv's words. One thing she had said he couldn't deny: he didn't fully understand the depth of the connection they had.

There was a warm calmness in the room as the two lights descended through the ceiling. They morphed from shape to shape, not landing on any one in particular. Everyone watched except for Ben, who couldn't look directly at them.

The smaller shape descended first, sliding easily into Nyx's shell. She stretched and twisted as she pushed her way back in. It was tight. It was unpleasant for her to confine herself into a physical form after being freed from it. She opened her eyes, watching the other shape hovering above.

It shuddered. Stretched apart like taffy, only to snap back into place. It exerted force against itself, resisting its own attempts to divide. They were unable to split apart. Once they stopped straining, two small, thin streams pulled out from the bottom. One headed toward each of the two empty shells. They unwove themselves the way threads of a tapestry would unravel until they were uncoupled.

Ivan found it difficult to enter his shell. It was tight, cramped, confined. He felt like a prisoner in his own body. It made him feel dim and diminished, already longing to be free of it. He understood why Nyx abhorred the physical incarceration.

Grace had an easier time coming back. She wanted to pass on what they knew. Her desire to see her sons was stronger than her resistance to the confinement. She wanted to know why they had felt Mikkel above the others for a moment. The tightening was undeniable. Unlike Ivan, she was comforted by the physical presence, even though she longed for the freedom she had felt in The Everything with Ivan. She was drawn to it. Yet, she didn't feel as imprisoned by her shell as he did. Without the amulet, she recognized she could leave anytime she wished. She didn't feel restrained like she had before when she wasn't able to rise at will.

The most difficult part of returning for both was the sense of loss. Being separated. They could still hear each other. They felt each other like the touch from a ghost. It was a strange sensation, no longer being one. Being split into halves again. Being only a portion of a whole entity. The adjustment was achingly solitary. Only the two of them could comprehend it.

The physical adjustment was hard, too. Figuring out how to work their extremities again. Feeling the aching of muscles that had sat still for too long. Cramming their vastly grown consciousness back into brains that processed thoughts far more slowly than they had become used to. The physical world worked significantly slower. Their power was masked, diminished, and heavy. Speech took effort.

Grace paused before she could make the words she wanted to say come out. Standing was awkward once she had gotten to her feet. Gravity had become cumbersome.

"We did it." It was all she could say before the group erupted into a flurry of questions.

Everyone talked over each other. She moved to Ivan's side, standing as physically close as she could get to him. Disappointed, she was unable to feel him the way she had when they had risen together. She didn't know what question to answer first.

Nyx stepped in front of them. "Give them a few minutes to adjust. They need some space."

She recognized the frustration they felt returning to their shells after the freedom of The Everything. She recovered her senses more quickly, having done the same many times in the past.

"They did well. Better than I could have anticipated. Coming back to the confinement of their shell requires an adjustment. It can be disorienting the first few times."

The group stepped back and gave them some breathing room.

"That's better. Let's see what questions I can answer while they recover a bit, shall we?"

Nyx directed the others to the plan table. She strode to the front of the center screen, leaving Ivan and Grace standing where they had been.

Nyx began, "Time is very different for us out there. How long were we gone?"

Sadie answered, "You have been outside of your encasements for nine days, eighteen hours, and twenty-seven minutes."

"For us, it seemed only a few hours. There's no proper way to mark time outside the rotation of a planet. Since they all rotate differently, time in The Everything isn't the same anywhere."

Nyx was unable to judge if they grasped the concept or not. Grace and Ivan were clearly astonished at the amount of time that had passed. Nyx continued.

"Sadie, how has the energy of this dimension changed in the time we were risen?"

"The energy in this dimension has increased by point zero, zero, eight, one, six percent in the positive direction in the time you were outside your encasements."

Nyx gasped excitedly. "Excellent! Quite a marked difference and they barely did anything compared to what they are capable of. I count it as a successful outing. Now, as for the rest of you, let's say you've had some slightly less successful endeavors?" She posed it as a question.

Nyx raised her eyes to Grace's. They had absorbed the knowledge of the last few weeks' events from Sadie as they passed back through her on their way in. Nyx was waiting to see if Grace and Ivan had caught up to that information yet. Grace took an extra two or three seconds to find what she was seeking. Ivan seemed to have landed on it first.

"Where is Frigg anyway?" Ivan addressed Mikkel directly. His tone was steady and concerned.

Ben snapped his head around, seeing the exchange between them. He didn't have any idea why Ivan would ask for his mother. Or why he would be asking Mikkel? He was unaware of the events of Mikkel's turn. Ben wasn't even aware it had taken place. He had assumed Mikkel's appearance out of uniform was due to the physical and emotional issues he had been going through as a result of not taking the turn with his brothers. Something else was going on. Something he didn't think he was going to like.

"I don't know where Frigg is," Mikkel replied, shaking his head.

Grace didn't want this to turn into a crucifixion by either Nyx or Ben. "I think we can discuss it with her later. I'm sure she's gained some insights into proper procedures."

She was regaining her wits, settling back into her physical form.

"Can somebody please tell me what in all hells is going on here?" Ben demanded.

"Frigg almost lost Mikkel's soul yesterday. She turned his empty shell, which tried to kill Lilly before I shoved him back in," Ami said flatly.

Ben stared wide-eyed across the table at her. He looked around the table at each of the others. None of them seemed the least bit surprised.

"WHAT?" He looked around again. He couldn't have heard that correctly. Then he turned on Mikkel.

"You took the turn yesterday, and no one thought to tell me anything?" Ben was shocked and angry.

"It was part of the brief last night." Viv still had some animosity toward him from their encounter on the training field a few minutes earlier. She wasn't about to tell him how she really found out. It was his job to keep up with what was happening. He was responsible for obtaining the briefs.

Violet, Viv, and Asta had heard about it from Erik along with Jack at dinner the night before. Neither was going to speak up about that against their mother, given her current attitude. It was in the brief, so that at least was accurate.

Ben ignored Viv, glowering at Mikkel. "That's not the point. I had a right to be there. I should have been told before it happened."

Lilly leaned forward, pushing Mikkel back in his chair to see Ben past him. "Mikkel had deteriorated significantly yesterday. It had to be done quickly. The only ones there were Mikkel, me, Frigg, and Ami. That's it. Did she make a mistake in the timings? Obviously. It wasn't her intention. Things got a little rocky, but everyone came out of it alive. We're the ones who have the right to be pissed about it and we're not. The rest of you need to let it go." She slumped back in her chair, throwing her head back against it.

But Ben was upset. He was being left behind. His last son had been turned and no one, including his own mother or his other two sons, had given a second thought to informing him. It had become a critical situation, and as the supposed leader while Grace and Ivan were away, he had not been told there had been an issue. He was more than upset. Rage blanketed his entire thought process. All of them had disregarded and disrespected him in his mind.

"Do any of you get the point at all? Not only is there the fact that I'm his father, but I was supposedly left in charge here. And not one person thought I deserved to be personally informed that there had been an issue that almost resulted in a catastrophe?" He turned on Viv next.

"Courtesy? Respect? Empathy? You people harp on it like it's a mantra. It's great to say. How about practicing a little of it? You think I don't deserve it because I'm not one of you? If it wasn't for me, none of you would be here."

He brought his fist down on the table, shaking it as he slammed himself back into his own chair. He was brooding.

Asta would not listen to their people being disparaged in that way. Especially not her mother. She knew better. Despite her fear of speaking up, she couldn't just let his outburst pass. She found a tiny bit of courage from somewhere.

"Ben?" she said timidly.

He glared at her without answering. She swallowed hard before continuing.

"Erik told us he left a message on your TAC yesterday when you wouldn't answer his calls. He wanted to discuss it with you before the brief came out.

When you didn't get back to him, he thought you had already heard, and he didn't want to discuss it with you when you were angry." She bit into her lip. Lately Ben was always angry.

She felt bad about outing him in front of the others.

He pulled his TAC out of his pocket and threw it forward, letting it clatter over the top of the table. Thinking it was just another thing he didn't want to deal with, he had ignored the blinking light. He clenched his jaw, not saying anything or making eye contact with anyone. He had been a jerk, and he knew it. In his mind, none of that mattered. One of them should have come to find him. Nonetheless, his stubbornness wouldn't allow him to apologize, no matter how wrong his actions were.

Nyx couldn't believe she felt sorry for him. Rescue wasn't really her thing.

"Well, I think we need a little break. Why don't we all get ourselves cleaned up and meet back here this afternoon for our regularly scheduled briefing?" She gave the group her usual too-sweet, just-for-show smile and popped her eyebrows as she clapped her hands twice, then immediately turned and walked to the back of the room. They had been dismissed.

Violet and Asta immediately got permission from Sadie and ported out. Viv wanted to talk to Grace, but Ami sped past her, grabbing Grace in an eager hug. Viv decided she would catch up later. Her time would be better spent speaking to Leo. She nodded to Grace and Ivan before porting out.

Mikkel and Lilly weren't ready to face all the questions just yet. Ivan smiled, nodding at him understandingly. He nodded back before they also disappeared. They had been planning lunch with Erik, Alex, and Jack and needed some mental preparation beforehand. They would have enough questions to answer from them.

"Okay, Ami, you can let go now. I'm glad to see you. Have you been here this whole time?"

Grace had thought Ami was out recruiting. She had learned from Sadie that Ami had been here keeping watch.

"Someone had to protect you." Ami was proud of herself for sticking by them.

"We're glad you did. Who's been recruiting while you were here?"

"No one. We've already got half a million on the list. Everyone is talking about it. There are more coming every day and we've only managed to turn about fifteen thousand."

"I know. Sadie already told me." Grace was concerned about the numbers.

"Frigg has a way to turn large groups all at once. That should help," Ami offered.

"I think she has some more work to do before that procedure is ready." Grace saw she didn't have the proper nanite supply for something of that size.

She had also gotten the information on the problems with Mikkel's turn. When Mikkel was ready to take over training groups, she would propose Jack work with Frigg. She would suggest it to Viv later. It would need to be her decision. Grace and Ivan had to concentrate on the balance full time if they were going to get it right.

"Thank you for saving Mikkel. Things wouldn't have turned out so well if you hadn't been here."

"You're welcome. I hadn't caught a soul in a while. His was hard to get back in. I'm out of practice," Ami joked.

Grace noticed Nyx approach Ben. That was a strange situation.

"You should do it. You'll never understand them if you don't," Nyx stated rather flippantly.

"And what do you know about it?" He was irritated with himself.

"I know you're struggling with it. I know you're on the outside looking in."

"Yeah. I am. The problem I have is, do I need to understand them more than I need to stay objective?" Ben shifted his jaw. He bit the cuticle on his thumb, took a few steps away from her, and ported out.

CHAPTER TWENTY-ONE

Mikkel ported Lilly back to his apartment. It was a huge three bedroom he had shared with his brothers until Erik moved out. He and Asta had gotten their new quarters a few days ago. Everything was basic. No décor other than what had come with it. A quick cleaning and you wouldn't believe anyone lived here. It was surprising to her that there was a total lack of personality.

"I know what you're thinking," Mikkel laughed. "It's been a long time since I had to live with my brothers. We agreed the common spaces would stay neutral. Trust me, it's more peaceful that way." He nodded as he said it.

"That's why I like living alone. I don't worry about what anyone else thinks."

"No, you sure don't."

"Well, you've seen mine. Show me yours."

"Right this way." Mikkel bowed, extending his arm toward his bedroom door.

Lilly opened it. It wasn't at all like what she had expected. It was orderly. White and navy. The wall screen behind the bed across from the door had an ocean view. The color of the water was off. It was a darker blue than she was used to. It hit her. The water appeared darker because it wasn't from Rasa or Earth.

The sky was deep blue, streaked at the very top with pink and orange from the setting sun.

The far-left wall was the standard closet setup all the apartments had with a bathroom instead of the last closet door. The wall behind the bedroom door had two large vertical tapestries with intricate designs placed on either side of a small worktable. Words written in a language she didn't understand covered them both.

She stepped inside, facing the wall the door was on. It had shelves and cubbies with a viewing screen in the center. One shelf held a sword in a display stand. If she had stood it on its end, it would have come up under her chin. It had been sharpened and shined to perfection. The blade was marked down the center with more of the strange writing. The hilt was as thick as her arm. It had shiny silver-colored metal underneath and thin strands of black braided metal over the top for grip. At the end was a large weighted pommel. Black, rectangular to stop the hand from slipping. Sharp edges worn round. She suspected it had perfect balance. It wasn't only a showpiece; it had seen extensive use.

She touched the blade. It was cold and slick, sharp enough to slice a single hair. When she reached for the hilt, Mikkel stopped her.

"That's not something you want to feel the weight of." His voice was solemn.

She pulled her hand back slowly, taking in the gravity of what he had said. She moved on. There were twenty or so knives of all types. Each one of excellent craftsmanship. Further down, hanging in one of the cubbies, were several ropes, all tied with intricate knots. Lilly smiled at the familiarity as she ran her fingers over them. She knew from experience some of them were very difficult to tie. Two were elaborate ties she wasn't familiar with. Mikkel sat down on the edge of the bed, watching her. As she moved further along the display, she could feel him holding his breath. She was getting close to something important, personal, or both.

There was a small flat disk sitting on the center of an empty cubby, eye level if you were sitting in bed. Lilly grazed it with her fingertips. A moving image popped out above it. It was a girl. She looked older than Lilly, yet younger than Mikkel. She had light-brown hair that wisped at her shoulders. When she spun around, Lilly could see that her eyes were golden brown, and she had freckles on her nose and cheeks. She had a smile that could stop your heart beating. She wasn't exceptionally pretty, but at the same time, she was the most beautiful thing Lilly could imagine.

The next image was the same girl, rolling in tall grass, laughing, under a tree. After a few more scenes cycled, Lilly could see this girl was important to Mikkel.

"Who's this? She's adorable," Lilly asked, mesmerized by the images.

"Faith. The last picture is the last one she sent me from home. It was her birthday." Mikkel laid back on his bed. He couldn't watch it today.

Lilly's stomach dropped a little, but she had to keep watching. Faith wasn't one of the one hundred and ten that were on Rasa. She grasped what that meant. When the very last picture cycled through, it was an image of Mikkel holding a younger version of Faith in his lap. She had an enormous smile of pure joy as he kissed her on the cheek.

Lilly's eyes burned; her heart dropped into her stomach. She knew why Mikkel blamed himself. He couldn't save her. She turned the disk off and stood with her back to him, unable to turn around for a moment. When she did, Mikkel was lying on his back, staring up at the ceiling.

"You asked for deepest and darkest. Now you've seen mine." He leaned up on his elbows. "Nobody knows mine either," he added.

"Not even your brothers? How can you hide that from them?"

"I have a dark little place where I tuck things away. Even we can hide things from each other when we need to."

"What about her mother?" Lilly asked timidly.

"She was a friend. Nothing serious. Neither of us wanted a partner. She didn't want Faith burdened with the legacy of my family, so she made me promise to keep her a secret. Faith was my hidden little piece of happiness. We kept her safe and happy. Until I couldn't protect either of them."

Lilly kicked at the floor. "Damn it! You're more broken than I thought you were." She kicked his foot a few times.

Mikkel sat up. Lilly bent down, giving him a sweet hug. "Good thing those scars don't show on the outside." She shoved him back down and took a seat on the far corner of the bed.

Mikkel rolled over on his side, leaning his head on his elbow. Now he was the one who needed to talk about something else.

"Now that we both know how royally fucked up the other one is, do you mind if I ask you a question before the others get here?"

"You can ask. Can't guarantee I'll answer," she chuckled nervously.

"Fair enough." He paused.

"I get that you're not looking for a mate. Neither am I. I mean, you get that, right?"

"I get it." She recognized he had his heart ripped out. That kind of pain made it hard to want to love anything you could lose again.

"What I don't get is, why do the turned even take mates? We can turn whoever we want. We don't need to procreate conventionally, right? It sounds absurd to me that you can sire fifty if you want, but you're only allowed one mate. How does that even work?"

"First of all, that's three questions. I think I can answer most of it by saying it's a reaction from a time after we were nearly wiped into extinction. Males and females did take on singular mates for procreation. They needed to blend in. The clans they created were meant to closely resemble families. They also fell into their human counterparts' traditions of weddings and such. A lot of the old clans still do. Mainly the ones who had difficulty letting go of being human." Lilly was searching for a good way to convey reality versus expectation.

"But not you." Mikkel's reply was a statement, not a question.

"No, traditional isn't my thing. I don't fit the mold."

"I can see that."

"Taking a mate wasn't something they started doing until a few hundred years ago. It used to be each clan had one main sire. He or she would turn a few, then each of the others would turn a few until you had a clan the size you wanted. No one was exclusive. You could be intimate with whoever you wanted. Intimacy wasn't really about sex, either. Most times, you just need someone to hold on to. To be physically close to. We would bathe together or sleep together in groups. Oftentimes, it would be feeding from each other. If I wanted to be intimate with the girl down the hall or the guy downstairs, as long as they consented, no one cared. If I was drinking a guy on the kitchen counter and someone came in to make a sandwich, they might join in. Or they might make a sandwich around us and leave."

Mikkel chuckled at the statement.

"There weren't all these heavy moral judgements and rules like the ones the Board started. Some of them make sense, like candidates should be mentally stable and have something to offer the community. Some of them don't, like you can only turn for mating purposes, and they highly encouraged it to be someone of the opposite sex. At least it looks like the last one is gone now since we're implementing sire lines again. I think it's a more pure, natural form of the process. We aren't being forced to pick someone to spend eternity with anymore. People grow, they change. If you no longer make each other happy, why should you be forced to stay together because you were once drawn to that person?"

"Is that why you never sired before? You didn't want to be stuck with someone for eternity?" Mikkel was curious.

"Part of it. Part of it was I didn't want to settle with any specific clan. I wanted to see if my sire was out there somewhere. See why they saved me, maybe? Why they didn't just leave me for dead? I wanted to be free, drift through clans as I pleased. Then when they made rules, I didn't want to be stuck with anyone for eternity."

"What changed? Why'd you agree now? Why me?"

"Everything changed. New planet, fresh start. Spreading through The Everything. And you're different. You don't want to be tied up either," she explained.

"Well, I didn't say that. I don't want to be tied up by the same person for eternity," Mikkel replied coyly.

"Still a dick." She shoved him off the bed. "Go change. They'll be here soon."

"I'm glad I got you as a sire. I think we kind of see the world the same way."

Lilly was a little worried. They were mixing so many species and cultures. She hoped they could figure out a way to make it all work without taking a huge step backward. While Lilly and Mikkel were having a mildly awkward lunch with Jack, Alex, and Erik, there was another lunch happening on the other side of the city.

Ivan sat down at the table where Viv and Grace had already started eating.

"Viv was telling me she went to have a talk with Leo."

Ivan tilted his head. "About?"

Viv replied, "Having someone in the community monitor Frigg's work. She's great with the genetic aspects of her research. If she had an engineer who understood what went into programming the nanites, the incident with Mikkel wouldn't have happened. I said it on the first day, we need teams, not egos. Everyone needs to work together." She mixed her vegetables into her rice, taking a forkful.

"I have a suggestion, if you don't mind," Grace offered.

Viv swallowed her food. "Of course, I don't mind. Who?"

"Mikkel is going to be ready in the next day or so to take over training. I think we could easily slide Jack into the lab. Frigg won't be intimidated by him, and he's amicable enough to put her at ease."

"And he's bright. Erik says he's got a real panache for engineering and science. I think he's a fine choice." Viv took a drink of her wine.

Ivan added, "You should run it past Ben. Make sure he's on board."

"That's something else we need to talk about." Viv wasn't sure how to broach the subject without sounding prejudiced against the unturned.

"What do you mean?" Grace asked, taking a bite of her salad.

"Ben's struggling. He doesn't understand the community. He doesn't get how we're connected. His strategies don't necessarily work for us without us being on the same page, and he's not discussing any of his plans with me, if he even has any. I've held up my end. I've got the training plan in place, group assignments, deployment schedules. I've got Sadie on board all of our ships and I implemented enhanced planetary security. He doesn't even watch his briefs or answer his messages. I don't know how to help him if he won't talk to me. I can't do my job and his too. And he's made some pretty nasty comments recently. Everyone can see his incredible animosity toward the turned Jur, especially Vaeweth. They're uncomfortable with his anger toward them."

"Can you really blame him for his animosity toward the Jur?" Ivan defended Ben in the only manner he could.

"Yes. I can. He doesn't have clean hands either. He's done a lot of worse things for a lot of worse reasons. It is not his place to judge someone else's heart when he cannot sense it. He says he's objective. I don't think he can be with the Jur. Any of them. Everyone sees it except for him."

Grace set her glass down. "What are you suggesting, Viv?"

She sighed. She didn't want to say what she was thinking, but she owed it to them not to hold back now. "You're not going to like what I think. In my opinion, he either needs to take the turn or step down. He can't keep shutting us out and expect us to follow him. He's not a monarch anymore. This isn't a dictatorship. He can be voted out, if necessary, but we prefer it to be his choice." Viv shouldn't have said we. She guessed Grace already knew she meant The Three. She likely wouldn't ask to confirm it.

Ivan could see her point. Ben had become angry. Angry led to reckless. Grace was having a harder time with what she had said. Ben had always protected her. He had been selfless when it came to her. But Viv was right about the other points. Something had to change. They ate in silence, contemplating the words.

Ivan spoke up first. "If he stepped down, who could take his place? There aren't a lot of people here with any type of experience. None that understand strategy the way he does. There's no one qualified. We can't afford to replace him with someone lesser."

"That's not true. We have two very capable options. Ben's definitely going to hate them both. You're probably going to hate them both. I'm probably going to hate working with them both." Viv didn't want to put either candidate forward. One had never led significant numbers. The other was plain difficult.

Grace exchanged a puzzled look with Ivan. "Who?"

Viv looked like she had swallowed something distasteful. "The first is Vaeweth. And before you scoff, he is an excellent strategist. Remember what he pulled off to get his people here? And that was a plan that took him all of twenty minutes to put together. The issue I have with him is he has only led small numbers. Raids, skirmishes. Would he have the chops to do that on a mass scale? Is he capable of scaling up since taking the turn?"

Ivan asked, "Dare I ask who the second is?"

"You'll dare. You'll like this one even less. The most qualified candidate is Nyx."

Grace and Ivan both looked at her like she had lost her mind.

"We need Nyx in The Everything," Grace emphasized.

"Not for much longer. She said it herself. I know you think I've gone batshit crazy but hear me out."

"All right," Ivan acquiesced.

"She has been strategizing on a level we can't even comprehend since the beginning of time. She has skills and understanding of things we couldn't imagine. Yes, she's a diva. Yes, she will need to be reined in. The benefits to Nyx are that she does understand us. She has the ability to feel our connection, even though she's on the outside. She has also proven time and time again that she can be the most objective of us all. The Everything's existence is crucial to her, and she's willing to go to any length to ensure it. And it doesn't hurt that she has history with entities and dimensions we don't."

"That history could hurt us too," Ivan added.

"Then you better hope you can talk Ben into taking the turn, Ivan," Viv challenged, appearing stern.

"You've given this a lot of thought," Grace said.

"I've been racking my brain for days. I could only come up with those three options. If you have something better to offer, please don't hold back."

"I really don't like discussing this behind his back. Ivan, I think Viv's right. You should be the one to talk to him." Grace felt anxious.

Viv added, "I'm not doing this to go behind his back. I've tried talking to him. I even confronted him this morning with the fact that he's done some pretty horrible things himself. He won't talk to me."

"I'll talk to him before the brief this afternoon," Ivan said wearily.

They finished their lunch. Ivan made a scan for Ben. He was alone in his quarters. Ivan shifted outside his door and knocked. No one answered.

"Ben, it's Ivan. I know you're in there."

"It's open."

Ivan entered the apartment. It was a studio, but much larger than Lilly's. The lights were off. It was dark. Ivan could see him slumped down on the sofa, drinking.

"Grab a glass if you want." Ben raised the bottle in his hand.

Ivan took a glass off the bar. Ben didn't have a kitchen, only a service panel and a bar. He sat down beside Ben, putting his feet up on the table in front of him. He held out his glass in front of Ben to fill.

"Ben. What are you doing? This isn't the time for you to fall apart." Ivan was concerned. Ben had been spiraling downward since the morning of the ceremonies.

"When *would* be a good time, Ivan? Can you schedule me for a breakdown in the next few days? When it's convenient for you."

Ivan sighed.

"I don't know. I don't have any idea what I'm doing anymore." Ben sounded forlorn. Grace didn't need him. The only goal he had since he was young had been to protect her. He was lost.

"Viv said you're not talking to her. She can't do this alone."

"Viv's done enough talking for the both of us." Ben took a gulp of his scotch.

"And? What did she have to say?"

"The truth," Ben scoffed, finishing his glass and refilling it.

"And what would the truth be?" It was like pulling teeth with him.

"For starters. I can see my own faults clearly in others even though I don't see them in myself at all. I have no empathy or compassion. I can't be what these people need if I can't understand them."

"What are you going to do about it? Sit here drinking alone in the dark?"

"I'm not alone now."

"Ben. Talk to me."

"I don't even know where to start, Ivan. Grace has turned out to be this all-powerful entity. My boys have all taken the turn. My world is gone. Everyone is joining the community, and I don't feel like I belong to anything anymore." He faced Ivan, knowing he could see him.

"When the two of you rose, I felt calm, peaceful maybe, even the slightest bit happy. I did feel a connection to them. But it faded. After a few days, I just felt empty, isolated." Ben had gotten himself into a very dark place.

"Have you considered taking the turn?" Ivan didn't want to push him.

"That's all I've thought about. If I take it. How can I be objective? How can I make the right decisions? If I do it and it's a mistake, there's no going back. And if I don't, I'm ineffective because I can't understand the way you're connected to each other. How you function together at the basic levels."

"Ben, do I appear in any way like I'm not objective? The turn doesn't take away who you are. It opens you up to who you can be. If you decide you want to do this, I'll sire you myself."

Ivan and Grace had discussed not siring anyone. They weren't the same as the others. But Ben needed it. What was more important, they needed Ben. If he got a few extra abilities out of it, then so be it. Ivan couldn't turn his back on him.

Ben thought about what Ivan had said. Ivan was objective. He weighed decisions carefully even when Grace pressured him. He did what he needed to do for the survival of the community and now for the survival of The Everything. If Ivan could be that way and be inextricably tied to Grace, why couldn't he?

"You haven't sired anyone before. Why would you do it for me?"

"Because I believe in you, Ben. I trust you. I need you to lead these people because Grace and I can't. We have our part. You have yours. Besides, you're the only friend I've got left and I'll be damned if I'm going to watch you sink into a self-destructive dark hole if I can save you from it."

"I knew I was your only friend." Ben poured them both another drink.

"Shut up, Ben."

CHAPTER TWENTY-TWO

Although Ben was awake, he wasn't ready to open his eyes yet. He let himself absorb everything around him. The smells, the sounds, the temperature of the room. Was it really morning already? He felt that moving would send his head into a dizzying reality he wasn't ready for. He wanted to be asleep again. He wanted his perfect dream to come back. He tried to force himself back into it, to no avail.

"Ben?"

The voice was familiar. He wasn't quite able to place it. It was rich and full and sweet as it whispered to him. He felt her leaning over him, shaking his shoulder. Warmth emanated from her body, spreading over him. He smelled a pleasant light scent on her arm, reaching close to his face. There was something a little synthetic about it. It wasn't a natural extract. More of an artificial scent, like a lotion or simulated perfume. The question was, who was it who was shaking him awake? Familiar, yet not quite. A touch that was soothing and firm. Did he dare open his eyes and shatter the illusion? If he didn't see her, she could be anyone he wanted her to be.

Ben still didn't open his eyes. He took her hand. It was soft, small, delicate. He pulled it into the center of his bare chest, holding it close. It was comforting. "Shhh. I'm awake. I just want to lie here another minute." His speech was slurred, sleepy.

He took in the room's scent. Honeysuckle, sweat, clean linen, starch, and stale scotch. There were other scents further off, but these were closest to him. The sounds were clear. Heartbeats close, crinkling material rubbing together with unseen movement, the light humming of electricity in the air. The almost unperceived tapping of fingers on the surface beside him.

The feeling was what captivated him the most. The feeling of not being alone. The calm peacefulness of being in this specific moment in time. No description could accurately convey what he was feeling. He felt alive and free in a way he hadn't since he was a small child. He feared it would all dissipate into smoke if he opened his eyes. It was perfect if he didn't see it. He wanted to linger in his perfect moment between sleep and full wakefulness, clutching this soft, warm hand against his skin. He wanted to hold this hand forever.

He felt the back of her other hand rubbing against his cheek.

"Hey, handsome. Time to wake up. Let me see those gorgeous baby blues," she drawled softly, leaning in close.

His eyes fluttered. He couldn't focus when he opened them. Everything in front of him was bright and blurry.

"There he is," she drawled again, running her fingers through his hair.

Ben sat up slowly, letting his legs dangle over the edge. He was dazed by the brightness of everything. He couldn't focus on the woman leaning against him. Her face was washed with light that seemed to be coming from inside of her. The light itself seemed to be swirling and shifting. He focused harder, blinking away the fog.

"Nyx?" His speech wasn't completely clear.

He reached out to touch her face. His arm felt incredibly heavy. He tried to stand up as the room swayed in front of him, making it difficult balancing his full weight. The sheet on his lap slipped down. Nyx grabbed it, holding it up against his abdomen as he stumbled into her.

"Easy there. Have a seat." She took his weight, lifting him back onto the platform.

The room began to come into focus. Ivan, Grace, and Ami were standing behind Nyx. Viv, Vaeweth, and The Three behind them. Jack, Violet, and Asta a little farther back and to the side.

His face itched. When he reached up to scratch it, he had a full beard. He swore he had trimmed it the previous morning. He had so many thoughts swirling, dancing, hopping around his brain. Back and forth. Different places. Different times and the same times. He pressed the heels of his hands into his eyes, then rubbed his temples.

Nyx saw his shell wasn't made for this amount of information. Even with the enhancements of being turned, it wasn't processing quickly enough or in the right order. She took both of his arms and gently pressed them down into his lap. She held them with one hand, placing her other hand against his forehead. With her thumb, she slowly rubbed the center of his forehead. Seeing the root of the tangled mess inside, she fit the pieces together like a jigsaw. When she finished, they locked eyes. They didn't need words. He understood.

When Ivan had sired him, it changed not only his body but his essence. It had turned him into a second-tier Primordial, like the children of Nyx or Gaia or the others. He could rise. He would have the ability to harness energy, change it on a small scale.

After his turn, he had risen from his shell. He went into The Everything. Nyx had gone after him and caught him. She encased him in her own essence. Out there, she was his sole companion. She showed him what was happening in The Everything. Why it needed saving. He had absorbed her knowledge. He absorbed her. They came back when they felt something wasn't right. Something had happened while they were gone. The thought snapped him back.

"How long ago did it happen?" Ben asked as more a command than a question.

"Three hours forty-nine minutes," Sadie replied.

"Has there been any destabilization in the surrounding dimensions?"

"No noticeable destabilization has been detected," Sadie replied.

Grace added, "Ivan and I did a recon on it. We stabilized the borders. We've also pinpointed where it came from, but it's gone now."

They had been waiting for the Council to make their move for months. This was one they hadn't expected. They had managed to collapse a dimension. It was the oldest and most fragile one. It didn't take much more than a nudge, but it had been a nudge no one thought them capable of yet.

Nyx started to move back a step. Ben had his hand on her hip that kept her from moving away. He pulled her into his lap. He couldn't stand creating space between them yet. Grace and Ivan were the only ones who understood what was going on with them. Nyx and Ben hadn't become one entity like they had, but they had been inside each other's essence in a very intimate way. The others in the room were confused by the action.

"Can someone get me some fucking pants? I've been lying here an entire month, and nobody could put clothes on me?" Ben was getting his bearings back.

He continued, more controlled. "Has a new dimension dropped yet?"

"No," Ivan replied, "there is one close to splitting. We were going to head there next and flood it."

"Good," Ben nodded. He twisted to look behind him. Thoth, Lilly, Leo, and Frigg were on that side. "Anything from Ma'at?"

Thoth's eyes widened. His mouth gaped. How could he know? It simultaneously dawned on the others that Ma'at had been embedded with the Council from the very beginning. They could now reason from where they had gotten some intricate pieces of information.

Nyx shrugged. "Sorry, Thoth. He's been in my consciousness."

Thoth stammered, "Not since last week. She … she hasn't answered today."

"Let's hope she's just somewhere she can't answer right now."

Ben stood up, holding Nyx in front of him as the sheet dropped to the floor. He was tall. His arm wrapped high around her waist. His open hand was on her ribcage. She felt him pressing into her lower back.

"Grace, Ivan. Go do your thing. We'll do ours." Ben's thoughts were streaming easily. They were coming fast and smoothly. His self-doubt was long gone.

Grace and Ivan pulled out two chairs, rising immediately. Their rise had become fast and fluid. Ben felt a pang of envy when he felt them rise. Nyx felt his body shudder. It was erotic for her. His total control, his draw to The Everything. All of it flooded her with feelings of lust. She was disgusted that she was thinking about those things. It had to be the connection of encasing him in her essence.

She rapidly shoved the thoughts away, even if she was unable to bear moving away physically.

Ben's thoughts were firing rapidly now.

"Viv, Vaeweth. Any info on how to track that thing?"

Viv stepped forward. "We're getting reports from different sectors. It's been jumping erratically."

"Jack, figure out the algorithm. Give Vaeweth coordinates on the next likely set of places where it's going to appear." Ben was rolling now.

"On it," Jack ported out.

"Vaeweth. How many troops do you have ready to go?" Ben knew Vaeweth had been doing his job while he was gone. He hadn't been bad at it. They both realized pretty quickly he was no match for this new version of Ben. Vaeweth was more than happy to go back to leading troops. Viv had been right about one thing; most of his animosity toward Vaeweth had waned with the turn.

"Half a million in The Everything. A hundred thousand in training," Vaeweth answered.

"Make sure you've got teams ready to jump the second Jack gets those coordinates."

"Yes sir," Vaeweth tapped Alex and Mikkel, and they ported out together.

Erik handed Ben a uniform. He took the pants, placing the shirt and boots on the platform. He handed Nyx the jacket, sliding her around to face him. She held it up, blocking the others' view of him. She looked him dead in the eyes while he put on his pants. Why did she feel it was wrong to look at him? She had never felt that way before about anyone. He didn't seem to care. Why did she? She wouldn't hesitate to ogle anyone else. She couldn't figure out why it was so difficult for her to objectify him.

"Nyx. Keep trying to contact Ma'at. If she needs to be pulled out, go get her. Don't wait," he said softly. He took the jacket from her, throwing it on the platform.

She nodded at him. He picked her up, sitting her on the platform and leaned forward, straddling one of her thighs between his. He was still uncomfortable breaking physical contact with her.

"Leo. How many are in the pipe? And how many can be turned at once?" Ben needed to calculate numbers.

"We've got seven million on the list. By tomorrow, we will be able to turn a hundred thousand a day," Leo replied.

"But they all need to come here?"

"Yes."

"We need to get this operation mobile." Ben swung his head around.

"Ami. Get the word out to anyone willing to give us a troop carrier, a cruiser, anything of substantial size. Get them to send Thoth specs to load Sadie and get fitted with defenses."

Ami was eager to be useful. She liked this version of Ben, even if he had this weird thing about touching Nyx.

"Got it." Ami ported out next.

Thoth said something to Lilly, who ported out after Ami.

"Leo, Mother, make sure you have enough technicians trained to interface with Sadie in the turn. We'll need at least two on every ship we can have fitted. And use any newly turned with medical training for their species. We need experience with foreign biology."

Leo and Frigg agreed. They had a brief conversation among themselves before leaving.

"Viv, where's Galin?"

"On T28-66 shaking the trees. Everyone is speeding up their timelines to get here. Most have already made the trip. There are around fifteen hundred left who are still coming." Viv wasn't sure why he would ask about Galin. She had been keeping him fully abreast of operations for the past month.

"We need someone who can keep the civilians calm. Get those who need to go to The Desert moved. Can he get back here?"

"Their government isn't strong enough yet. It's going to take another two or three months at least."

Ben didn't want to leave the community on T28-66 exposed. He couldn't bring Galin back until they were ready.

"I can do it." Violet stepped forward.

Ben didn't know much about Violet. He hadn't interacted with her at the ceremonies. He saw now that what he had mistaken for vanity then was an expectation of perfection. It had been so obviously inherited from her mother.

"Qualifications." He didn't have time to be anything except succinct.

"CEO of a global corporation. Acquisitions, shipping, a lot of hand-holding and coercion."

"That works for me. Viv, hook her up with Morgud. They'll have to walk over the bridge once she ports in. We don't have anyone available who can shift them over. I want anyone under the consent age who hasn't taken the turn and any of the turned with children who haven't already moved to get priority. Clear?"

"Asta."

She was shocked to hear him say her name. She wasn't certain he remembered it.

"Yes."

"Go to The Desert with Violet. Make sure we have enough quarters set up. Take some service units with you."

"Yes, Ben."

Viv stepped up. "It's good to have you back, Ben. We needed you." She nodded to him.

He nodded back. Viv opened a port large enough for her, Violet, and Asta to walk through.

Nyx placed her hand on Ben's shoulder. "I got her." She slid down, turning to face Thoth, wedged between Ben and the platform.

"She said the Council is in an uproar. There are protests and rioting. She couldn't hear Ivan earlier. She barely heard me. It'll take an hour before she can find a quiet place."

Nyx felt sorry for Thoth. It was an emotion she didn't like much. She had absorbed some of Ben's emotions in The Everything. She liked the new him; she wasn't certain she liked the new version of her. Her hope was that it would fade away. Somehow, she didn't think it would. Much to her dismay, they were connected now. She felt a small piece of him burning inside her essence.

Thoth was mildly relieved to have heard from Ma'at.

"Let's meet back here in an hour. I need to get rid of this mess and take a shower." Ben stroked his uncombed, unwashed facial hair. Next time, he would leave strict instructions on his grooming requirements.

"All right. An hour." Thoth attempted a smile, falling short. "Thank you. Thank you both."

Thoth ported out.

They were alone. Ben's body felt filthy, but he wanted to talk to Nyx before he left her. He moved back far enough for her to turn around. He placed his hands on the platform on either side of her, pushing back, opening a little space between them.

"I need to thank you, Nyx. If you hadn't come to get me after I rose, I don't think I would have come back. I don't understand why I can't make myself pull away from you. It's strange. And I don't even like you much." He widened his already huge blue eyes, giving her an embarrassed half smile.

She couldn't help but smile back. Her smile was one of sadness. She placed her fingertips in the middle of his chest. "I think we got a bit mixed up out there. You have a piece of me, and I have a piece of you." She touched her own chest. "I don't believe there's any way to fix it. What I do know is you most definitely need a shower. And you need to do that alone." She looked up at him, smiling with her own gray-blue eyes.

His face was pained. She was right. They couldn't live their lives physically attached to each other. Maybe some distance would be best.

"We can figure this out when this crisis is over, okay?"

"Yeah." Ben fought the urge to grab her and rise into The Everything and not come back. He had to get himself away from her.

She took that decision out of his hands by shifting away first. It was painful for them both. Physically and emotionally. What had they done to each other? His was the first essence she had to completely encase in order to control. She didn't have any other explanation. She felt a piece of him inside her. There was no question in her mind that he felt exactly as she did. Worse, maybe.

She thought she had shifted to The Desert, but she had shifted to Tartarus when she thought of home. It was her real home.

Ben stood straight, shoving himself off the platform. He adjusted to being by himself. He wasn't alone, there just wasn't anyone else in the room with him. While he had a piece of her inside him, he would never feel alone. He somberly shifted to his quarters to clean himself up, not recognizing what he had done.

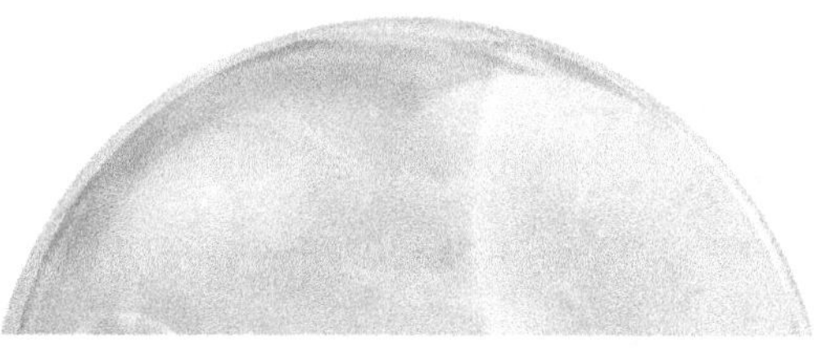

CHAPTER TWENTY-THREE

Thoth was at the plan table when Ben shifted in.

"Hello, Ben. Would you care for a beverage?" Sadie greeted him.

"Shurian Nectar, Sadie. Full cask. Three glasses." Ben sat at the table, leaving an empty seat between him and Thoth. Nyx would need to be in the center to pull them both into the conversation. The cask appeared on the table with three glasses.

"Enjoy your beverage, Ben," Sadie said.

"Thank you, Sadie." He wasn't sure "enjoy" was the right word.

Ben poured three glasses, slid one to Thoth, downed his, and poured another. He wanted to brace himself as much as he could. The nectar was the strongest drink they had. He didn't believe it would help him anymore, but he could try.

When Nyx shifted in, she was wearing her uniform. It was probably the first time outside of her fitting she had it on. She was fully covered except for her hands and face. It didn't help. She sat in the chair between them. Ben slid a drink in front of her, avoiding touching her. She drank it, sliding back the empty glass, avoiding eye contact. He refilled it and slid it back.

"You boys ready?"

"Yes," Thoth replied eagerly.

Ben didn't reply. He was ready.

"Sadie, can you project my thoughts on the plan table?" She wasn't certain if they had the link functioning yet.

"Please place your hands flat on the green squares in front of you," Sadie replied, creating two green squares in front of Nyx.

Nyx complied. "Guess they got that working."

She and Ben were both relieved she wouldn't need to touch him. He didn't think he could let her go again if she did. A blank, cloudy shape appeared in the center of the table.

Ma'at. Can you hear me?

Ma'at's voice came through. She was whispering. *Yes. I hear you.* Her image followed. Not a full clear image, but it was her view of a small room. A closet or storage room of some kind. It was dark.

What happened? How did they manage to collapse the dimension?

It's hectic here. They're saying Kali and her little band of psychopaths managed to build a weapon that can collapse an entire dimension on their own. I don't see how they could when the Council hasn't been able to. Word is they've run. They're out loose in The Everything. Pantheons are fighting. There are protests. They can't agree about what to do with them. They have listed them as terrorists, but no one seems to be going after them. The Council is afraid the population will retaliate against them, too. They are aware we're turning bigger numbers than they had accounted for. They are also aware we have more supporters every day. There's something else going on here. It doesn't feel right. They are afraid of something other than Kali. They've called for Gaia.

Who called? They need three from the High Council, Thoth asked.

Mab, Shiva, and Amun.

Have they been monitoring the energy shifts? Ben asked.

I don't know. We felt a shift when the dimension collapsed. I overheard them discussing that their stabilizers hadn't helped at all. They're a long way off from it being finished. They said they weren't supposed to feel the impact inside the barrier at this stage, Ma'at added.

Can you get close to Amun? Would you be able to slip him a message that I wanted to talk without giving yourself away? I am still officially a member of the Council. He's required to answer me either way, Ben asked.

I can try. I can get Osiris to help. He's been vocal about trying to meet with Grace and Ivan. With the way things are, I'm not sure how long it would take. How could I let you know if he accepted? How would you even get here if I could?

I can get there. Don't worry about that. Do you have something to write with?

She searched through the storage room, finding a sharp piece of metal. She flipped up the hem of her skirt and pricked her finger.

"Sadie, give me a secure message code to my TAC," Ben ordered.

"Secure link code xj724ry-/," Sadie replied.

Did you get that, Ma'at?

Got it.

Tell them to monitor the lower dimensions. Grace and Ivan will have a new dimension split off in nine hours if they keep up their current pace. If they don't, contact me after that. We're coming to get you out. Ben hoped she could get to Amun.

I'll do what I can, Ben. I have to go.

Stay safe Ma'at, Thoth added.

The feed went off.

"Now what do we do?" Thoth asked.

"We go forward with our plans. And we wait." Ben drank another full glass of nectar.

The others drained theirs, too.

Nyx studied Ivan's and Grace's shells. "I hope they can pull this off."

"Don't we all," Ben added.

Thoth was distracted. The statement made by Ma'at was troubling to him.

"That's the second time she said that."

"You mean something bigger? That caught my attention too." Ben poured another drink.

"Yeah. And how could Kali and the others have slipped out from under their noses? She's not the greatest strategist. She's more of an in your face, down your throat type. All the ones she's with are. They aren't the kind that run," Thoth added.

"No. They're not. I guess we'll find out tonight. The Council is getting a visit, whether they invite me or not."

"You shouldn't go alone." Nyx was thinking along the same lines he was.

"I was thinking about making it a family trip." He hadn't been on an outing with his boys in far too long.

Nyx sulked in her chair. She wanted to go. He could tell what she was thinking. There was no need for a connection to see that. He also didn't need her distracting him.

"One of us needs to be here until they get back." Ben nodded to Grace's and Ivan's shells.

Nyx sighed and kept her mouth shut. She wouldn't get into it with him in front of Thoth.

Ami ported in behind them.

"There you are," she addressed Ben.

"That was fast, Ami. Why are you back so soon?" Ben spun his chair around.

"I went to see the Ljósálfar. They said they were neutral." Ami stressed "neutral" and rolled her eyes. "I think they're waiting to see who wins. Anyway, some Neufl… something said he owed Leo. Told me to bring him these." Ami put a clear cylinder the size of a large thermos on the table. "I thought I should bring them to you first."

Ben examined the cylinder. It looked empty. As he turned it in different ways, he could almost make out tiny clear dots. It could have been a trick of light reflecting through.

"Sadie, what's in the canister?" Ben placed it on the table. Sadie scanned it.

"The canister contains nanites in suspension."

That piqued Thoth's interest. "Sadie, what's the volume?"

"The canister contains one trillion units."

Thoth's mouth dropped open. "That's enough to turn …" He was calculating in his head.

Sadie was faster. "Five hundred thousand per session."

"Ami, get these to Leo immediately. Then go get us some ships." Ben was very pleased.

"Wow, that's a lot!" Ami opened a port, examining the canister intently.

Before she stepped through, Ben added, "Good work, Ami."

She left with a huge grin on her face. She didn't remember Ben saying anything nice to her in the past. Thoth pushed his chair back from the table.

"That takes some of the pressure off. I need to get back to the lab. Let me know if you hear from Ma'at."

"We will," Ben replied.

Thoth ported out, leaving Ben and Nyx alone.

Nyx spun her chair to face Ben, placing her fist on her hip defiantly.

"What's the real reason you don't want me coming with you? They'll be back before you leave. You don't need The Three for this."

He turned his chair to face her.

"Because you're a distraction for me. That, and I can't spend the entire time worrying about your temper. You don't make the best decisions when you're angry." His voice was as flat as he could make it.

She arched one eyebrow. "You don't either," she paused. "Fine. I'll stay here." She stretched before placing her elbow on the table to the side and slightly behind her. She leaned her head against her hand, elongating her body and pushing her chest forward. "Wouldn't want to distract you." Her voice was soft and seductive. She flashed a sinister smile, showing lascivious intent.

Ben sat a little straighter. "That's not fair."

"What's not fair? I haven't done anything." She feigned coy innocence, batting her eyelashes, placing one foot on his chair between his legs carefully to avoid touching him.

"You're not fair." His eyes narrowed and his mouth was slightly open. He was tempted. It took everything he had in him to lean back in his chair with his hands on his thighs.

She shoved his chair with her foot and stood up.

"Guess I'll go home and find something to read for my night alone." She flashed him a triumphant smile. It hadn't taken much to work him up.

She shifted out, leaving him alone. He drank another glass of nectar, leaned his head back against the chair, and rubbed his face. With an audible groan, he rose from his seat and cracked his neck. He thought about hitting the gym. Then he thought about Nyx again. He tried to shake it off, but his body had other intentions, forcing him to shift. Next thing he knew, he was standing in front of her on Tartarus.

His sudden appearance took her by surprise; however, his presence did not. They stared at each other in momentary disbelief before he firmly grabbed her around the waist. She reached her arms up, digging her hands deep into his thick curly hair. She kissed him with a thousand years of hunger. He reciprocated with ten thousand more.

They tore at each other's clothes, digging roughly into skin. The tension between them culminated in hours of unadulterated passion, each trying to force their bodies to become one, as their essence had been inside each other when they had risen. The aching of being separated by flesh created an intuitive demand for each to satisfy the other.

They both expected it to be good. Neither expected it to be cathartic. There was no guilt or explanation. They cleansed each other of outside judgment. There was a mutual yearning between them. They fulfilled each other. It was no one else's business what had been created between them.

As Ben lay holding her, he thought to himself that he was finally free to be who he was. He was free of the burden his mother had placed on him. Free of the burden of his birthright. Free of the stranglehold Grace held on his heart since his earliest memory. The need to maintain constant physical contact with Nyx no longer consumed him. He carried a piece of her inside of him and could find fulfillment with that. He wanted her to be close, but he didn't *need* her to be close like he had before.

She rolled over, laying her head on his chest. "What time is it?"

He tapped a spot behind his ear. "Nineteen ten."

"We should get back to The Six. They'll be finished soon." The thought of duty or allegiance sounded absurd to Nyx coming out of her own mouth. She was changing, but she didn't have the energy to fight with herself over it.

"Look at you. Concerned about others," Ben teased.

"You've done a terrible thing to me, Ben. Giving me feelings." She grabbed his face, shaking it playfully.

He squeezed her, kissing her forehead.

"All right. Where's your shower? Do you have a shower?"

"Better," she grinned, pulling him out of bed.

Ben trailed behind her as they walked naked down a dark corridor. Nyx stopped, turning at a heavy wooden door. When she swung it open, a thick blanket of steam rushed past him. He stepped in after her, attempting to see where the vapor had emanated from. A few steps inside, the air cleared to reveal a natural spring at least twenty meters long and nearly as wide. The far end had a waterfall flowing over high stacked stones, spewing warm mist from its blue-tinted stream.

The pool was strewn with honeysuckle and jasmine flowers falling from vines growing over the entire ceiling. He realized this was why she smelled the way she did. Soap rocks floated throughout the pool, creating patches of bubbles on the surface. He would be content if he could spend the remainder of his days in this chamber.

Nyx entered the water slowly, submerging herself. When she came back to the surface, her loose wet hair fanned out behind her. The water came up almost to her collarbones. The room was as pleasantly cool as the water was deliciously hot. Ben slid in and swam to the other end, standing under the waterfall for an extended period of time before he moved forward, shaking the water out of his hair.

"You don't do anything halfway, do you?" he asked.

"What would be the point in that?" she answered with a question of her own.

This was definitely a place he was coming back to. He turned, facing the rock. He stretched his back by placing his hands high on the stone. Pressing his shoulders forward, he leaned into the falling water, letting it rinse through over his head and down his back. It felt like washing away years of torment and anger. Nyx watched him while she lathered herself.

"Wash up. We mustn't be late. You'll have a difficult enough time explaining why you smell like me," she laughed, throwing the soap rock at him.

He turned, catching it swiftly, enjoying the rare sound of her laughter. A real genuine laugh. It was the first time he had heard one from her.

"I don't need to explain myself to anyone. It's not their business."

"You say that now," she quipped, prompting him to emit a pleased chuckle.

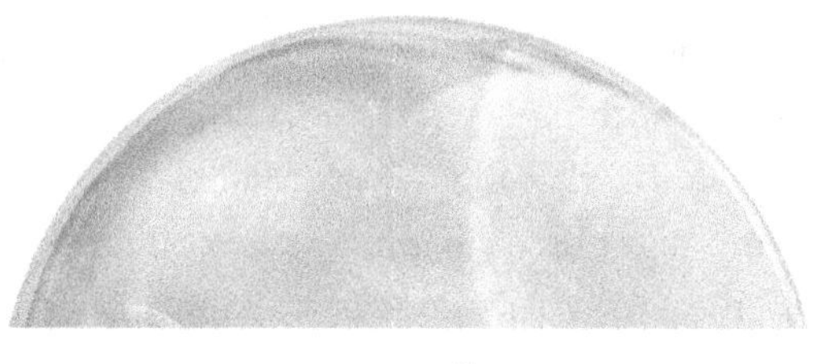

CHAPTER TWENTY-FOUR

When Ben and Nyx arrived together at The Six, most of the group was already there. Ben was in his usual uniform. Nyx was in her normal, over-the-top attire. Her outfit of the day was a short black skirt with over-the-knee stiletto boots and a long black kimono-styled shirt with a single closure in the center of her chest. The only unusual thing about her appearance was she wore her hair in a loose French braid that ended in the center of her back instead of the tightly braided crown she normally sported.

There were five minutes remaining before the brief would begin. Someone had shifted seats at the table for vacant spaces at the top where Ivan and Grace would sit when they returned. Directly to the left of Grace and Ivan's place was an empty chair for Ben. Further down the left side of the table was Viv, Vaeweth, then The Three and an empty seat for Ami. The right side of the table had Leo, Thoth, Lilly, an unoccupied seat for Jack, Violet, Asta, and Frigg. Finishing the line was an empty seat for Nyx to occupy.

This would be the farthest removed Ben had been from Nyx for any length of time since his turn. They were both finally comfortable with the space, accepting their seats without complaint. Viv's face was painted in surprise at their joint arrival, although she said nothing. Mikkel and Lilly exchanged a pleased glance. None of The Three were overly judgmental, Mikkel least of all. He wanted his father to grasp onto any slight bit of happiness he could.

Ami ported into the entry. As she was walking to her seat, an alert came across the right upper screen.

"Sadie, play alert," Ben commanded.

"Dimension D0212 has dropped."

A sweep of relief came over the room, followed by a celebratory cheer. Ivan and Grace would be back shortly.

Jack ported in the entrance chamber to the room, appearing slightly disheveled.

"Sorry I'm late," he apologized, heading for his seat. There were still two minutes left. He hadn't been late to anyone outside of his own standard. To him, unless you were five minutes early, you were late.

Ben called the gathering to order. Starting on the left, they went around the table reporting statuses of the tasks they had been assigned. Training was going as planned. Jump troops were in place. Most of the remaining families had been moved to The Desert. There were a few holdouts with unturned minors within a few weeks to months of consent age. Their reasoning was understandable. The consent age had been one hundred on Asgard and they hadn't thought to make any adjustments since they had been here. The consensus at the table was, as long as they passed the mental stability evaluation, they would be allowed to take the turn.

Ami had secured two troop carriers and a battle cruiser, and the Phailents were giving access to set up a turning facility on one of their space stations. It had a good position in sector sixteen on the far side of the universe. The only condition was their people would have priority access, and they were also willing to provide another six trillion nanites from the station. It would add another half million to a list that had grown to over one hundred million already. That was still well under one-half percent of the population of this dimension alone; but to them, it was significant. The list had been doubling each hour since the incident that morning. Now that Grace and Ivan had successfully opened the new dimension, Ben expected many times that amount would request to be added to their growing community.

Ben told Sadie to start tracking the universal date on one of the screens and add it to the uniform visors and TACs. It would be easier to coordinate if all their systems ran at the same time and date structure. It was also easier to convert than a star day. Each universal day was fifty hours, which worked well for Rasa since each day here was twenty-five hours. Every two days on Rasa was one universal day. A universal year was one thousand universal days. Two hundred universal days in a Rasan year meant there were five Rasan years in a universal year. The math was clean for their planet. Others would have less difficulty with the conversions than trying to go from planet year to star year to Rasan year in order to figure out meetings and events. There were also no months considered in the universal calendar, making it even simpler.

Leo reported twelve fully trained technicians, with another thirty enrolled in the program who would be ready in the next few weeks. He volunteered to go to the Phailent station, set up the facility, and give their technicians initial training. He would work on setting up the carriers and cruiser while commuting to complete the Phailent training before returning to Rasa.

Jack reported he was close to deciphering the algorithm of the vessel they were tracking, which was carrying Kali's crew. The last two times, the jump team had only missed the ship by a few seconds. Jack was confident he could capture it before morning.

The brief was nearly complete when everyone felt Grace and Ivan returning. Ben felt the growing pang of envy as they descended from The Everything. This time, their descent was as effortless as their earlier rise had been. They were getting good at it. Three short minutes later, the pair moved their seats to the table, sliding them close together.

Ivan turned his face, rubbing his forehead to shield his eyes from the table once he caught Nyx's scent on Ben. He winked at Ben, who quickly raised his hand to cover a smirk. It was an intimate joke and reaction shared between a sire and his sired. No one else would dare force a smile on Ben in front of others.

"Great job, you two," Viv complimented Ivan and Grace. Her words started a round of applause.

After the applause died down, Ben asked, "Did you get the brief on the way back through?"

"Yes," Ivan said. "Anything from Amun yet?"

Ben held up his TAC. "Nothing yet. If I don't get a message in the next fifteen minutes, I'm taking The Three and going to get Ma'at. She's been there long enough. The risk she's taking isn't worth it anymore." He peered down the table toward The Three. "What do you say, boys? Family trip?"

They replied concurrently over each other.

"Hells yes!"

"I'm in."

"Let's go get her."

Grace addressed Jack. "Jack, I realize how hard you've been working on the algorithm. Don't worry about it. Ivan and I will take care of her."

Jack sighed with relief. "Yes ma'am. It's been a difficult one to chase. The base keeps shifting for no apparent reason."

Grace continued, "Nyx. Could you go talk to Gaia? If the Council thinks she knows something, I want to find out what it is."

"I'm uncertain I can make sense of anything she would have to say." Nyx shook her head slowly, wrinkling her forehead.

All eyes turned toward her, causing an uncomfortable shift in her position. "I guess I could try," Nyx yielded. She absolutely did not like this newfound sense of loyalty Ben had cursed her with.

"I can go with her. Gaia and I are at least friendly," Frigg volunteered. She had been staying isolated in the lab since the debacle with Mikkel. This was the first time she had been to a brief in a while. Everyone had gotten over it after a few days, but she seemed to be punishing herself anyway.

"I agree, you may be able to make more sense of her than I can," Nyx said, nodding.

"I guess we all have something to do." Ben stood up. "You boys ready?"

"Shouldn't we bring our swords? Not to use. They're just so much more intimidating than these stun blasters." Alex tapped the energy weapon strapped to his leg.

"What would a family trip be without them? Be back here in five," Ben ordered. He nodded toward them and shifted out to his quarters, followed by The Three departing, along with most of the others.

Grace and Ivan went to clear their minds before they went to get Kali.

Nyx slid her chair out. "Frigg, could you excuse me for a moment? I need to find something before we leave. It will only take a minute."

Frigg smiled, grasping Nyx's wrist. "I know what you're doing. It won't work. He will eventually see through your façade."

"There isn't anything to see through. He sees exactly who I am. He's seen everything I am, and I've seen everything he is." Nyx was earnest about what she said.

Frigg was suspicious, but she was the outsider. She wasn't connected even in the way Nyx was with her link through Ivan. She couldn't fathom the idea of Nyx being a committed partner to anyone, let alone her son. All Frigg could see in their future was soul-crushing heartbreak, and Ben had enough of that from her own actions already. She let go of Nyx's wrist, allowing her to shift away.

Ben had expected her. He was strapping his sword on his back. It was thick and ornate. The pommel was embedded with The Helm of Awe, a beautifully woven design holding a large sapphire in the center.

"Be careful." She reached out to buckle the strap across his chest as he held the weight of the sword.

"Always." He was flattered by her concern.

"Good." She gave him a quick peck on the cheek, smoothing out the wrinkles on his uniform from the strap. "Can't have you getting yourself killed now, can we?"

"No. We can't have that," he replied as he wrapped his arms around her waist. "Who would be here to torment you?"

"Who would dare?" she teased.

"You be careful too," he insisted, causing her to look up at him.

"Go. I need to get a peace offering." She pulled back, pushing his shoulders.

Her escape wouldn't be as easy as she expected. Ben pulled her closer, kissing her lips, soft and quick, before he stepped back and shifted to The Six.

Nyx paused for a moment, taking in his lingering scent, resisting the pull to follow him. Her thoughts reflected on this unusual feeling inside of her. One that had taken root and grown into something mysterious and comfortable at the same time. Unable to decide if this was something she should resist or embrace, she shifted away in another direction.

When Ben arrived back at The Six, he Three hadn't returned yet, and Frigg was still there, sitting in her same spot.

"Where's Nyx?" Frigg asked him suspiciously.

"I thought she was going with you?" he asked, sounding convincing. It wasn't her business, and he didn't need her judgment.

"She said she had an errand. I thought she went to see you." Frigg peered at him.

Mikkel ported in, giving Ben his much-desired escape from the conversation. Ben shrugged at Frigg and began walking toward Mikkel. Alex and Erik appeared close behind their brother.

"I want you camouflaged. When we get there, go find Ma'at and bring her back to me," he directed.

"Heard," they said in unison.

Ben shifted them to Amun without touching them. That was new. He wondered if Grace had figured out that one yet.

The office they appeared in was CEO-sized, not lower management–sized. There was a desk on one side and a seating area with two sofas and chairs on the other. Amun was in one chair, with Osiris and Shiva on one sofa and Mab standing on the table in front of him. As soon as they arrived, The Three ported out of the office to find Ma'at. The group was surprised by Ben's appearance.

Shiva spoke. "Ben, we were just reviewing your request. How did you get in here?"

"I thought I'd save you the trouble. I figured you'd call after you saw the new dimension drop," he said, having ignored the question. They were nervous but held their composure.

Mab flew up, hovering a few feet in front of Ben. She was small enough to fit in the palm of Ben's hand, although he dared not touch her. Fairies didn't like anyone pointing out their stature. The last thing he needed to do at this moment was insult her without provocation. Her wings flitted noiselessly to others, even though Ben could hear them loud and clear.

"We were hoping we could speak with Grace." Mab's eyes were large for the size of her face, clear and without fear of him or anyone else, he'd imagine.

"I'm technically still on the Council, and she's been a little busy creating a new universe and all. Made better sense for me to come."

"Understandably. Please, have a seat." Amun extended his arm to the chair across from them. Close enough to watch him, far enough away to make them comfortable.

"It's difficult to sit with this," he said as he patted his sword. "Thank you for the offer."

Ma'at ported in close to the desk, stumbling awkwardly.

Osiris's eyes widened. "Ma'at? What are you doing here?" He didn't want her involved in this. He had told her he would keep her out of it.

"Uh," she stuttered, "I was, um, summoned."

The others were confused.

"We didn't summon you, Ma'at," Amun finally spoke.

"My apologies. I summoned her. I'm taking her back with me."

"She hasn't done anything. You can't come in here and kidnap people at will," Osiris protested.

"Camouflage." Ben amplified his point by snapping his fingers. The Three appeared out of thin air surrounding Ma'at, swords at the ready. Ben felt the power dynamic shift further in his direction. Everyone was terrified of The Three.

Mab flitted back to the table. "What are you going to do with her?"

"Taking her back to Thoth."

The Council members protested. Ben read the room. Ma'at was giving a stellar performance of being afraid. Everyone except Osiris was buying it. He saw the truth in what was happening. They were rescuing her. Osiris was relieved. Wanting to give her every advantage, he leapt to his feet, moving close to Ma'at across the room, offering a realistic push to the illusion. Alex dropped his sword in front of Osiris, warning him to stay back. He stopped a few feet in front of them and Alex lifted the weapon. Ben raised his hand, silencing the room.

"This isn't up for discussion. What *is* up for discussion is how you were able to collapse the dimension." The situation was working the way he had planned. They would be able to get Ma'at out without outing her as a spy.

"We didn't do it, Ben," Mab answered more timidly than she had spoken to him before.

"Let me rephrase the question. How was Kali able to collapse the dimension?"

Shiva calmed himself. "She didn't."

Beivve came crashing through the door holding a device pinging wildly with lights. "There are Primordials here! We need to evacuate!" she exclaimed. She scanned the room, seeing Ben and The Three. She shook her device, scanning the room again.

"Beivve! You're interrupting," Amun exclaimed harshly.

"But!" Beivve protested, shaking her device again. She wasn't wrong. She just didn't know that Ben now carried that signature too.

Amun decided he couldn't let her leave the room. "Beivve. Sit down and be quiet."

They had no idea what was going on. Beivve sat in the chair Amun had offered Ben earlier. Ben swept through their minds. The prevailing thought was she was only picking up The Three. They were each half. It justified the readings to them. Beivve suspected something else was going on. Ben hadn't been discovered, and Beivve had been silenced. She glared at him. She had four Primordial signatures, not three.

Ben continued, "If she didn't do it, why is she running?"

"She's not. She's trying to locate what did," Shiva answered.

"Then why would you send an alert into The Everything naming her and her crew terrorists?"

"We needed someone to blame. We needed to restore order and keep the people calm. If they think we don't know how this happened, mass hysteria will break out among them." Amun answered this time.

"How's that working out for you?" Ben felt the panic, not only in this room but also in the hundreds of thousands that were there.

"Not well." Shiva was a man of few, well-placed words.

"Why should I believe you? This was your plan, wasn't it? Collapse The Everything. Live inside your bubble?" He could already see the truth. They didn't need to know he could see it.

"We suspended that plan. We were waiting to see if Grace and Ivan could save The Everything. Our energy device isn't functional yet. Our stabilization isn't complete. Maybe not for thousands of years without them to stabilize it," Amun spoke truthfully. Ben had already extracted that thought from him.

"Why call for Gaia?" It shocked them he could know that information.

No one outside of Amun, Shiva, and Mab were supposed to have that information. It would cause mass panic. They believed they had sent a secure message to her.

Amun glanced furtively at Beivve before he answered. He hadn't wanted her to let this information out, and he knew she couldn't keep something like this to herself. Outside of the fleeting glance, there was no exterior sign he had lost his composure.

"She has a connection to the planets. There were over a million viable planets left in that dimension. She may have an idea of how they were all destroyed at once."

Ben was satisfied with the conversation.

"Thank you for taking the time to see me. This meeting has been very productive." Ben's words were calm in opposition to the menacing look he presented.

"What are you going to do with us?" Mab was tentative in her question.

"Oh, that." He kept his gaze on them. "One of you boys want to clean up here?"

The room flooded with panic. Everyone was yelling. Ma'at grabbed at Osiris, slipping the BAT that Erik had passed her into his hand. It was a temporary secured unit coded to her species since they didn't have her genetic material to use. It would work for Osiris if he needed to contact them. Alex pulled Osiris away from Ma'at, pushing him back, speaking to him in silence.

Emergencies only, Osiris. For your own safety, don't let them catch you with it.

Osiris nodded as he stumbled backward.

Mikkel went over to Beivve, who shrank back into her chair, screaming. He whispered something to her, entrancing her into forgetting why she was there, and took her device so she had no evidence. She had gone mute when he stepped back. Her eyes were blank. Her thoughts removed.

The other deities had all been struck dumb. The level of panic subsided when they saw what Mikkel was doing. At least they wouldn't need to worry about Beivve saying anything. Then the stench of unadulterated fear took over when they realized what that meant. The Three had turned. They were more lethal than before, if that was even possible.

"Now then. Until next time. Enjoy the rest of your evening." Ben shifted the five of them back to The Six where Thoth was waiting.

Ma'at immediately ran to him, embracing him with tears of happiness and relief.

"What reason did you give Beivve for being in the room?" Alex asked Mikkel.

"I told her Amun called her to his office to have sex with her," Mikkel chuckled.

"Dude! There is something really wrong with you," Alex laughed, slapping him on the back as he shrugged.

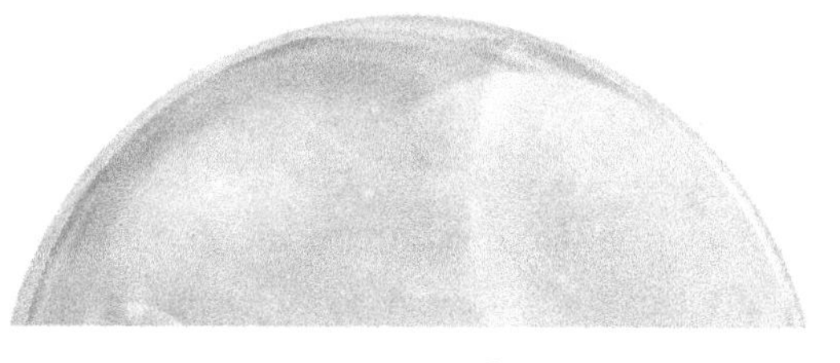

CHAPTER TWENTY-FIVE

Grace and Ivan needed a few extra minutes of recovery time after pulling off what they had. They would need all their senses intact before taking on Kali. While rising and descending had gotten much easier, today took a lot of effort. Knocking it all back into place would take some extra physical contact, too. A quick shag was all it took to get Grace's adrenaline pumping. The euphoric effects of manipulating the amount of energy they had needed to transfer had put Ivan in a good mood, but to him, Grace was more like a junkie riding a wave. He was concerned the feeling was going to make her reckless.

Grace tapped Ivan's shoulder twice quickly. "All right, let's go."

He rolled onto his back. "A tap out? Whatever happened to romance?" he jested.

"No time. I'm ready to rumble." She was already out of bed and in the bathroom.

"Wrestling references? What *have* we come to?" He groaned and rolled off the bed.

"Hey! Wrestling is an ancient and revered sport," she emphasized, being overly serious.

She smacked him on the backside when he walked past her. "Make it quick."

He suppressed his urge to laugh and continued his trek toward the shower, hoping her high would wear off sooner rather than later. Ivan took his time getting ready.

"What's the plan?" he asked.

"Don't know yet. We'll figure it out when we get there." She gave him a cheesy grin.

"Great. I love that plan," he replied sarcastically.

Grace winked at him and concentrated on Kali, shifting them to her.

"Finally. What took you so long?" Kali stood in front of them with her arms crossed.

"Excuse me? What took us so long?" Grace was irritated.

"We expected you to catch up to us hours ago," Kali spat with attitude.

"Oh. I'm sorry. We were busy creating another entire dimension because you and your little minions decided it would be a brilliant idea to collapse one." Grace gave back an exuberant amount of attitude, moving in fast on Kali.

Zeus shot an energy bolt at her back. She could have phased and let it hit Kali. Instead, she absorbed it. Raising one eyebrow at Kali, Grace shot back a highly accurate and disabling amount of pain directly into Zeus's groin, causing him to drop to his knees while grabbing at himself.

"Delicious," Grace remarked, licking her lips. "Ivan, would you be a dear and take away his toys?"

Ivan chuckled, taking the shield and thunderbolt from him. Zeus leaned back against the bulkhead with his arms crossed over his lap. Kali had a hint of a smile when Grace turned back to face her.

"Let's try not to destroy the ship. Everyone put your weapons down before you end up killing us," Kali ordered.

The remaining crew members did as she commanded.

Ivan scanned the room. Something was missing.

"Where's Ker?" he asked.

"What do you mean, where?" Kali answered.

"We heard Ker was working with you. Where is she?"

Kali stared at him as if he were an idiot. "Ker is completely unhinged. How could you possibly think we'd be working with her? You're standing in *The Ker*. It's the name of the ship."

"Seems things aren't always what they seem, are they?" Grace had the sinking feeling any information was a matter of interpretation.

"Speaking of things not being what they seem. We didn't collapse that dimension," Kali stated point-blank.

"Then why are you running?"

"We aren't running. We're tracking."

"Tracking what?"

"Whatever took down that dimension has been jumping around, destroying little pieces of other dimensions. It's leaving an energy trail. Look for yourself." Kali pointed to a screen. Grace decided to take a walk through Kali's thoughts instead.

"Shit."

"Yeah … shit," Kali mirrored her tone.

"Why wouldn't you come to us? Let us know what was going on? You know, ask for some help?"

"After the little stunt Nyx pulled at the ceremony? Sure. We'll all be best friends. She made us look like the enemy in the most publicly embarrassing way possible. We don't trust you." Kali chose the wrong words.

"Trust us? You. Don't. Trust *US*? You've been lying to us, manipulating us, and trying to control us since the minute you met us." Grace put her finger aggressively in Kali's face. "It's us who can't trust you."

"We don't know what Nyx has been feeding you or what her motivations are."

"At least she's been feeding us something besides bullshit."

Kali didn't back down. "You sure about that, Grace? Besides, how were we supposed to handle it? Oh, Grace, by the way, you're a bona fide Chaos-created Primordial being and you've been in a relationship with the wrong guy for the last seven hundred years. We need you to end that and run off with his best friend sitting next to you. Would you mind doing that right now? We didn't have time to wait. We need you to save The Everything. Until *you* brought *him* into that Council chamber, we were oblivious to who you were." She pointed vigorously at Grace, then at Ivan.

Grace yelled back. "That was three years ago. At no point in all that time did you think maybe you should let us in on the rules of the game? Nyx found *me*. I didn't go looking for her. We didn't have any idea what we were until she showed up. She's the one who got us to the point where we were able to fix what happened today. We'd still be sitting on Rasa with fifteen thousand turned and a few Æsir with our thumbs up our asses if it wasn't for her!"

"You lost your mind for a while, Grace. Remember the museum incident? We didn't know if you were stable. You were making some rash decisions after that. Plus, the fact that no one knew what you'd turn into after you took that thing off your neck. All-powerful and insane, taking lessons from Nyx was exactly what we needed!" Kali spat back with words dripping in mockery.

"I lost my mind because of you!" Grace retorted angrily, pointing her finger in Kali's face again.

"No, you lost your mind because of Ami!" Kali defended.

Grace clenched her jaw. Kali was right. If her memories had been released properly, with explanation, she wouldn't have been overloaded and caused a tear in her own mind. That didn't negate the fact that Seshet should have seen it before the second memory upload and tried to mitigate the damage.

"What about what you did to the Jur? That was rash and completely unnecessary. Why should we believe *you're* sane?"

"That *was* sane. It was strategic *and* necessary. You were pissed, Grace. Second time I'm saying this. All powerful, irrational, pissed off. Not a good combination. We needed time to get away from you. And since you brought it up, what about what *you* did to the Jur?"

Ivan and Ares exchanged uncomfortable glances. The rest of Kali's crew were staring at the floor or their hands. Anywhere except at the two women.

"Ladies," Ivan addressed them calmly.

They both snapped their heads around.

"WHAT?" They both yelled at him.

"What do we do next?" He pointed to the screen flashing beside them.

Kali turned to the blinking screen on her right. "Shit! We're jumping!"

The ship made a jerking movement. The view screen at the helm streaked white as they folded space, jumping through stars. It came abruptly to a halt outside the border to The Nothing.

A voice came from the ship. "This ship is not equipped to move forward. There is no more available tracking data."

"Well, that can't be good," Grace said as she and Kali stared out the helm screen into The Nothing.

No one had any idea what to do from this point forward. Grace and Ivan decided to shift the crew back to The Six to convey their information to the rest of the group. Sensing unauthorized foreign beings, Sadie turned off all the secured data feeds when she noted their presence.

"Impressive," Oro whispered to himself.

Ben and The Three were seated at the plan table, cleaning their blades. They hadn't used them. Traditionally, once a weapon is unsheathed, it needs to be cleaned. Fortunately, Thoth and Ma'at were nowhere in sight.

"How was the trip?" Ben asked.

Ivan passed them the information.

"Shit," Mikkel said.

"How was yours?" Grace asked Ben.

She thought he would tell them. He reciprocated, passing the information to her and Ivan.

"Learned some new tricks, I see," Ivan said. "Now them," he directed, pointing to Kali and her crew, who were all utterly confused.

"Really?" he asked.

"Just the highlights," Grace smirked.

Ben passed the information to Kali and her crew. Minus the Ma'at-being-on-their-side part and the Thoth reunion. It disoriented them. Kali realized what he had done before the others. She had no idea how he had done it, and she didn't want to appear shaken by it.

"Tad bit aggressive, don't you think? What did you do with her?" Kali was trying to give the impression of still being in charge.

Ben smiled at her.

"Sadie, get Viv and her second down here," Grace requested.

"Yes, Grace. Would you care for a beverage while you wait?"

"Set up a bar. I think we're going to need it," she replied.

A well-stocked bar appeared in the center of the table. Ben and The Three were unfazed by its appearance directly in front of them. Kali's crew was surprised at the scale. The entire surface of the plan table also worked as a service panel.

Grace headed to the bar. The others followed. Once everyone had their drink of choice, Ares took a seat next to Mikkel.

"Hey, Mikkel. Haven't seen you in a couple hundred years. What's up?"

"Not much. Home world was destroyed, end of The Everything crisis. The usual. Got some new teeth." Mikkel raised his lip, letting his canis drop.

"Damn. All three of you?"

"Four." Mikkel nodded toward Ben.

"Anything special come with that or is ripping out throats the extent of it?" Ares half joked.

"Ten times stronger, faster, and more lethal. Nothing much," Mikkel said casually as he oiled his blade.

"Yeah," Ares gulped. "Not much at all." He appeared to have taken on a slight green shade to his skin.

Viv and Vaeweth ported in. Kali's eyes got huge. Her mouth gaped. Then it registered. Pledge until death. They killed him, which led to turning him. Why wouldn't they have? She would if she had the ability. Her choices were coming back to haunt her with a vengeance.

Viv was across the room before Kali had the time to register what was going on. Viv took a hard swing, connecting with Kali's jaw. The hit sent her flying through the air and onto her back several feet away. She rubbed her jaw, shifting it around as she got back to her feet. Viv walked to the bar, pouring herself a glass of wine like nothing had happened, while Vaeweth smiled.

Kali moved back beside Grace. "Memories, I'll assume."

"Yup," Grace answered.

"Should I be expecting any more attacks while I'm here?"

"Not from my people."

"You're not going to tell the rest of them?"

"Not much point anymore." Grace took a swig of her drink.

Everyone took seats at the table, indulging in uncomfortable conversation. Kali and her crew were on one side, the turned on the other.

"What are we waiting for? Shouldn't we be doing something? Making a plan?" Kali was agitated.

"We're waiting for Nyx," Ben answered.

Kali's jaw clenched, sending a minor jolt of pain into her temple. "And why are we waiting for Nyx?" she sneered.

"She went to see Gaia," Ben replied calmly.

"That's always turned out well. Gaia has her own version of, shall we say, reality," Kali remarked, rubbing her jaw again.

~~~~

"Gaia. Are you here?" Nyx called out.

Nyx and Frigg were standing inside a greenhouse the size of a small town, stuffed bottom to top with plants.

"Go away, Nyx. I'm not in the mood for you," a wary voice called out from far on the other side.

Nyx nodded in the direction of the voice, prompting the two women to weave their way through the lush foliage. Plants of every imaginable type grew from unseen containers covered in ivy and mosses bursting with color. Even with the dense foliage, it was bright, and the air was moist. Scents of vibrant flowers mingled with fruit and nuts, and grasses glided over them, blending and changing as they pushed forward.

Nyx was not wearing the right footwear for trudging through wet grass and dirt. Her boots would be ruined by the time they got out of there. The idea caused her demeanor to sour as they plodded through before stumbling into a thinned area.

She pulled back a large branch, revealing Gaia lying on a chaise, sipping tea from a delicate cup covered in tiny byzantine flowers.

"Nyx, I told you I wasn't in the mood," the woman whined.

Gaia was a tall, large woman. Handsome, but not what anyone would think of as pretty. She was dressed in an oversized white shirt and khaki pants tucked into high green rain boots. There was a sunhat and a trowel on the small table
~~~~

beside her. Next to those, a saucer matching the cup in her hand. Her shirt was clean. Her gloves and the knees of her trousers were irreparably stained with soil.

"I came to see how you were doing after the incident. I understand how upset you must be," Nyx cajoled.

Gaia didn't reply.

"I brought a gift, and a friend," she added, stepping aside and revealing Frigg from behind her.

"Frigg!" Gaia exclaimed excitedly. "Please forgive me if I don't get up. It was incredibly horrible. I don't know how long it will take me to recover."

Frigg went to her side, sitting on the edge of the chaise.

"I'm so sorry. You must be completely beside yourself."

Nyx and Frigg would have to entertain Gaia's overly dramatic need for attention if they wanted to get any information out of her. Nyx was unsure how accurate it would be. If she knew anything at all, it would certainly be wrapped in monolithic exaggeration and paranoia.

"I am. It was so horrible, so unexpected. It was far too early. Far, far too early," she repeated, trailing her words into quiet sobs.

Frigg patted her hand. "There, there. The good news is that Grace and Ivan have already given you an entirely new dimension to fill."

"Good news? That's not good news at all! I'm not prepared. Look around you. My greenhouse is only half full. I have so much work to do." Gaia sounded distraught. She placed the back of her hand on her forehead, shrinking back on the chaise while theatrically feigning a near-fainting incident.

Nyx bit her tongue, holding out a box she had produced from nowhere. From what she had seen on the way in, the greenhouse was packed to the brim, but this wasn't the time for contradiction.

"I brought you this. I know it's small, but I hope it will help."

"What is it?"

"Open it."

Gaia took the box, opening it carefully. "Queen of the Night. Oh Nyx! Thank you!"

Nyx added, "Not any old Queen of the Night. It's from Tartarus."

"Nyx. This is so sweet, so unexpected. You shouldn't have." Gaia was genuinely grateful. This strain of flower was extremely rare. Gaia placed it on the brim of her hat as gently as most handled a newborn.

Frigg wanted to ask while Gaia was still excited about the plant.

"I'm sorry, Gaia. We must ask. Do you know what happened? Why the dimension collapsed? We're trying to fix the balance. If this is going to happen again, I don't know how much we can do."

"It was Chaos, of course. All destruction comes from Chaos," Gaia fretted. She leaned forward, whispering, "Everything bad comes from Chaos. The more you fix it, the more she breaks it. The more she breaks it, the more you have to fix it. It never ends. Never ends." She shook her head.

Nyx sat on another chaise across from them.

"Gaia, why would Chaos have done it? She wants us to fix The Everything. What would be the benefit of breaking it?"

"There's always a benefit. Old things decay and die in order to feed the new. That's what the entire cycle is about."

Frigg didn't think what Gaia said had made any sense. Collapsing a stable universe wouldn't give way to anything new. Frigg wanted to get her more to the point. "That's understandable if it happens in the natural time. If it weren't for Grace and Ivan, the new dimension wouldn't have been created. The Everything is already precariously out of balance. Something is causing it. I don't think it would be part of Chaos's plan."

"Chaos's plan?! Chaos's plan?! What would you know about Chaos's plan? She's evil, you know. She ruins everything she touches." Gaia's eyes darted around as if she were waiting for Chaos herself to appear and strike her down. "Your Grace and Ivan were supposed to correct the balance. I'm saying it is Chaos's fault it's unbalanced in the first place. Everything is Chaos's fault."

"I still don't understand. What would cause a dimension to collapse early? What if it happens to a full dimension next?" Frigg was becoming exasperated by her answers. She didn't like creating stress for Gaia. She was normally very calm and sweet, even if her reality wasn't the same as theirs was.

Gaia sat up with an exaggerated groan.

"In the beginning when The Everything was created, Chaos didn't understand the cycles. She didn't understand anything. She didn't see that one collapsed, another opened. It's a simple thing in my opinion. But no, Chaos couldn't wait. She couldn't watch to see what was going on around her. She wanted everything now. It always had to be now. She was too impatient to wait." Gaia sipped her tea.

"… and?" Frigg led her.

"Chaos began creating other beings, us at first, to correct what she saw as an imbalance. Nothing was out of balance until Chaos began to fix it. She made it that way. By the time it needed a real fix, your people saw the problem." Gaia rubbed Frigg's arm.

"You created Grace, which was fine. She didn't have powers by herself. Not ones that mattered. Not by herself. It was him. When Chaos changed him, there were many issues and many, many, many failures. Each one changed the balance, made everything worse. He was such a sweet boy, not like the others, before she turned him into that. Do you understand? She always made everything worse."

"Not entirely. What do you mean each one changed it for the worse?" Frigg asked.

"What I mean is there were dozens of her monstrous little creations running loose. 'Little creatures,' she called her children. Disgusting, nasty little things, running, laughing as they tore grass from the soil, ripped beautiful flowers from the ground. They were destructive to my beautiful little lovies." She reached over to the gift from Nyx and ran her finger between the cactus needles.

Nyx glanced at Frigg. "Gaia, how did they make things worse?"

"None of them could control their energy. Each one pushed The Everything and The Nothing closer to colliding. I was glad when Chaos ate them. She had failed to create them properly, so she killed them and ate them. She finally took the only good one, but before that, one of the other little monsters got away. He fled into The Nothing. She couldn't be bothered with going into The Nothing to find him, so she gave up. She probably thought he would just stay there. But no. He comes into The Everything eating up bits and bits of it. If you watch, you can see that there are bits and bits and bits missing everywhere. Everywhere." Gaia's eyes darted around the greenhouse.

"Now he's hungry. He's taking bigger and bigger and bigger bits. Grace and Ivan can't keep up with him. The Everything will fall back into The Nothing, and no one will be able to do anything about it." Gaia seemed almost gleeful about the destruction of The Everything.

"So, you see, if Chaos had left everything alone, none of this would be happening. It's *all* Chaos's fault. It's always Chaos's fault."

"Oh dear. This is far worse than I imagined." Frigg was worried about Gaia and The Everything.

Nyx was wondering how much of that was based on truth and how much she had pulled completely from her own imagination.

"Yes, it is. Soon we will all be taken into The Nothing. I won't have any of my lovies to grow and care for. Nothing will grow there at all. It will be quiet. We can all rest in the quiet." Gaia displayed a sickly grin, nodding as quickly as a bobblehead on a car dashboard.

Nyx couldn't take much more of Gaia. "I'm so sorry we upset you, sister. We'll leave you to rest now."

"Yes, yes. Thank you. It's been a lovely visit, lovely visit, but I do need to rest. I have work to do. So much work to do." Gaia laid back down and sipped her tea, staring off into her greenhouse.

Nyx whispered to Frigg, "I think she's been indulging in her mushrooms again. She was even more paranoid than usual."

Nyx took Frigg's hand, shifting them back to The Six from there. She was not inclined to go back the way they had come.

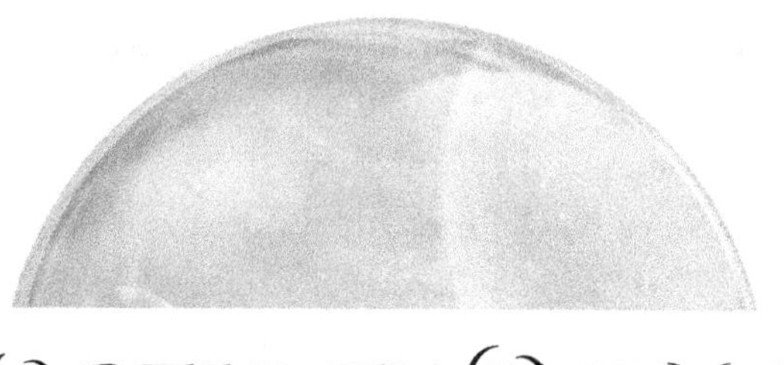

CHAPTER TWENTY-SIX

"Do none of your people stay dead?" Irkalla asked Ben when she saw Frigg shift in with Nyx.

Ben shrugged at her. "We try not to let them stay that way."

"What are they doing here?" Nyx didn't know whether to be confused or angry, letting her tone take on a bit of each.

Ivan directed them to take their seats. Nyx flopped into hers, annoyed at both the company and being told what to do. He transferred the information from both of their excursions to the two women.

"Shit," Nyx uttered.

"Seems to be the consensus," Grace replied.

"What about your trip?" Ben asked.

Nyx utilized the table to transfer their encounter with Gaia to the group. "Take it with a grain of salt. Gaia's gone pretty far around the bend."

"It's not that far-fetched. Who in this room hasn't killed an enemy and drunk their blood?" Kali knew if a single one of them denied it, they were lying.

"I'm not so sure that was the case here. They weren't Chaos's enemies. They may have been dangerous to The Everything, but they were still her children. I can't see that being something she would have done." Ivan remembered the visit he and Grace had with her. They heard the children.

"I spent quite a bit of time with Chaos while we were figuring out how to create Grace. I certainly don't think this sounds like something she would have done." Frigg thought she knew Chaos well enough to defend her.

Nyx didn't think she would have either. "I can't see it myself. She didn't kill me or my siblings, and we certainly gave her cause. I don't understand why you wouldn't think she could, Ivan. You don't even know her."

The look on his face gave him away.

"Ivan! When did you see Chaos? How? When Ben and I were in The Everything?" It was the only thing that made any sense to her. How else could he have hidden a visit with Chaos from her?

Ivan took it as an out so he wouldn't have to reveal when they had gone in front of everyone. It would be better if Nyx thought they had gone when she wasn't there.

"Yes, Grace and I went to see her." He omitted when. As he was about to explain why, Nyx cut him off.

"What do you mean, you went to see her? You don't drop in on Chaos for a visit. Chaos finds you."

"Grace was able to find her somehow," Ivan explained while Nyx glared at him. "There were children in the place where we met her. From the sounds of it, lots of them. We think she took their essences into hers and created a place for them to thrive in." He hoped he wasn't out of line dragging Grace into it.

Kali was attempting to rationalize. "So, if we take the view that Gaia thought Chaos had killed them, but she really drew their essences into her, she hadn't actually killed them. That part of Gaia's story, no matter how misinterpreted or embellished, is true. Is everyone in agreement with that statement?"

They all agreed it was logical, so Kali continued, "Should we also conclude there's some truth in the remainder of the story as well? One of them somehow got loose and is wreaking havoc on The Everything?"

They all agreed the basic conclusion was also sound.

"What can we do about it?" Ben questioned.

Grace contemplated. "I think right now all we can do is mitigate. We need to track them and repair the damage done until we can find out more. Stopping this child isn't something we currently understand how to do, and we don't know if what they're doing can even be stopped. What we can do right now is be vigilant about strengthening the weaker dimensions."

Irkalla added, "All of that is well and good. What I'm most interested in is figuring out if this is some playful child who doesn't understand what they are doing or a fully grown malevolent entity."

"Does it matter? Either way, it is dangerous. We need to find a way to eliminate it." Zeus had no qualms about taking the kill shot first and figuring out the rest later. His preference to refer to the child as "it" glaringly showed he didn't want to acknowledge sentience in this being at all. Some of the others on their crew agreed. Neither Kali nor Ares was remotely convinced elimination was the correct option.

Ivan settled the rumblings. "I think we need to calm down. Trying to kill as a first response could make things much worse. It would make better sense to find out what we are dealing with and assess the situation before considering that road. If this child has abilities many of us at this table have, it may be more advantageous to try to negotiate or contain them in some way."

Not everyone was happy with the suggestion. They eventually agreed to track and assess for a few weeks. Monitoring the child's patterns could give them some insight into whether these actions were conscious decisions or if the patterns were random. Ivan had Sadie set up monitoring using the tracking information from The Ker. Grace and Ivan would resume shoring up dimensions that were the farthest out of balance for their stage. They also agreed to try contacting Chaos again.

Ben agreed to mend fences with Amun, Mab, and Shiva, getting himself actively back on the Council. Unfortunately, that would most likely entail delivering Ma'at back to them. With his new abilities, he would be able to monitor the other members as well as the overall feelings of their people. Kali begrudgingly took responsibility for the behavior of her crew. They were still on the interdimensional terrorist list. It was in their best interest to keep a low profile.

Once Kali and her crew had been returned to their ship, Ben shared the information with the community through Sadie. They shared nearly everything, even if not always the specific details. Some plans were tedious and intricate, so highlights of the big items worked best. If anyone had questions, they were free to ask, but most rarely did. They were satisfied knowing the main parts. Ben did not reveal the exact conversation with Gaia. No one needed to know how paranoid she had become. He gave them the pertinent facts or, at least, what they believed to be the facts.

Ben did share the information of Ma'at and what she had done for them by staying with the Council, and her likely fate of returning. They also let the community know that neither Kali, nor her crew, nor the Council had been involved in the collapse. None of the turned would be involved in hunting or capturing them. It was the Council's lie. They would not be responsible for promoting it as truth.

Lastly, Ben shared that the community would be trying to work with the Council to address the issue of the unnamed child. Ben would be taking an active role with the Council, whether they wanted him to or not. This action in no way meant that they could be trusted or that it would be a permanent partnership. That would be left up to a vote of the turned once the current crisis had ended.

It wasn't that they considered the Council evil. The issue they had with the Council was that they perceived the Council as prizing power and control over what was in the best interest of the people they were supposed to be protecting. They used information as a weapon and a shield. The Council's reasoning was that average people weren't capable of handling or understanding most of the facts. The Council's stance was they were protecting the common subjects by keeping things from them. Many of the situations that happened in the last few years with Grace and Ivan specifically could have been avoided if they had been trusted with the truth. Then again, the turned community wouldn't have grown as it had if they hadn't been pushed to it.

The turned community saw things differently. They believed sharing information helped foster an atmosphere of trust among them. They could feel when they were being lied to, so there was no reason to do it. Involving their people and letting them know what was happening let them be prepared. Giving them a vote gave them a sense of being able to shape their destinies. Their connections gave them a bond of togetherness that the pantheons within the Council leadership would never be able to attain. Comparatively, the turned were more peaceful and reasonable. They wanted better for The Everything. They weren't afraid to work together to realize their dream of balance.

Days went by. Then weeks. Then months. Grace and Ivan spent most of their time in The Everything. At first, they were filling holes, shoring up the two weakest dimensions. They created and repaired, and they moved through, finding soft spots Sadie couldn't detect.

Care of their shells had been given over to Leo. He found placing them in a light stasis field kept them clean. It kept their hair from growing, and they could easily free themselves from it upon returning. Their shells kept them healthy. Any minor discomforts from lying still for long periods would dissipate shortly after their return.

There had been only a few incidences of the unnamed child coming into The Everything. They hadn't been able to decipher any patterns from so few visits after Kali's chase had ceased.

Grace and Ivan had made three attempts to see Chaos again. They were able to go back to where they had met her. She hadn't revealed herself, although she had allowed them to meet some of the children. The beings appeared as children, anyway. Their essences were innocent, although filled predominantly with negatively charged energy. They were sweet and playful as only young children raised with unfaltering love could be. Grace and Ivan felt it best not to stay close to them for long, for fear their presence would injure them. Their essences were much stronger than the children's. They also felt the longer they stayed, the less they wanted to leave. The place seemed designed that way so the children wouldn't want to wander.

Ben had begrudgingly made amends with the Council. He was placed back onto the active Council, not as a representative of Asgard since it no longer existed, but as a representative of the turned; a Rasan delegate. The population of the turned community had soared to nearly half a trillion, with another trillion waiting to be turned. It was a population growing so quickly the Council had no choice but to move his seat to the High Council. The community outnumbered some of the other pantheons already, and there was no denying they were multidimensional. While Ben's appointment displeased some of the members, he remained unbothered. Those were the Council's own rules, and they were unable to deny him his seat.

Between dealing with the politics he despised and attending briefings back on Rasa, he took every opportunity he could to rise with Nyx. He had learned how to control small amounts of energy and matter on his own. He could rise on his own now too and not become overwhelmed by the freedom he had. It was still his preference to rise with Nyx. Their connection had grown strong. They brought stability to each other. Their energies had shifted too. They had both become neutral, carrying both positive and negative energies in equal amounts. He had gained some of her abilities and she some of his. She no longer needed touch to read others.

But Nyx and Ben hadn't merged as Ivan and Grace had. Nyx didn't have any of the turned abilities like entrancement or canis. It was likely only because her shell was a synthetic biology. She only received enhancements from Ben's essence, making them quite satisfied with each other.

The charges against Kali and her crew had been dismissed. They had been found innocent of their involvement at Ben's promise not to reveal the truth to the other pantheons if they were exonerated. Kali and Ares had been appointed as liaisons to Rasa at the Council's insistence. Since they had Ben in their camp, they felt it was only fair to have their own people on Rasa. It had been a bit tense at first, but Kali and Ares were reasonable. They had no illusions about why they were there or how much they would be listened to. After a few weeks, it had become easy for the others to see what they were thinking. They all had the same goal, only different ideas of how to accomplish it.

Ami's recruiting and procurement efforts had been stellar. They had hundreds of ships and four turning centers based on planets and space stations throughout several dimensions. They were turning over two million each universal day.

Mikkel and Lilly had started a comfort station on Rasa. All turned species and genders were welcome to associate in whatever ways they saw fit without judgment or stigma. Whatever anyone wanted was fine given all involved parties consented. They didn't promote sexual intimacy, although they did have rooms set up on the upper floor for it if anyone wanted to use them. For the turned, connecting intimately with others was more important than sexual urge.

The station had activities, gaming, sporting events, dancing. It was a place where those stationed outside the main community on Rasa could come when they felt isolated or wanted to interact with others. The place had an ambiance that blended the qualities of a social club, casino, and sports pub. It was a popular place for informal gatherings, especially for the unmated.

Violet had gotten her wish as well. She was carrying the first child that would be born a native of Rasa. There was a sense of stability within the community. Life had become routine. It could be centuries before The Everything was fully in balance. There was a sense of hope they hadn't felt before. It was a peaceful time, and they would cherish it for as long as it lasted.

ALSO BY

JOYCE SERRANO

THE TURNED GODS SERIES

Original Grace - Book 1
Immortals in the Everything - Book 2

THE TURNED GODS - CHARACTER COMPANION SERIES

Galin's Alley
Lilly's Game